For my wife, my sons and their partners

A BEGINNING

Coyote lingered in the shadows contemplating his next move. Fall was coming. It was etched on the leaves of trees, on the faces of humans bent into late September breezes. North winds swirled down, filling his nostrils with hints of colder days. He felt mangy; a dirty tiredness permeated his fur. He did not like the city. Instead, he longed for open fields, grasslands, stunted bushes, the laughing playfulness of river waters. These rigid forests of concrete, steel, and glass had stolen his sense of humour.

By day, he slinked into the dappled sparseness of available parkland and waited chameleon-like, quiet, aloof, resting. Re-emerging at night, he would follow terrain back along alleys and laneways looking for leftovers living or dead—rats, mice, raccoons, an unsuspecting small domestic sniffing outside for relief. All prey succumbed to his skills. When not up for the challenge of stalk and chase, garbage offerings eased his hunger.

Coyote was not here out of choice. He had come as if in a dream, propelled along by a current of memory that carried all things. As he tracked and observed, he longed for a return to a more natural wildness.

Up above him somewhere—nestled in treetop branches, black and hidden by the night—was Crow. Coyote sensed him. He was aware of his cackling interjections, his merry conjectures, his indignant intelligence. Despite their differences, Coyote knew he was their eye in daylight. Crow could move from sky to ground, caw and peck, and not evoke attention. Unlike Coyote, he had become accepted in this landscape as just another bird—one more downtown scavenger, though not as irritating as a seagull or pigeon. In truth, he was as much a trickster as he, a formidable shapeshifter not always to be trusted.

On this occasion, they were working together, watching their quarry with similar intent—a man they had travelled through time with since childhood, a man who did not know himself and spun in circles on a wheel he did not control or yet understand. Coyote and Crow were both elated and saddened by their undertaking. Though prophecy was still beyond their scope, they knew two roads stretched out ahead for him, and only seven days remained to reach the fork.

Chapter One

DAY ONE

THE PRESENT

I stood outside the gallery entrance scanning the street, unsure whether he would come. Frustrated, I jammed my hands into my jacket pockets. I wore my jean jacket today, which was faded like my jeans. Not being a workday, I left my usual skirt, blouse, and moderate makeup ensemble behind. I still wore a scarf and earrings to add colour. I blew out a breath of late breakfast, my lunch as it turned out: eggs, bacon, toast, and coffee. I should have brushed. I put a hand up to my mouth and blew again. Not bad. Still, it wasn't my main concern. I wasn't particularly trying to make an impression.

This was the third time in as many weeks that I had encouraged him. I thought briefly of baseball, the Blue Jays, and the long ball drifting slowly up, up, and away under an open dome and into a blue sky. It was almost the end of the season. For him too, maybe. Third time, third strike. Was he even going to take a swing?

"Be here at 1:45p.m.," I had told him. It was now after 2:00p.m. Not that it mattered. We would get in. My membership would see to that. It was the fact that he might blow me off again that really pissed me off. I kicked and pawed at the pavement, my red Converse high tops scratching out sandpapery riffs on the sidewalk. *Fuck, Fuck, Fuck.* Five more minutes, and I'd go in myself. I wanted to see this exhibit, and, right now, alone would be just fine.

Saturdays and Sundays were busy here. For people like me with Monday to Friday working routines, weekend slots had to be taken or lost. I knew it was best for him too. He could drag himself out of a drunken stupor or a drug-induced haze and still salvage part of the day as long as it was late enough. "Nothing before noon," he had joked, "got to get my beauty rest." This was the pattern I had usually worked around and had come to expect since first meeting him over a year ago. I shook my head at this but managed a smile. His genuine sense of humour often won out over darker shortcomings. He wasn't hard to look at either. I sighed. Was this why I was putting more effort into his reclamation than anyone else? Unprofessional, Jesse. Unprofessional.

I whirled and kicked at the steps leading up to the gallery doors. More images of my job began to drip into my head as I waited, a leaky tap I could never completely shut off. A four-year sociology degree had initially provided paper access into the helping profession. A year ago, at age 23, it had landed me a "summer temp" job at a downtown smorgasbord of housing, work placement, and counselling services. There, inside a cube of brick and glass nestled in Toronto's CAMH neighbourhood, we sweated our butts off as an underpaid, understaffed collection of government employees, offering a turnstile approach to support as best we could. And who did we serve? The indigent primarily; the young, the old, the restless, the marginalized, the physically beaten, and the mentally harangued; those living in shelters, infested apartments, on street corners, under overpasses, in valleys and parklands; hands out, heads down, hidden away in plain sight. An ever-broadening swath of humanity lying fallow. I had fallen into this rabbit hole like Alice, a new, unfamiliar, and sometimes disturbing world. It had scared me at first, this constant migration of shadows.

But here was the kicker. They seemed to like me there. The way I handled people, I guess. Whatever the reason, I got a permanent job and stayed. I sometimes wondered why. Maybe it made me feel good to know that I was better off than those who wandered in, flitting their eyes from side to side, securing a bag to their bodies, their inner demons perched on shoulders that often sagged as they shuffled and lurched.

Maybe I thought I was helping; that this job was meaningful and said something about me as a person. If truth be told, I knew that I could do my job without becoming attached to anyone. My parents had helped instill this trait in me. Being an only child, they had provided me with a home base, a compass, and the independence to find my own way. I often shared a beer with colleagues after work but had never developed any friendships I could call meaningful. The same could be said for my high school and university days. I had friends in sport, in the classroom, and circulated with them at parties and other events, but never made them a part of my life. After leaving, I had never looked back. As for my clients, they were lost souls that I simply tried to point in a positive direction, then turned loose. A few phone calls, some paperwork, a smile, and out they'd go. When they'd regularly drift back to me, I would attach another rudder, a lifeline, and send them off to sea again. My contact with them was mostly quick bumps at the dock.

Until he had walked in.

He was tall at around six feet, and his dark hair flowed back in an unkempt mane. An earthy complexion marked him as someone used to the outdoors. *He could have some Indigenous blood*, I thought. His clothing—a hooded, unzipped jacket, T-shirt, jeans, and running shoes— though clean-looking, revealed their tiredness. He had noticed me almost immediately, adjusted the backpack on his shoulder, and sauntered over calmly and unhurriedly. It was only when he got close and was about to place his hand on the empty chair across from my desk that I had noticed his piercing blue eyes. They quickly took in my desktop surroundings, lingered on my nametag, and then zeroed in on my face. My cheeks warmed a little, and I shuffled some papers in front of me. I was immediately attracted to him. *Get a grip*, I had told myself. *You're an adult now, not some giddy school girl.*

"Hi," I had said. "Can I help you?"

My standard greeting was met with a nod, nothing more.

"Would you like to sit down?" At that moment, I was the one who had felt slightly intimidated, and I had wanted to level the playing field. He was hovering above me like a bird of prey, and I wanted him seated. Again, he nodded and eased himself onto the chair, his backpack bolted to his lap, hands hanging down over the top, securing it like roll bars on a midway thrill ride. It was then that he leaned in, reducing the distance between us by several inches, and waited.

I broke my reverie long enough to skip up the steps to the gallery entrance and peer through the glass doors. I wanted to go in but grudgingly delayed, ticking off more minutes as I returned to thinking about our first meeting.

Jesus, I had thought. *Maybe this guy's a mute, or something worse.* I remembered I had quickly looked around for possible support. I had also returned to more paper shuffling and had unconsciously grabbed a pencil before breaking the silence one more time.

"So, what can I do for you?"

He had sensed my unease at this point and finally managed a smile. Some sunlight began to wash over his earthy veneer, and his eyes sparkled, pulling me out from the cloud I was starting to move behind.

He had glanced at my name again and then said it. "Jesse, I need help gettin' a job." He had leaned back and dropped his backpack on the floor. As it settled beside him, I had noticed a lone black crow's feather attached to one of the straps. It fluttered for a moment before coming to rest. I had thought of asking about it but put the notion aside.

And so, the paperwork began, a picture of him inching into focus as I attempted to draw out answers to my questions. It was like shucking an oyster, I recalled, as I pried at the shell he had put around himself. Dash, a unique but real name it turned out, had been in the city for a few weeks. Good weather allowed him to wander outdoors for the most part. Sleep was gathered in bunches on park benches, at drop-ins or even the Y, but he preferred fresher air and the anonymity that open spaces provided. He realized, as his meagre savings had dwindled that he needed work. I, as part of the system, had been his first reluctant port of call.

The "system" is my word, not his. It is a casual reference my colleagues all use—mechanical, mundane, and all-encompassing. It is elusive in that it defines everything and nothing. If you wanted help, you had to play the game and come inside. If you weren't in the system, you were off the grid, on your own, an outlier. Out there, your luck came in the form of a paper cup and the guilt or sympathy of passersby. In here, you had a chance at a porcelain mug, at the possibility of something more stable and less transient. The mug on my desk boasted the centre's name on one side in green, and a bold "We Can Help" in red on the other. However, I came to realize that not many clients had permanent faith in the slogan. Over time, dust had settled on the mug's lip, the open maw now a repository for paperclips and a wilting bouquet of pencils and pens.

Surfacing again, I scanned the shops lining the street across from the gallery. A corner, British-style pub welcomed everyone under the banner of The Village Idiot. I had always loved the name, and the food was good. During the summer and on lovely days like these, the front windows were opened wide to allow patrons a patio feel along the street. Small boutiques offering assortments of clothing and art were connected in rows as one moved down the block. Even a couple of professional offices offered up their services. This area of the city, just minutes from my first-floor apartment, appealed to my sensibilities. It was artistic, lively, diverse, close to the University of Toronto, Chinatown—anything I could want really. It was what kept me enthused about living here.

"Asshole," I said aloud. He was still missing in action. A mother with a younger child in tow gave me a look and a wider berth as she passed. I attempted an apologetic gesture, which was lost in the moment. I returned to my broodings on time and his absence.

A couple of weeks after I had met him at the centre, I had managed to get him a job. He had several strikes against him, which became evident as we worked through the lengthy application process. I only had his story to go on. He told me he had drifted in from out of province, a tumbleweed uprooted and blown in from the West. His education, although not terrible, was a few credits shy of a high school diploma. When I asked why he hadn't finished, he had shrugged, saying he had grown bored with the routine of book and seat work and the people around him. I took this to mean he had felt penned up, like a wild animal, and had just wanted out. A final hurdle was that his resume from then on had been a trail of undocumented experiences, a few odd jobs he had held for weeks and months at a time. Money had trickled in and out.

His personal life and family were topics that I touched on briefly but pulled back from when I gauged his sensitivity. He had been raised by his mother in a small Saskatchewan town. His father was only a name that he recalled, blowing in, seeding the ground, and then leaving when he was four or five. They—his mother, a new boyfriend and he—had left for Edmonton when he was fourteen. Things weren't too bad for a few years, aside from a few scrapes, a couple with the law. He wouldn't elaborate, but I knew there was more to tell. Then, after a tragic incident involving his mother and boyfriend, his life had changed. He turned more to drugs and alcohol to ease his pain. He found himself spinning out of control. Eventually, with nothing but his memories to keep him there, he decided to leave and try something new. At 20, he began following the Trans-Canada Highway and ended up here.

The first job I got him was washing dishes at a greasy spoon, an early morning locale that specialized in cheap breakfasts and lunches and closed by four in the afternoon. It was not a great job, but it was a start. The owner had a big heart, and I thought he was in, scrubbing away at his past. But early mornings did not work for him. Drugs and drink continued to be his reliable companions, and belligerence, anger, and frustration surfaced. He lasted a sporadic month, then went down in a heap, taking his resolve with him. We had to start over, twice now in the past few months, the rock he pushed, never quite able to crest the hill before rolling back down on him. He was in the process of rolling it up again.

I shook off the recollection and headed for the gallery doors. Enough is enough. My patience was done. "Stupid bugger," I hissed out loud, "I'm not doing this anymore."

And then my name sliced through the air. Turning, I watched a figure angle and bump over streetcar tracks at the intersection, then mount the sidewalk leading to the gallery. It was him. I didn't know whether to smile as he approached and dismounted from his bike or wind up and punch him in the head.

* * *

Dash peered out through slits, and tried prying them apart but couldn't. They were dried and cracked; two parched and burning riverbeds. His fingers kneaded and kneaded them into a doughy mixture, rubbing them awake. He found and rolled eye pus across his skin and flicked it away, finally looking out and into the blurry world around him. Distant drums, once echoing deeper in his sleep, pounded to the surface of his head. As he moved, they grew sharper, like horses galloping across his temples. They quickly reached the furrowed ridge of his brow and stampeded across the plain that was the top of his skull. He needed a handful of Tylenol or maybe a restorative drink. He had to tame the wildness that was still swirling from last night before he could begin to function.

Last night. He spliced his recollections together randomly like a bad movie editor. Jumbled actions had him moving from scene to scene, faces swirling around in no specific order. He had roamed around from room to street to room again in a small herd, shouting, laughing, arguing until he had ended up here.

The darkness of the room gave way to a muted orange, sunlight sifting through and around the thin sheet that passed for a window blind. He groaned and pitched off the couch and onto a pizza box.

"Shit." He put his hand onto the floor. It slid over some spilled beer—at least that's what he hoped it was. "Fuck." He heard movement on the couch across from him, a semi-clad image stretching from a fetal position and then curling back and turning into the cushions. A cheap coffee table drew attention back to his plight, and he reached for it. Placing his weight on the end, he managed to get himself into a kneeling position.

Christ, I should pray more. He chuckled, but the pain in his head at this felt like retribution for his ongoing tradition of sacrilege. The gods circling above—a confusing collection of spirits drawn from a murky past—had never been helpful. He had run from their wisdom and embrace at a young age. Instead, he had put his faith in Our Lady of the Immaculate Deception, the LCBO, and certain street corner minions of illegitimate repute.

Thoughts of his mother flooded back. She was lost to him, a smooth stone that he skipped across the waters of his mind from time to time only to see disappear into the shimmering distance and sink from sight. He pulled himself back to shore. This is where he was now, and he had to deal with it.

But where was "here" exactly? The fog was slowly lifting. He searched for landmarks. The abused couch across from him, screaming cigarette burns, food stains, and housing human sprawl caught his attention again. There was definitely a female curled up on it, but she was still unrecognizable to him. Other sticks of furniture, including two wooden chairs and a small corner table heaped with bottles and cans, marked their territory around the room. Further on, a doorway opened into a small kitchen. To the left lay a short hallway, which led to the bathroom and two tiny bedrooms. It was coming back to him now. He was at Tania's, his sometime girlfriend, who had a roommate if he was not mistaken, both sharing two halves of the cost of a hole. He chuckled again at his masterful attempt at humour, but the effort cost him another burst of pain. He clutched his head. There must be a few others crashed somewhere in the bedrooms. He couldn't imagine them all drifting off if they were in his condition. Of course, he had done the same many times, so why not? There were always other places to wander to, other watering holes that dotted this area of downtown Toronto. Under the cover of darkness, they opened to travellers who knew the passwords, the language of the damned.

Anchored securely to the table, he decided it was time to move into the day. He pushed up and waited for the crashing in his head to subside before stumbling toward the kitchen. As he passed the couch, trying to get his land legs while avoiding the minefield of assorted debris in his path, he now recognized the form on the couch as Tania's. His motions were clumsy and erratic, like a stringed puppet being manipulated by an amateur. He was still wearing his sweatshirt, jeans, and shoes, so he had obviously passed out rather than dropped off into sleep.

Arriving at the kitchen archway, he positioned himself spread-eagled against the doorjambs and surveyed the pantry that had been party central. Some lingering pot lay abandoned in an open bag; knives crossed themselves in penance by a stove burner, their hash-coated tips beaten black and blue. Glasses and dishes littered the countertop and piled themselves as landfill in the sink. Small numbers, a pale ghostly green, came into sharp relief above the stove. 1:30 p.m. A kernel of light appeared in his brain, then it flashed into full light bulb mode. He made his way back out and to the living room window and pushed open the sheet. Daylight blazed in, temporarily blinding him. Shit, it was 1:30 in the afternoon. He remembered. "Jesse will kill me. Fuck."

There was little stumbling now. The hangover and general buzz from whatever had happened overnight were replaced by a syringe of adrenalin and a feeling of impending doom. He found the bathroom down the hall, pissed, stripped, and stuck his body under a burst of cold water. Life was returning. Towelling off, he rummaged for pills that might help his head. Finding nothing, he dressed in the same clothes, ran a finger's worth of toothpaste over his teeth, and, as he moved toward the front door, opted quickly for plan B on the headache front. He found a couple of ounces of bottled elixir lying dormant, uncapped it, and drank it down. Whiskey and peppermint. *Christ.* And then he reached for his backpack.

Uncanny, he thought. No matter how much he drank or smoked, no matter how much brain matter he found discarded in the dumpster the next day, he always managed to know where his backpack was. In it, he stored a couple of pieces of ID, a cheap android cell phone, some protesting remnants of clothing, a light jacket, and his bike lock and key. The latter was his most valuable.

His bike was a used fixed gear, a Miele he had picked up shortly after arriving in the city. Back then, he still had a good portion of his money. For about a year, in all kinds of weather, it had guided him down streets and through parks, stood by him, kept him company, stopped and started on command, weathered and aged without much complaint. He unlocked it from its outdoor porch stall, stuffed its lock and tether into his pack, bounced it down three steps, and headed north.

The quickest route for him would be to hit Dundas Street and go west across to the gallery, about two kilometres. Traffic and lights would slow him a little, but his alcohol-laced body was the real culprit concerning speed. However, 2:15 p.m. was still a feasible target, although his legs felt like a bison hit by gunfire, out of control and pitching forward onto awaiting ground. *Keep breathing,* he told himself as he pumped madly.

Jesse mattered more to him than anyone in his life right now, though he was sure she didn't know it. He had sent out signals, but they had been obscured by his failures. As he rotated forward, he thought of all her help, trust, support, and kindness over the last year and likewise his repayments of fuckup after fuckup. She had bet on him, and he had yet to win, place, or even show. The chain clicking over and over on his front ring reminded him of this. A telling breeze picked up and moved along with him, clearing his mind, but it didn't help him feel any better. He hoped she was still waiting for him when he arrived.

* * *

I manufactured a stance, arms folded across my chest, brows furrowed. I hoped he sensed, no—even better—could feel my frustration, a red-hot poker ready to sear him the moment he pulled up beside me.

"You shit. You almost screwed up again. I was on my way in without you."

His breath came in short gasps, but he managed his trademark smile. "I know. Late start. Sorry."

I smirked and nodded. "Late start. It's almost 2:20. You're fifteen minutes away. How can you not get your bike and ass in gear to make it here on time? It's not like we were meeting at 8:00a.m."

He bounced his bike sheepishly, then pulled off his backpack. "I know. Things were a bit of a blur. I just remembered about an hour ago. Stuck myself under a cold shower, pulled on some clothes, and here I am. How do I look?" His breath wafted toward me, a mixture of what I couldn't tell, but it reminded me of stale booze and cheap mouthwash—his effort at a rise and shine cocktail. I didn't want to go down the road of yet another of his dead-end nights. He was here, and that was something, so I moved on.

"How do you look?" I stepped back and feigned a critical pose. "Let's see. Jeans ripped at the knee, and what's that there?" I pointed to a spot on his left thigh. "Pizza sauce, maybe? Then there's the frayed and fading sweatshirt. And, of course, the discoloured and treadless rubber bands you call running shoes. Inside, you could pass for a starving artist." I tilted my head and forced a smile.

"Or some guy livin' on the street," he added, sweeping my eyes and the city around him.

He was playing the sympathy card, but I wasn't biting. "Your choice. You can turn things around any time."

"You don't think I'm trying?" he said with a half-hearted attempt at anger brushing through his voice.

"Not really." I headed away from him and up the steps toward the doors lining the street.

Suddenly, a burst of heat hit me from behind. "You don't know what I've been through!"

I peddled back to him. "You're right, Dash. I don't. You know why? Because getting you to talk about your past is like tunnelling through a mountain with a spoon."

We both looked at each other with resentment. Then he laughed and pulled his "aw shucks you caught me" routine. "Yeah, I know I'm not easy to work with, but I swear I'm gonna change. I know I have to. I want to."

Yeah, but I don't see it is what I wanted to say. Instead, I focused on his blue eyes, piercing their way into me. Despite his problems, there was no doubt I was attracted to him—always had been since that first day. However, where could that go? Anywhere? I sighed and smiled. "Look. That discussion can wait. For now, let's get inside. It's almost 2:30 for God's sake." He nodded, locked up his bike, and we moved in together.

Whenever I enter the AGO from the main entrance on Dundas Street, I always take a deep breath and stand for a moment. I want to take it all in. For me, it's like moving into a spiritual space. The world outside cannot get in; the pace of life slows down and becomes more meditative. I am about to enter a world of colour, reflection, and beauty. And it starts with the building itself and Gehry's architectural interpretations.

In front of me is a wide, gently meandering ramp that moves upward like a winding river. Wide, full banisters curl along with it. Everything is constructed in beautiful polished wood. Wooden stairs are located to the sides as well, an offering for those more able or interested in a short climb. These are both subtle elevations, taking patrons mere steps to the next level where they queue to enter the gallery proper. To the left, a large gift shop is easily accessible at both the entrance and secondary levels. Coat check is to the right of the entrance, and to the right again on the second level are the ticket kiosks. This panorama of space is the first visual rendering everyone notices as they push through the revolving or single doors and prepare for the various art experiences that await them.

I moved Dash to the right. "Come on. You have to check your backpack before we go in." He followed along, taking in everything as we went. Reluctantly, he handed over his bag to the attendant and pocketed his tag. We headed up the steps to grab our tickets.

As we waited in line, I threw out a question. "You like baseball?"

He looked at me. "Yeah, it's all right. Played a little when I was younger. Why do you ask?"

I shrugged. "I don't know. I was thinking of the Blue Jays before you showed up. I wondered if you were going to take a third strike and not make it again."

"Like I said, I'm here."

"But why did it take so long? It's such a great place."

"I guess art's not really my thing."

"Yeah, well, I'm sure we'll find something in here you'll like. They have many great exhibits, like the one we are about to see, and they change them up all the time. But they also have their permanent galleries to enjoy whenever you want to drop by." I could see that I was waxing a little too enthusiastic and pulled back.

He smiled. "Glad you're so passionate about it. But remember, I don't have the money to drop to come in here."

No, but you can spend it on booze or drugs when you need to or walk away from jobs when you get pissed off, I thought. Instead, I sucked up my criticism and said, "Well, that's why I told you this one is on me. You had no excuse this time. I wanted you to come. Shake you up a little. Get you to see something different."

"Appreciate it, but don't expect too much."

It was now our turn, and we moved up and secured tickets. "Tell me what you think after we're done. C'mon, let's go."

We moved toward the expansive and central hub of the gallery, Walker's Court. This huge rectangular space could be walked through to the other side, or one could climb to the second floor where many of the galleries were situated. It also opened to the levels above either by elevator or the mesmerizing baroque staircase that could be accessed from the courtyard's far end. This intricate wooden structure writhed its way to the top floor like a serpent uncoiling. Its wide staircase allowed people to stop and look out from various windows at Dundas Street and parts of the skyline around. It was a wondrous atrium that people could simply pause in to enjoy the moment or, if so inclined, sit and relax more reflectively. The ceiling was a spider's web of steel and glass segmented into different sight lines that opened to the Toronto sky. Windowless openings—portals, if you will—on the second floor above allowed patrons to walk around the entire open courtyard and gaze at it from any of its four sides. It reminded me of what a beautifully sculpted and palatial Greek courtyard might have looked like. All the many gallery rooms in the AGO housing exhibits radiated from this heart which pumped life's blood into every corner.

I pointed these things out to Dash as we walked, my interpretations and opinions filling the air. Finally, he laughed, touched my shoulder, and remarked, "I have eyes, you know." Suitably chastened, I smiled, and we climbed to the second floor and joined the line for the exhibit.

"Wow, there are a lot of people here," I noted. We inched along together, his face remaining impassive and unreadable. I hoped he would be excited at this opportunity, or at least enjoy the diversion somewhat. Not my worry, though. My own anticipation ruled out any concerns as we entered.

Alex Colville was a Canadian painter of contemporary realism, and over one hundred of his paintings hung throughout a series of rooms in this designated space. We needed to slither quietly sideways, apologize for the occasional bump, tilt, and bob and weave like a boxer to gain vantage points. I lost myself in the simple yet complex interpretations of each piece we saw, in the relationship that Colville managed to convey, specifically between animals and humans; animals and landscape; humans and landscape; and animals, humans, and landscape. There was an edge to much of his work. For me, his everyday scenes captured nuances of the inherently dangerous. Innocence was not an image that came easily to the canvass at times. I wondered what Dash thought as we took it in. Nothing had been said between us for about ten minutes. I couldn't help cutting through our shuffling silence to get a response.

"What do you think so far?"

"I like it. It's so real. Almost like photos rather than paintings."

"Nice initial observation. Anything else?"

He smiled. "Ah, so now you want me to be a critic. Never had much of an imagination. I don't spend much time thinking about art and deeper stuff. But you've said that to me before."

"Said what?"

And he whispered playfully in my ear, "That I don't think."

I ignored this slight dig and nudged him into a space that had opened up. It was in front of a painting I loved. "You don't give yourself enough credit. Take a look at this, *Horse and Train*, one of Colville's most iconic…"

"Most what?"

"Well-known, OK?"

"OK."

"What do you think of when you look at it?"

Dash knew I wasn't going to let this go, but would he decide to tag along against his better nature?

"What do I see? What do I see?" He placed a hand under his chin, forefinger tapping rhythmically against his lower lips, then crossed his arms and furrowed his brows. He was imitating my stance outside the gallery earlier, and it was quite good. I laughed.

"C'mon, smartass. Humour me."

"*Horse and Train*. Just like the title says, you see a beautiful black horse galloping down a set of railroad tracks toward an oncoming train. It's either late night or early morning, but whatever time it is, there is still moonlight above. It's out in the country, open prairie. There's nothing else except the landscape, the horse, and the train. The steel rails stand out, reflected in the moonshine, parallel lines leading away from the horse and toward the train. The locomotive shines a beam of light toward the horse. Neither one's gonna stop."

He ended then and just looked deep into the painting.

"How do you feel about it?" I asked.

"You want more?"

"Sure, if you think there's more. To me, this is a pretty disturbing painting. It's beautiful but dark and brooding. It has always stuck with me when I see it. I wondered if you saw anything similar."

Dash gave a sigh. "To me, the horse is determined and scared. His ears are back, sensing his danger, but still running hard toward it. It's a deadly game of chicken. The viewer knows who will win out, though."

He paused, and I was about to interject, but he started up again. "Maybe the artist, what's his name again?"

"Colville."

"Maybe Colville is showing the last gasp of civilization against nature. The horse is the old and the train is the new."

"Yeah, that's sort of what I..."

"Colville's Canadian, right?"

"That's right."

"Maybe the horse is like the Indian then," Dash said, getting increasingly louder. "You know, taking one last shot at an invading culture, a society that keeps kickin' its ass to the curb, year after year." I looked over at Dash at this point, noting his increased agitation. "But the horse keeps coming, ears back, head up, legs flying, leaning toward that black box of metal and grinning, 'Give it your best shot, you fuck. I'm not going anywhere!'" Dash's voice echoed throughout the space.

And there it was. Anger had splashed out, a bold, bright stroke across a blank canvas. I wondered where it had come from. People around us receded a little, moving quietly on to other paintings, but measuring the words that brushed the air around with furtive glances. Nothing was said between us. Instead, we soon melted back into relative obscurity, sliding frame by frame, until we reached the end of the exhibit. The ripples he had created within himself seemed to have stilled, and he was the first to break the silence.

"That was great. Better than I expected."

"Really? Good to know. I never would have guessed that."

"Why?"

"Well, it's just your reaction to that one painting. Then nothing for the rest of the show."

He shrugged. "That was a moment, all right."

"You seemed pretty upset. I shouldn't have pushed you."

"Don't worry about it. It was nothin'. Lots of things get me upset."

I couldn't help myself. "What made you connect the horse to an Indigenous reference?"

"Indigenous. What's that mean?"

"It's a more acceptable term for Native these days, I guess. You haven't heard it?"

He frowned. "Yeah, I have. I guess I'm not as politically correct as I should be, eh?"

He started walking away from me, and I walked quickly to catch up.

"No, it's not that. I just wondered why you made that comment, that's all."

We came upon one of many areas to sit, and he decided to plop himself down. I slid in beside him and waited. He leaned forward and rested his arms on his legs and began tapping his fingers together. After a few seconds, he stopped, stretched back into the seat and looked over at me. "Something I haven't told you before. Never wanted to, but maybe I should now." He drew in and expelled a long breath, then said, "My mother was Metis."

"Cool."

"You think so?" He stared back at the floor.

"I guess. I don't know." I tried to keep silent to let him talk if he wanted.

"No, you don't." There was a pause and then a half-hearted smile, "but I don't really know myself."

"What do you mean?"

He looked down at his hands, then stretched them out and pushed away at the empty air in front of him. "I loved my mom. She did her best, but the accident took her away before I had any time to find out who I was. We lived at the edge of our town, but not in it. We lived near a reserve, but not on it." He paused for a second. "My mom had friends in both worlds but no one close; no one that stuck. I took my cue from her. I was my mother's son."

"You could still find out, right? Do some digging?"

At this, he simply clamped his hands down on his knees and stood up. "No. Better that I just move on to some kind of life that doesn't remind me of that. It's a puzzle with too many missing pieces." And he started to head off and for the stairs. "But thanks for this today. It made me remember how much I actually like art. Well, at least some types of art."

I thought of something and blurted it out. "You know, there's something else we could check out while we're here." I hesitated.

"What's that?"

"Well, there's a permanent display of Native art at the AGO. Lots of neat stuff, old and new."

"Yeah, like what?" He didn't sound particularly enthused.

"I don't know, masks, carvings, beadwork, paintings—beautiful art of different kinds."

"I think I'll pass. Not really in the mood, but maybe another time."

"Sure. Just a thought." I hoped there would be another time. At least that was encouraging.

I kept stride with him as we moved down the stairs and out into the lobby. Suddenly, he stopped, glanced over at the gift shop, and made a beeline for the entrance. By now, I had given up on trying to figure him out, so I just followed along.

I must admit, I was glad he had come in here. I love this part of the gallery, the final stop before leaving. Whenever I go into one, I think of *Exit Through the Gift Shop*, the movie about Banksy. That's what every gallery wants you to do. Go through, browse around, and pick something up that might help sustain it. It was a noble pursuit or maybe just a money grab, but I didn't care. I was not of the monied class. Still, I never entered the gallery on my own without flowing around each eddy and pool in the shop, eyeing each worm on the hook, but wary of striking.

Dash was honed in, though. His lingering thirst drove him to the small oasis on Colville, where he began drinking. I knew without asking that Colville's art was what he wanted, the opportunity to bask in the visual rather than the biographical.

"Found anything you like?"

He held one up. "This one, I think."

Good choice, I thought. Dash had a hardcover copy of *Colville* in his hands, encapsulating the artist's history in a form Dash would appreciate. The question of whether he had the forty-five dollars plus tax to buy it rose out of the depths and toward me like the Kraken. I knew the answer, but I waited stonily for his response. He said nothing, just patiently and quietly kept thumbing the pages.

Finally, I stated the obvious. "I'm thinking you want this book."

"Would be nice. Great pictures. Fits easily into my backpack..."

"But..."

"But, no money...as you know." He never turned toward me; he just kept leafing through the pages, a fisherman casting out his line.

Finally, I bit.

"OK, look. I'll lend you the money for it, how's that?"

He turned toward me, smiling. "You're kidding. You don't have to; you already bought me today's ticket."

"Another thought," I said, "if you're worried about money. There's a place called a library where you can likely find this book, no charge."

"Yeah, but then it wouldn't be mine. I'd have to return it, meet due dates, get a library card." He smiled again. I couldn't help but join him.

"You prick. OK. Let's get our backpacks and the sacred wallet that holds my magic credit card and come back. But listen, you owe me." I was as serious as I could be, given my elation at his interest. Whether I'd get the money back was irrelevant, anything to help him focus on something positive for a change.

We pushed outside into the freshness of the late afternoon. It was still recognizable as day; the sky skittered with pink waves cresting a growing purple sea. The sun was moving more and more into fall. The buildings around captured and held its radiance, but it was cooling and moving away from us. It would not return in full again until spring renewal, but merely poke out in ever-fading rays of warmth as it grappled with the coming darkness.

Dash had *Colville* secured in his backpack and seemed genuinely happy. He hinted at our departure, though, as we headed toward his bike. Something was tugging at me, emotions that had been bubbling to the surface since his arrival today. I should have just nodded when he unlocked his bike and turned to say goodbye, wished him good luck with his job hunt, and given him a "see you again sometime soon", but I didn't want to let him go. I was still hooked on other possibilities. Like a fish out of water, I flopped around for a bit then resigned myself to fate.

"You doing anything now?" I asked, instead. "I was thinking maybe we could go into Chinatown, grab a bite to eat. Talk a little more." Dash hesitated, rolling his bike back and forth in short, quick motions.

"I'm not really a lover of Chinese food. I'm more of a traditional eater. Pub fare is usually my thing."

"Fine then. We could just stroll across the street to The Village Idiot over there."

Dash smiled. "What? Is that a dig at yours truly? Besides, haven't you had enough of me for one day?"

"Of course, I have," I joked. "You're a jerk, but there's more in that trap," I said, rapping his skull, "than you let on. I'd like to open it up and see what else is inside."

"Nothin' much. Cobwebs and dust."

"Bullshit. Besides, other than coffee and donuts a few times over the last year, I don't think we have ever been out for a meal. What do you say?"

He hesitated. He had twelve dollars in his pocket meant to last into next week. Jesse had paid over eighty for him so far today. Now, she was asking him out for food and conversation. He was a fucking leech, no doubt about it. He thought of Tania then, his sometime girlfriend who he had met a few months ago at the strip club where she was working. He existed with her in a turnstile relationship of sex and partying, living in his moments of ups and downs. As far as he knew, she was too.

Jesse was much different. She was a tough, no-nonsense person, and he readily admitted to himself, a natural beauty. There was nothing fake about her. He admired her, and she was right. He was a prick, a jerk, a taker—all those things. She had been good for him, a rock that he didn't deserve. However, he decided to say yes to the invitation and to throw in the little money he had at the end if she would have it. Besides, he hadn't told her the good news. He had an interview tomorrow for a job as a bike courier. He already had a bike that would do what he asked. How hard could it be? Jesse would be happy with this new prospect. It was the third or fourth shot at a job—he couldn't quite remember—since he had met her. He knew he had blown the first few. This piece of luck he had found out for himself from a biker he had bumped into on the street. It had been a good day so far. He was happy. Jesse was happy. Yeah, things could work out.

"Hey," she burst out, interrupting his good vibes, "I've got a better idea. Let's nip down McCaul Street to Queen Street and duck into The Rex for a bite. They have great jazz and blues there.

If we're lucky, we'll get in before the evening rush and maybe catch a set while we eat."

Dash was about to note that he didn't like jazz or blues that much, that the psychedelic and acid rock of the 60s and 70s was his usual choice of sound, but he managed to save himself. He was learning. Instead, he smiled, turned his bike around and chirped, "Sounds good. Lead on!"

* * *

Crow sat atop the distinctive external architecture that defined the AGO. The beautiful shimmering facade, a pulsating stylized canoe of aluminum that ran a block's length above the currents of car and pedestrian traffic flowing underneath, allowed him to think and observe.

He sharpened his beak on the metal and preened himself for action.

Below him, two rivers converged. He saw this confluence and drew himself up to full height on the summit of his perch with a raspy cry. There was hope in their mingling, an opportunity for new knowledge, acceptance, and change. But history ran deep. The past flowing toward them, cutting into the banks still threatened and reflected in the blackness of his eyes.

On the horizon, another shape was beginning to emerge. Unclear yet, it gathered in the wind that started to blow around him.

The night was approaching, and soon Coyote would appear to carry on their vigil. Crow lifted himself into the wafting draft of air, allowing two feathers to drift out and spiral to the ground. The first alighted unnoticed on the pavement, footsteps behind the departing duo, soon becoming part of the street's detritus. The second grappled with gravity more intricately, fluttered and danced out ahead of the two. It was ultimately noticed by the male, who stopped, and holding his two-wheeled machine, stooped to pick it up. He stroked it and put it in his bag. He would soon hang it with the other.

Picture #1: *Nude and Dummy*

Observer's description: A naked woman with her back to the artist gazes over her shoulder at a clothing dummy in the foreground. She appears to be in the attic of a house. The smallness of the room is accentuated by the peaked but close ceiling above her, lending an air of claustrophobia to the space. She is standing in front of an upstairs window that reveals sunlight and an open field outside. The scene is both natural and disturbing. An innocence that may soon be lost sweeps across the vista. What does she think as she looks back at the dummy unclothed as she is? How does she view her body in relation to this armless, legless hourglass? What is this headless scarecrow stump on a stick telling her?

Chapter Two

THE PAST

Usually, Miriam's anger came up like a summer storm. Dash could see it gathering, approaching on the horizon. His hope was that it would blow past and drain itself quickly with some cursing, hurled objects, and even sobs of frustration or despair. To be safe, he would start tying things down, moving shrapnel that could become airborne into nooks and crannies for their own protection. When it hit, he would run for cover and wait until her fury expired. Sometimes he headed outside and walked the lane. Sometimes he propped himself against the shed behind their small wood-framed bungalow. Here, he would look off across the open fields that skirted the periphery of their small town and pull weeds or grasses that sprang unbidden from the dirt inhabiting their backyard. If he chose to walk over the open ground, edge through scrub brush, and hop a fence or two, he could stroll unimpeded onto the reserve.

His mother's tornado-like winds erupted mostly toward the day's end, which he came to realize were connected to the type of day she had had. Often, her rage was work-related. "Fucking bastard" became a code for her manager at the restaurant where she waitressed. "Fucking prick" or "fucking bitch" were reserved for the various patrons she served who were cheap with tips or who left none at all. "Fuckers" was her blanket term, sometimes prefaced with "mother" for anyone who had disparaged her by name or had made lewd or suggestive comments. And when her anger had been compromised to a degree that she lashed out indiscriminately, he could also become the brief focus of her wrath. His part in seeding the clouds was never clear to him. It could come from a misinterpreted look, an ill-conceived word, a gesture or action perceived as defiant.

Whatever the cause, he knew that the youthful, playful, smiling aspects of his mother would always return like a flower pushing through earth to reclaim him. He just had to wait it out.

In his eyes, she was beautiful, and he would catch himself tracking her movements. The natural sway of her body and hair reminded him of prairie grasses gently tossing in a breeze.

Occasionally, he had seen her naked. He would sometimes get up in the middle of hot nights, walking, dreamless. The door into her bedroom would sometimes be open; her covers strewn or bunched around her. Her body was a sculpture of beauty fashioned into positions she formed without effort. She was at her most innocent here, making him want to reach out to touch her, to reassure her.

He regretted that her body was not lost to the eyes of other men, but for different reasons. In the past, she had even allowed one or two to stay for a time. Their indifference toward him had been evident, but her need for more than his companionship as a son made her blind to this reality. These intrusions into his life had ended quickly enough with a final creaking protestation of her bed and a "catch you later", which thankfully never came. She seemed happy about that as well.

At least now, Miriam had Eric, a regular who stayed over a lot, helped pay for things, and treated her with kindness—a boyfriend, as his mom called him, something more permanent to latch onto, a gate she could close and maybe keep from swinging open.

Eric also didn't drink much; an occasional beer, a glass of wine, but never enough to get him drunk. This trait had helped his mom cut down too—something she had repeatedly told Dash that she wanted to do, but couldn't conquer alone. It had been months since she stepped out from under that cloud. Others still gathered from time to time, fueled only by her anger at the inequities of life. These bursts reminded him that silver linings were at best elusive.

Today was a good day. She had brushed her hair until it shone lustrous and full, and she had wrestled the crow's feet that took hold around her eyes into submission. She put on new clothing Eric had helped her buy and hummed a tune as she danced about the house, washing dishes that lay caked and forgotten in the sink, sweeping crumbs from the squares of cracked kitchen linoleum at her feet, dusting various sticks of furniture, and shaking out tattered rugs into the morning air. Best of all, during these brief interludes without Eric shining brightly into the centre of their world, she would let him in, talk to him, and ask him how he was doing. She would be his mother.

At age thirteen, and in these shared moments, he peppered her with a spray of the same requests, family questions that he flashed in front of her like an old film flickering on a tattered screen. These were the times when he could push and get a response that might initially feel like a change in the weather but never trigger a gale or squall. His mother might stiffen at first or turn away as if to do something else, suggest that a wall was beginning to build, but then bend or turn into the wind he had created and enter the conversation. It would always start directly and at the source of his longings.

"Tell me about my dad."

The tolerant half-smile would appear. "Again? We've been through that." Her hands would then move through her hair or over her clothes as if tugging or brushing at the past.

"I know, but you never say much of anything." And this time, he added, "At least that I can remember."

"Memory's not always a good thing. Besides, you weren't that old when he left, right? Five or six was all." She picked up a rag to keep busy now and dusted around him. He had a small bag full of remembrances from a year or two, penny candy that he opened from time to time to gaze at before selecting one to suck on and enjoy, like putting a worm on a hook, driving in their truck, roughhousing on the floor or outside. But these soon scattered like a flock of startled birds and disappeared into trees or sky.

"Where did you meet?" He looked down at his hands as he spoke.

"You know this. I told you before." She was right, but he needed her to say it, to remind him of who he was, to make her enter the story he wanted to hear.

"He was from away, right? From out of province."

"Yeah, from the East, the 'Big Smoke' he had said. Toronto." Here she smiled for a second. It was a place his father had described to her, and she now passed on to him, full of lights and sounds, skyscrapers and shops, big lakes and parks.

She rarely spoke about her past, the time of her growing up. How her parents, the grandparents he had never met, had left her. How the different schools his grandparents had been forced to attend first shaped them into objects they could not recognize, then spit them out unable to remember their real names. They had each drifted along separately, blown like dandelion seeds until they met. Together, eventually with her in tow, they existed until their spirits had broken. Her father left her at sixteen; a year later, her mother departed. "For better places," she would say when asked, "gone from this world."

At seventeen, she was also just an object, a cup dropped, many times cracked, chipped, dirtied. But she rose up, left the limitations of her public education where habits and collars had muddied her name. She schooled herself with work she found in restaurants and bars, her looks and natural intelligence winning her employment. She kept going, lived cheaply in a one-room basement apartment that one of her bosses had found for her until a year later, she met him. "Your dad," she would say.

He had cobbled this vague history together in a loose fashion. His questions allowed him to puzzle several pieces of his mother's life into place, but the edges were absent and too many pieces remained missing. His father was just one of many that lay jumbled on the table of his memory.

"We met when I was eighteen." She slapped the rag at a fly walking on the coffee table and watched it flip to the floor. Bashing it one more time for good measure, she picked it up, carried it to the front door, and threw it outside. "He was nineteen and called me to him from his truck, a pickup that dropped rust along the street like dead skin. I was heading home from the greasy spoon I was working at then. Seems he had seen me walking out and about before but hadn't had the nerve to introduce himself."

"What was he doing here?"

"Another answer I think you know, but what the hell? He had come out here for work after school. Didn't know what he wanted, but knew he needed a job and a different place to be. There was a company out of Regina laying pipe for the town, gas and sewers, I think, and he was working for them." She looked over at Dash. "I didn't care about what he did at that point. He was good-looking and funny, and I was an Indian with no real prospects. He opened the door, and I got in." She pulled at a few cupboards and drawers and put the odd dish away as she recounted this. When finished, she wiped her hands across her jeans and smiled. "In the beginning, we had most of our good times on the seat of that truck."

"What do you mean?"

She laughed. "What do I mean? That's where we partied. Driving out on country roads, we would park, have a drink or two, talk, look at the stars." She messed up his hair affectionately and said, "That's where I had you."

He felt himself warming at these words, a fire slowly burning inside him, but he wanted more before the moment slipped out of reach, before she decided to shut down and bring her memories back inside herself.

"I don't remember him much. Why did he leave again?"

A flash came to her eyes. "Does there have to be a reason? Things change. People change."

"Yeah, but..."

"Look. You came along, right? It was too much for him. We got this rental; he got another job after the pipeline work finished. All that responsibility and us so young, he still wanted to party and have a good time. We lasted four years, almost five, not bad, but I could tell he was restless, not sure of what he wanted, so he up and left one day. Greener pastures. End of story."

He knew not to push it any further, but she took a breath and finished a thought as if it needed air. "He loved you. His decision to go wasn't easy, and I don't blame him now." Then she brightened a little, took him by the shoulders, and looked directly into his eyes. "But you and me, we're still here and together. That's not gonna change."

This reassurance, something he always craved, made him feel good, comforted. He knew there had been knocks at the door over the years, conversations with officials about her suitability as a single parent. Sometimes it had been about her lifestyle, sometimes about her ability to provide. But she had fought these interlopers tooth and nail, a mama bear protecting her cub. She would do whatever it took to keep him with her—straighten up and stop drinking, work more hours if she could, and even talk to an elder for advice if she found herself visiting the reserve. But this kindled a shame in her she could not explain or understand. She often felt lonely there, a shadow walking.

He did his part by going to school, limiting his truancy, staying out of trouble. They had been a team in this respect, flying under the radar of the institutions and their rules.

"Nope, not gonna change...Do you miss him?" He would end with this question, then moved toward the door and outside sun as if to prove this to himself.

"At first I did," she said quietly as she followed his movements. "Awful sometimes, I won't lie. He was a part of me and you, but that part's gone now, so I had to let it go." She paused and looked at him. "You should too."

He nodded. "I'm going outside for a bit."

"You do that. Let me know if you go anywhere, though."

This part of July, the last two weeks or so, had been dry. As he stepped onto the dirt laneway that ran right to their door, dust spun up and around him with every kick of his shoes. The mini bowls he created drifted out over the ground and disappeared in the air. There had never been grass on their scruff of property that passed for a lawn. Anyone who arrived in a truck or a car just drove up the lane and parked on anything available. Their home, not their own, was clumped like others along the main road leading into town, a mangled arm, limp and hanging, but still connected to the body. They existed between the two communities of reserve and town, a no man's land that both sides ventured back and forth through as it suited their purposes.

Mr. Gibbons, the town's largest real estate owner, had bought up this land years before when people had left for points further West and better jobs, his mother said. He bought them for a song, dropped a little money into improvements, such as better wiring in places and a couple of new appliances, and offered it to his parents. They could afford the rent together. Then his dad took off. Dash kicked the ground hard at this, remembering, and dug his toe further and further into the hole he was creating. Gibbons knew this and the predicament it was causing and made his mother an offer. He would drop by every couple of months or so—afternoons, evenings—and would receive his payment in other ways. His mother never complained, never talked about these visits, but she was always sullen afterwards, and a bottle was never far from her side.

Dash picked up a handful of loose stones and began chucking them at the shed door, its beaten and buckled aluminum announcing each successful strike. Beside it stood the decaying wood of a doghouse, its small roof sagging, a metal peg protruding, and rusting in front where the animal had once been tied. His mother called the dog a mutt and said it was better off after the car hit him, wandering as he often was when he got off his chain, back and forth along the ditches that flanked the roadway. His dad had got him—a cheap investment from the humane society. Another being, it turned out, for him to eventually leave behind.

When Digger died, the town came, threw his carcass on a truck, and drove away. That was two years ago. His sadness had passed, been sealed up like most other disappointments in his young life. The subject of another dog or pet of any kind had never been raised since.

As he bent to choose another stone, Dash heard a distinctive rumbling sound. He rose to look and saw Eric's blue Ford pickup brace for its habitual turn off the main road and into their narrow laneway. The tires caught dirt and grit and fishtailed toward him, gulping air. Dash flipped the stone in his hand, hurled it at the shed, and then waited for the truck to slide to a stop. The engine coughed twice and died. Eric emerged from behind the creaking driver's door and stomped his cowboy boots on the ground.

"Hey kid, what's up?"

"Nothin'. I was just messing around, throwing stones and stuff."

Eric smiled. "When I get some time, we'll get a baseball out and throw it around."

"When I get some time" was a phrase that kept rolling around in Dash's brain. "You got a couple of gloves?" This was his immediate response. Not that he expected Eric to cough up money for everything that he knew other kids at school had, and seemed to take for granted, but if he was going to be his mom's boyfriend for real, then was a ball glove too much to ask?

"No, I don't, but we don't need gloves, do we?"

"I guess not, but it would be better if we did."

"Yeah, well, we can't have everything," and as if to end the conversation, Eric turned away and moved toward the bed of his truck. Reaching in, he pulled out a tool bag and a case of Coke. Months earlier, it would have been boxes of beer that made their way into their home. Occasionally, when his mother had been distracted or drinking herself, Dash had stolen a bottle or two from the fridge and gone off to consume them privately. The taste was bitter, but he enjoyed the buzz that helped him escape the moment. However, since Eric's arrival, this had changed, which worked in his favour as he preferred the taste and fizzy carbonation of Coke much more.

"Your mom in?"

Dash jerked his thumb toward the house. "Inside."

"Great. Got a few little jobs she wants me to do. We'll throw the ball around soon, OK?"

"Sure." Dash reached down for another stone to throw.

"I'll put a few cans of Coke in the fridge. You can come in and have one in a bit when they get cold if you like." Eric then moved toward the house, whistling a tune. Dash knew that he meant well enough. And since he had become more a part of his mom's life, Gibbons had stopped coming around. He fired his stone over the truck and into the field beyond. The eye he and his mother had been in closed just a little when Eric opened the screen door and walked in. It was their time now, and Dash didn't want to be around. He thought of Digger again for a moment, picked up another stone and fired it at the doghouse. It drifted wide and ended in the dirt. He wanted to clear his head for a bit, so he decided it was time to go elsewhere.

* * *

Picture #2: *Hound in Field*

Observer's description: It is late winter/early spring. A bush line stretches across the background at the top; the open field in front is sparsely snow-covered in places, thickets of wild grass poking through at intervals. The hound at the focal point, its coat a mixture of whites and browns, blends into its surroundings. It is intent on sniffing for scents. Its head close to the ground pulls its body to the side, preparing to turn. His one visible eye is set and immovable in its gaze, a yellow glass reflecting what it sees. Its nose points the way, and the eye follows, both focused on a sight off the canvas. The dog moves comfortably in this environment, an animal in tracking mode, nature in motion, instinctive.

At times in his life, Dash had been a thief. Usually, this hadn't bothered him because he only stole small stuff, like chips and chocolate bars, the baseball he had in the shed, the odd comic book, things that any kid he knew would take, items that he figured were plentiful and wouldn't draw attention when gone. But the drawing kit was something else; it always made a surge of guilt course through his body when he picked it up. School was often a black pit. His life on the periphery of both town and reserve, somewhere perpetually in-between, often followed him to class. He was only one of a handful of Metis attending his school, and those that shared his reality were either younger or older, leaving him a nebulous being at best, a cloudy apparition that was looked through. He had no status. Friends were scarce and fair-weather. Most of his classmates stuck to their cliques, and entrance into their domain was by invitation only. In class, he sat in silence, participating when the teacher insisted, but otherwise not drawing attention. Outside, he observed quietly, interacted when he could or bounced around from bully to bully when they were bored. Sometimes his anger surfaced like a struck match, and he pummeled a tormentor into submission and bloodied his face. This gained him a modicum of respect and relief for a time, a break from school if it had been decided that a cooling-off was required. But the name-calling would return, a virus latching onto his body and mind and never fully letting go. His mother often came to his defence, her distance from the school measured by the nature of the offence. She handled a minor infraction by phone, but if a major incursion toward her son occurred, she was known to rage into the office, nails out, teeth bared. It was a sight to behold, but Dash felt he ended up no better off.

Art was a solitary activity, something created at his desk that could be cut off from everything else. At this allotted time of day, he could fold into himself, block out the chatter, reflect, and push his vision onto paper. It was different than words, which were often expressed in anger. Here, he was as good as anyone else, maybe better if his work was compared. Over the years, he had moved from the frenetic movement and vagueness of crayon to the refined possibilities and nuances of pencil. People gave him trouble, and he rarely drew them, but landscapes and animals he worked at capturing over and over. He was sorry to see the class end, to have to shut up his creations in his desk for another day. They were as imprisoned as he until their next opportunity at release.

And so, at a particular moment almost two years ago, just weeks before Digger died, he had returned to school, having forgotten a booklet he needed for homework. A back door by the trash bins was still unlocked, providing seamless re-entry to his destination. His grade six classroom door was open, and his teacher was nowhere to be found. Mr. Emslie, the janitor, was the only sign of life piling up dust with shakes of his mop at the far end of the hall. He walked in toward his desk and there, sitting on the worktable in the corner of the room, was the pencil drawing kit. Mrs. Weatherby, his teacher, had forgotten to put it away. It was a treasured resource in the classroom. Mrs. Weatherby had purchased it, so it was hers and hers alone to share. He had often heard her complain at the end of the day when a thoughtless colleague had borrowed and not returned it.

Dash felt anxiety begin to move through him. His brain was racing, and he felt his face begin to flush. This was not a bag of chips or a baseball; this was something larger with potentially more consequences. He found his desk, reached into it, grabbed his booklet, and shoved it into his backpack. He set his gaze on the kit again and moved back toward the table. A noise outside brought him back to himself. *What was he thinking?* He shouldered his backpack and moved to the door, then looked out. The sound had dissipated, moved elsewhere. Mr. Emslie was in the other wing, he guessed, and Mrs. Weatherby likely in the office. Anyone could come in here and rifle through stuff, even other teachers. In an instant, he was at the table, his backpack hungrily chomping down on the kit he had slid inside. Then like a wary animal, he was back at the classroom door, made a quick check, and exited the building. He grabbed his bike leaning in wait against the brick wall, and pedalled around to the street and then toward home, the rush of stampede pounding in his head.

Most students brought their own writing utensils to school at the beginning of the year. Part of a collection of items listed in a package sent home and which his mother consistently had misplaced or thrown out. He had a backpack, which he was grateful for, but anything beyond the basics of a couple of pencils and an eraser, like coloured pencils, a good ruler, a math compass, or protractor, were persona non grata. Luckily, Mrs. Weatherby, and other teachers he had had, would raid the school stockroom for collective classroom needs or even provide out of pocket, which he always thought was generous, so he got by. The art kit, though, brought out from time to time as incentive or reward, was special. It was full of quality products, a true artist's treasure trove. The kit included drawing pencils, a flat sketching pencil, a charcoal pencil, a sharpener, a kneaded and a rubber eraser, an artist's triangle, a couple of tortillons, a sandpaper block, drawing paper, a pad and an instruction booklet. He did not use much of these materials properly, so he would regularly skim the booklet for knowledge and pictures to help ease his frustration. He was impressed with what he saw each time it opened, his desire to have it a seed that grew and grew as the year progressed.

The dust had settled around his past actions; only his memory remained, a brushstroke he had smudged, but not erased. His teacher had conducted an investigation that involved questioning the class, other teachers, the janitors, even parents, but weeks later, she had given up. No new kit had emerged as a replacement, and her faith in the integrity of the world was reduced, and for this, he had felt bad. Dash had kept his head down, nodding or shaking it in response to questions, mostly silent as the grave. Suspicion hovered above him, a hawk he felt ready to strike. But no talons had impaled him, no blood had been drawn. His body remained intact. He had managed to scurry to safety, squeaking with relief. His mother was oblivious to what he had done. The kit—his kit—was secure in his bedroom closet, a place his mother never ventured into. It could be worked within the relative privacy of his room, or at the kitchen table when his mother was out. Most times, though, he would simply put it in his backpack, jump on his bike and head off to somewhere private where he could be alone.

Dash entered the house after half-heartedly lobbing a final stone. Eric and his mother were in the kitchen. She was propped up on the counter, legs splayed, Eric between them with his hands on her thighs. His tool bag dangled from a kitchen chair. Their infatuation with one another was obvious, and Dash wondered how much actual work would get done. One thing he did know was that Eric would stay the night, so getting away was a good thing. In his bedroom, he brought out his art kit and stuffed it into his backpack. He briefly entered the kitchen, interrupting the laughter, and opened the fridge.

"Can I grab a couple of Cokes?"

Eric glanced over. "Sure, buddy. Take what you want."

Dash found the coldest and shoved them into his pack.

"Where are you off to?" His mother slid off the counter and approached him.

"Just heading out on my bike for a while," he said and started to move.

His mother put an arm on his shoulder. "Where to?"

"Around. Nowhere in particular."

"You'll be back for dinner, though, right?"

"Maybe." He slid away from his mother's touch.

"Dash. I want you back by eight. Well before dark, all right?"

He balked at this, a colt wanting its freedom. "I have a light."

"Doesn't matter. I don't want you on the road out there after dark. Guys around here drive like shit." She glanced over at Eric, who knew enough to nod at this point. A response from her son was still expected.

Pawing at the floor, he finally relented. "Yeah, OK."

Dash knew that she worried about him, and it sparked a warm glow when he thought about this. Sometimes these expressions of concern had been hard to trace, especially when alcohol had surrounded her. Not that long ago, before Eric had emerged, a white cowboy riding in on his one hundred fifty horses, a warning of return before dark would often be lost, submerged in a boozy halo of forgetfulness. He could be out all night back then if he chose, but often, if the weather was right, he would come back and sleep out under the stars. The outdoors gave him extra peace and comfort when needed. Recently, with sobriety, a ring that his mother had been holding onto successfully, her tracking of his whereabouts, irritating as it could be as he grew into a teenager, was a welcome change. The summer they were heading into, he hoped, would remain mostly sunny and free of rain and cloud. He shouldered his backpack, pushed open the door, and headed for the shed.

His bike was a hybrid of sorts, its tires wider than a road bike's but narrower than what a mountain bike offered—something in between like himself. It was forest green, had a rear pannier and more gears than he used, but the saddle was comfortable on his ass. There were shifters on the grips at the end of the handlebars, which were straight and not curved like a racer's. He liked this feature. Although his bike was slower because of his upright position and broader tires, he felt more under control and not as nervous on the town streets, and especially the main strip of highway he often needed to use to get to where he wanted.

This bike was the one meaningful contribution to his life that Eric had made so far. A recent purchase at the end of the school year; a graduation and early birthday present combined. Eric had gotten the Raleigh from a friend whose son had outgrown it. It had been tuned up and was in good shape. Dash had been riding it around everywhere since the surprise had been lifted from the bed of Eric's pickup. He would be fourteen in less than two weeks and leaving the public school in September for his beginnings at the local high school. There was no excitement in this transition for him. He had moved mechanically through the early grades, one foot in front of the other, doing enough to get by or enough to be pushed on. High school would be bigger, harder, and scarier. At least the summer months allowed him to forget what was coming for a time.

When he was nine, he had had another bike—his first. It was a cheap garage sale purchase that his mother had allowed him years after his father left, but as it turned out, it was no good for anything. The owner knew this and was trying to make a buck off anyone who couldn't afford more or who might be able to fix it. "Take it or leave it," his mother had said. So, he did and rode it up and down the dirt laneway and around their dirt yard for a time until winter came when it was buried under a blanket of snow. He recovered the carcass in the spring, then lugged the guts behind the shed where it still lay four years dead, a forgotten sculpture of cracked rubber and rusted metal, disappearing more and more into the arms of resilient weeds and grasses.

Dash decided that he would ride out to the dump, but not the official one to the north of town surrounded by fences. That one was only accessible by the main gate. A bulldozer and front-end loader were kept busy daily sifting, heaping, and burying the community's unwanted history. Where he ventured was unofficial, loosely created at the end of a long, winding dirt track where the cheap and environmentally challenged members of society made their donations. They came at night, undeterred by signs reflecting off their headlights that threatened five hundred dollar fines for trespassing. Security was provided for them by the surrounding thickets of bushes and trees, a minor forest that enveloped these unnatural deposits. The response to these transgressions was a flurry of activity, which predictably began with angry letters to the local newspaper followed by indignant sighs and chest-thumping from the town council. Occasionally, culprits were caught and publicly shamed, and then an annual clean-up would ensue. Ultimately, though, like the seasonal cycles of migratory birds, the flotsam and jetsam would slowly return, creating nests of refuse like growing families chirping and longing to be fed.

For Dash, it was everything an almost fourteen-year-old boy could want. He could ride there in under twenty minutes, first briefly taking the main road before cutting down a couple of side concessions toward the bush. Propping his bike up against a tree, he would wander and investigate as the products of man and nature spread out around him. He was never sure what he would find. Old pallets rotting into the folds of roots and earth, metal rebar bent and rusting, household appliances, loose wires and tubing snaking through grasses, broken chairs, bound magazines and papers yellowing with old news. Any of these things could be sifted through before he would head to his favourite location, a rock outcropping large enough to accommodate his backpack, his drawing kit, his whole being.

If lucky, and if he was quiet enough, a wild animal or two might venture through attracted by various scents. Pitched garbage bags oozing kitchen scraps was a delicacy at varying times of day or night. Squirrels, raccoons, assorted birds, coyotes, even bears had crossed his path. Sometimes he had scared them out of their foraging upon arrival; other times under his watchful eye, he could see them sniff, scratch, tip, and cart away a treasure. If prepared, he might capture a pose for posterity on a sheet of paper, lines roughly and feverishly thrown down to be worked on later. Digger had been a mainstay of his work. Several attempts at capturing him running, howling, and sleeping were evident in his pad. He would transfer the pieces he thought were worthy onto drawing paper, but those were few. Horses and birds were also represented. He had attempted his mother once, a work in progress he had never returned to.

* * *

Picture #3: *Crow Up Early*

Observer's description: The image of a giant crow, larger than its surroundings, floats in the sky. It occupies a point at the top of the painting. It is early morning. The landscape it drifts over appears somewhat muted to accentuate the crow's darkness or show that life has not yet arrived on the scene. The crow's blackness is layered over the heralding hue of the sky that is awakening from the night. The crow is majestic in its singularity. It is the first to see the day, the first to bask in the openness and beauty of its surroundings. But what does the day hold given that the sky is a pinky red? He searches the masthead of his memory for the sailor's portent and flies on.

Dash settled himself on the large rock, pulled out his kit and one of the Cokes. He started drifting, his mind mixing into the soft cadence of the quiet around him. He was not sure what he might try to draw. Suddenly, the staccato snaps of branches being stepped on roused him from his reverie. He focused on the sound and what it might be. Stepping out of the bush with what appeared to be a gun in his hand was Billy Priestly. "Shit," Dash whispered to himself and the air. Billy was a year older and had moved on to grade nine this year, a reality that many students and teachers alike had celebrated. He was a lumbering bully who, throughout the school year, had still returned periodically to his old haunt to pick up where he had left off. Those like Dash, who were younger than him and therefore still ripe for his taunts, were preferred targets given that he was now back to being a little fish in a bigger pond. He had not seen Dash yet, but would when he moved entirely into the clearing. Dash managed to slide the still unopened drawing kit back into his pack and then waited fretfully to be recognized and acknowledged.

"Well, well, if it isn't Dash alone with the trash." Billy walked toward him, chuckling at the poetic witticism of his greeting. Before Dash could reply, Billy noticed the Coke nestled on the rock. Suddenly, his mood changed. "You got another one of those?"

Dash didn't want to give anything to this prick but realized what he had to do. "Just two, but you can have the other one," and he reached into his bag for it. He pulled it out and offered it to Billy.

"Thanks. Don't mind if I do." He leaned his gun against the rock and snapped the top. Taking a swig, he eyed Dash and then smiled. Bullying never mattered as much when there was nobody else around to watch, so he decided Dash could be his friend for a while today.

"What brings you out here?" he said, looking around. "You like the smell?"

Dash ignored the remark and shrugged. "Just wanted to go for a ride. What about you?"

"Me. I come out here every so often to use my pellet gun."

Dash wanted to say something about it just being a toy and not the real thing, but luckily, he stopped himself. Instead, he put his drink down and asked if he could pick it up and have a look. Billy nodded, the cola adding to his unexpected friendliness. It was a Daisy model rifle, all black with sights, and a strap for carrying. It was light in weight, but nothing fancy. He sighted along the barrel and moved the gun slowly across his field of vision.

"Here, gimme it," Billy said, finishing the last of the Coke and throwing the can in the direction of the dumpsite. "I'll show you how it's done." He took aim at the can he had thrown some thirty feet ahead of him and fired. A metallic pop was heard, and the can jumped a little. When they ran up to check, a hole could be seen where the pellet had entered. Billy picked it up and shook it. The pellet was lodged inside.

"Nice shot. Can I try?" He had watched Billy squeeze off the round and was confident he could do so as well.

"Sure. Have a go, but while you do that, I'm taking a slug of your Coke."

Half of it was gone, and it was getting warm anyways. It was an easy compromise for Dash to make. "Go ahead."

His choice of target was a paint can that he noticed tilted forlornly on top of a fusion of flattened cardboard boxes. He would put it out of its misery. He poured his eye along the barrel, found the notch and the paint can, and pulled the trigger. The gun jerked slightly, and the pellet whistled into the cardboard with a soft thump that spelled miss. Billy laughed. "Try again, dimwit. There are still some pellets in the magazine." Dash made an adjustment to his aim, focused, expelled his breath slowly, and fired. The pellet pinged off the can as it moved slightly.

"A hit." Billy nodded and, without a thought, finished the Coke.

They spent another twenty minutes or so setting up targets and testing their skills against each other, imagining the field of combatants they had dropped before them. Then Billy made a pronouncement. "Let's stop makin' noise for a bit. I want something else to shoot at."

"What do you mean? What else is there?" They had shot at everything in the area, refuse of all shapes and sizes. *What was left?* Dash wondered.

"Just be quiet," Billy hissed. "We're going to wait for the animals for a bit. See if anything shows up."

Dash was incredulous. There was a chance something would arrive, but he had never thought of shooting it. "What animals are you waiting for?" he whispered. He couldn't imagine anything big.

Billy just sneered. "I'd shoot at a critter like a coon or a coyote, but birds mainly. Crows in particular. Big, black fucks that need shooting, right? They'll come driftin' in soon with any luck. Always curious, always scavengin' around."

"Why would you want to shoot birds?" The question sounded stupid when Dash asked it.

Billy looked over at him, puzzled. "Why the hell wouldn't you want to shoot them? It's target practice is all, a chance to take out something alive and that moves around. A fuckin' can isn't going to give you that rush, is it? Besides, what's a few birds or animals matter?"

Dash could not comprehend the idea of shooting anything living. The only animal lives he had ever taken were when he had gone fishing a few times. Even then, he had only kept the large ones and released the small fry. His mother had reminded him of that. "Only the pan-sized ones come back with you," she had said when he had occasionally ridden off with an old rod his dad had left behind. And so, he had started to protest ever so mildly, "Yeah, but why..."

"Look, bugger off if you want to be a wimp, I don't care."

Dash felt the sting of Billy's remark, the quick push back into the realm of the unwanted. Relegated to the status of a whiner, he knew he could quickly become fodder for the bully. His Coke had been the offering that granted abstention from the role of Billy's periodic whipping boy.

"Nah, I'll hang around. See if you scare anything up." Bravado was now his momentary hope. At this point, though, Dash went for his backpack and threw it over his shoulder in case he decided to head for his bike and home at some point soon. Shooting wildlife was not his thing.

As it turned out, Billy had not been wrong. After ten or fifteen minutes of sitting, poking at dirt with sticks, picking at scabs that were healing over from forgotten scrapes, a sign that foragers had arrived appeared. First, they gathered in the treetops surrounding the pit, a gaggle of conversation occupying their time. Perhaps these were raconteurs, adept at telling stories about past conquests of dump cuisines; perhaps they were reconnaissance, sent in to map out the possibilities of safe access to the riches below. Whatever their arrival announced, one by one, the group descended until five or six carpeted the terrain at strategic intervals.

Billy had already positioned himself before their feathered descent, taking advantage of tree cover close to his trajectory. He was locked in, something deadly wavering in his eye. His sight fell on a crow perched on a torn garbage bag. He shot, saw the slow tumble and roll of his target as the collective flight launched in surprise, fear, and shock, a frenetic spiralling toward treetop vantage points. They had reacted instinctively to the one body finishing its death rattle, feet curled skyward. A deferential silence had invaded their domain for an instant.

Billy whooped at his success. Turning, he blurted, "Now I'll search the trees. Drop them where they sit." Dash shook his head. He knew that as soon as Billy spewed his first projectile, the crows, not idiots themselves, would take off. Perhaps one would die if Billy's aim was true, but Dash was not convinced. As Billy made for another shot, Dash headed for the downed crow. He found it pliant, as though it was resting, and bent to take it in. He did not know why he picked it up and placed it in his backpack, but a certain rage was growing in him, coursing up through his body and bubbling toward eruption. His mother's image came to mind. Despite her problems and her bouts of anger and depression, she had always instilled in him a respect for animals and nature. Where it came from, he had never fully understood, but he carried this awareness within him. Even Digger, his mutt, had been loved by her, despite her periodic frustrations at his willfulness. As he stood, his eyes smouldered and smoked, but he put out the flame.

"Shit. Missed the fuck," Billy grunted.

"Too bad." Dash was thinking of leaving. He had had enough of this. "Look, Billy, I've got to get going. I need to get back home to do a few things." He threw his backpack over his shoulder and headed for his bike propped by a tree on the dirt track about thirty feet up.

"Yeah, you run back to momma." Billy's cruelty surfaced then, an inner demon that he was unable to suppress. "Course you might stumble onto her doin' some guy, right? Then what would you do?" He laughed. Dash managed an over the shoulder "fuck you" as loud as he could, but Billy simply laughed more intently at this and returned to his search for other winged victims. Dash was a mere footnote in his twisting psyche.

* * *

Crow had come down in that final exchange. He saw hurt and anger mingle with derision and contempt and waft up into the air. Perched on the metal handlebars of a young girl's discarded pink bike, a streamer on one side hanging down torn and limp, the other missing, he waited. The bike's body propped itself awkwardly against a heap of graying insulation, adding hints of chipped and fading colour to the mawkish mixture around it. Its white plastic carrier was filled with garbage.

Crow's black eyes were fixed on Billy, willing him to turn and take notice of where he was. The other boy was moving off down the winding laneway toward his bike. Billy saw Crow, moved as close as he dared, lifted his weapon slowly and took his bearings. He watched as the black body loomed up large through his scope unperturbed and seemingly unaware. Here was a gift unable to miss.

Billy smiled and squeezed the trigger. But he did miss. Instead, the pellet ricocheted off the bike and back to its owner, like a dog returning on command expecting a treat for good behaviour, poking its muzzle into Billy's left leg before sitting at his feet.

Crow sailed off into the treetop, listened to the screams of pain and frustration that hopped Billy around the dump for a time, and then left.

The other boy heard the cries and shouts as well but did not turn around. His inner thoughts pushed him up and onto his bike, and toward home, death concealed in his backpack, waiting to be acknowledged and released.

* * *

Chapter Three

THE PRESENT

We walked south together along McCaul Street. The late afternoon September sun was still evident, but would soon slip below downtown buildings. Turning left, we sauntered onto Queen Street and joined the human stream of pedestrians bent on their own end-of-day destinations. Crossing St. Patrick Street, the Rex entrance opened to us within steps of the intersection.

"Here we are," I said. "You know this place, right?"

Dash nodded. "Yep. Just never been inside." He found a spot where he could lock up his bike, and we headed in.

The Rex Hotel had been around for decades. Family ownership stretched back some fifty years or more. Originally, the beer hall was at the back with a men's clothing store occupying the Queen Street side. In 1960, the clothing store was replaced with the expanded bar. Jazz and blues, nineteen shows a week, were introduced in the 1980s. Upstairs, there were twenty-six rooms to occupy travellers from all walks of life. Over the years, the hotel had been slowly renovated to bring back its old lustre. It was this history, plus the great music, that brought people back, locals and tourists, regulars and newbies, again and again.

Inside the pub area, a large bar occupied center stage and wrapped around toward the back. Tables and chairs filled all the remaining spaces around it. To the left was a slightly raised area where musicians set up and played. An upright piano permanently resided there for band usage. The stage was currently littered with a drum kit at the back. A stand-up bass, sax, trumpet, and oboe horseshoed out in front; each stood upright in their stands, waiting for the skilled touches of musicians that would serenade them into performance. We also stood, waiting for a waitress to find us a table.

"Looks pretty busy," I noted, "but I see a few tables in the back."

Dash simply nodded and continued to look around. Ceiling fans spun slowly at intervals. Hardwood floors stretched off, reflecting various stages of colour and wear. Black coiled water heaters festooned along the baseboards radiated warmth when needed. Light became less and less evident further to the back where windows shed their presence. It was inviting and filled with a kinetic vibe that only history and live music could create. A waitress eventually ushered us to a table mid-way back that allowed us a view of the stage, but at a distance that Dash appreciated. He didn't want to be at the front, held captive by sounds he might not enjoy.

"A second set should be starting pretty soon. Since it's Saturday, we're getting the benefit of a late afternoon session before the evening band kicks in."

I was a little more nervous than I thought I would be at this spontaneous adventure of ours and so continued to chatter on. Menus and cutlery had arrived. "Food's pretty good here, but I guess I said that before."

Dash smiled. "You did, but that's OK. Never hurts to remind me."

The waitress asked about drinks, and Dash surprised me with water. I said I'd have the same for now.

"You could have ordered a beer or something," I said when the waitress had gone. "I don't mind," I added, even though I did. Still, I felt it was his choice to make.

"I know," and then his visage clouded for a second as he played with his spoon. "But I think it's time to cut back, give it a break. So, I'm good."

We surveyed the menus in silence. Prices were always reasonable here and the portions generous.

"I think I'm going to have the chicken quesadilla and a house salad," I said. "Got to watch my figure." Looking down, I played with my cutlery. *Why did I say that?*

"Nothing wrong with your figure," Dash remarked with a turn of his head to me. "I think I'll have the steak and fries. Got to watch my figure too."

I laughed. Well, there it was. I guess we were officially flirting. God.

It was in a moment of silence that Dash had reached for the feather he had stored, retrieved it, and secured it with the other to his backpack.

"You starting a collection?"

He smiled. "Not really. For now, I'll settle for the two."

"Anything significant about having them?"

He sat for a moment before speaking. "I don't know too much about their meaning. Feathers can mean a lot of different things. The first one I got was years ago, growing up. I took it from a dead crow that had been shot. I tried to draw it a few times before giving it a proper burial. I was just a kid."

"Sounds like that incident had a big impact on you at the time."

"I guess. I just don't like killing or hurting animals."

"And the second?"

"Two feathers are a sign of good luck or good news. At least that's what I believe."

"You think you're in for some good luck or good news?"

"Maybe. I'm here with you, aren't I?" He smiled.

I could feel the heat rising in my face and grabbed for my water. I thought of my job. I was stepping beyond propriety, into the realm of the unknown. True, we were just having dinner, enjoying a few hours together. Nothing wrong with that, right? Then why were my feelings for him going beyond the realm of decorum? *Get a grip. You're fantasizing. Come back to Earth.* I took another sip.

When the waitress returned, we placed our orders. Soon after, I started running my finger around the rim of my glass. I wanted to start a specific conversation but wasn't sure where it would go. Then it hit me. "You know, you never told me where you got the name Dash from. You just shrugged it off when we first met."

Dash shrugged again, but this time with a grin.

"Come on, humour me. Was it a nickname from school? What?"

"OK, where to begin?" He paused, took, and then expelled a long breath. "I think I told you that I didn't know my dad very well. He left when I was around four or five." I nodded. "His surname was Dashiell. He was French, and in French, I think, or old French, *de chiel* translated into English meant Dash. At least that's what my mother told me. Anyways, my dad was a bit of a cut-up, a card you might say, a funny guy. He was always laughing and smiling. He decided, and I guess my mom went along with it, to call me Dash. A bridge between English and French, which nobody would get except him."

"Didn't you have a more formal first name when you were born?" I asked.

"Nope, not that I know. Besides, once I started walking, my parents decided it was the right name for me. I wanted to run all over the place. Anyways, there you go. That's it."

I took a drink of my water and decided to push a little further. "So, you don't have any brothers or sisters?"

He sat and looked at me for a five-count before breaking his gaze. "Nope," he said and gulped some water.

I could tell he didn't want our talk to go too far in that direction, but I was stubborn and wouldn't let go. "So, what was your mom like?"

He picked up his knife, fiddled with it and looked around. "Look, Jesse, I know I should be able to talk about my mom, but I don't, with anyone. Not yet. It still seems too early for me. When I do, though, you will be the first to know. I promise."

"That's OK. Anytime you feel like it, though, you know I'm here to listen."

He smiled at this notion. "You know, this counselling stuff really suits you. You're a natural."

"I didn't mean it that way. It's just that I'm someone who believes that opening up can help. Keeping things bottled up isn't good."

Before he could respond to my therapeutic insights, our food arrived and became a welcome diversion for us both. After a few bites, Dash decided to reverse the flow of conversation.

"So, what about you, Jesse? What's your family's story? Any skeletons knocking around?"

"Actually, the closet's pretty clean. Nothing sinister to report." I knew he wanted more, so I carried on. "My parents had me late, an unplanned sexual romp. My dad's still a practicing doctor with a few years until he retires, and my mom does research work part-time for a private company. I am their one and only, and because I was a surprise, never got as much nurturing as you might think."

At this point, we both took note of the band returning to the stage.

"So, are they close by?"

"Ottawa. We text or talk, usually once a week or so. I go down for Christmas. They've been here once or twice. I fended for myself most of the time. Did a bit of travelling to Europe after high school before deciding on university. My folks pretty much let me be."

Just then, the band grabbed our attention with the introduction to their next set, and we settled back into finishing our meals and listening. Over the next forty-five minutes, they covered some Coltrane and Monk and a couple of their own creations. It was good to see Dash tapping along to some of the songs. We never said much during this time, just let the music wash over us. The waitress came over to clear our plates. We both asked for coffee and passed on dessert.

It was when the coffee arrived, and the band was finishing up that Dash decided to announce his latest opportunity.

"So, I've got an interview tomorrow for a job. Thought I'd let you know."

"I'm impressed. Tell me more."

"Well, it's not much, but I'm excited. It's for a bike courier."

I sat back at that point and folded my arms. "A bike courier."

"Yeah." He noticed my folded arms. "I'm getting the sense you don't seem too impressed now."

"Dash, it's not that so much. It's just that, well, it could be a pretty tough job with not a lot of perks."

I could see that I had made him defensive because he took a sip of coffee, crossed his arms on the chair, and looked around, frowning.

"I thought you'd be pleased," he blurted out. "Something I'd done on my own for once."

"Sorry, I am. My bad. Really, good luck. I'm happy."

"Thanks. And don't worry. I can handle it. The only thing I do well is ride a bike." And he smiled again. "Besides, I haven't even gotten the job yet."

"You will. I'm sure of that."

We sat through another band's set before I decided to settle the bill. Dash sheepishly pulled out a few bucks from his pocket to give me. "Next time," I said. "When you get that job and have the money rolling in."

We left. It was getting dark; the sun was completely gone. Night lights cast cooler shadows on the ground. Dash would likely cycle back to his flat. I hoped he would get that part of his life sorted too. I knew what the added pressure of the circle he moved in cost him. We walked together for awhile before gauging our different directions. There was a reluctance we both felt at this departure.

"Good luck tomorrow," I said. "Let me know how you make out. Drop by the office Monday, or you can always knock on my apartment door tomorrow if you like. I'm usually around in the late afternoon on Sundays, doing my laundry and clean up stuff." My head exploded at this revelation. What was I doing? I thought of work again, and my colleagues' reactions: jaws dropping, eyebrows furrowing, bodies concretizing before asking, "What were you thinking?" But I gave him my address nonetheless.

"Thanks. 28 Beverley. It's burned into my brain. I might just drop by. And thanks again for everything today; the art, the book, the evening."

I added nothing at that point, not even a counselling comment about his alcoholic abstinence at dinner. I wanted to end our day on a positive note, keep my foot out of my mouth.

Then he hugged me. Spontaneous and deep, one hand holding his bike, the other arm pulling me into him. It was an embrace that I wished would go on a little longer. I tried to hide my feelings after we separated, but my face was hot and, if not for the evening's help at disguise, would have shown a reddening burn, peaking at the colour of my running shoes. By then, he was on his bike, and with a backwards wave, heading off. I floated on toward home in a blissful fog.

* * *

Coyote was taking a chance by being out this early on an open street that only now was growing dark. He huddled in a closed doorway and, utilizing his skill at blending into shadow, felt relatively safe and obscure. He watched the entrance to the Rex, waiting for their eventual emersion.

The Rex. It sounded like a dog's name he had heard being called out on occasions in the past when he was mobile and loping behind residences. It was the call from masters for their Rexes to return to the warmth and safety of the indoors for the night, the call that separated them from him. He had no masters. When needed, though, he could simulate a dog's more domestic movements, shift subtly in appearance and motion and pass into their realm.

Eventually, he noticed the couple's exit, ultimate separation, and then individual movement toward their respective homes. He would have to choose who to follow. His preference landed on the woman because of her more leisurely gait. He was tired and had no desire to attempt the exertion needed to keep up with the man and his bike. Crow could pick him up in the morning. Besides, there was a park situated in her direction in which he could retire for the night. There might even be enough energy left in him to track down some dinner before rest took over. So, he became a dog, tucked in closely to parked cars, and with his head down sniffing, he tagged along, unnoticed, behind.

* * *

Picture #4: *Sleeper*

Observer's description: A naked woman stands bent over the messy covers of her bed. Either she is rising into the morning or is up in the night for some reason. Only her back, buttocks and one breast are visible as she leans on the bed. Curtains are drawn in the background, keeping out the light or ensnaring the dark. The painting is in black and white, suggesting a mixture of innocence (white sheets) and culpability or loss (dark blankets/her posture). A foot is protruding from under the blanket. She is not alone. Is this a washroom excursion, insomnia, or a bad dream that has taken her from her bed? Is this even her bed? Is she going to return to it or grab her clothes and leave?

Chapter Four

DAY TWO

THE PRESENT

It is hot. I am on a beach somewhere in Cuba, getting away from it all. My feet are submerged in the warm sand, and the sun's rays are baking me. I begin to turn, moving onto my stomach, but the beach towel I am on, big and heavy, is coiling around me, tightening like a constricting boa. I start to flail and kick, trying to free myself, to tame it into compliance.

Then I come out of my dream, damp hair stuck to my pillow, one eye cocked open and visible. I get my bearings. Sunday beckons through my bedroom window. I sigh. "Damn it, Mr. Garrison," I mutter. "I know it's almost October, but do you have to crank the heat already? Christ."

Mr. Garrison is the owner and landlord of this house I call home. At seventy years of age or more, he is conscientious in most ways except for the heat. Friendly when we meet, willing to chat and fix a problem promptly, he lives alone, a widower, in the expansive apartment beside me. Two couples occupy the larger flats on the second and third floors above. Mine is the smallest of the four, but it suits me.

Mr. Garrison snowbirds south for three months in the dead of winter, but as early as October, starts preparing for his escape. Hitting the thermostat, he prematurely ejaculates his fears of frigidity into my apartment. Unfortunately, he controls everything.

I tried to nudge him gently in the direction of moderation and conservation in the first winter of my stay here, but he only nodded and smiled, commented on his old bones and told me to open some windows until the snow flies. He is a sweetie; I can't complain about rent or anything. The location is so great for me, central to work and play. Still, it is fifteen degrees or more outside these days and could be for a while with this global warming shit all around us. "No more sauna, Mr. Garrison, please," I yell at the walls, "my sheets and I will thank you."

I rip at my shell and let it slide to the floor, a skin I no longer want covering me. I sleep naked, au naturel because I love the feel. I don't want anything against me in bed. Some soft sheets when it's cold; maybe another body sometimes.

I have had a few boyfriends over the years, but nothing long-term. I have needs like anyone else, but no one yet has measured up, yelled out that I'm the one. That's fine. An exchange of sweat and fluids doesn't hurt from time to time, I tell myself. I just haven't found Mr. Right. I am meeting Greg for lunch this morning at 11:30 a.m., someone I have been seeing for a couple of months. We are nearing an end. He just doesn't know it yet. He is definitely a Mr. Wrong.

I think of Dash and wonder, but shake my head as if to clear away an image that shouldn't be there. Yesterday was great, though; his farewell embrace maybe more than a friendly hug. I sigh, staring at the ceiling. My eyes track a thin crack that meanders its way diagonally across a three-foot corner, completing a small triangle. A spider occupies a tiny space directly where the walls and ceiling meet at the top. It waits patiently to do what? Cast a web? Create a cocoon? Stretch its legs and then move on?

I perform a snowless angel stretch on my bed, willing my perspiration away and psyching myself up for the day. I think of the most important task ahead. *Tomorrow, and tomorrow, and tomorrow, creeps in this...* I can't remember any more of that

Shakespeare line. No matter. Greg's tomorrow has come. I just hope all will be well when I break it to him.

Pivoting into a sitting position, I look at the clock on my bedside stand. It's 8:30a.m.—not bad for a Sunday morning. It's the only day in the week I can sleep in if I want. Pulling myself into a stand, I step over my prostrate sheet and head for the bathroom for a much-needed shower. Afterwards, wrapped in a fluffy towel tamed and emptied of sand, I relax with some coffee, a small bowl of granola, yogurt, and some fruit. Then I finish my washroom duties, dress, and get ready to go out. Another image of Dash flashes into my mind, but I push it aside. First things first, I don't want to get ahead of myself. In fact, I can't think like this. Dash and me. How could that be? How could that even work? I ping pong thoughts of Greg and Dash back and forth until they blur. I step out and into the day—time to get on with it.

This morning, I am going to walk. It is beautiful outside; sunny, a light breeze playing with the leaves on trees across the street. They strike poses of red, yellow, and orange, but cling to their branches, chorus lines shimmering and refusing to exit the stage. They will kick and twirl for as long as they can, reacting to the wind's music, the temperature's decreasing tempo, and take several blustery encores before bowing to the ground. Winter will cover them until new protégés return in the spring for their budding auditions. On with the dance.

Leaving at 10 a.m. allows me plenty of time to stroll leisurely, take in the sights, reflect on strategies I might need to use with Greg when I break the news. I think of his reaction, the anger and argument that will likely unfold when I do. No matter, it must be done. I turn my key and get set to hit the streets. My loyal Converse tap out a soft shoe riff as I skip down the front steps. Across from me lies Grange Park, an oasis within the community. It is already filling up with the treasured migration of Sunday patrons, individuals, couples, and families bent on enjoying a lazy Sunday outdoors. I will wander north to Dundas Street and beyond, cut through the University of Toronto campus grounds to Bloor Street, make a left for a few blocks to Madison Avenue and then amble up to my destination, the Madison Pub.

There are several small, independent art galleries and studios within walking distance of my apartment. I had no idea how important this would become as the months moved on here. As I walk along, I think of high school and the art classes I took. My parents, both professionals, allowed me the freedom to choose what I wanted to develop in myself, as long as I was happy. I could handle the sciences, hated the maths, liked English well enough, but really latched onto art. I could sink into it, create quickly and experimentally, and see the results displayed in front of me. I could tear down and rebuild, rip up and reform, use a variety of mediums to express myself. As a teenager, my teachers told me I had the skill and that I should continue to explore my talents at a university or an art school. While university did ultimately beckon, after a preliminary year or two of taking smatterings of English, Fine Art, and Psychology, it was Sociology courses that finally drew me into its area of specialization.

The AGO loomed up at me on my right, becoming a visual component of my running inner monologue. As always, when going by, I perused its outer façade before turning my back on it and this time, moving west along Dundas Street. At least I had decided to minor in Fine Art for my last two years and completed a handful of courses that kept me practicing. In fact, next Saturday, I planned to take my first art class in almost two years. A re-introduction to various mediums: oil, pastels, water, pencil, and charcoal. I will renew this flame as a hobby, nothing more, I believe. But this return to a creative undertaking has me nervous and excited. I can hardly wait. Bright new art books and canvasses to be drawn in and painted on, a healthy break from the cracked, faded, and battered portraits I handle at work every day. At this moment, I think of Dash again, my favourite frameless, smudged, bargain-basement discard. Restoration is in order. I smile and continue on my way.

* * *

Foot and pedal power, the two modes of transportation Dash uses most. He has never driven, does not have a license, never wanted one. He has often hitched rides or out of necessity uses buses, streetcars, and subways when distance dictates a compromise, a practical alternative to time compressing around him. In a city like this, vehicles are merely obstacles to get around, erratic metal projectiles clogging air and space. He has only ever been a temporary passenger in their presence. An Iggy Pop song flashes into his head as he rides.

It is just before 10:00a.m., an ungodly hour to be up and cycling, given his usual nighthawk existence. He has kept his wits about him, though. After leaving Jesse and a great evening of sitting, talking, and he had to admit, listening to some pretty good music, he had gotten in around 10:30p.m. He had braced for people hanging out and partying, but the place had been empty. He had not formalized his relationship with Tania enough to always be here, but he crashed with her most nights. Tania was probably out working her pole and floor routine somewhere. It was her act that had drawn him to her. He circled with her for a few nights until he finally bought her a drink after a set. The dance had continued from bar to bed, but now he wanted off the floor. He had looked around the apartment for something to take the edge off. When he found the mickey of whiskey, he had moved to crack it open but then remembered Jesse and his desire to cut back. Instead, he had sat under the soft light of the corner chair and cracked open *Colville*. It was filled with the pictures he remembered seeing in the gallery earlier that day. Now, he could focus longer on each, take everything in silence. As he leafed through the pages, reading in places that caught his eye, a meditative mood gathered within him. He thought of his younger self and a stolen art kit, the summer he had drawn and created before things had changed. When he had finished, he returned the book to his backpack for safekeeping and decided to crash. Tania might not return tonight, which was fine. It didn't matter. He had reminded himself of his interview, set an alarm clock by the bed, and was up by nine, getting ready to go.

So far, Sunday morning was a quieter day for traffic of all kinds. The day would pick up if there was a game in town, the Raptors and Leafs having both come out of hibernation and awakened the yearning fans that clung to them, flies buzzing in a spider's sticky web, waiting to be cocooned slowly for months and eventually sucked dry. He had tried his hand at pond hockey a few times growing up, knew the basic rules, but basketball eluded him. He could run, though, kick and throw a ball, so soccer and baseball helped him develop some skills at school. But sports were mostly a team activity and he had never been part of a team for long. The teasing and friction that came with being the odd man out in a mostly white community would eventually track him down even at sports and he would find himself lashing out, mixing it up with teammates in anger, then walking away. Attending a baseball game now could be fun, although this season was almost gone. Hockey could be good, maybe even basketball, but no one had offered him a ticket. He knew it was his fault because any money he had, went mostly to Our Lady, and she washed it away before he even realized it. How had he let drink become his religion? Was it weakness, self-pity, self-loathing? Like a rug, he needed to be put on a line to air out, whacked a few times with a broom to drive out the dirt.

Today could be different, he thought as he mounted his steed and rode off. Money could flow in again if he got this job. This time, things would improve; he would control his urges and not let them get the better of him. Jesse's words came back to him from the day before. She was right to be angry and disappointed in him.

Her words had burrowed under his skin like a tick and infected him. He had to do better. There was something to prove to her that had him feeling both optimistic and scared. And he knew something else. His feelings for her were changing, morphing into more than friendship, but that had to be for another time. He needed to get this job first and earn some new respectability.

Dash was meeting Derrick, the owner of Y.E.S., at a small café on The Esplanade. He knew the place because a housing co-op was sprawled just across the street. Jesse had asked him if he might be interested in considering such an option, and this place had been mentioned. There were rules to be followed in belonging as well as responsibilities, but affordability was also a key factor. He had nodded but had declined the notion. He told her that something else would work out. What he did not say was that there were too many people there and too many possible conflicts. He preferred to maintain his nomadic wanderings. Then he had met Tania and settled into a tumultuous four-month entanglement, her door opening and closing on their mutual needs and desires. Another relationship Jesse had said needed to change when it came up at one of their recent interviews if he was to have any chance. She was right again. He drifted more into thoughts of Jesse until a red light brought him out of his daydream and back into concentration.

Bike courier. It had a feel to it, a tangible look and appeal that fit his personality. Dash could see himself, packages lashed to his body and his machine, accosting the streets and weather, a maverick, a desperado, his pony express always getting through. He had seen couriers crisscrossing the downtown core, and they looked pretty cool. Defiant drumbeaters, tough and self-assured, giving as good as they got. That's how it had to be when you rode against time, when you measured your motion against the tick-tock of other aggressive pedestrians and drivers. He had witnessed exchanges between a few of them, bikers squaring off at intersections or on sidewalks, the wrath on both sides blowing up quickly and without warning in the public domain. As if on cue, a taxi cut in on him as it pivoted onto Front Street, causing Dash to bounce off the curb and struggle for balance. He laid on his horn, a long verbal barrage of curses and insults that ricocheted off the driver's retreating bumper, and disappeared into the air. Taxi drivers. The worst. Dash fumed on down Berkeley Street until he reached The Esplanade. He tried to compose himself as he approached his destination. Blustering into a first meeting might not work in his favour. Another flaw he had to sort out—his temper flared up like a geyser, a hot blast that had become more unpredictable since the loss of his mother. He arrived and popped his bike up onto the sidewalk in front of the café. Securing it to a well-heeled post, he re-slung his backpack, took a calming breath, and prepared to enter.

* * *

I was a few slow minutes from my destination, the pub within view in the distance. I took a deep breath as I moved on, reluctant, yet determined. I had rehearsed several ways this could play out but didn't know what would happen. Greg would have driven his car, public transit never an option for him. His apartment was a mere forty-five minutes north of here by foot, but walking rarely appealed to him. He loved his car, and that was that. Any suggestion on my part that he leave it behind was met with derision. I had mentally checked this off as one of the detriments in our brief time together. A second was his drinking. We had met months ago at a party, a friend of a friend introducing us. Initially, he was charming. He seemed genuinely interested in what I was doing; he asked the right questions about my job and interests. He was neither loud nor abrasive nor opinionated early on. He drank very little as I remembered.

We went on a few dates after that. It wasn't until we got into bed together, became more serious and committed in his eyes, I guess, that his truer colours started coming out. Beer was his go-to beverage, but the hard stuff was now a recognizable sidekick. When in tandem, they brought out the boozy bigot rather than the witty charmer I had first met. Most ethnic groups would find their way into his sights, but the Indigenous—Indians he always called them—were maligned the most. His rants about them stemmed, he said, from his experiences in the West and elsewhere. I thought of the unfortunate coincidence this presented, given the other man rearing up in my life. My complaints at these attitudes always fell on deaf ears. He would laugh, insist he was just kidding, but I knew this wasn't a one-off. This was who he was. Why had I gotten involved with him in the beginning? My radar must have been way off. I decided that I was not going to invest any more time in trying to reform someone I saw now as indeed an asshole. While the sex, as short-lived as it had been, was good, I was ready to tweak the Bowie line and, with no more wham, bam, thank you, man, part ways.

Madison Pub is a big place, six British style pubs connected inside three Victorian-era mansions. Crowds of students and professionals flock here at night, particularly on weekends, but this is Sunday morning at 11:30 a.m., so business should be light. I chose this time for two reasons. It is less likely that Greg will be in a mood to drink, making what I want to say more clear and definitive, but I can't count on this. More importantly, though, I can extricate myself from any mess that occurs and walk away in the daylight. At a busy pub in the evening, his party lights blink on, listening skills turn to mud, and he is more prone to disagreements, even insults. I walked through the iron gates bordering a front patio that waited for one last gasp at an outdoor sitting before the end of the season and headed up the few stairs to the main door.

Inside, one of many rooms opened up to me. The traditional wood of the bar and its brass trim accentuated the velvet reds and golds of the cushioned seating. It was dark enough at the moment, even with the light of day filtering through the beautiful windows. British influence for sure. It was a little over the top for me. I preferred The Rex and last night to where I was now. Greg noticed me first, and I was serenaded with a ringing "hey, babe" and a hand wave from the booth beyond the bar. I cringed at the greeting, but smiled and moved toward him. I could see as I arrived that he was already nursing a beer. I was ready to blurt out my decision then and there, but I kept silent and instead chose to sit down. For now, I would have a coffee and something light to eat as I fumed. Give myself some perspective. There was still time. It was not yet noon. The title of a novel I had heard about at university, but not read, popped into my mind: Arthur Koestler's *Darkness at Noon*. Somehow, it seemed appropriate. He should enjoy his last meal with me before I purged him.

* * *

The café Dash entered was nondescript. Small and clean, it offered coffees, teas, and fruit drinks along with the usual assortments of sandwiches and desserts. Its few tables were occupied, but Dash singled out his man, Derrick, sunglasses pushed up on his head, the company name and logo on his sweatshirt an obvious giveaway. He eyed Dash as he came toward him, pushing out the second chair at the small table with his foot.

"Glad you made it, and right on time. Always a good sign in my business." He held out his hand. "Dash, right?"

"Right." Dash peeled off his backpack and sat down.

"Interesting name, man. That a handle or for real?" Derrick smiled, and Dash instantly liked him.

"No, it's for real." Dash wondered how far to go with his explanation. "My mom's idea, a moment of inspiration, she said."

Derrick nodded. "What inspired her to call you Dash?"

"She said I was a quick, easy birth. As soon as I came out, I started moving and wouldn't stop. I was never sure if she was serious or not, but that's what she told me." Dash looked out the window.

"Sounds like a funny lady."

"Could be, sometimes." Again, the window drew his attention. Derrick astutely changed the topic.

"You want a coffee and a scone? That's what I'm having. My treat."

"Sure, thanks."

"What do you take in your coffee?"

"Nothing, black."

"Plain, cheese, or fruit scone?"

"Ah, fruit, I guess."

Dash tapped his fingers nervously on the table as he waited, right leg bouncing in time to his beat. He brought his solo to a close as Derrick returned mugs in one hand, scones on a plate in the other.

"There you go, man. Coffee's good here, scones are always fresh. Enjoy."

Dash took a sip. Hot, but Derrick was right. He felt the caffeine ease into his system, and he tried to relax.

Derrick had moved off to grab cutlery and butter.

"Blueberry scones today," he said as he sat down. "Hope that's OK."

"Love blueberries," Dash replied, and he picked up a knife. For an instant, the recollection of picking wild blueberries with his mother on a walk strolled into his mind, but he covered it with a slather of butter.

Once they had settled into a bite or two, Derrick began the discussion they were to have with a natural segue. "I saw you ride up. Figured it was you. That's quite a beast you have there."

Dash fidgeted a little and took a mouthful of coffee. Was that a veiled criticism he wondered? Didn't matter. "Yeah, it's that, all right, but no complaints. I get around no problem."

"As long as it works for you. Guys who ride for me come in all shapes and sizes, and so do their bikes. Getting from A to B is all that matters in this game."

"That's all me and my bike do is get from A to B, so I figure I'm good."

Derrick laughed. "You know your bike? What I mean is, are you good with breakdowns, tune-ups, repairs, that sort of thing?"

It was Dash's turn to laugh. "You saw that machine. Not a lot of working parts. But yeah, I can keep it mobile."

"Good, because you're pretty much a one-man show out there." Derrick paused for a drink and a layer of butter on the second half of his scone. "What made you decide you wanted to try this?"

"I've biked on and off most of my life. It's always been the main way I get around other than on foot. The job, being outdoors and riding around, it appeals to me. I think I could do it."

"It's not as easy as it looks or as much fun, you know?" Derrick was honest here. "Weather can be a bitch. Traffic crawls up your ass all day long, clients get pissed off if you run late or make a mistake with the delivery. We're in competition with other couriers for business, so if you screw up, it's on you. Turnover on the job is high, although we do have some guys who have been at it a long while too." Derrick stopped and smiled. "That make you feel like you still want to do it?"

Dash sat quietly before responding. "I want to give it a try, at least. It's better than what I've been doing so far, odd jobs I've had inside packing boxes, cleaning dishes. This excites me."

Derrick looked hard at Dash, arms crossed, taking in what he had been saying. He didn't know him, didn't know his background, where he was from—nothing. But at this point, what the fuck? He would give him a shot because he had been given one as well and what goes around comes around. Besides, and Dash would soon find out, the romantic notion of courier delivery wore off quickly. Many of those who started the job as students in summer or young men looking for something new and different often packed it in when winter began to surface. And winter's first surge was likely just a couple of months away.

"OK, then, if that's what you want, let's settle in, and I'll explain the basics of the job to you." Dash nodded. "We'll start training tomorrow. I'll introduce you around, show you the ropes. Then I'll put you with Blake, one of my best long-term couriers, for a couple of days to ease you in, then off you go on your own toward the end of the week. Sound good?"

"Sounds good."

They would spend another half hour there, replenishing coffees and chatting. Learning the job involved being ready to go at eight in the morning, using the cell phone provided, memorizing routes, figuring out short cuts, respecting the clients, not getting pissed off, maintaining one's bike, getting appropriate clothing, and staying sober and off drugs. In general, being responsible. Derrick also mentioned pay, which started at fifteen dollars an hour plus any tips he might receive for good service and stellar communication. Dash needed to bone up on communication for sure, but he could do this. He had to do this. Jesse would expect nothing less.

* * *

I couldn't help myself. My mouth opened of its own accord as I slid into the seat opposite Greg.

"Getting off to a pretty early start, don't you think? Coffee not good enough?"

Greg leaned back and took a sip of his beer. "Don't worry about me. Just a little pick me up after last night."

I knew I would regret asking. "What were you up to last night?"

"Out with a few boys from work. Hit some bars." Greg chuckled. "Got pretty wasted, actually. Made it home in one piece, though." He pulled at his beer again.

He was waiting for me to say it. I didn't disappoint. "So, I guess you guys had a DD, or maybe you all took a taxi afterwards?" Before he could respond, our waitress arrived and asked me if I wanted a drink. I looked up at her. "Water and coffee, please."

"A little more time with the menus?" she asked.

"When you get back. Thanks."

During my brief exchange, Greg had almost finished his beer. "To answer your question, I drive. I always drive. You know that, babe."

I bristled. "Even, like you said, when you're wasted. And stop with the 'babe'. I don't like it."

"Whoa, OK, ba…", but he pulled back, hands up in mock submission, laughed, and tried to backpedal, "I was exaggerating. It wasn't that bad."

"Don't give me that." I scanned the menu. "I've seen you at parties."

"Yeah, and everything was fine. Everything worked out."

I couldn't believe his cavalier attitude, but I've seen it in a lot of guys. This macho "I can handle my drink" that paints every yahoo's response to alcohol. I simply shook my head. Fortunately, the waitress returned with my water and coffee. I almost decided then and there to pass on food, but I was hungry. I ordered the chicken Caesar salad. He went for the hungry man's breakfast and a second beer. Another one of his traits was to eat big, along with drink big and talk big. I guess it was part of his Western code. No Stetson adorned his head though, which I was thankful for, only the occasional ball cap. Such a change from our first contact. How had I let this chameleon hang around?

He was originally from Calgary and had moved here a couple of years ago. I had been to Calgary when I was much younger with my parents, a two-day stopover as we wended our way to the B.C. coast. Everything was big there as I recalled—big hats, big boots, big trucks, big oil, but maybe it was because I was only twelve or so and everything seemed big. We missed the Stampede, and I was glad of that. I love horses, but not the images I had seen of how they are worked, either bucking wildly to off a rider, running down a steer to be lassoed and hogtied or worse, pulling chuck wagons around a track at speeds bent on killing them and everybody on board. And although the mountains were great to see looming up around us as we drove and the countryside had its beauty, nothing about Calgary had impressed me then. Too homogeneous. The city has changed now, I understand, and is much more diverse. Still, I've never had the urge to go back—my prejudice to deal with.

"So, what were you up to last night?" His question brought me out of my reverie and into the present again. He had finished off his beer and while waiting for his food and another drink had opted for conversation.

"I was out with a friend for a bit, nothing much."

"Doing what?"

"We met at the art gallery in the afternoon, then decided to go for a bite to eat after. That was it." I could see Greg's eyes glazing over when I mentioned the gallery. Not his thing. Nothing to do with the arts was, come to think of it. He was into cars, hockey, and partying. Suddenly, my eyes started glazing over. What was I doing with this guy? I mean, really.

"So, your friend. What's she like?" And there it was. Two assumptions made on his part. One, that my friend had to be a woman because art was involved and two, I couldn't possibly be out with a guy somewhere on my own. After all, your honour, isn't possession nine-tenths of the law? This irked the hell out of me. Well, let's see how he takes the coming revelation.

"Actually, my friend's a guy."

Greg looked at me then, incredulous. "A guy. What kind of guy?" Interrogation 101 was beginning, and the air was getting a little frosty.

"What do mean what kind of guy? A guy, a couple of balls and a dick kind of guy, I assume. What does it matter to you?"

"What do you mean, what does it matter?" Anger was setting in. "What does this guy do? Where did you meet him?"

Our waitress returned with our food—another timely break in the action that I needed. When she asked if there would be anything else, I opted for more coffee. Greg decided he wanted a chaser to go with his beer and asked for a Crown Royal neat. Things were not going to go well. He dug into his plate, impaling potato and onion onto a slice of bacon. "Well?" and he rammed the forkful into his mouth.

"Well, what?" I sifted through my Caesar, mixing in the dressing, plucking at a piece of chicken.

"Where did you meet this so-called friend?" I tried not to focus on his churning pie hole, the food becoming more and more masticated with his attitude. Good form, Greg. Good form. "How long have you known this guy? Do you work with him?"

"I've known him, funnily enough, for longer than you. A year or so if you want to know. And yeah, I work with him." This was, in actuality, no lie, depending on the interpretation. I wasn't going to say much more about Dash, though, or who he was. Greg's whiskey had arrived at this point, and I took his distraction with this as a chance to start eating. By the time I had finished my first bites, a third of his beer was gone and his whiskey had disappeared.

"So, what's his story?" I was beginning to feel harassed.

"What's his story? He's a friend. That's all. End of story. If you can't accept that, too bad."

"Listen to me." His fork had now become an instrument, a weapon pointed toward me as he gestured. I wasn't picking up on his words at that point, but I had struck a nerve, and the venom was oozing out—green-eyed jealousy. I thought of my high school Shakespeare. He was playing his Othello off against my Desdemona. Thank God there were no pillows around, or I'd be a goner. I caught the end of his diatribe, and it snapped me back into anger. He was attempting to lasso me toward him with threats of a branding, put his mark on me as his own. In his world, a male friend independent of his circle was not going to happen, and he wanted him cut from the herd. I had had enough. I put down my fork.

"Who do you think you are? You'll never tell me who I can have as friends. Male or female. Do you understand?"

He brushed my words aside, a flick at a pesky fly. "I want to know who this guy is, what he means to you." He was really good at not listening. His booze was having its way, shaping his words into a truer representation of himself. He finished his beer. His eyes signalled that he wanted more, and he looked around for the waitress. This was it, my time to go. I reached for my bag and pulled out my wallet. I put a twenty on the table beside my unfinished lunch. I no longer had an appetite. He was slow on the reaction to my visual cues, so I spelled it out for him.

"I planned to talk to you today about us...about where we are and where we're going. Two adults hashing things out calmly and with some respect. You've just made my talk unnecessary." Here, I slowed down for a minute to let him absorb my last few words. "You don't own me. Nobody does or will. You can't tell me what to do or who to be friends with. I don't like your attitude. I don't like your drinking. We should never have hooked up. I don't want to be around you anymore. We're finished." I got up to go. Luckily, there were only a few heads in the pub that had picked up on our exchange. As I walked out, I felt their eyes riveted to my back. I heard my name called out and a command to return, but I never looked back.

* * *

Dash walked out of the café with Derrick. He felt good about the meeting and the guy who had just hired him. Derrick was in his forties, an old road warrior who now organized and sent out his minions. But he still donned the apparel when his crew was strapped for time, or someone was under the weather and commandeered the routes. This is where his message to Dash had become loud and clear. Riders couldn't afford to be sick, couldn't afford time off. Obviously, because of the money they would lose, but also because it put the entire operation in jeopardy. One downed courier was a chink in the armour, a weakness that undermined and opened the core. If the work was there, you rode five days a week, sometimes Saturday, if needed. Derrick was compassionate and understanding enough, he had said, but not a believer in excuses. Either you could do the job or not. Everybody had their problems, but recovery from whatever ailments you manifested had to be cured on the weekend. Dash got the point. Taking care of yourself was the first credo in approaching life and the work; taking care of your bike was second.

He moved toward his mount and looked around. "No wheels with you?"

Derrick shook his head. "Don't need 'em today. I live across the street."

"You live in that cooperative?" Dash was surprised.

"Sure, why not? It's a great place. I'm on my own in a one-bedroom for about a thousand a month. It's close to everything I need and want right now."

"A thousand a month." Dash thought of his regimen of crashing here and there over the last year, his somewhat tentative living arrangement with Tania, and wondered if he could ever get his own place. "A good deal, I guess, but still too rich for me."

Derrick looked at him, kindly. "The nice thing about the co-op is that all types of people live there. Young families, fixed pensioners, people with disabilities, new immigrants all have a shot if they're willing to follow a few rules and work with each other to keep the place a going concern."

Jesse had told him as much, and he had been quick to walk away from the idea. He had made up excuses in his mind like he was too much of a loner or wouldn't fit in. Maybe he could consider something like that after all. He'd talk to her again about it when he had a chance. For now, he was more concerned about getting ready for the next day. He had his bike, check, his mobile phone, check. He would be given a courier bag for the small packages and letters he would be distributing, and a T-shirt and sweatshirt. The rest was up to him. Derrick had mentioned a bike shop that the company used exclusively for tune-ups, repairs, replacement parts—whatever. They got a discount when used, but those were bills that the couriers had to pay. "Keep that bike pristine or in your case at least functional," and he had laughed.

"Thanks, man, for everything so far, for the chance." Dash was not good at ingratiation. It made him feel like a loser, like he was getting a handout. He knew the stereotypes that had followed him around for most of his life, the diminished expectations and the calculated discriminations. "Just bend over and take it" was the much-maligned mantra he was used to. But Derrick had not made him feel this way. Whether he knew instinctively of his Metis roots or not, Dash appreciated his candor, so his thanks had been unscripted and given with feeling.

"No worries. I'll see you tomorrow. Eight sharp. We'll go over stuff again, you'll meet Blake, and we'll see how things go." And they parted ways, like friends it felt. Dash thought of Jesse again. Maybe he could ride over to her apartment, let her in on the good news. But he mulled this idea over and thought no. Better to have a day or two under his belt then tell her. Nothing like a little success to up his status in her eyes. Instead, he would head for a neutral space, a park somewhere, dig out his art book and pass the time in quiet reflection. There was no rush in getting back to Tania's. No telling what was going on there. He had to keep focused on Monday and stay away from temptation.

* * *

I made it onto the street and several steps south toward Bloor Street before I was accosted. That's what I'll call it. I felt a hand on my shoulder. It was not a touch, not a tug, more like the grip of something that meant business, a talon securing flesh before tearing into it. I knew who it was. I flinched and froze, wondering if a blow was to come. I didn't know, couldn't predict what he would do. He'd had a few drinks. My basic instinct was that we were on a public street, secure in the eyes of passing observers and that fellow pedestrians would rein in any rash response he might have. I turned warily, pulling away from his reach. He let go. There were no words at first. We just stood eyeing each other like wary boxers waiting for an opening. I was still angry, but also tentative and a little afraid. He held a set of keys in his hand that he fiddled with. Finally, he broke the silence.

"What do you think you're doing?"

"What does it look like? I'm leaving."

He tried to keep himself under control, but his voice cracked with emotion. "Just hang on a minute. Let me say something."

I wouldn't let him in. "There's nothing more to say. I've said it all. Please go. I don't want to see you anymore."

Then he popped, and his anger filled the air. "You can't do this!"

I just looked at him and shook my head. Then, utilizing a former Prime Minister's famous line, I said, "Just watch me," and turned away. Shots rang out and careened off my body. "Bitch" caught me on my right shoulder, "you fucking bitch" ripped into my left, and then a longer barrage of "you goin' to see him, you whore" strafed my back, but I never went down. And he never followed me. I expelled a deep breath, wiped some tears from my eyes, a salty mixture of pain and relief, and kept walking into the sunlight. I hoped he would just find his car, drive away, and that would be the end of it.

* * *

Crow had perched himself on top of Madison Pub and sat taking in the morning air. Sunlight caught his feathers from time to time as it filtered through the trees. He enjoyed the warmth when he could, recognizing that colder air was moving in. Soon the trees and city landscape would take on a more barren reality. Fall was on its way. Below him, he noticed the appearance of the girl again. Coyote's call had instigated a tracking switch, and now it was he who had followed along her meandering trajectory to here. She had been with another inside, a darker spirit, but she had emerged alone, walking purposefully back in the direction she had come. Then the other surfaced, a predatory gait driving him, and Crow had become vigilant. Their exchange had been brief, but the girl had been wounded by a string of heartless sounds that drove Crow up onto a higher tree branch nearby and away from the words. He watched as the man stood for a time before retreating to search for his car. Crow did not intervene in any specific way, but he would comment on the altercation. Lifting off, he found his target, a shiny black metal object parked further up the street, and daubed it with his milky signature, a simple abstract of splashes that steamed for a moment with artistic freedom. Then he turned back to check on the girl. He felt lighter at heart, and a croak of laughter escaped him.

* * *

St. James Park is one of many green spaces within the city that offers respite from the hustle and bustle of daily life for foot and pedal travellers. Bounded on three sides by Adelaide Street to the north, Jarvis Street to the east, and King Street to the south, it contains trees, gardens, walking paths, a gazebo, and a water fountain. Assorted benches to rest on are scattered here and there. A nineteenth-century style garden presented by the Garden Club in 1980 is part of its appeal and is noted on a plaque within the grounds. Enclosing the park from the west side is the majestic Cathedral Church of St. James, part-owner of the park along with the City of Toronto. The beautifully appointed cathedral boasts a Gothic Revival design, has the second tallest church spire in North America next to one in New York, and boasts a series of incredibly rich-sounding chiming bells still used regularly. It was this location that Dash decided to seek out after his meeting with Derrick. While the church itself beckoned to tourists and parishioners alike, Dash had never been inside, his feelings about religion in general, leaving him as cold as the stone with which the edifice was erected.

In the western town where he grew up, he remembered three churches, Baptist, United, and Catholic. Likely, this was to offset the competition of the three bars that also welcomed believers into their midst. The bars always had the upper hand, though, being accessible every day, but Sunday. Bernie Dobson, the local bootlegger, helped offset this one-day aberration, often using one of the church parking lots late at night on a Saturday or Sunday to run his own service. From the pulpit of his trunk, Bernie would absolve sins, hear confessions, break bread, and pass the cup. Dash smiled at this. A few Indigenous from the reserve attended church in town, and he had wondered why. However, many saw Bernie as their priest or pastor of choice too.

His mother had friends on the reserve. Sometimes she visited, and he had tagged along. Occasionally, a drum circle and dancing were involved, but his mother never joined in. She observed stoically, met with a friend or two, and then they would leave. He spoke of these events with her out of curiosity, but always received vague insights or none at all. She could not tolerate white religion, yet circled around Native spiritualism but never entered.

Dash had adopted this aloofness as well. To investigate would open wounds, and he opted to keep the Band-Aid on, his past covered. He came back to his present and the cathedral before him. It was the intimate nature and beauty of the park itself that drew him here, not the tribute to a god that had never favoured him.

Propping his bike up behind a bench, he placed his backpack beside him and pulled out his book. He stared at the cover before opening it. The image of a young woman standing on a boat and looking directly at him through a pair of binoculars filled the space. A man's arms draped across a deck seat behind her, face unseen, and the rising outline of a lifeboat behind them, leading off to a final vision of blue sky and water, completed the picture. She held him in her gaze. He wondered what she was really looking at as he flipped her over past the brief forwards and introduction to the first picture and the *Welcome to Colville* article that prefaced his collected works. Dash wanted to get to the images that he knew made up most of the book, but he skimmed the words and found himself captivated by certain imagery that he noticed and, in particular, quotes that stopped him and caused him to lift his head from the text and stare off into the park. Two lines pulled from the Talking Heads song, "Once in a Lifetime", which addressed how people get to where they are in life, catapulted him back into a burst of memories. Childhood, home, his mother, these recollections of joy and pain held him for a moment until he shook his head and returned to the pages. And then another that Colville offered from his own thoughts, comparing what he saw as the goodness of animals to the lack of goodness in people. Was he good, he wondered? In his constant arguments with himself, he rarely found a reason to say that he was. Digger then sprang to mind and their days of running free together. Those days had been good. Dash would spend another hour there focused on the book before deciding to put it away. It was time to make a choice, and he wasn't sure of the outcome. Shouldering his backpack, he hopped on his bike and headed out.

Tania's apartment was on Mutual Street, just south of Dundas Street. A few high rises surrounded a small row of dilapidated brick row houses, one of which she and her roommate had managed to get. It was a cramped enough living space, mainly when people arrived to party and ended up crashing. He was never sure who might end up there, and he was always surprised when no one was around. As he pulled up to the front steps, he heard music coming from inside and knew then that he wasn't alone. Securing his bike, he swung open the front door and was greeted by the unmistakable aroma of weed. Tania, her roommate, and two other guys he vaguely recognized were sitting on the couch and chair, drinks in hand. She greeted him with an insincere "where you been?" and before he could respond, a "join the party." It was then that he moved toward his ill-conceived plan.

"Can't right now. Just came back to grab a few of my things." He headed for the bedroom. Tania followed him lazily with her eyes before finally broaching a response.

"What things?"

Dash had forced a few clothes into his backpack and now was in the bathroom, grabbing a toothbrush. As he turned, Tania confronted him in the doorway. Looking at him, she said again, "What things? What are you doing?"

"Some good news. I got a job. Start tomorrow." He started to move past her.

"So? That means you'll have some more money to contribute here, right?" and she put her hand on his shoulder.

Dash looked at her for a moment, frowned, and then said, "Actually, I'm going to stay at a friend's for a while. I need to focus on the job and get my act together."

She had brought along her drink, her signature rye and coke, and took a long sip. "Get your act together?" She laughed. "That's a good one. Who's your friend? Do I know him?"

"No. She's someone who's been helping me try to get straight for a while and…"

"She!" There it was. He'd stepped in it. "You fucking prick! She!" Dash started moving now as she bounced her words off him. She wasn't wrong with most of them, he thought, as he passed the threesome in the living room watching the show. "Well, get out then, you shit. You never gave me much around here anyways except your dick, and I can get that anywhere and anytime."

Dash turned as he opened the door, looked at her, then smiled. "Oh, I know you can." He pulled the door closed just in time to block the arrival of her flying glass. He was only halfway there now and less certain of his next step. The ride over to Beverley Street filled him with dread. What if Jesse wasn't there? What if she refused to take him in? What if? What if? This question repeated itself over and over like the clicking of his pedals as he moved along Dundas Street. His arrangement with Tania had always been fluid, nothing he felt or wanted to be permanent. The streets had been his alternative before; if Jesse did not let him in now, they might have to be again.

He arrived at Jesse's apartment more than a little out of breath. He put it down to his nerves and not his conditioning; otherwise, tomorrow could be a very long and punishing day. As always, his timing was not that good. It was just pushing five. Maybe she had dinner plans or worse yet, someone over, maybe even living there. He didn't know anything about her friends or relationships. *This could be a bad idea,* he told himself. He stood on the street, counting off the minutes before finally taking a deep breath, stepping up onto the porch, and ringing the doorbell. Time ticked away. He thought of turning around and simply going… somewhere. But then there was an unlocking sound, and the door opened.

Jesse stood in the doorway, a look of surprise plastered on her face, some laundry tucked under her arm.

"Hi, Jesse. Sorry for showing up like this, but…"

"You decided to drop by. That's great," she said. "Like I told you, Sunday afternoon is usually cleaning and laundry. Boring stuff, right?"

Dash shifted on his feet. "Maybe I should come another time."

"Don't be silly. Come in. I'm almost done. You can chain up your bike out there." She turned away, the door wide open.

Dash secured his bike, hesitated for a second then crossed Jesse's threshold to the inside. He hoped she would still be as welcoming when she heard the rest of his story.

*   *   *

Picture #5: *Horses in Field*

Observer's description: The image is muted, almost a grainy depiction of the scene, perhaps suggesting a hot summer day. There are two horses in the foreground, one lying down head erect, the other standing beside it eating grass. The artist uses shades of blended yellows, greens, and pinks to help depict the grass's drier consistency. Around the open field are trees and shrub brush, which are tinged a blueish-green. The sky above is cloud covered, looking in places like they are gathering for rain. The roofline of a barn is partially seen in the distance. The horses look healthy, relaxed, and content in each other's company and their surroundings.

Chapter Five

THE PAST

Summer had pushed lazily into July. Dash had spent the first two weeks since exiting school sleeping in, biking to various locations in and around his town, and trying to privately improve his drawing skills. He had finished his final year of treading water in the elementary pool, and there were hints of change coming. He had overheard the occasional quiet conversation between his mother and Eric. There was talk of a move, but he didn't know what that meant and who was involved. He had let his questions go unasked, preferring instead to lose himself in the moments of a ride or the movements of his hand over paper. Most of his time had been spent alone; his desire for companionship less sought after than his wish for solitude. His mother had expressed concern, suggested that maybe looking for a part-time job might be warranted. Her periodic cajoling had ended with a tussle of his hair or a sigh to his shrug. The issue had finally died.

Dark clouds had appeared overhead a week earlier and had taken a few days to dissipate. In a moment of free-range searching, his mother had entered his room and then his closet and had uncovered his art kit. When he had come in from outside and his daily regimen of stone-throwing, she had presented her find to him all nicely opened and laid out on the kitchen table. In a fit of anger and outrage, he had raced toward her, responding to her initial query with "none of your business" and citing invasion of privacy. She had rebuffed his verbal attack by raising her initial question to the level of an accusation and demanded an answer.

He had collected his supplies and tools roughly, thrown them into the box, and hustled himself off to his bedroom where he had closed his door. To her credit, his mother had let him be, had gone about other things until an hour had passed, and then she had knocked on his door. No response.

"Dash," and she had knocked again. "I'm coming in."

He sat cross-legged on the bed, his art kit closed by his side. He picked bird-like at the bed cover with his head down. His mother had perched on the edge of the bed.

"That's a beautiful art kit. Anything you want to tell me about it?"

Dash shook his head. "No."

"Dash, look at me." His head came up slowly. "Where did you get it?"

"From school." He continued to pick.

"So, you borrowed it?"

He looked down again and remained silent.

"Dash?"

"I took it, all right?" His anger began to bubble up again. "All the other kids have stuff, mom, art stuff that they bring from home—nice paper, pencils. I don't. I just use the crap they've got there." He stopped for a moment to gather his thoughts. "And I like to draw."

His mother sat for a while and picked away with him, both eventually creating their own tiny piles of fluff.

"You know what you did is wrong," she quietly stated.

Dash didn't respond, just sighed and pushed a hand through his hair. He was waiting for her inevitable decision—one he knew would involve him returning the kit with whatever was left unused to its rightful owner. But what good would that do? School was out. He was done with Grade 8 and all its shit. He'd be branded a thief by his teacher, the school and would probably have to pay for everything he used, or his mom would have to. He sat there with feelings of guilt, embarrassment, shame, and anger washing over him and waited for the axe to fall.

But it never happened. Instead, she had said, "Come on out to the kitchen table and let's take a closer look at what you've got." They had sat down at the table together, opened the kit, and laid out its contents. Before they went further, she had reprimanded him again on his actions and told him that what he had done would not happen again, but there would be no returning his lifeline. It would be their shared secret. Dash had looked at her with bewilderment and then a burst of love. A smile painted his face. He could keep it, and now that she knew of this passion, she said she would try to help him with materials when he needed them. Then something even more surprising had occurred.

His mother had picked up a pencil and pulled out a blank sheet of paper. "May I?" she asked. Dash nodded. On the table, there was a mug and plate left from earlier. In a few minutes, she had captured the essence of the objects and transferred them, while not precisely, to the waiting sheet with confidence and flair.

"I didn't know you could draw. Where did you learn?"

"First, I don't really know how to draw, at least not that well. And as for learning," she said with a quick frown as she laid the pencil down, "there were some things at school that I didn't find useless and insulting." School had always been a sore point with her. Maybe that was part of why she did not press him to return the kit. He could see her looking at him.

"You never talk about your school days," Dash finally said. "They couldn't be much worse than mine, right?"

She laughed and reached out to run her hand across his cheek. "It's something I try to forget, but I guess I should tell you a little now since we're fellow artists and all." Dash smiled at being acknowledged as both a confidante and an artist.

"My parents never had much, and because they never had much, I got taken away from them when I was eight or thereabouts." She stopped for this to settle in, but Dash remained quiet.

"The foster home and school I had to go to after that was, let's say, less than perfect."

"You didn't like it?"

"Not much, really. I was never harmed in a bad way like some I knew or heard about, but I never felt loved or treated with respect. I felt lost and alone most of the time. And the bad part was I never got to see my folks again."

"Your mom and dad?"

She looked at her hands and nodded. "When I was sixteen, I took off. I wasn't going to stay there anymore. It wasn't easy, though. I took odd jobs until a little later, I met your dad, and here we are." She picked up the pencil again and began to shade in a bit more of her drawing. "But at least I learned to draw a little, and that gave me some comfort."

Dash knew that he was only getting a crash course in her early life. She had left out the darker periods of self-destruction and anger that festered in her, compounded with too much drinking. But she had found her way back, and throughout it all, had held onto her promise of not letting him go, and he could see the difference in her now. He hated to credit Eric's part in this too much, but it was there and had to be accepted. Dash felt an urge to push for more before another of their moments ended.

"Why did you never get to see your parents again?"

His mother picked up the pencil and worked some paper with it, at first just long lines flying out to the edges. Then a wide circle began in an unused section that she tightened until it darkened into a black dot at the centre where all the whiteness lay buried.

"You see this circle, Dash?"

"Yes."

"Well, this circle was like my family. In the beginning, we opened wide to each other. We had our culture, our ways to keep us going, to tell us who we were. Then when times got hard, things changed, and the circle tightened around us. My parents forgot themselves, became something else and let me go in the process. It wasn't their fault. They were forced into this shifting by outsiders who didn't understand what they really wanted or who they really were. I was taken away, supposedly to a better place, which was the final tightening and the black dot lie." Here she poked the centre until the lead broke, and a pinhole appeared. "A better place I was told where everything I knew was forgotten and my name became a memory. And my parents, well, they got drawn into that black hole so far that they vanished before I could get back to them." She could see the look of confusion and pain cross Dash's face, and she stopped. With a sigh and a smile, she took his hands in hers. "But you, I haven't forgotten, and never will. Whenever I'm sad, I just have to think of you, and everything is good again. OK?"

Dash nodded as he tried to absorb her words. He thought he understood. When she let go of his hands, he found himself running his finger around the circle, feeling the indentations she had made and the tiny ragged puncture at the core. It was enough for now.

* * *

It was Saturday, July 25th, and the town's annual stampede festival was taking place. Saskatchewan towns were dotted with these summer blowouts, but their town of over 3,000 people had one of the larger ones. Folks from different communities, often as far as a hundred kilometres away, would drive over for the day or the weekend. Some would camp at the lakes nearby and make a holiday of it; others would book rooms for a couple of nights at one of the three hotels in town. Whatever the reasoning, the stampede boasted a large parade on Saturday that wound its way through downtown streets, eventually ending up at the massive fairgrounds. Here, visitors could attend the various rodeo competitions, the vast array of vendor displays inside and outside the arena, grab assorted food truck offerings in the park and chase them down with cold beers at the beer tent, or hit the midway and games alleys in the fields set up nearby. All of this was within easy walking distance.

Dash had asked his mother if he could attend. She was working an extra shift at the restaurant from noon until eight, and Eric was helping a friend with a garage door problem. The money for the day at work would be good because of all the visitors in town, so in a mood of overwhelming generosity, Dash thought, she had given him twenty dollars. This would cover his entrance fee, a few rides or a souvenir if he wanted, and some food. He was told to be careful and, regardless of what was going on, to be back before dark. Dash had nodded in agreement and grabbed his backpack, which always housed his art kit, jumped on his bike, and headed off.

Living on the edge of town meant a longer ride to the fairgrounds. Dash would head down their lane to the main road that brought people into town. Then he'd cycle about a kilometre along it past the two-grain elevators that marked the landscape until he turned onto Main Street. Both roads were nice and wide. From here, he could zigzag across side streets, some of which were still dirt, until he found himself at the fairgrounds. First, he would find a place to stop, maybe a tree where he could lean his bike and watch the parade go by. Cars would not be allowed on the parade route, so would be parked wherever they could find a spot in parking lots and side streets all around town. A bike was the best way to go.

The parade was long enough, taking over an hour to thread by spectators who lined sidewalks along the route. Local businesses and charities were represented with floats that included musicians, waving children, and adults dressed in various outfits. All were pulled by large tractors or trucks. A few marching bands from surrounding areas also participated. The mayor rode in an open convertible at the head of the parade, clowns threw candy at the kids as they walked by, and a string of old combines, threshing machines, and other pieces of antique farm equipment was hustled into service, belching a sometimes-reluctant tribute to the old days. An Indigenous float representing the reserve to the east of town was also colourfully involved. Dash gave this closer scrutiny. His eyes locked onto a couple of teenagers, a boy and girl, dressed in bright traditional garb. A slight pang of envy and regret rose in him. He wondered if their smiles and waving hands were genuine or just for show. Were they happy in the knowledge of who they were? Were they proud staring down the gawkers lined up below them as they passed or could they hardly wait to remove their handmade clothing in favour of the more subdued and imported trappings of the surrounding citizenry? Sirens suddenly blasting from the local fire trucks bringing up the rear of the parade jerked him out of his stupor. The parade was over. Dash had been most impressed as he reviewed the hour with the beautiful horses that intermittently pranced by, their manes ribboned, saddles flashing gold or silver trim, riders bearing flags or simply doffing their Stetsons as they bounced along.

Dash figured that it was just past 2:00 p.m. He guessed this because the parade began at 12:30p.m., and he had found a spot to watch midway on the route. The lead floats were just beginning to arrive at a cordoned-off area of the fairgrounds where they would wait out the day until they were torn down, and the wagons and trailers were returned to their owners or sponsors.

Dash noticed some of the midway rides like the Zipper, the Ferris wheel, and the Roundup spinning off in the distance. He would take a closer look later. Right now, he would pay his entrance fee, a three dollar cut into his twenty dollars because of age, and then head off to get something to eat. French fries and a Coke shaved another three dollars off his total, but his stomach growls subsided. He looked around at the gathering crowds and decided that he would go into the arena and check out some of the stalls.

Like many of the stampedes or fairs that took place, the arena was filled with a variety of offerings and displays. Down one side of the vast floor were a host of tables advertising science projects from local high school and elementary students all vying for coveted contest awards, a first, second, or third prize ribbon acknowledging their fellow participants' betterment. The same categories existed for adults in areas such as baking, quilting and even, Dash noticed, arts and crafts. He thought of the art kit he had tucked into his backpack and wondered whether, with practice, he could beat some of the work he saw on display. Other parts of the arena were reserved for vendors who were selling their wares. Foodstuffs such as homemade preserves, pies, and meats could be sampled and bought; cowboy paraphernalia such as hats, boots, kerchiefs, and bolo ties could be found at different specialty tables; posters and cheap variety store knick-knacks such as whistles, balloons, trading cards, and candies were available for kids with only a handful of change at their disposal.

Dash passed them all until he came to a series of tables that featured Native art of various kinds. He was captivated by what he saw. Drum kits, medicine wheels, dream catchers, spirit chasers, talking sticks, peace pipes, and beaded wrist bands were all laid out for people to admire and purchase. He thought of the money he had and wondered how easy it might be to lift something small when a table was busy, a simple sleight of hand, a transfer magician-like to his backpack. His face began to burn when he recalled his mother's words, and he vowed not to give into the temptation. He would take a closer look and see if there was anything he could afford.

For a time when he was younger, his mother had dream catchers. He was just a child then, but he recalled them hanging from a metal pole outside, twisting and turning in the wind. There was even one kept inside suspended from the window in his mother's bedroom. He never recalled asking about them; he just admired their beauty and wondered at his mother's desire for them. That was years ago now, and they had weathered and disappeared. Perhaps, he should get her another one. The Native vendor behind the table noticed him.

"See anything you like?" Dash nodded and found himself eyeing a small red dream catcher suspended on a peg behind the woman. She looked back at it.

"You like that one, eh? Good eye." She leaned back and plucked it from its mooring. "Take a closer look if you like" and she held it out to him.

Dash accepted it and turned it over in his hands. The small circle was carefully wrapped tightly in red leather, thin strips that overlapped the metal circle. Leather strips of red hung down, complimenting a series of soft white and black feathers that he stroked. Within the circle, thin strands of thread or hair of some kind crisscrossed in a shimmering pattern.

"That's actual horsehair," the vendor said, "and those feathers are from a pheasant. Fluffy and soft, right?"

Dash nodded. He finally asked, "How much?"

"Ten dollars, son."

He hesitated. Doing the math, that would leave him four dollars for the rest of the day. He wasn't sure what he still wanted to do and wondered if four dollars would be enough. Sensing a dilemma, the woman smiled. "You wanting this for yourself or someone else?"

"My mom."

"Well, that's a nice thing for a young man to do. What have you got?"

"Fourteen, but I still wanted some left for food, maybe a ride or two."

"Well then, let's leave you with half. You give me seven, a lucky number, right? You'll still have seven left. How's that sound?"

Dash beamed. "That sounds pretty good," and he handed over a ten. He placed the dream catcher, which the woman had wrapped in thin paper, into his backpack, took his change, remembered to thank her, and headed toward the doors and outside. He was happy with his decision and hoped his mother would be too.

Just as he emerged, a PA announcement was made. Native dancers would be performing along with drummers at the large gazebo. With his curiosity peaked, Dash moved in that direction. There were six dancers in all, three male and three female. They all wore beautifully appointed costumes. Off to the side, four males sat around a large drum waiting to aid each dancer on their individual interpretative journey. Each had their own distinct movements beginning with their feet, their bodies crouching, bending, turning, moving like wind through tall grasses. Dash particularly enjoyed the hoop dancer's skill as he emulated a great bird weaving and arching through the sky.

It was mid-afternoon when the dancing and drumming finished. People were everywhere now. Dash wended his way over to the midway and games area. Barkers called out to him as he passed, trying to entice him to part with some of his money on a game of skill or chance. He watched various people attempt to knock over pins with a ball, burst balloons with a dart, throw a ring around a bottle, shoot a hoop with a basketball, or fire a gun at a moving target. He noted that while an occasional winner scored a big prize, most ended with nothing or a trinket or the realization that they had to play a game many times to make it pay off. He opted for a two-dollar cone of chocolate ice cream and stood watching the rides. When he had surveyed them all, he headed toward the Zipper.

All the rides here moved in circles. The Ferris wheel carried people up and over slowly in a high arc; the Roundup spun riders rapidly around in a standing position, sometimes causing the weak-stomached to throw up all over themselves and many of those unlucky enough to be in the path of the frothy projectiles; the eight-armed Monster lifted people up and down and rotated them around in a more comfortable seated position. However, the Zipper had everything. Here, one or two riders were strapped into an enclosed cage that spun in a complete circle so that the rider was often upside down, much like careening through space in a capsule out of control. Add to this the fact that the entire ride, comprised of at least a dozen cages, could elevate itself up and down like the motion of a zipper, and you had a ride that was much more varied and intriguing as far as Dash was concerned. As he waited for his turn to get on, he noted a bucket close to the operator. As he moved up in line, he saw that the bucket was slowly filling up with coins, nickels, dimes, quarters, even loose keys and jewelry. Anything not secured could evidently come free and fly around the enclosed cage until ultimately finding its way through the openings in the metal mesh and onto the ground below. A tidy extra sum was being raked in by the carneys in charge here as they gathered up money around them like manna from heaven. Dash made sure that anything loose in his pockets went into his backpack before embarking on his journey.

The ride itself lasted all of three minutes but was worth it. When Dash had finished and regained his land legs, he decided to look for the area where the animals were housed. A small series of fenced-off enclosures allowed visitors to see a variety of farm animals such as goats, pigs, chickens, and sheep. But it was a separate and larger space that Dash was particularly interested in, a riding paddock where owners who had trucked their horses into town would walk and trot them around the enclosure for people to see. There were three beautiful horses visible when he arrived, a pure black colt, a grey, and a piebald. He watched them for a while until an idea came to him. There was a small knoll behind him, an elevation of some five or six feet under a tree that allowed him to see the horses while seated on the grass. It was an opportunity to take some paper and a pencil from his kit and capture what he was seeing.

His excitement started to build. He settled into position, his back against the tree with his knees slightly up, kit closed on his lap and acting as a table. He took a breath, focused his attention on the black colt that now stood resting in a corner of the pen, its head a perfect profile waiting to be drawn. Dash began, first hesitantly, but then with growing confidence. He became lost in concentration, willing only his subject to be there. All other sights and sounds were muted. He didn't notice the shadow that appeared behind him until it was too late.

"Well, well, what have we got here?" Dash started and turned toward the voice. Billy leaned over him from behind and peered down. Before Dash could react, Billy had reached down and snatched up the paper. "Let's take a closer look at this."

"Give that back, Billy." Dash pushed his kit aside and jumped to his feet.

Billy ignored the demand and instead made a move toward the box on the ground. "Why don't we take a look at what you have in there?"

"No." It was here that Dash instinctively moved in front of Billy and put up his hand. "It's not yours. Leave it alone."

"A tough guy, eh?" Billy smiled. And then with simple precision, he began to rip Dash's picture into pieces.

The reaction was swift and unexpected. Like a tornado touching down, Dash attacked. He lashed out with a punch to the nose that caught Billy entirely off guard and which drew blood. As Billy's eyes welled up, Dash kicked him in the groin. A fury of blows to the head as Billy was going down to the ground was only halted by two adults who came running over from the corral and pulled him off. Billy lay crumpled in a heap but was being vocal enough about his situation for the men to know that he was going to be all right. The men helped Billy up and dusted him off, muttering about teenage boys and their need to beat each other up before walking off. Dash left the scene before Billy gained his feet, with the art kit and the pieces of his torn picture stuffed in his backpack. He figured that Billy would come after him at some point. He was a bully, and he had been humiliated. Despite it all, though, Dash felt elated in some ways. His picture had been destroyed, but he had stood up for himself, smacked down a foe and come away on top. He located his bike, hopped on, and made for home.

* * *

Two weeks had passed since the incident at the fairgrounds. Amazingly, Billy had remained a ghost, so Dash had put the altercation behind him. His mother had noticed the bruised and scraped knuckles of his hands, but Dash's insistence that he had hurt them while tripping on concrete at the arena seemed to placate her. She had loved the dream catcher and displayed it prominently from her bedroom window. Dash had decided to stay around the house, for the most part, venturing out for rides on occasion but mainly content to improve his sketching of fields, bushland, and birds—anything that caught his eye and forced him to challenge his artistic perspective. It was later in August that his mother approached him one evening while Eric was away, finishing some tile work for a client. She sat across from him at the kitchen table, and her question had come up softly like a gentle breeze.

"What would you think of moving away from here?"

His reaction had been a mixture of shock and surprise. "Move? Where to?"

"A bigger place. Edmonton."

Dash hesitated. "Edmonton. That's like a city, and it's pretty far away."

His mother smiled. "Not that far. A few hundred kilometres. We can get there in a few hours."

"Why would we do that?"

His mother folded her hands. "Well, Eric has a chance at a really good job there starting in September. He's already checked out an apartment, and he wants us to come with him."

Dash was getting used to Eric's presence now. He was a pretty good guy, and he treated his mother with respect. They were good together, but he was feeling scared about leaving what he knew. His mother sensed this.

"I understand you're nervous about this. To be honest, I am too."

"Really?"

"Of course. But I look at it like an adventure, something new, right? I can get a job there, maybe better than here. It will be a new chance for all of us, Eric, me, and you."

Dash didn't feel that enthusiastic about his mom's description of a better life and a new chance, but what did he know? When he thought about it, there wasn't anything that was keeping him here. The move was still a week or so away—enough time to get used to the idea. He headed outside before it got dark to throw a few stones and take in the sunset.

* * *

Picture #6: *Coastal Figure*

Observer's description: A nude female lies stretched out on a sandy beach gazing at the water beyond her. She rests easily on her left forearm with her body extended comfortably, right leg raised to support her right arm. Her body is a golden brown, blending into the sand beneath her. The picture gives off an air of warmth and reflection. There is a small island or sandbar immediately beyond her and then a line of land at the horizon in the distance breaking up water and sky. Her face is not visible. What is she thinking as she gazes outward? Who is watching her?

Chapter Six

DAY THREE

THE PRESENT

Sweat clambered for purchase on Greg's body, pooling under his armpits and then trickling in tiny rivulets down his sides. His mouth crackled, cinders and soot coating his tongue. The late morning sun magnified itself through his bedroom window and bored into his brain. He tried opening his eyes, but the light pushed his ostrich head under the covers. He rolled to his left, dropped onto the Berber rug, and pulled himself unceremoniously toward the cooler tiles of the bathroom floor. Hauling himself up and over the porcelain receptacle, he spewed his guts into the welcoming bowl. Mission accomplished. Better. He flopped back onto the floor, a fish sucking air, and waited to die. But death did not come for him and, moments later, he decided to stand. "Oh, God," he muttered as he placed his hands on the sink and gazed at his reflection in the mirror. "What the fuck happened?" But his doppelganger could only stare back at him red-eyed, dishevelled, flecks of salmon-coloured sick dotting his chin. It was day, he guessed, but he wanted no part of it just yet. Splashing water on his face and into his mouth, he towelled off and turned back toward the bed he now recognized.

But another form loomed up in front of him. Legs, an ass, the bare, freckled backside of someone he did not know. Clothes draped on the bedroom chair indicated an overnight stay. His first thoughts were of Jesse, but as the body stretched and turned, the illusion was broken. Large breasts greeted him, attached to the body of someone not particularly young, as well as unfamiliar.

"You look like shit, sweetie," the smoky voice whispered before reaching for a sheet that would cover her.

"Who the hell are you?" Greg's abrupt rudeness was matched by a rising wave of nausea, and he lurched back to the bathroom.

"Marcy," was what he thought he heard when he re-surfaced. Marcy. Nope. Nothing yet. His befuddled silence produced another turn, her head now propped on her hand.

"We met at the pub up the street last night." Still, a flounder floundering. She frowned back. "We came back here, obviously. One thing led to another. Here I am. Ta-da."

Fragments began to slowly emerge and paste themselves back together. He parked himself on the edge of the bed. The drive back to his apartment after his disaster with Jesse, his parked car, he assumed in the lot at the back, a decision to walk the two blocks to the pub he often frequented for a couple after work. He rubbed his hands over his face and eyes.

"You came in pretty angry. Sat at the bar." The woman pulled herself up then, and hugged her knees, the bed sheet draping her like covered furniture. "I left you alone for a bit, then after you'd had a drink and ordered another, I came over. You bought me a couple of drinks. You had a few more. You were more pissed than I realized."

"So, you're a hooker?"

Laughter, then a pillow careening off his head, helped him begin to clarify things.

"You prick. No, I'm not a hooker. A little easy, maybe, lonely for sure, but I'm not a slut."

"Sorry, it's just that…"

"Forget it. Turns out, you're the sorry shit. Not me."

Greg got up and stumbled to his closet door. His pants, shirt, jacket all lay in a heap in the corner. He had managed to pull on his underwear at some point, or maybe he never took them off.

"Did we…you know?" and he waved his hands around as if their motion would somehow improve his articulation and memory.

Again, that laugh. "You gave it a go, but the best you could do was get your flag to half-mast, so I let you pass out, and we ended the tragedy. I could have left, I guess, but what the hell? Why get dressed all over again, right?"

"Right." Greg began searching in his pants' pocket.

"If you're looking for your wallet and keys, Einstein, they're on the kitchen table where I put them. Don't worry, everything's there. I didn't rip you off." With this, she got up and headed for the bathroom. "I'm going to freshen up and then get out of here."

Greg watched her grab her clothes and move into the bathroom. She was not at all self-conscious, not a bad figure either, but he figured she was at least ten years older. Not that it was a problem. But it was good that she had said she was leaving. He was feeling awkward enough without having to ask her to go. Glancing over at the bedside clock, he noted that it was almost 10:30a.m. *Christ.* At first, he thought he was late, really late, and wondered how he would square this with his boss, Graham. Then, as the fog continued to lift, he remembered he began a shorter shift at noon today. Luckily, he was only scheduled for five hours in the afternoon. Thank God. But should he call in, say he was under the weather, or suck it up and go? Fucking great job too, he snorted, delivering automobile parts to various dealerships around the city. What crap, but he liked to drive, and maybe it would clear his head. It would take him twenty minutes to get straightened up and out of here, and fifteen minutes to get to the head office in his car. Plenty of time. Just then, he heard the shower turn on. He'd have to get Marjorie or Mercy or whatever her name was to get a move on. In the meantime, he'd get dressed, maybe see if he could keep down some toast and juice. Jesse came back into his mind again, and a slow burn began to take over. He needed to track her down, apologize, get her to listen to reason. There was no way he could let her walk away, not with another guy lurking around.

* * *

A series of sounds that Dash couldn't identify at first began clanging around in his head until they raised him from his sleep. Eventually, he recognized them as pans, drawers, and cutlery, all playing a harsh melody of rise and shine. Throwing off the remainder of the blanket that covered him, he lifted his head and noticed Jesse hard at work. He managed a croaky "morning" before stretching into a sitting position. Her one-bedroom apartment came into focus. It was a comfortable open space. It included this couch, a couple of chairs slouched around a coffee table all facing a television, and a cabinet in the corner. A tall, narrow bookcase, IKEA, he guessed, stood along one wall. Several paintings hung discriminately throughout, adding colour. The kitchen where Jesse stood was at the end of the room, separated from this area by an island. Three large stools circling it served as the eating area and a repository, it turned out, for mail, keys, and any other paper paraphernalia needing a home. Jesse's bedroom and the bathroom were accessed through dual doors against the final side. All nicely contained in a big rectangle that, if you added the bathroom and bedroom, might be about 500 to 600 square feet. *Nice,* he thought.

"Morning. How did you sleep?"

"Great. Good that you have a longer couch."

"Yeah. It helps if someone needs to stay over."

Dash looked over at Jesse sheepishly. "Look, thanks again for letting me stay. I won't make it a habit."

"No worries." Jesse had the fridge open and was pulling out eggs, cheese, mushrooms, and an onion. "Stay as long as you need until you see if this works out."

"I promise. It's going to work out." *Enough excuses and fuck-ups,* he reminded himself. *Time for some results.*

Jesse was wise enough not to reply to this. "So, it's just after seven. We both start early today. While I make this delicious omelette for us, why don't you use the bathroom and get dressed?"

"Sounds like a plan. I won't be long." He folded up the blanket—a small gesture of help—grabbed his backpack and headed off. He decided not to shower. Work was likely going to get him sweaty. He took a piss and pulled on clothes that he hoped would do, making a mental note that shopping was going to be in order soon. Splashing water on his face, he looked at his reflection in the mirror, then shook his head. What had happened to the young boy? Where had he run off to? A heaviness began to grow in his chest. "Nerves," he whispered. "Just nerves. Get a grip." He splashed his face again, towelled off and opened the door.

"Breakfast is served," Jesse chirped. "Have a seat."

"Thanks. Looks great." He waited for her to join him, and then dug in.

"Can't promise this service every morning." She offered Dash some juice from a pitcher on the table. "Sometimes I just have granola and yogurt, grab a piece of fruit and run."

"That's fine. I wouldn't expect it. I don't even know what my routine's going to be yet."

Jesse nodded. "Kind of exciting, though, isn't it? How do you feel about it?"

"OK. A little nervous for sure. I guess I'll let you know tonight."

"It'll be fine," and she put a hand on his for a moment, a quick but definite touch of reassurance, which he appreciated. He smiled. "Thanks for the vote of confidence."

When they had finished, Dash insisted on cleaning up. Dishes were cleared, washed, and stacked to dry. It was 7:35 a.m., still plenty of time since Y.E.S. had its location on Adelaide Street, which was only blocks from here. Still, it would be good to be early, so he made ready to go. Jesse surprised him again with a big bag of mixed nuts and dried fruit.

"Energy food," she said while handing it over. "I snack on it all the time."

He accepted but reminded her she was doing too much.

"And I'll get an extra key made for you, just for now. It's not like we're a couple or anything," and she smiled.

"No, of course not," Dash joked. "How would that look?" He put on his backpack and opened the front door. A brisk breeze greeted him, but it was a nice morning. *Good for riding*, he thought. Let's hope his bike and he were up to the task.

"See you later tonight, I guess."

"Looking forward to hearing how your day went. Have a good one."

"You too," and he was off.

Jesse closed the door to get ready for work herself and let out a huge breath. This had better work out. For them both. She pondered what this could mean as she got ready. No one at work could know about this. One day at a time was the obvious mantra.

* * *

Coyote was glad to see the sky begin to brighten around him. He had been on the move for most of the night. He had watched the man stumble home from the bar in the arms of another before heading out, secure in the knowledge that he would remain there. A brief but nasty scuffle with a young raccoon behind a large bin in an alley as he had wended his way along had satiated his growling stomach. There was something about facing off with another creature, even as tired as he had been, that rejuvenated him, made him feel like he was who he should be—a predator. Garbage was not the same. When he arrived back at the small park, all was quiet. He kept his eyes at the ready, observed the increased noise as the city began to awaken. Curled up and secure in a small treed enclosure, he saw the man leave on his bike and the woman close the door before leaving minutes later. It was up to Crow to follow now. All Coyote wanted was to rest and dream of other places he would rather be.

* * *

Magnus Automotive served a huge swath of the Toronto area. Multiple routes crisscrossed the city that every driver had to know. These could be revised weekly, depending on client changes and needs. Still, once the truck had been loaded up and Greg could get out on the road, his view of the day often improved. Fuck-ups with traffic, he knew, were always going to happen, but knowledge of the streets and how to avoid major tie-ups was part of the job. He enjoyed the challenge of untying knots and snarls and still getting to his destination unscathed and on time. Granted, when he got boxed in or forced to a standstill, even a snail-paced crawl, he would heat up like his engine and fill the air with curses and horn play, a banal display of misplaced testosterone that resolved nothing. Inevitably, in these moments of sober or often less sober reflections, he would cast the blame for these outbursts and his personal frustrations at life on his family, more specifically, dear old mom and dad.

Greg had grown up in the Inglewood area of Calgary. Formerly known as East Calgary or Brewery Flats, it was heralded as the city's oldest neighbourhood. The Bow River, which cut a wide ribbon through the city, was close by, as were the Stampede Grounds, the Calgary Zoo, Fort Calgary's Historic Park, and numerous trails and pathways. It was not a wealthy community overall, and in Greg's time, it had become home to more and more immigrants, which had never impressed him. He didn't like the fact that foreigners were popping up everywhere, Blacks, Asians, East Indians and, of course, their own home grown Indian. But his dad had seen this as an opportunity to make money by investing early in old buildings and turning them quickly into condos and apartments. He had raked in the money over the years, built a beautiful and spacious home for himself, his wife, and three kids, and kept adding to his collection of properties. And yet, despite his father's ability to make money, he couldn't make himself a father. For Greg, there was no time to throw a ball, come to a game or share a laugh or a story. Even his mother, by the time of his arrival, seemed to have expended all her energy and love on his elder brother, Craig and his sister, Kate. They at ten and six years his senior had gone on to careers in finance and teaching. He had opted for recognition as the class clown, the party animal, and ultimately, the unfulfilled procurer of odd jobs, the family screw-up, who had money thrown at him in the hopes he would smarten up or simply go away. At twenty, he had opted for the latter, thumbed his finger at mom and dad, bought himself a new black Corvette, with an infusion of family money, and drove out East. He found work in a Northern Ontario town at a sawmill and stayed for over two years until he was driven out. Then it was on to a pipeline crew in the Sault for another year, drifting ever closer toward his current destination. Now, having been here for almost two years, he had settled into a job that at least involved something he liked: driving.

One thing his father had taught him was how to drive. At sixteen, he had been taken out of the city onto quieter country roads where he had learned the art of the stick, clutch, gas pedal, and brake. Soon, he transitioned to the city and learned road rules at a quicker pace. It wasn't until he was seventeen and could release himself from the dictates of parental supervision that speed became a necessary addiction. He would take out the family car when available, exit the city, and scream onto the ribbon of highway that stretched between Calgary and Edmonton for twenty to thirty kilometres before turning back. Only when he had received his first ticket and been docked points for speed more than 160 kilometres an hour, did his father clip his wings and the privilege of solo driving for a time. His anger at having to cool his heels, at only driving periodically as a chauffeur for his mom on errands or with his dad to odd jobs, had only increased his use of alcohol to cope with frustration.

Greg pulled up to an intersection that had red-lighted him and waited. In his passenger rearview mirror, he noticed a cyclist manoeuvring past cars along the curb and up beside him. More often than not, they pissed him off with their expectations of equality while at the same time, flouting the rules of the road. He was always on high alert when one was in the vicinity in case an inadvertent door opening or a quick turn or a lane change caused an incident, a toxic public exchange of verbiage or worse. Greg had never hit a cyclist, but many times had thought of grinding one into a parked car or a pole as he went by if they were giving him grief with their erratic road behaviour. As the light changed and he shot out ahead of his two-wheeled adversary, he recalled the one time in Dryden, a Northern Ontario town within a couple of hours of the Manitoba border, three years earlier when he had hit someone and how lucky he had been. It had not ended up so well for the other guy.

The pulp and paper industry had fizzled by the time Greg arrived on the scene, but there were still smaller sawmills around, and he had latched onto one of these. For a short while, he kept a room in a motel just off Government Street until an apartment was found, and he moved in. Dryden was small, and a young man wheeling into town in a black corvette attracted attention, mainly when he stayed. The friends he made at work were locals who taught him the ropes, accepted his offers of drinks at the bar at night and fast rides out to Wabigoon Lake, where they would party most weekends. Of course, his friendship never extended to any of the Indians he ran across in the town. He gave a wide berth to the two who worked at the mill, and to the many more he saw on the streets who, in his addled mind, were always either looking for a handout or stumbling around drunk. Despite his own drinking habits, he was white, had a cool car, and enough money to put himself on a different level, a higher plane of privilege than the Natives he looked down on and often joked about.

Sometimes he wondered where his prejudice had come from. Over time, it had crept into his bones like a cancer and eaten away at him. When he acknowledged his inadequacies, self-loathing, and failures in moments of clear-headedness, he knew that the Indians had become his salvation. They could be stereotyped, put into a box, a portion of his brain where their struggles and shortcomings shone out like a beacon beyond his own. If he stood above anyone, it was the Indians and their general freeloading natures.

Wheeling into his first destination, he motored to the back of the dealership and the parts office. With smugness, he noted the rows of cars, a variety of coloured sameness passing as unique. Not like his beloved, a car now four years old but still purring with power and sleek lines. "Settle for an import if you want, losers," he muttered as he exited the truck, "but North American is the only way to go." He had offered this advice to Ron, the parts manager on occasion and every other manager on his route, along with his trademark smirk, as he grabbed their signatures. It never hurt to brag about black beauty. They would just say, "Yeah, yeah," and nod, sometimes make a lame attempt in defence of the growing import market, sight quality, price, dependability, even looks, as trump cards in their hand, but he would just laugh and shake his head. Company lackeys with no imagination. But it was a foreigner of sorts that had given him grief years ago, he recalled, as he headed off to his next stop.

His job at the sawmill had been outside Dryden, a few kilometres away and just off the main highway. It was a Friday, and he had just finished his shift. The weekend was here, and he, Doug, and Mark were making plans. Drinking was to be a big part of the scenario and to start it off right they crowded into Doug's pickup truck in the parking lot to enjoy a cold one from a cooler he always kept in the bed. Just one each was all they had. Greg would hit the Beer Store on the way home. They planned to meet at his apartment to start, then fan out from there like some brush fire into the night.

An old Allman Brothers CD was blaring through his speakers as he cruised into town on Government Street. And then out of nowhere, it just happened. An Indian lurched out onto the road in front of him, and Greg cut him down, a scythe laying shafts of wheat to rest. There was the screech of tires, the contact, the body flying up and over his hood, and the crumpled deposit behind him in the rearview mirror as he came to a stop. It shook him to the core for a moment. By the time the cops had arrived, whatever semblance of alcohol he had in his system was frightened away. The investigation was quickly ruled an accident. While not dangerous or erratic, his driving had been determined to have been fifteen kilometres above the designated speed limit. For that, he was fined, and the incident disappeared over two weeks after occupying some talk and a short article in the paper. It seemed there were others in the community, including the police, who did not want to waste time on any in-depth investigations or concerns over Native issues. Case closed, and Greg had breathed a sigh of relief.

It turned out the Indian had been drunk. Afterwards, Greg announced to his friends at work that this was predictable. "What do you expect, right?" However, his jokes and talk did not sit well with the two Indigenous men also employed there. Days after the dust had settled on the tragedy in the town, he woke up one morning for work and headed to his car. He remembered the shock as if new, a gut-punch draining all his wind. His pride and joy had been keyed everywhere, a sadistic torturer taking pleasure at his task. What's more, his tires had all been slashed. It was a thorough job of mutilation without the noise of breakage or the screams of terror and pain—a stealthy quiet attack in the night by unknown culprits. His anger had grown, multiplied like vultures circling carrion, but he was smart enough to know that he was a target now, and could be for some time. Within two weeks, he had dropped a shitload of money on fixing his car and then disappeared south toward the Sault, hatred a series of red embers still burning in his chest. Each time he resurrected the assault in his mind, replaying all his remembered images, he blamed the Indians solely. He was the victim, he and his car. This recollection soured him for the rest of his day as he zigzagged across the city, a knife on edge, slicing through skin.

* * *

Picture #7: *Cyclist and Crow*

Observer's description: A cyclist fills the foreground of the painting, bent over and pedalling a white Peugeot touring bike. She is wearing a white top, beige shorts, and white sneakers. The trail she is on suggests a hard-packed gravel road in the country. Behind her and moving back toward the horizon of the painting is a field of wheat, their golden heads giving way eventually to the green grasses of a different crop until finally, a wall of dark green trees at horizon marks an end to the fields and the frame of the picture. The woman has her head turned away and toward the field, so her features cannot be seen. As she rides, she is watching the one black object in the painting, a crow gliding parallel at eye level just in front of her. Both are captured in a moment of pleasure and tranquillity, a journey on this day they are undertaking together.

His hands were shaking slightly, and his heart was racing when he stepped off his bike. Dash wondered if it was withdrawal, the effect of not having had his usual intake of booze to get him through his periods of anxiety or anger. He had not had a drink in a couple of days. This was more to do with Jesse than anything. Breakfast had been great, the coffee necessary. No, he chalked this brief segue toward delirium tremens up to nerves. He noticed his reflection in the glass front of the company office. *Take a deep breath, make it a few, actually, and calm down*, he told himself. Securing his bike, he opened the door and walked in. It was a simple enough layout inside, he noted. A couple of desks and chairs to the left, a counter across the back, a small office to the right with its door closed, and another two behind the counter. The smaller door was marked "washroom", the other larger double door, which swung back and forth, was blank but suggested a larger space behind, perhaps a warehouse section or storage of some kind. Before he had more time to reflect, the office door opened, and Derrick appeared.

"Morning rookie, you made it." He strode over to Dash with a smile and held out his hand. "Good to see you."

"Thanks. You too."

At that moment, the double doors swung open, and two people entered. Both nodded. The woman headed behind the counter, the man out and around to the front.

"Time for some introductions," Derrick chirped. "The young lady behind the counter is Cindy. Sometime courier, sometime dispatcher. She basically runs the show."

"You got that right," she quipped. "Welcome aboard." And immediately she began shuffling papers on the countertop and reaching for a cell phone. Dash put her a few years older than him, maybe in her late twenties, around 5' 5", a sleeve tattoo colourfully decorating her left arm, her frizzy dark hair partially hidden under a bandana. Dash suspected that she was a no-nonsense girl for sure.

"And this is Blake."

Blake eased out away from the counter like a cat, his motions fluid and self-assured. At around six feet, he wore a black zip full-sleeved hoodie, the hood down to reveal shoulder-length dreads. A sling bag adorned his back and shoulder. Khaki style green shorts and what Dash figured were high-end bike shoes finished his ensemble. A three-day growth of beard adorned his face in a manner that could have suggested personal grooming or simply no interest in shaving. He had to be at least thirty-five years old. As soon as he opened his mouth, though, Dash thought, *The Big Lebowski*.

"Hey, dude. Saddlin' up with me for a couple of days, I hear."

"Yep, that's what Derrick told me."

Derrick nodded. "Blake has been with us for ten years. A real road warrior. Knows every inch of the downtown city section where we make our bread and butter."

Blake shrugged off Derrick's accolades with a slight grin. "Good day to start. Weather's supposed to be pretty outstanding for the week. No high winds or raging rainstorms."

"And no ice and snow," Derrick joked.

"No, but that'll come, and then everything changes." Blake looked right at Dash. "That is if you decide you're cut out for this and want to stay that long."

"I guess I'll find out soon enough."

Derrick smiled. "That you will, but Blake is a great person to shadow until you find your bearings. So, let's get started. Any questions right off?"

Dash looked down at his feet, then blurted. "Just one for now. Where did you come up with Y.E.S. for a company name?"

"Two places, really," Derrick laughed. "First, I like music as most people do, but I prefer the old prog rock stuff from the 60s and 70s, stuff with drive and some theatricality thrown in. Give me bands like Jethro Tull; Emerson, Lake and Palmer; and early Genesis with Peter Gabriel at the helm, and I'm a happy guy. Among these groups was another favourite, though, and that was a band called Yes. Lots of members over the years and still going. There was wild musical talent in the band from the likes of Steve Howe and Rick Wakeman. Great stuff."

"And the second reason, dude?" This quick interjection came from Blake, who knew Derrick's musical tastes by heart. Derrick was always espousing his belief that the 60s and 70s were the best eras for music. For his part, Blake would counter with a reggae compliment that included Bob Marley, Peter Tosh, and Jimmy Cliff, and would remind Derrick that other cool styles existed. On many occasions, they had ridden down this musical road together after work with a couple of spliffs and a drink or two, educating each other on the finer points of each pedigree, the various strains of their chosen heroes blasting from behind the office door.

"The second. Right. As you know, there are all kinds of names for courier companies in the city. I wanted one that was positive and personal and easy to remember, so I thought of Y.E.S. An acronym that I decided would mean 'Your Express Service'. It reflects one of my favourite bands and is a word many people use when happy and excited. Yes," and Derrick pumped his fist.

"I'll have to check them out when I get a chance," Dash said. "Now, the name makes complete sense."

"After work someday soon when we have the time, I'll introduce you," Derrick offered, "but for now, let's get you ready to work." And with that, Dash prepared to face some music of a different kind.

* * *

Greg eased the van into its parking space at the back of the office and turned off the motor. It was 5:00p.m. Another shit day over with. He expelled a deep breath and sat staring off at nothing. His head was pounding, short, sharp staccato calls, a shifting and clanging like the packages and boxes he had banging around in his truck with him, hour after hour. He needed a drink. A quick visual remembrance of Macy, or whatever her name was, and the night before flashed across his mind but then was replaced by one of Jesse. Pulling out his cell phone, he tried her number. She needed to listen to reason and not walk away from him. Their last contact continued to anger him. No answer. *Fuck.* He got her voicemail and left a message. He then locked up the van and headed for the office to sign out. He would jump in his car, head home, have a shower and a drink or two, and wait. If she didn't call, maybe he'd drift over to her place to see what was up. Sounded like a plan. The darker shadow of her "friend" drifted into his subconscious, and he frowned. Just who was this guy that Jesse had been spending time with? Someone she worked with, she said. Another do-gooder? Some office nerd? Whoever it was, he needed to know more, and Jesse had to be set straight. He rubbed his eyes, pushed open the door to the back lot, and headed across the pavement to his car.

* * *

Dash had been out on a cliff edge for most of the day. Luckily, he had been tethered to a man who knew the terrain well and was willing to allow him time to grab a new foothold. But his coaching wasn't beyond occasional criticism and frustration. Blake couldn't allow slip-ups and miscues to slow him down by much.

"Relax, man," he had said at a stoplight where he perched and had waited for Dash to catch up. "You're all tense. Forget the traffic. Keep yourself in the moment, and don't let the jerk-offs around get you rattled."

Dash had simply nodded, then took the few seconds they had stopped to catch his breath. *Easier said than done,* he thought as he inhaled the fumes from around him. He had shared his annoyances during the day with drivers of all shapes and sizes—taxi, truck, and tourist, as well as wayward pedestrians, sometimes causing Blake to just shake his head, laugh out loud, or on one occasion, get him off his bike to ream his ass when he had kicked at a passing car that had brushed by too closely. Time was money, and he had to get that through his head sooner rather than later. Anger just slows you down and sometimes gets you into unwanted shit that fucks up your whole day. It had been a hard lesson, and Dash could only promise to try to keep his feelings in check.

It turned out that starting on a Monday had been wise and for his benefit. Businesses were just coming to life again after the weekend. The week would only get crazier from here on in. Most of their route had also been in the business corridors of downtown boxed in from Front to Queen and Spadina to Yonge streets and all the arteries crisscrossing in between. A controllable venue, Blake had told him, that might expand like a bleeding wound on certain days. You had to be deft at applying a tourniquet. "Always be prepared for the unexpected is my best mantra, man," Blake had stated.

Dash could only mumble, "Yeah, well, everything's fucking unexpected right now." He put the thoughts of a drink or two, something harder than water, out of his mind and kept pedalling, his lifeline getting away yet again in the crowds of metal and flesh that loomed up around him.

* * *

I had to admit, I was having a great day. I rarely, if ever, can say that about Mondays. I don't suppose too many people can. An old Boom Town Rats tune came into my head, and I found myself humming its dark but catchy refrain. I was way too young to know anything about this band, but I had heard Bob Geldoff's name from my parents and the work he did for world peace in his day through music. This 70s lament, their big hit, was based on a true story. A young schoolgirl went home, got her father's gun, and decided to shoot kids with it just because she didn't like Mondays. I looked around the office space where scatterings of walk-ins parked themselves in various states of cognitive impairment, waiting for help. How many of them didn't like Mondays, either? What might they decide to do about it if their own thoughts became too unhinged?

I shook off my macabre daydream and returned to the reality that despite Sir Bob's unexpected musical bullets to my brain, I felt good. I knew deep down that Dash and his unexpected arrival at my door last night was making me feel this way. He was causing illogical and subjective disturbances to flit around me all day, little fireflies of blinking light and electricity. I couldn't deny them. Now, what was I going to do about it? I'd wait and see I supposed as I tidied my desk absent-mindedly and looked at the clock. Almost 5:00p.m. My shift was ending.

Shelley mimed to me by pointing at her watch and raising her hand containing an imaginary glass. She was planning on going for a drink after. Did I want in? I smiled but shook my head. I wanted to get back home to be there when Dash arrived. There was a pang of fear tinged with exhilaration at this. What would his arrival signal? Good news or bad, anger or elation? The sudden ringing of my phone startled me out of contemplation and into the moment. I picked it up and recognized the number on the screen. God no. It was Greg. I put it down. Seconds later, I knew that a message had been left. I listened to it, a tone lacking in remorse, more demand than request or plea. "Call me. We need to talk. You can't just end things like this." Can't I? But his message gave me concern. This was not going to go away easily, I realized. A small cloud started to accumulate over my head as I prepared to leave. Maybe Geldoff had something after all.

* * *

Picture #8: *Target Pistol and Man*

Observer's description: A figure sits facing the viewer. He has shortly cropped hair, wears glasses, and is staring resolutely forward with no expression. His elbows are on a large wooden table that occupies the entire base of the painting. His hands are crossed together in front of his chin. He wears a long-sleeved black sweatshirt. In front of him, sitting to the left of the table, is a pistol, the butt of the gun toward him. Behind him, large windows reflect a winter scene outside. The focal point of the picture is the man's eyes followed by his hands, followed by the gun, a line deliberately drawing the observer into this trajectory. What is the man thinking? What is he planning to do with the gun? What has he already done?

Chapter Seven

THE PAST

Dash remembered the four-hour journey from his home to Edmonton as if it was yesterday. But it had been three years now, he was seventeen, and his small-town recollections had been slowly replaced with a new city reality. The apartment that Eric had found for them was close enough to the downtown core that biking, bus or even walking was simple. Eric had found steady work in the building trades, and his mom had started part-time as a waitress in a greasy spoon but had recently found employment in a clothing boutique, which she really liked. He thought of her transition again. She had only had two slip-ups with booze that he recalled, both when Eric had been out of town for a week or two on a job. Dash guessed that it was the time alone on a Friday or Saturday night that had gotten the better of her resolve. That and boredom, the fact that a city of this size could still leave you feeling like you didn't belong, that you were invisible, that no matter what you did, you would still be who you were. He loved his mother and, despite these lapses, knew that she was there for him. She had always been strong and had managed to rise above the day to day humiliations and frustrations that plagued them even here. He had not been so lucky, and his alienation at school and in the wider world of the city had gotten the better of him at times. Suspensions for fighting, experimentation with drugs and drink, and associations with kids on the street struggling with similar battles had left him at odds with himself and even his mom.

"You can't keep butting heads with me, Dash," she had said on numerous occasions. "I know life can be shit at times, but you can't let it get the better of you."

When he felt guilty, he would nod and pretend to agree, but when his anger got the better of him, he could intentionally be hurtful."Hey, mom, I'm just learning from the best. Booze and pills. That was your motto, right?"

He could see that his words hurt, but her anger would never surface. She would allow them to wash over her these days, recognize the troubled source, and do her best to reconcile, often through an apology. "Yeah, you're right. I've been a hypocrite at times," she'd say. "I should know better, should be a better role model. But I'll tell you one thing; I won't give up. That's all I want you to do too." And she'd leave it at that and hope her words would sink in, flow into the ground of his being and provide some sustenance. It did for a time. He would take her words to heart, make an effort, even dabble with his art in moments of quiet reflection. He continued to hold this part of his life close to him and would visit the page with a grim outlook one might reserve for church or a funeral parlour. Out of the emptiness, he would create the feathered flight of birds, the loping or galloping gaits of dogs and horses, the landscape of open ground nettled with brush, shrub, or grass. But never people. He could not capture their essence in any meaningful way. His mother had been attempted a second time, in a moment of recline, deep in sleep on the couch. A picture in pencil yet unfulfilled, still requiring colour and facial acuity. He had never enrolled in any high school art classes, even at his mother's encouragement. The thoughts of revealing himself on paper and in public, awakening the potential voices of criticism or ridicule, had kept that pursuit at bay. He would practice alone and at his own discretion, even though these intervals had lessened over time. Then he met Manny, and things changed again. His art kit closed once more, and personal therapy took a different route.

It was a hot day in late June. Dash had just finished his last exam at a school that didn't matter to him. He figured he had a fifty-fifty chance of passing his courses. If he did, he might be walking away from his Grade 11 year with as many as eighteen credits. Of course, he should have twenty-four by now, he figured, if he could trust his math calculations. But life had gotten in the way at times. The life of an outlier, part French, part Native, both halves lost to him so that the whole was just a cosmos of spinning particles riding the rim of a mighty maelstrom waiting to be sucked in.

Manny was Italian and appeared to him on a skateboard in a park. Dash had leaned on a tree and watched him attempt to perform a few tricks on some steps and a railing nearby. With each fall and reaction, Dash's grin had grown wider until a final outright laugh drew Manny's ire. He grabbed his board and walked up to him.

"What you laughin' at?" He was a couple of inches shorter than Dash, but his eyes were fire. Dash immediately reigned himself in.

"Nothin' man. Just watchin' you." He started to turn away.

"Hang on. Hang on. You think you can do better than me? Show me what you got." He threw down his board. Dash wasn't sure if he wanted him to fight or to get on and ride.

"No, man. As bad as you are, I'm a hell of a lot worse, for sure."

"You think I'm bad?" Again, the full stare.

Dash took a breath. "I know you are," and clenched his fists for what might be coming.

Whether Manny had noticed that defensive move or not, he paused for a second and then smiled, "You're right. I suck." The laughter on both sides of the divide eased everything.

"I'm Manny," and he put out his fist.

"Dash," and the bump was made.

"That your real name or a handle you go by?"

"No, it's for real."

"Cool." Flipping his board up into his hand, he followed with, "You live around here?"

"Close enough. I can get home easily on my bike or a bus. Walking takes me about forty-five minutes."

Manny looked around. "Where's your bike at?"

"On my dogs today," Dash replied. "Where you live?"

Manny carried on as if his life was an open book and Dash his confessor. "Me, I live right over there," and he pointed to a six-storey high-rise. "A shithole if you ask me, but what the hell?" He said this in such an offhand way that Dash wasn't sure whether he meant it. "Yep, just me and my dad. Bit of a dick, but I just put up with it."

"And your mom?" The question came out without any real thought or pretense.

A cloud settled over Manny for a few seconds. "She died a few years back. Cancer."

"Sorry."

"Manny shrugged. "Shit happens, right?" Dash sensed that the shit was still sticking to his new friend, and it was hard to get off. "You?"

"Just me and my mom. My dad took off a long time ago. Never really knew him."

"That's tough."

"She has a boyfriend, though, who is OK, treats her right, so..."

"So." Manny sensed the conversation needed a turn. "You want to hang out for a bit?"

"Sure, why not?"

Their first chance meeting had turned into weeks. Manny's dad mostly worked the graveyard shift at a plant to the north of the city. A pattern of sleeping days and working nights had left Manny on his own a lot. At eighteen, a year older than Dash, he knew he needed to find a job, but he had dropped out of school, making it harder than he had realized. His old man was not happy about his decisions, which he called his lack of incentive. A host of other things in life, like his mom's death, had also soured his dad and caused him to drink more. They pretty much kept out of each other's way. Dash could relate to this. His mom and Eric had both wanted him to get a summer job, but he had balked and had started staying away from home more and more as summer progressed, avoiding the growing confrontation. Most of the time, the duo would hang out in parks, on downtown streets, or at Manny's apartment. They would bike and board, shoplift food, lounge around, and go to the odd party.

One highlight of their early friendship ended up being Klondike Days, a huge summer festival, spanning ten days in mid to late July that took the boredom and routine of sameness away for a bit. While they didn't always have a lot of money to throw around for the giant midway and food truck offerings, there was a lot of free stuff. Free pancake breakfasts with sausages, bacon, and hash browns kept them filled for most of the day. The North Saskatchewan River meandering through the city heralded an entertaining river raft race between Terwillegar Park and Rafter's Landing, which they participated in, throwing water on contestants as they passed. Sometimes their light-fingered abilities got them souvenirs from vendors' tables of one form or another—T-shirts, key chains, sunglasses, and hats. They would trade these with Manny's friends for dope, which they would enjoy, particularly on midway rides at night that manufactured skylines of colourful turning lights. They ran and whooped and laughed. Dash and Manny were two young amigos, like a host of other free spirits they bumped into, a contradiction of feelings and emotions rolled into tight balls, bouncing off each other and the world around them. Then one August day, an opportunity arose.

Through the crackling airwaves at a party that Manny had just attended, he found out that a pound of dope had surfaced and was available for sale. If you had a connection, you could make a deal for some, maybe all of it. Ronny, a big talker and acquaintance of Manny's, said he knew the guy and could hook them up for a meet. He had scored a couple of ounces from this dude in the past and said he was cool. Manny asked Dash if he wanted to tag along. "It's on for today, man," he had blurted out enthusiastically.

"I don't have money to buy dope," he had said.

"No problem. I lifted some cash from my old man. Enough to get an ounce or two." Manny was always happiest when he had a plan brewing, a scheme to get his brain moving. "Ronny said the guy would bring what I want to a street down from a little park. I know the spot. We make the exchange. Simple."

"Who is this guy with the dope your friend seems to know?" Most of Manny's friends were floaters. They bumped into each other on the street, congregated together at parties, and kept their heads down around cops. A few even disappeared for months at a time, more hardened around the edges when they returned, benefits of time spent behind bars. Many were years older than Dash.

Manny shrugged. "Far as I know, he's a university student making extra money." He gave a smile. "Not some heavy gangster type, man. Relax."

Dash inhaled and let out a breath. "Seems pretty straightforward, I guess."

"Sure it is," Manny chirped. "We still have a couple of hours to kill, so let's go back to my place to grab my backpack and drop off my board. Then we'll head to our rendezvous."

Uncertainty still tracked Dash, a predator that lurked at the back of his mind, ready to pounce. What if this guy was a narc? What if he was just a thug with friends who only wanted to take this dupe's money? What if cops arrived on the scene tipped off by Ronny, who had turned and was an informant? *Get a grip*, he kept telling himself. Everything would be fine.

They opted to walk rather than take city transit. The closer they got to their destination, the less talkative Manny became. It was as if he was sinking further and further into himself with each step. Dash was picking up this feeling more and more. As they crossed 105th Street and moved toward the small park that was now visible, his uneasy feelings began to build too.

A nice grassy area, shaded with a couple of trees, was tucked back a little from the sidewalks at the street corner. Their guy was at one of two picnic-style tables. Manny picked him out from the telltale description Ronny had said to watch for, including a Yankee's ball cap and a University of Alberta sweatshirt. His legs were bouncing under the table as he looked around like some death metal drummer on double bass.

"See, what did I tell you?" Manny crowed. "A university boy just looking to pay for his books." Dash wasn't convinced that someone wearing a logoed ball cap and sweatshirt was who he said he was, but he kept his mouth shut. This was Manny's game. The dealer focused on them as they approached, his feet ceasing their two-step with the ground. He kept his arms loosely out in front of him on the table. He spoke first.

"You the guys Ronny mentioned?" He folded his hands in an attempt at relaxation.

Manny just nodded. "You got the stuff?"

"Yep. How much did you want?"

There was a hesitation before Manny responded. "How much you got?"

"Still ten ounces to unload."

Dash wasn't sure why Manny needed to know this since he said he only had enough money for an ounce or two, but he continued his straight man routine. Manny whistled and just smiled. "Two ounces is all we want."

"Where's the money?" The dealer wasn't moving, but he took on a warier tone.

"Right here." Manny unzipped his backpack and pulled out an envelope.

"Not here, dipshit." The dealer rose to his feet. "I'm not carrying around dope in my pockets. We'll take a walk to my car up the street." And with that, he looked around and lead the way up the block and onto a small side street. No one said anything on the short hike, but as they turned the corner, Dash noticed a police car pull out of a Subway shop. It eased out slowly and gave them a look, but turned away from them and headed off. His heart was racing. The dealer seemed unperturbed.

The dealer's car was an older model Toyota, dark blue. Rust curved in a half-moon around the right fender and circled the trunk's keyhole. The bumper had been scraped repeatedly and dented into submission on the left side. It had seen better days. After glancing around quickly, the dealer popped the trunk. There was nothing inside.

"What the fuck are you trying to pull?" Manny growled.

The dealer just smiled and threw back the trunk's cover, revealing the opening where the spare tire was supposed to sit. Ten one-ounce bags of pot were arranged inside. "A little extra precaution in case I get stopped. Now, give me your money, and you'll get your deuce."

"Sure, man." Manny put down his backpack and reached inside. "But I changed my mind. I think I want it all." When he stood up and turned, he had a gun pointed at the dealer's head. "Keys."

A boa constrictor had just dropped from a tree and was tightening itself around the whole scene. The dealer was frozen. Dash couldn't breathe or move. "Jesus Christ," Dash managed to force out of himself. "What are you doing?" The dealer had taken a step or two back.

"Last chance," Manny cried. "Throw me the keys or take a bullet."

The dealer glowered at Manny. "You fuck. You'll never get away with this." But he tossed them over.

Dash felt his legs buckling. "Don't do this. We're fucked if we do."

"Shut up. Grab my backpack and get in the car." Manny grabbed the bag and made for the driver's seat. Dash remained inert, unable to move.

"Your pal's right. You're done if you drive off."

"Fuck off. Who are you going to tell? The cops? I doubt it." And to Dash. "Get in now. I'm leaving with or without you."

Dash glanced over at the dealer and then stumbled toward the passenger's door. Manny already had the car running. With a quick look in the rearview mirror, he threw the stick into drive and took off. Dash looked over his shoulder at the dealer and saw him pull a flip phone out of his pocket. He was calling someone. He already felt the noose tightening around his neck. Manny brought him back to reality with a whoop as he pounded the steering wheel.

"In the clear and on our way, man," he sang out as they turned a corner and slowed down.

"In the clear? Are you out of your fucking mind?" Dash punched the dashboard repeatedly. He looked at the gun that Manny had tucked between his legs. "Where did you get a gun?"

Manny took another left. He was wending his way toward Jasper Avenue. "I grabbed my old man's target pistol. He shoots sometimes to relax. It isn't even loaded, but he didn't know that." And he laughed.

Dash just shook his head. "But, you ripped him off and stole his car!"

"You worry too much, buddy. I'm going to cut across Jasper and back onto a quiet street close to where I live. Leave the car on the street, load the dope into my backpack, and skedaddle. Then we celebrate."

"Celebrate? Are you crazy? That guy knows exactly who we are. The word is going to get out. Edmonton is not that big a place, you idiot."

Dash was still fuming when the cop car pulled out and in behind them. The whole episode from beginning to end had taken about ten minutes so far, but now time had slowed to a crawl. Manny tried not to panic. They had just turned onto Jasper Street. He looked for an opportunity to get off the main drag and onto a quieter street, see if the cop followed or if it was just a coincidence. Dash's breath was coming in audible gasps, and his heart was pumping, the alien beast inside ready to crack his sternum and burst through. Manny signalled and slowly pulled around a corner and onto a side street. The cop turned with them and then flashed on his lights. They were approaching a two-way stop on their street, the other having the right of way. Two cars were approaching behind one another from their left. Instinctively, Manny reacted and took off through the intersection in front of them. The police officer was momentarily slowed down as the other vehicles tried to avoid a collision.

Dash grabbed his head in disbelief. "What the hell are you doing? Pull over for fuck's sake. We're done." The cop was catching up quickly as they manoeuvred down another street. Manny's eyes had become huge, and his head bobbed around like a chicken as he searched for any way out of the coop they were in. As if to provide an answer to their predicament, the Toyota began to lurch and sputter and then sigh into silence. The gauge showed empty. All three were evidently out of gas. They drifted into the curb as the police car screamed up and pulled in front of them. Manny grabbed the pistol and threw it under his seat. Two cops emerged quickly from their vehicle with their guns drawn, and approached, one on each side. Dash closed his eyes, put his head back, and waited for the trapdoor to open.

* * *

Crow and Coyote had watched the unfolding of this event from different vantage points. In this rare moment of duplicity, they shared realities. Tracking had been easy for Crow as he floated and swooped from tree to pole to rooftop along the erratic trajectory that developed.

In a skulking and shadowy fashion, Coyote became Dog, relying on Crow's raspy directional reports to allow him time to find shortcuts. Jasper was his biggest challenge, but humans in Edmonton, at times, accepted the presence of Coyote or Deer, even Bear, on some of their streets as part of the inevitable wildness that surrounded them. Their worlds could intersect for a moment without significant panic and then separate and disappear again as if all were awakening from a dream. They took in the final scene from the security of a selected treetop and empty alleyway and waited until the boys, dejected, disheveled, and handcuffed were rustled into the back seat of the police car and driven away. The distraction of a tow truck summoned to remove and impound the forlorn and abandoned Toyota as additional evidence, allowed Coyote the opportunity needed to slink back into seclusion. Crow, uncaring and unworried, called out his departure in a series of curdling cries, and then lifted up into the shimmering sky.

* * *

The noises and conversations around him seemed otherworldly. They came in bunches, fragmented, rumbling, discordant, a slow and ponderous medley of disharmony. Dispatcher barks from the front seat of the police car, doors opening and closing, footsteps back and forth at a precinct where voices instructed, cajoled, demanded. The blurred marching from room to room where waiting seemed interminable stretched out like a rubber band ready to snap. Dash had sunk into silence, a stoic praying for some form of release from the nightmare he now found himself in. He and Manny were no longer together, their once tethered existence separated by different rooms and different questions. He knew about radar. Knew that bats had it in spades, used it to avoid obstacles, catch prey, see in the darkest of dark places. He had had it too but left it on the street only hours ago. His senses told him that things were not right out there, that Manny's deal was too good to be true. And it was—everything from Ronny the snitch, an informant passing as a friend, to the narc fronting as a dealer, to the cops at the ready to lasso some outlaws. Everything had been choreographed, a public show where he and Manny had become the unsuspecting lead actors. They had performed beyond the original script's requirements, Manny's outrageous adlibs and asides ending in a hasty exit with no chance of an encore.

Dash had eventually been told that his mother was on her way. It had taken time to reach her, but on her return from work, she had checked the messages on her phone and was descending toward him now, Dash imagined, a hawk with talons bared, beak sharpened. His life had shifted in an instant from cliff top to cave. Worry and shame were his only companions. When his mother finally arrived and was led in to see him, he was not the recipient of any harsh words from her. This was not the time and place for that.

The process unfolded quickly from there. Dash had age on his side because he was a first-time young offender. After discussion, instruction, and more waiting, he was released into his mother's care with the stipulation that he re-appear with her at a later date in court, where his case would be heard in front of a judge. As they exited, Dash looked around instinctively for Manny, but he was nowhere to be seen. It wasn't until later that he found out that Manny, a year older, would be tried as an adult. Their paths, short-lived and incendiary, never crossed in friendship again.

The ride home by bus was quiet. They took turns, staring out at passing buildings and people until the doors opened for them at their stop. The walk from there to the apartment was equally sombre, a procession of two behind an invisible coffin. It was early evening, time having moved from the heat of the afternoon to a cooler version of the early night, the sky beginning to ease into the pinks and purples of a coming sunset. Dash was starving, his stomach knotted and writhing, clawing at him to be fed. His mind wandered to an image he had seen on television a few months back of an eagle's nest cam high in a fir tree. In it, two young eagles not yet able to fly waited to be fed. Mouths open and cast skyward, they clung to the desperate hope of food that arose each time their parents appeared. The bond between mother and child was evident in the day to day footage that could be watched and enjoyed. Dash looked over at his mother's face as they walked, her chiselled features revealing nothing and wondered whether his actions would cause him to be thrown from the nest, a fledgling still trying to fly.

"You hungry?" His mother's instinctive query as they entered the apartment caught him off guard. He could only nod and croak out a parched "yes", his vocal cords a dry riverbed needing water.

"Thirsty, too, I'll bet." She reached for a glass and poured him some cold lemonade from the fridge. He gulped it down. "We've got leftover pizza, some chicken, beans, potato salad. Take your pick." She looked hard at him.

"Anything is fine," he said and plopped down exhausted onto a kitchen chair.

His mother gave a slight smile, a small curve of the lips that Dash did not notice. "I'll put it all out on the counter, and you grab what you want. You can warm up the pizza and chicken in the microwave."

Dash nodded. "Cold is good. Where's Eric?"

"Away on a job for a few days." She pulled out the food, plates, and cutlery and laid them on the counter. "Help yourself, and when you're ready, we're going to eat and then talk, something we haven't done for a while."

Dash looked at her and nodded. "OK." He stood and filled his plate, his mother watching his every move. Then she joined him. When they had seated themselves and had both taken a few bites, she said, "Now, from the beginning, spell it all out. Tell me your story." After a pause, he began, a tentative breeze blowing at first, but soon, a gale-force wind spinning out his tale, mixed with the rain of his own tears. His mother took it in without interruption, a beacon fixed against the storm. They would both get through this, she hoped, but there would be some fire, some scorching of the ground before things could grow again. Her own experience had taught her this.

* * *

Chapter Eight

DAY FOUR

THE PRESENT

It was Tuesday. I smiled. A day without a feel. I had resurrected this notion after recalling an episode of Seinfeld, a show I had watched in re-runs after my parents had insisted I would like its style of humour. Memorable characters; smart writing. Each thirty-minute infusion, a poignant commentary on the mundane aspects of day to day life, somehow turned epic. It was funny as hell. The scene I relived included Jerry, Kramer, and Newman, three of the principal characters. The debate they were having was about which days of the week had a feel. Newman philosophized that while Monday had a feel, Wednesday had a feel, and Friday had a feel, Tuesday had no feel. The start of the workweek, hump day, and the last day of the workweek before the weekend, he argued, all had distinct feels, but Tuesday was just there, indistinct, melodramatic, simply needing to be over. Normally, I might agree with him, but my desire to have one man enter my life while desperately needing another to leave was making every day of the week one of feeling, much of which I couldn't seem to control. Sorry, Newman.

Monday evening had been a blur. It had been rife with emotions, at first a series of warm winds blowing until the weather changed and swirling gusts appeared, picking up funnels of dust and dirt that got into your eyes and nose, coated your clothes and left you gasping before everything settled, the residue lying inert at your feet. Dash had arrived shortly after my return, a sweaty collection of stories unfolding around him as I asked about his day. He was excited, for the most part, unusually talkative, his re-telling of events a tragi-comedy unfolding before my eyes. I laughed, shook my head, furrowed my brows, and took it all in. Over his eight-hour day, he had managed to crash twice, once into the back of an illegally parked van, his fault, once into a cab that cut him off, not his fault. He had argued with motorists at stoplights unaware of how to traverse city streets, with pedestrians unaware of how to traverse city sidewalks, with pigeons unaware of how to traverse, period. He even blustered and complained to Blake, who was just there to help him deal maturely with these realities and prepare him for Wednesday when he would begin soloing. He recounted all this with feverish gesticulations and passionate pacing about my apartment.

When finished, I said, "This has got to go into a book. You're a great storyteller."

He just smiled and dropped onto the couch.

"Now that you've settled, what's your overall impression of the job?" I opened the fridge as I said this. "I mean, I know it's just been a day."

He sighed. "Actually, I think I can do it. I just have to stay calm and not let things get to me."

I had pulled out a couple of cold beers, forgetting for an instant to whom I was offering one.

He took it, though. "Haven't had a drink since last Friday." Then added, "But I am back in control now, Jesse," he said earnestly. "I'll make this my beverage of choice for now and have water with supper."

"Supper," I pondered. "I was going to have fish, vegetables, sliced tomatoes with a bit of feta and basil on top. Sound OK?"

"Perfect." He took a swig of beer and then parked it on the end table beside him. "If you don't mind, I'm going to peel off my work clothes, shower, and change into something else."

"Sure. You'll find clean towels in the bathroom. I'll get started on supper."

"I won't be long, and then I can help you." And with that, he headed off.

I found myself in a really good mood at that point. My day had been typical and had gone reasonably well. Dash had survived and was moving forward. There was the residual problem with Greg that kept invading my mind, but I put it behind me for now. I clanged a few pots around and began to pull out the vegetables. Then the doorbell rang. I skipped toward the door and pulled it open. It was as if I had been turned to ice, frozen like a department store mannequin, my eyes enlarged, my mouth open, staring at something I could not react to. He stood there on my porch, cell phone in hand.

"You haven't returned any of my calls," he said belligerently, holding up his phone to me. "I told you I wanted to talk."

It took a few seconds for my voice to thaw, for me to break out of the freezer that I had momentarily found myself in. "What are you doing here?" was all I could manage to say at first.

"I told you, Jesse. I want to talk, straighten things out between us. Can I come in?" And he took a step forward.

"No, Greg. You can't come in. I'm making dinner. There is nothing to talk about anyway." I stood my ground and crossed my arms, but this was to minimize my nerves. Besides, I wanted him outside, in public view, as much as possible.

"What's for dinner? Maybe I can join you while we chat?" He wasn't listening, his body language indicating that he still wanted past. Then he noticed the bike locked up on the porch. "Whose is this? Doesn't look like something you would ride?"

I ignored his question. "I want you to leave. We have nothing more to say to each other. I don't want to see you anymore." And with that, I put out my hand and started to back through the door. In an instant, he had me by the wrist and was yanking me toward him. "I'll tell you when we're done, right?" I tried to twist my wrist free, yelling for him to let me go, and then the door flew open. Dash was standing there behind me. Shorts, bare-chested, a T-shirt draped over one shoulder, towel rubbing through wet hair. Both Greg and I were entranced momentarily by the beautiful tattoo that adorned much of his torso.

"Heard you yelling. Everything OK here, Jesse? Who's this guy?"

Greg let go of me. "Who am I? I'm the boyfriend. Better question is, who the fuck are you?"

"You are the ex-boyfriend, Greg," I yelled. "Ex. Get that through your head."

Greg was seething, his fists clenching and unclenching, his body swaying back and forth like a boxer at centre ring facing down his opponent and waiting for the referee to finish his instructions.

"And this is the new boyfriend. That what you're telling me?"

"I'm not telling you anything. It's none of your business. Now, please leave." I wanted him gone, off my porch and out of my life.

He gave a hard look at Dash, who had remained calm throughout this unwholesome exchange. "Looks like you've gone a little Native there, Cochise, judgin' from the paint you're wearing." Then he burned his eyes into me. "This isn't right, Jesse and it's not over."

It was then that Dash said, "That sounds like a threat." As if to make his point clearer, he moved forward one or two steps.

"Take it any way you want, you prick. You'll both be seeing me again." And with that, Greg stormed off.

We returned to the kitchen. Dash tossed the towel over the back of a chair and put on his T-shirt. I had lost my appetite, the thought of preparing a meal disappearing into the fog around me as I sank into a chair.

"You OK?" Dash had put his hand on my shoulder, a reassuring touch that I acknowledged by grabbing it. I held onto it for some time, I remember, before letting go.

"Yeah. I just need a moment." Eventually, I smiled briefly. "Thanks for riding to my rescue."

"The guy's a bit of a whack job if you ask me."

"You think?" I tried to joke off the altercation at first.

"I'm not kidding, Jesse. I've seen guys like him before. Guys who can't back down from a challenge to their manhood." He had pulled another chair in front of me and sitting, leaned forward as he spoke, trying to drill his words into me so that they would stick. I still balked.

"I'm sure he'll calm down. He knows I'm serious and he thinks you're in the picture now."

"And that's good, how?" I just looked at him as he continued. "The guy's a bully, someone with a chip on his shoulder. He wants to be in control. I don't think he's just going to go away."

"So, now you're a psychiatrist?" and he had just shrugged. But I had pondered this as we sat until Dash, hungrier than I, offered to get supper going. I relented, watched as he bumbled his way through the kitchen, hunting for things. Finally, I laughed and joined in the ritual.

We had eaten together and chatted. As the night drew on, we managed to unearth kernels about ourselves that we shared, stories that released intimacies long held inside, away from the prying minds of the curious. He had asked about my parents and my life growing up. A couple of days earlier, I had given him snippets of what it was like to be an only child shackled to the lives of busy career parents. That the love they conveyed, while genuine, was often awkward and stilted. That the feel of a hug was rare and comforting words random. I elaborated on this and other themes for a bit now. It was as if my father knew how to deliver babies, but not how to care for or raise them, and my mother knew how to research about motherhood, but not naturally apply the knowledge. And so, I was left to my own devices as I grew, which was usually reading and drawing, although I was, I told him, a natural tomboy as well, engaged in athletics and sports at school, enough to keep me loosely connected to and accepted in the circles that mattered. I travelled with my parents to Florida in winter a few times; coast to coast in Canada, which I loved; to New York and the eastern American seaboard; and once, my first time in a large airplane, to London and Paris, a trip my mother wanted and which my father reluctantly agreed to after much cajoling. These family excursions, I had to admit, had likely given me the bug to travel for a year after high school, the proverbial attempt at finding myself that countless other young adults engaged in before committing to University, College, work, or the often-unintentional hedonistic pursuit of continuing to drift.

When asked, I had even opened up to him about my love life. He had raised the question casually, like asking for an after-dinner liqueur to finish the meal. "It won't take me long," I had joked, and quickly moved through my first kiss with a neighbourhood boy at eleven years old to my one high school year-long grope in Grade 12. I had had a brief romance—my first intimate exchange—while travelling, and one more extended relationship at university. It had ended amicably when the guy moved away to another city and university to do a graduate degree. I did recount one incident for Dash when I was travelling in Italy that had him laughing out loud. While I had joined in with him, at the time, it had freaked me out and put a damper on my travels for a bit.

"I was in Rome taking in the sights," I had said. "It was a beautiful day, the sun was out, and I was walking along a quiet street at the time, trying to get my bearings. A convertible with the top down pulls up beside me and a young Italian guy, one arm resting across the passenger seat, the other on the steering wheel, asks if I want a lift somewhere. I look over and down at him and finally notice that besides the big smile he is giving me, he has his dick out of his pants. Well, my jaw dropped, I turned white, and I started looking around in a panic before I managed to get control of myself and scurry off toward what I hoped was the safety of a group of tourists. The guy called after me, "Hey, hey, beautiful," a couple of times like nothing had happened and then drove off. Later, I was told by other young women I had met that this kind of thing happened all the time there. Sex and women; women and sex. That's what a guy wants, and that's what a guy should get."

At that point, I had brought up another Seinfeld episode that I recalled. Dash knew of the series but hadn't watched any of them. It was a scene where Elaine, another principal character, recounts a date she had the night before with a friend of Jerry's. Jerry had insisted that this guy was nice and that Elaine would like him. In the scene, she sits back on the couch in Jerry's apartment when Jerry asks her how the date went. She looks up at him, takes out her glasses, cleans them, and says, "Oh, the date, the date." Breathing on her glasses she adds, "he took it out." Jerry still mystified at this point, says, "Took it out. Took what out?" Elaine breathes on the glasses again and says, "It." Jerry repeats, "It," and Elaine says, "Out," and Jerry repeats, "Out." And then it dawns on him what Elaine is saying. Jerry says, "Well, that can't be." Elaine assures him that, "Oh, it be," and ends with something like, "You got any other friends you want to set me up with?" I wasn't sure if I'd managed to capture the true essence of the scene for Dash, but he smiled, even chuckled at the story. He never asked me about Greg at that point, the last and worst of my dalliances, which I appreciated, and so this ended my history lesson for him.

Getting Dash to open up had been a little more difficult, though. He brushed over episodes in his life quickly and mechanically like some used car salesman trying to rush through a deal. I had to slow him down at points and ask for more details. However, I felt his elaborations still needed substance. But it was a start for us. He talked of his small town in Saskatchewan a bit, how as a Metis growing up between reserve and town often made him feel like an outcast in both worlds. He spoke of his dog and bike, of his love of the outdoors at the time, but never about friends. There were only acquaintances, kids at school that he fell in and out with, and bullies he avoided or fought to carve out some peace and quiet for himself. He alluded to his father, the man who helped make him and then who just as soon decided to leave. Then there was his time in Edmonton, a dark patch of history for the most part that he bumped over, giving me just enough information to form a fuzzy picture. But he had focused on two things that I could tell meant something to him, his mother and an art kit that he had had. He spoke of them with much more light in his words, much more colour and definition. I could tell that they hung on the walls of his being with an importance that other memories he had spoken of just did not have.

It was then that I had asked him about his tattoo. I had seen the image before, but I couldn't remember where. Maybe an art history book. "Let me have another look at it."

Sighing, perhaps a little self-conscious, he had obliged and removed his T-shirt again. The tattoo covered the fullness of his chest and down almost to his navel. I wanted to reach out and touch it, but restrained myself. "It's beautiful. When did you get it?"

"Out West. In Edmonton, just before I decided to leave."

"I've seen this image before. It's kind of famous, I think."

"You mean, like, iconic?"

I burst out laughing. "Right. Smartass. Well, tell me about it. Why this image in particular?"

"Story's a little long." He moved to put his T-shirt on.

"We've got lots of time and no, leave it off a little longer," I said brazenly. "It should be looked at. After all, it is a piece of art." And I added, "on a pretty nice canvas too if I do say so."

He crossed his arms and smiled. "Maybe I should charge admission."

I playfully pulled his arms open. "Too late. My gallery. My rules. Now talk."

"OK. I've never told anyone this before. Not too many people have even seen it."

"Nice to have the privilege of a private showing then. I'm feeling honoured."

He began. "After the accident, I was feeling more lost than ever. I walked the streets a lot when I wasn't high or drunk. It was a low point. I ended up going into a music store one day. They had a great selection of vinyl as it turned out, and I was just randomly thumbing through albums, looking at the jackets. Then I saw it and froze. The image was so powerful. *Surf's Up* by The Beach Boys."

"The Beach Boys, of course." I interrupted. "I remember that cover too. My parents loved the album. Sorry, go on."

"I found out that the picture was of a sculpture called *End of the Trail* by an artist named Fraser. I think a cast of the original work he did a long time ago is in a U.S. town somewhere in Wisconsin. You can see it shows a Native American man with his head hanging down, braids down, spear down, limp on his horse that also has its head down at the edge of the Pacific Ocean. The artist was trying to show what it was like to be Native and damaged by an invading European and American culture. Even the horse as it dips its head to drink at the shoreline looks defeated."

"It's so powerful," I said quietly. "So moving."

"Yeah, it is. I knew that I had to have it, so I bought it. Not to play. I didn't have a turntable for vinyl. I took it to a tattoo parlour, made an appointment, and got it done. A piece of me I would always have." He reached for his T-shirt at that point and covered up.

"So, you do think about your roots?" I said.

"Sure. Sometimes. Who doesn't?"

"You should keep searching."

He had simply nodded at that. The evening had opened a door that I wanted to enter more often. Reluctantly, we retired separately to sleep, but the chemistry between us was building. I think we both wanted it to go somewhere.

As I sat at work the next day, shuffling through my recollections of the night, the random papers strewing my desk cried out for attention. I reviewed my suggestion to Dash before bed. After work tonight, I had told him that we were going back to the art gallery. At first, he had been silent, but with some encouragement had agreed, thought it was a good idea. It was something we could both look forward to, a few hours out of the apartment. My day then moved on predictably. I talked with clients, wrote and filed reports, and met with colleagues until the phone call at lunch. Greg. I didn't answer. Then the texts followed, a barrage of three or four up until mid-afternoon, each more aggressive than the previous. Dash had been right. I was naive to think that this would just go away. I worried that I might have to get the cops involved if he didn't stop. It ruined the remainder of my afternoon. I needed to get home and put this behind me for now.

* * *

Quasimodo was up in the rafters of Notre Dame Cathedral, hump-backed and shouting as he pulled on the ropes that started his giant bells ringing. Reading was not Greg's thing. He had experienced too many public humiliations when called on in the classroom, his desire to be moving or jumping around overriding the calm concentration needed to follow and interpret the page. But he had seen the movie, loved the ugliness of Charles Laughton, and the rage that he could resurrect out of the despair at his own mistreatment. *He was the lucky one*, Greg thought. At least he was deaf to the raucous pounding that rang all around him.

On the other hand, Greg was still infected with a belfry full of bombs going off at intervals when he so much as turned his head. Hunched over the wheel of his car, he popped two more

Tylenol and willed himself on. He should never have gotten out of bed, but he needed to work and keep his mind on something other than last night. He relived the moment again on Jesse's porch, standing there just wanting to talk, her bitchy refusal to let him in, and then the arrival behind her in the doorway of the mystery man—the "friend" he was sure was more than that. It had stunned him, angered him, enraged him to see these two standing there, taunting and belittling him. He had left a seething mass and driven in an incendiary ball back to his apartment, where he shrunk the flames to a smouldering heap with a series of beers and shots before extinguishing himself on his bed.

But Tuesday had not taken his pain away; it merely dulled it. As he stripped off his clothes in the morning and stumbled from shower to water and pills to clothes again, he imagined his next steps. Justice, retribution, a hearing, this is what he demanded. Jesse could not just cast him aside, not this time. Women had done this to him before—flirted and laughed and promised and fucked, yes even that, and then left. This time, it was going to be different. This time, there would have to be a reckoning. He was owed that much, at least.

As he backed his one true love into its space and shut down its purr, a set of blue eyes drifted in front of him. Jesse had got herself an Indian, the realization dawning more and more on Greg as he unspooled and spliced and replayed their meeting. He knew the telltale signs. He'd been around them before. The tattoo he had seen front and centre on his body had sealed it for Greg, though. How could she? Did she know what could happen? The kind of trouble she was inviting. Lava bubbled up, threatening to explode again beneath a surface that was impossible to cool. Who was this guy? Some charity case from her job? Her do-gooder stray of the day? He banged and tossed and cursed his way through the loading of his truck, screaming out on four wheels into a morning that left his manager trailing briefly behind in his wake, his hands on his hips and shaking his head.

As Greg throttled the steering wheel and moved his metal chess piece along the city's asphalt board, Calgary's streets emerged. He thought of his old man, smug and supercilious, pontificating on what it was to be a success. His dad had cajoled, badgered, pushed him into various menial jobs after school meant to toughen him up, make him a man, but they had only made him more sullen, more determined not to succeed. He had hated lugging drywall or timber around as a flunky for his dad's crew as they patched and repaired apartments in preparation for new tenants. He hated pushing brooms, cleaning up scrap, moving in sticks of furniture or painting, any of the physical slavery his dad encouraged and demanded to welcome the outsiders moving in. Worst of all, he hated being there when these occupants, often foreigners with limited English and odd smells, moved into the spaces he had worked so tirelessly to get ready for them. And despite his dad's vetting, his pronouncements that these were good people from different backgrounds who just needed a break, Greg sizzled, the meat of his brain turning to a blackened char. These interlopers were usurping his birthright. Who were they, these funnily dressed, multi-coloured, racially suspect nomads with their sense of new world entitlement? Go back to your own expanses of dirt and leave us alone.

He signalled and turned into the second of his destinations, laying on the horn and laughing at a cyclist he had forced to brake quickly as he cut her off. Stupid, helmeted bitch on a weathered touring bike, pink running shoes and a skirt of all things, rear pannier laden and battened down with items. There ought to be a law. "Get off the road," he yelled to nothing but his windshield as he pulled to a stop. Tumbling out of the cab, he wrenched open the back doors, grabbed the small trolley inside and fired on the three-box order that needed to be trundled into the shipping department.

His day would continue like this, stops and starts of reflection and anger, a streetcar on screeching tracks he could not will himself to get off. And the image that continued to recur, to rise up red at various intersections in his mind was of the one group he railed against the most. The Indians, not the East Indians, although there was much to disparage about them too, but the Natives, the Indigenous as they were supposed to be called now, a politically correct term he refused to utilize. Why were they so special? What made him less native to this country than they? He was born here. His grandparents and parents had helped build this country, this province, this city much more than the Indian. What had they contributed with their arrows and bows, teepees and drums, feathers and dances? Hadn't they been separated like chaff from the wheat and blown onto the reserves and streets? Hadn't he seen them growing up loafing in front of bars and mission houses, zigzagging drunk along alleyways and into parks, mumbling words he didn't understand, looking through hair at him with haunting eyes that darkened his soul? How were they better than him?

His last stop had him only a mile or so from home base and forty-five minutes ahead of schedule. He had carried on through lunch again, had some time on the clock left and wanted a drink. Just one. Scouting around for a pub or bar would take too long, and he had to park. Instead, he opted for a Beer Store that loomed up ahead of him. A small lot and a six-pack were all he needed. He would sit quietly afterwards in his van, snap a cap, and drain one before moving off. A simple plan. They were cold, and the first had disappeared in a rush and a belch within five minutes. He decided on a second but would try to relax, take his time. He still had to get back and finish up the day. If he timed it right, he would arrive just a little late, the flurry of people rushing goodbyes as they headed for their vehicles and home allowing him relative anonymity.

With his next pull at the can, he was back to remembering his time in Sault Saint Marie, a shovel in his hand, wedged into a trench laying pipe. He had descended from Dryden across and down the Trans-Canada Highway, tail tucked between his legs, testicles shrivelled like squirrel nuts in a winter nest. His anger had driven him on through Ignace and English River, to Upsala and then Thunder Bay. Here, he had stopped and worked at a gas station for three months, his only friends a downtown bar and a hooker he brought back to his apartment once a week. Then it was on to Nipigon, Rossport, Terrace Bay, White River, and Wawa. His trajectory had been unplanned, his stops random, here a day, there a week, his boredom with each place equal to the durations he remained. And then he was at the Sioux. He had found it picturesque, this small city bordering the U.S. along St. Mary's River and cut into rock close to the watery expansiveness of three Great Lakes, Superior, Michigan, and Huron. He had found a job, rented a small bungalow on Pardee Avenue off North Street and hunkered down. His car was kept in the garage, locked up and hidden, unless he wanted to take it out on weekends for drives into the lake areas around. It would not be left vulnerable again. His work was within walking distance and was destined to go on for months as trenches were dug for new sewage lines on streets that looked like they could use the investment. The workers were either locals or transients like himself, labouring for a company that moved from town to town where contracts were found, a circus sideshow of trucks and heavy equipment bringing occasional gawkers and critics and changing the landscape for a time.

"Shit," Greg croaked. A police car had pulled into the Beer Store parking lot and jerked him out of his reverie. He put his open can back in the case, a slight paranoia beginning to creep in. The cop looped around the lot slowly and stopped by the exit facing the street. Was he just going to sit there? Maybe he was tracking speeders or taking a break. Greg decided not to take any chances. Perhaps he had been sitting here too long, drawing attention to himself. Whatever the case, he decided it was time to leave. Turning on his van, he eased slowly out of his space, passed the motionless police car, and turned right out onto the street. He exhaled loudly when the cop did not follow. "False alarm. Thank God." Regaining his composure, he reached for his beer again. It could be finished just as easily on the road.

Cecil Philips. An image began to appear as he drove, his beer resting on the console. He was his one friend in the Sault. Not even friend, a drinking buddy torn from the same cloth. A drifter of sorts from Winnipeg who had lived there for over two years. He had worked at everything from short-order cook to fisherman to labourer, his pastime a TV at the apartment he rented and beer at a local bar the name of which escaped Greg, but which featured pool tables, live music, even a karaoke night. It had been a good place to pass the time after work for a few before turning in and readying for the grind again the next day. Greg downed the last of his beer. He was about ten minutes from the shop.

He and Cecil had agreed on one thing, saw eye to eye on it. Wherever they seemed to go, Calgary, Winnipeg, Thunder Bay, and now, here, there were too many damn Indians around. Even their bar, what the fuck was its name, was full of them sometimes, drifting in to hang out, play pool, drink, stumble off or pass out, nuisances pure and simple. Greg's anger increased as he recalled one incident where he had been humiliated. It was in the washroom at the bar. He was having a piss, Cecil outside buying another round, when this older Indian stood up beside him at a urinal, looked over, had a peek, and said, "You're a little guy," and laughed, a chuckle really before turning back and spraying the porcelain. Greg, in one of his wittier states of mind brought on by a couple of quick beers, felt that his comeback of "Yeah, well, remember, chief, it's not how long you make it, but how you make it long, and your women aren't so particular" was a pretty good one. But this Indian, after just insulting him, didn't seem to be able to take a joke in return. With barely enough time to zip up, Greg had been grabbed by the throat and shoved up against the bathroom wall. "You be careful around me, or your dick will get even smaller." He had glared at Greg after that, then simply smiled, chuckled again, let him go and walked off. Greg banged his steering wheel at the recollection. When he came out, the guy was at another table with a couple of friends, heads together and laughing. These fuckers were always getting the better of him. Always.

His thoughts returned to last night and the doorman at Jesse's apartment. Another unjust turn of events, another humiliation. And this time, his girlfriend was a willing part of the charade. She had shut him out in favour of this drifter, someone who was obviously using her, someone untrustworthy, perhaps even dangerous. His destination loomed up ahead of him, and he signalled in. Parking, he surreptitiously transferred the remaining beer to his car before heading indoors. He would sign out, go quickly home, and then down to Jesse's again, where he would wait and watch. She obviously didn't know what she was doing or who she was doing it with.

* * *

Dash was finding out a lot about the bike courier business from Blake. As they sat and took a break, he also found out more about his boss, like the fact that Derrick was a "straight shooter, an honest no bullshit employer that didn't fuck with his guys." Blake had started to open up about the job and how hard it really was to work for ninety percent of the other courier brokers or companies.

"There are hundreds of courier outlets in the city," he had said on one of their breaks. "Some are overnighters run by big national or international owners. More cars and vans in their case and usually better pay, but we, guys like you and me," pointing at Dash and himself, "same-day delivery dudes, have a lot less stability. Unstable hours and…and," here he became more animated and outraged, "are treated as independent contractors, sometimes paying more for insurance and repairs and downtime than we can make. Because of that, there's often no loyalty. You work for more than one company; you dig and scratch and compete with everyone else. You give up a lot because of this, but most companies don't care because there's always another fish to reel in. Its dog-eat-dog, man, and everybody's got a bone to pick."

"So, how does Derrick manage to throw us the good bones all the time?" Dash had asked. "Keep everybody happy?"

"Don't ask me, man. I haven't got a nose for business, but I've been with Derrick for years. He's like a brother to me. We hang out together, and you don't do that with your boss, usually. He dispatches, still rides sometimes, and keeps half a dozen of us working full- or part-time in the downtown core. A small operation by most standards, but he pays as good as he can, treats everybody fairly and in return…loyalty, he gets back loyalty and respect, man. That's what everybody needs, right? A little respect." Dash had to agree. Respect was a good commodity to have. Of course, it had to be earned, and he had not earned it yet. Now, he had a chance to prove himself and earn it from people like Derrick, Blake, and especially Jesse.

"There's another thing on Derrick's side." Blake had taken a quick call on his phone and was mounting his bike. Their break was over.

Dash stood and stretched. "What's that?"

"Customers. Derrick has managed to keep a string of satisfied customers with him, even add some, like this pick up we just got on Bay. He treats everybody well, has riders who do their part as best they can," and here he looked at Dash directly, "and keep their cool. Everybody wins, and that's a good thing. Let's go."

Most of their runs covered the downtown core from the lake north to Bloor Street and from Bathurst Street east to around Jarvis Street. The bread and butter of their operation was in this hive of activity, an occasional forage getting them out further to Trinity-Bellwoods or maybe east toward Allan Gardens. They were like bees moving from flower to flower, picking up and dropping the door to door pollen that ultimately sustained each plant and collectively drove the honeyed economy. They came back sticky from a day's work, wings torn, legs frayed, into a small colony that would commiserate briefly together, maybe share a cold drink somewhere before settling into their own waxy worlds for the night, readying for the heat, cold, or wind of another day in the elements.

Today had been a mix of successes and failures. The weather had not been a key factor in either, but a lack of confidence and self-control had buffeted Dash on occasion. He had been given a little more responsibility, Derrick offering him the bulk of the courier drops to ferret out and deliver. Tuesday had not been terribly busy, and this had helped with time. It was his response to being cut off in traffic by cars or by pedestrians, the gruff response by a concierge at a desk if he needed direction to another floor or office, the crackle from his phone wondering where he was on a certain route that whittled away at his psyche throughout the day and made him question himself. Blake had been a big support. He had let him muddle along, which turned out to be the best approach, intervening only when needed, correcting an assumption or mistake quietly, giving advice discreetly and keeping, as best he could, self-doubt and anger from spilling out into the open. "Remember the old saying," he said after Dash had resurfaced from an office maze, fuming and shaking his head at the curt reception he had received for being a few minutes late with his package, "as much as it may be bullshit in your mind, the customer is always right."

Dash had just looked at him. "The guy was an asshole, Blake. But whatever. Where to next?"

"Hey, man. I'm serious. Particularly the assholes. It might be hard, but park the attitude outside with your bike. Better to apologize even if you feel you've been wronged than to go off on some dude who is having an equally bad day at that moment and decides you're going to be his lunch."

"But that guy just..."

"I know that guy. His name's Darryl. He sits at a desk all day in the front lobby, drinking coffee, eating doughnuts, flipping through magazines, thinking he's an almighty gatekeeper with power over everybody who enters." Here, Blake stopped and waited for Dash to give him his full attention. "Darryl hates himself, man. He's got nothin' in his life but that chair and that job. No respect that I can see, no dignity. I've talked to him when I'm not in a rush, and he's got nothing to say about anything—music, politics, life, the weather. He's just a blob going through the motions. I used to feel sorry for him, but not anymore. He's a piece of furniture with a mouth, man, and that's filled most of the time. Don't worry about him. He's not worth gettin' upset over. It'll just ruin your day. You got to figure that part out for yourself."

Dash had nodded and smiled. A piece of furniture. Good one. He would try harder not to let personal affronts take hold of him. Stay calm. Represent the company, not himself. All these tiny truisms needed to become embedded in his consciousness if he was going to get through the next day. Then he would be on his own, and that prospect unnerved him. But tomorrow was another day. The customer is always right. The world is full of clichés and assholes. And right now, he was both. So, wheel, wheel, wheel, he thought, like a hockey player churning up ice. Stick handle up to Blake and focus, focus on finishing the day with a goal. There is still tonight, Jesse, and the gallery to come.

* * *

"So, you ready to go?" I had grabbed my backpack and was waiting by the door.

"Almost there. Just one more shoe." Dash stretched on the last runner and started lacing.

"You call those shoes?" I laughed. "What do you do, wrap the laces around your feet a few times to keep the bottoms from falling off?"

"Yeah, yeah, laugh if you like, but they get me around." He stood up from the couch and grabbed his pack.

"You know you could use a couple of slices of bread and some elastic bands and be further ahead." I shook my head. "Promise me that you will get a new pair when you get your first paycheck."

"Aye, aye, captain," and a mock salute followed.

We had enjoyed a simple supper of grilled cheese sandwiches, a mixed green salad, and an apple. Dash had wolfed the food down. I knew he was still hungry. We would need to do some shopping tomorrow if these living arrangements were to continue. Breakfast stuff was all I had left.

We exited the apartment and started moving up Beverley Street. It was just pushing 7:00 p.m. The gallery would be open until 9:00 p.m., giving us a couple of hours to walk around some of the other exhibits Dash hadn't seen. My hope was that he would want to take in some Canadian artists like the Group of Seven, Emily Carr, and maybe the Indigenous offerings. Colville could come at the end if he really wanted to go through again, but there wouldn't be a lot of time to do everything. I wouldn't push, just play it by ear. I was just happy that he had agreed to go. Something positive was happening to Dash, and I didn't want to jinx it by coming on too aggressively. A turtle was coming out of its shell, and poking it with a stick was the worst thing I could do. We cut across to the other side of the street, passing Grange Park. The September evening was still warm, but the skies were beginning to fade and blend into a canvass of pinks and purples. By the time we left the gallery two hours from now, darkness would have closed in. City lights would be twinkling artificially along streets and from the windows of countless high-rises. Evening breezes would be bundling people along more quickly toward their destinations.

To every time there is a season. I was reminded of this old biblical line made more contemporary by the Byrd's as we strolled.

* * *

The broken branch that Greg had snapped from a tree had helped him pass the time as he waited in the park across from Jesse's apartment. He had raced from home to McCaul Street, where he had decided to park in the underground lot adjacent to the art gallery. He didn't know how long he might be there. He didn't know what he was doing, really, he was just there. Putting one foot mechanically in front of the other, he had walked to the park at the back of the gallery and to a bench. From here, he could watch the apartment in relative seclusion, sit or stand back from the street and observe. He did not consider himself a voyeur or a stalker, merely an unfortunate victim who deserved better. He could see the bike on the porch and lights on inside, so he knew they were there. What to do? He had walked around with the branch, idly swatting at grasses, lopping off the heads of an occasional flower. Each poor blade and petal that was felled spurted out anger, a bloodletting on the ground. Should he confront her again? What was going on behind those walls just fifty metres away?

He was hungry too. Aside from a bag of chips, he hadn't eaten all day. But he couldn't leave, not just yet. He cracked the branch against the back of a bench until it broke, and just as it did, her door opened. They stood for a moment, taking in the evening air before she had locked up. As they descended the steps, he had moved back behind a tree, his presence undetected. When they passed, he dropped the remains in his hand and eased out discreetly, a detective on a case he was making up as he went along. He followed them to Dundas Street, watched them turn right, and then sped to catch up. Rounding the corner tentatively, he saw them go up the stairs and into the gallery.

"Fucking art. Of course," he spat out under his breath. None of his high school friends had cared about art. Not a guy thing. They and he were more into good times, partying, cars, watching sports. That hadn't changed since arriving in Toronto. A couple of times he had been asked to come here by Jesse. But the thought of wandering through an art gallery and looking at pictures bored the hell out of him. He had laughed at the notion, pissed Jesse off with his attitude, and brushed off her own inclinations to draw and paint, something she had mentioned to him that she wanted to return to, as a joke. "Why would you want to waste your time on something like that?" he would say. "You any good? Can you make any money at it?" These were all worthwhile questions in his mind, but here he was at last, in front of this hulking piece of steel and glass, wondering if he should go in. He didn't want to have to spend the money, but he needed to know what they were doing.

"Idiot, make up your mind." Then his stomach barked at him, clawing at a portion of his gut in a desperate bid for attention. Looking down the street, he noticed another idiot staring back at him, in fact, a village of them, and he made up his mind. He would go to the Village Idiot pub at the corner where he could sit, have a drink or two and some food, and watch the front doors. When they came out, he would follow them, see what they did next. He liked this plan much better. Turning away from the gallery, he allowed his dogs to lead on.

* * *

As soon as we spun our way through the revolving doors, I took a deep breath and stopped in my tracks. I always performed this ritual, paid homage to this mystical space I had entered before moving on, this five-storey ark of intricate and complex architectural design, this monumental repository for some 93,000 individual pieces of varied artistic history. Dash stood beside me, less engaged in my dotage. After my brief meditation, we moved on to the coat check to drop off our bags. Dash remembered the drill and was already steps ahead.

"You're not particularly interested in ship models, are you?" I mentioned to him.

"Ship models? Why do you ask?"

"Down in the concourse below, there is a Thomson collection of ship models, quite impressive, actually."

Dash paused. "So, did he like, build them himself from kits and such?"

I laughed, perhaps more heartily than I should have given the startled and irritated look I got.

"What?" He shrugged.

I wasn't sure if he was serious or kidding, but I played it safe. "Sorry. No, these are incredibly crafted reconstructions of actual ships built with similar materials of wood, metal, rope, and paint. Military, luxury, leisure; sail and engine powered; a collection of old and new; and all under glass, of course, but some several feet in size.

"Well, since you put it that way," Dash said, "then no, not interested, really."

"Didn't think so. Not a boat or water person, I gather."

Dash shook his head. "It's not that." He was thinking of the few times he had been fishing at the lake close to his childhood home, bike resting on the grasses along the shore, his cheap pole in hand, waiting to be readied and released. And the one time before that, where his dad and mom had taken him when he was very young before his dad had drifted away, out in a canoe. He always remembered that day as one of sunlight and laughter, the blue of lazy waters lapping at their bark as his dad and mom propelled them along, he safe between them, surveying the shoreline and the open expanses around. This was a memory he held onto, fighting with it like a fisherman wrestling with a catch, drawing it up from the depths, hoping to keep it on a hook and line that bent and twisted as it attempted to get away, only to disappear again into the deep. His mother had had friends from the reserve who fished, sometimes even brought over pickerel, walleye, or trout to fry up or freeze. Eric had promised to take him out once or twice, but it hadn't happened. Usually, if the urge hit, he'd take an old rod left by his dad and would head off on his bike alone to try his luck.

Dash then jerked the line to his past and pulled himself back into the present.

"Nice to see you back. Penny for your thoughts?"

"Nothing really. Just thinking of a canoe ride I took once. I'll tell you later."

"I look forward to that," I told him, then paid for his ticket and ushered us in before he could react to my gesture. *I'm making a list,* I told myself, *and checking it twice.*

"Third time's a charm," he said.

"What do you mean?"

"Just that the next time we come here, it's going to be my turn to pay."

"So, there might be a next time?" I quipped.

"Maybe. Don't see why not." He smiled and looked around.

"Great. I'll hold you to it. Let's go."

We first made a twenty-minute sweep through the suite of galleries on Level One that held the Thomson Collection of European Art. More than nine hundred objects of northern European sculpture and decorative arts from early middle age periods to the 19th century, both sacred and secular, spread out around us. Baroque ivories, silver, boxwood carvings, carved portrait medallions. Dash took it all in, occasionally pausing to read an inscription or take a closer look. I moved in close tandem, but back a bit, a secondary observer having been through many times before. It wasn't until a certain large painting appeared before us that Dash stopped to take in something fully and with great intensity. *The Massacre of the Innocents,* a masterpiece by Flemish baroque artist Paul Rubens, had overwhelmed him. He was looking at a fabled depiction of Biblical slaughter, King

Herod's soldiers eradicating male babies to prevent the prophesied King of the Jews from taking his throne.

"Your thoughts?" I finally said.

"Graphic. Grim."

"Well, that's true."

"But, you want more." He looked over at me as he said this.

"I didn't say I wanted more. Did I say that?"

He continued, though. "The violence, suffering and fear, the struggle for survival is all so real. Muscular men with swords hacking away at women who are desperately trying to protect their babies from death. What can I say? It's another example of the strong beating down the weak." He stood for a time, then turned and walked away. "Love the artwork, though," he called to me over his shoulder. "The guy's good."

Rubens would be pleased with the nod to his art, I thought.

Next, I guided Dash quickly up to Level Two. Here, I hoped to get him interested in Thomson's Collection of Canadian Art. Maybe look at the Henry Moore sculptures and call it a night. There was a lot to see if he gave it a chance. His eyes brushed over much of the 19th-century stuff, giving Krieghoff a bit of time. Much of the Group of Seven caught his attention, MacDonald, Carmichael, and the outlier, Tom Thomson, their landscape interpretations drawing themselves to him. But Harris, I could tell from his body language, the way he wanted to reach out and almost touch the pieces, seemed to grapple with him the most. The range, he said in the end, from the realistic capturing of a scene of the Ward in Toronto or a building in Halifax to the majestic, almost spiritual renderings of Baffin Island, Lake Superior, and various mountain ranges, as well as the simplicity of the lines and the burst of colours, purples, blues, whites, and browns that made up his art, all left him wanting more. I never asked him to explain, elaborate, and interpret his feelings; I just followed along, content within his experience.

I skipped the suggestion of Henry Moore. We only had about thirty minutes left before everything would shut down for the evening. I wanted him to at least get a taste of some of the Indigenous offerings, not so much the collections of sculptures and masks and trinkets that had been amassed for public perusal, but a few representative pieces of more contemporary paintings. I specifically wanted to hunt down the one example by Norval Morrisseau, a great Canadian Indigenous painter, that I remembered was somewhere here. *Just for comparison,* I told myself, *to see if the spark continued in his appreciation*. What a conniver, but what the hell? We might not get back here for a while despite what Dash had said earlier. Ten minutes of scurrying uncovered the gem I was looking for, *Man Changing into Thunderbird*.

"Here," I said. "Look at this." We had stopped in front of something I thought was beautiful—a colourful representation of Morrisseau's changing vision of spirituality, his shamanistic journey toward enlightenment. Dash stared, not saying anything. I started to fill him in a little more on what I knew about this artist without seeming too teachy. I was definitely no expert.

"This is the first of six panels that this artist did on his Thunderbird theme. It took him fifteen years or more, I think, just to feel that he could do it, to get to a level where his life could emulate his art. Each panel gets more colourful and complete until his full spiritual realization is finally released in the last panel when he becomes Copper Thunderbird." Dash continued to remain mute. "The last panel even has a copper finish to the background, unlike this one, which is a more yellowy-gold. This is the first in the series."

"It is something," Dash admitted. "His human form at the centre but then the birds, fish, sun, and, I guess planets. All part of what is inside and around him. It comes together. And the colours. Wow. Beautiful primaries that just jump out at you. Different than the other paintings for sure. Kind of like the Harris stuff I liked in terms of lines, but the colours. You said there were more?" I couldn't hold in my elation at his response. He'd never positively said this much about art yet.

"I don't think there are any more exactly like this, at least not on display. We can always look up Morrisseau, though, and find out more about his art, and other Indigenous artists too if you like."

He became reflective and silent again, moving back into himself for a moment. After giving the painting another scrutinizing look, he asked if we had time to go into the gift shop.

"Sure," I said. "We still have about fifteen minutes left before the gallery closes." I instinctively thought of my credit card and yet another purchase I might be guilted into buying.

"What are you looking for this time?" I asked as we hustled ourselves into the shop.

He stopped. "Don't laugh. But tell me where they keep the sketchbooks, pencils, stuff like that."

"Not sure, but I think back in this area." We moved away from the books and toward the end of the upper level. "Why?"

"I think I want to start drawing again. It's been a while."

"Really." He had only mentioned his beloved art kit to me once as something lost and perhaps forgotten inside him. "That's great."

"I don't want anything too big or fancy. Something simple, compact, that I can carry around. Probably just for doodling. You know."

"Tell you what," I said as he was poking around. "You're not really going to find much here, to be honest. Lots of books, puzzles, T-shirts, posters, stuff like that, but not sketchbooks so much. Let's look at a couple of art shops I know in the area tomorrow." He seemed a little deflated at this and continued to look around. "More selection and better deals there as well." He finally agreed, and we headed for our backpacks and the door.

"I'm glad you're thinking of drawing again," I remarked as we wandered outside. It had gotten darker and cooler, but not uncomfortable. "Shall we head back?"

"Sure. And don't worry. I'm buying the sketchbook and pencils. Just so you know."

"I wouldn't want it any other way," and I punched his shoulder. He reached out and put his arm around me.

"Thanks for tonight. It was a great idea." I briefly put my head on his shoulder before he let go. "You're welcome."

"And I haven't forgotten about Colville, by the way. I'd like to see his stuff again."

"Of course. There's still time to do that." What a transformation. I couldn't believe it. And just in a few days.

"You know they called Morrisseau, the last artist we just saw, the Picasso of the North."

"Who's Picasso?" And he started walking away stone-faced.

I looked at him and strode to catch up. "You'd make a great straight man."

* * *

An empty glass slammed down on the table. Greg stood up abruptly and moved toward the till to pay. Three beers and two shots, but the food, a burger and fries, had kept him occupied and sober enough. A light night of drinking by his account. He had seen them exit the gallery, noticed the embrace, the head lean and had busted out of the pub like a wild horse from a pen intent on bucking its rider. They had turned back down Beverley by the time he had managed to cross the street. *Fuckers!* He picked up his pace, an awkward jog that had him panting for breath by the time he reached the corner. There they were, half a block away. He tracked them in the shadows of the darkening night until he was at the park. They had reached her porch, the light at the door illuminating them for a minute until her key was found. A final burst of laughter, the door opened, and they tumbled inside. Greg crossed the street and paced back and forth on the street. Should he confront them now? He mounted the stairs and stood before the door, fists clenched. He decided he would not. *Let them think they had won,* he thought. He needed to see Jesse alone, without her sidekick. Talk some sense into her. For now, he would slip away into the shadows, but not before letting the air out of this bastard's tires. He would prefer to slit them, to carve them up into pieces, but he needed something sharp to do it with, and he had been on the porch too long already. No sense drawing attention to himself. Another time.

* * *

Crow watched from his perch on the AGO. It had become familiar to him, this odd construction that absorbed light through the day then threw it off at night. People scurried about below him, oblivious to his presence. He had observed what unfolded, and now that evening had appeared, was prepared to let Coyote carry on. By now, Coyote should be in the park, having found his way surreptitiously there under the growing cover of darkness, his dog day just beginning. Let him determine what the next hours would bring. Crow turned his gaze to the underground parking lot from which the car would soon appear. Within minutes, he saw it emerge and screech north onto McCaul Street. Lifting himself, he drifted over the road, and at the stoplight where the vehicle and its occupant waited impatiently, he once again strafed the car's rooftop with his deposit. He cackled as he flew on. That trick never got old.

* * *

Picture #9: *Coyote and Alders*

Observer's description: In the immediate foreground of the painting, alders rise up amidst a cover of fresh white snow. A coyote intent on tracking something beyond the observer's sight is moving stealthily through the growth. His coat is a healthy grey and white mixture, blending him into his surroundings. His ears are upright, left paw raised, his whole body focused on what lies ahead. Behind the animal, the thicket of alders closes into one dense mass of darker brown until, as the observer's eye tracks toward the top of the painting, their tips blend with the sky's hazy yellow, suggesting a coldness to the day. Only the alders know what other animal is lurking in its protective confines, perhaps seconds away from a chase. It is only an imagining at this point, a thought in the observer's mind that has wandered beyond the frame and pushed reality into the realm of fate. What lies beyond the canvas borders cannot be determined.

Chapter Nine

THE PAST

Luck. Just a word, but like a two-headed snake, it pulled in different directions. He would have to agree that most of his life had been one of bad luck to date. Not knowing his grandparents, not really knowing his dad. Like a prospector, Dash had sifted through the few stories his mother had told him, panning for gold, but finding only the occasional small nugget. Getting into trouble at school, not making friends, always outside looking in had been a pattern. Was this because of his background, because his blood could be traced back through two different tributaries, both leading to a sea of uncertainty? That had something to do with it. Had he been born under a bad sign? He started quietly singing the lyrics to a version of a song he remembered about being born this way. This bluesy take on the original Albert King song was first heard by him when famous powerhouse trio Cream re-invented it. He had always loved it. Jack Bruce gutting out the lyrics behind his fretless bass; Ginger Baker stoically drumming along with a slow thunderous beat; and old, slow hand Eric Clapton, electrifying the notes, blowing them up and out for everyone on his Fender Stratocaster. Several decades ago, they had dusted it off, put their own spin on it, and thrown it onto their *Wheels of Fire* album, long before he was born. There were certain groups from that era of the 60s that he knew and liked. This song still tripped across his mind when he was feeling sorry for himself.

But the last couple of years had been filled with some good luck as well. He couldn't forget that. He had walked away with his mother from the courtroom without any jail time. That had amazed him, but luck had been on his side. At seventeen, the judge had noted that he had no other offences chalked up against him. And the dealer, in truth, a narc, who had honestly noted his bewilderment at Manny's actions, at what he believed was his unintended participation in anything but the purchase of an ounce or two of pot was also helpful. Even the cops had given him the benefit of the doubt. He had cooperated and told the truth, so the judge had given him a year's probation. After all, he had gone out to buy the dope that had ultimately begun to roll their giant snowball downhill. He was sent on his way with the guarantee that he would attend school or get a job and continue to live at home under his mother's eye. He had complied without reserve, but it had not always been easy.

School continued to see him as a pariah. Friendships were unwanted, and his one friend, Manny, was away at an institution where re-education was also a mandate, but Dash expected was much less enjoyable. He refused to fight at school, to get baited into releasing his pent-up anger. This was more in keeping with his mother's commands than the judge's edict. Words and threats would often be exchanged, though, and if these blew up beyond school property and onto the street, then Dash would not back down. Skirmishes were resolved unreported; he would explain the bruised knuckles or the black eye as gym miscues and accidents. And so, he had plodded along like an old draught horse pulling a heavy load until after a year of frustration and having secured only four more credits, Eric had found him a job. At eighteen, he would enter the world of work full-time.

Paul Driscoll was a small, wiry man in his mid-fifties. He was a Scotsman and had come over from the old country, as he called it when he was in his early twenties. With a cigarette always dangling from his lips and a twinkle in his eye, he told everyone who would listen that he had picked up a paintbrush soon after he arrived and hadn't put it down since. Houses, apartments, schools, factories, no job was too big for him. A friend of a friend told Eric that Driscoll was looking for someone, a good worker who could be taught a painter's trade, and since one of his own boys had packed up and moved back to Newfoundland, there was a space available in their posse of five. Dash had shown up for an informal interview on a Saturday, and ten minutes later, he was handed a roller and a tray of paint and been instructed on how to use the tool properly. He had followed the more experienced Roddy, who was doing the intricate cutting work around the rooms for three days until his first job was complete, a two-bedroom apartment in a complex, acquiring new tenants. Days off could be at any time or, in some cases, not at all if a job's deadline loomed up ahead. But he got used to this and began to even enjoy the rhythm that came with applying paint of many colours to different textures.

It took a few months, but eventually, Dash mastered the finer tricks of brush usage, specifically the steady, quick eye needed to cut along trim. When he could do it without tape and too much daubing with his ever-present cloth, when speed and accuracy outpaced mistakes, his rookie status was stripped from him, and he became a full-fledged member of the team. Although friendship was never extended in a big way, primarily because Paul, Roddy, Jim, and Phil were all family men and at least twenty years older than him, there were occasions when they would stay after work at a location and have a beer or two. The back of a truck was usually the pub and Paul the bartender, dolling out a cold can or bottle from a case he had bought earlier in the day and had on ice. The conversation was lighthearted, the banter involving rival sports teams or weekend plans or local politics. Dash was silent for the most part, chipping in on something when it suited, but just with a sentence or two. When asked about family, he often felt cornered and uncomfortable and would provide a minimum of information until Paul would shift his body and break up the awkwardness with an "anybody want another" or "finish up boys, I've got to get going."

When Dash would head home by bus or on foot after these exchanges, he would reflect on his reluctance to open up to "the boys" at work. They were always talking about their wives or their kids, about arguments, problems, humorous encounters, sibling rivalries, school conflicts, academic failures and successes, and neighbourhood disagreements—an endless array of personal topics that they felt was everyone's business. One-upping each other at a break until all four were chiming in was a favourite pastime: "That's nothing, you should have seen what my wife came home with last week" or "I told my son that the next time he pulled that, he'd feel the back of my hand" or "Damn teachers don't know shit" or "She's a good little player, but she needs to listen to the coach more" and on and on.

Dash knew more about the other families than his own it seemed, and he began broaching this with his mother. Whether he caught her at the kitchen counter before or after dinner, or with her feet up on the footstool of the La-Z-Boy, TV tuned to *Wheel of Fortune* or *Jeopardy*, a cloud of darkness would settle in around her initially at his request. He would wait patiently for a sigh or a movement, perhaps for a dish towel or the mute button, when she might deign to begin. It was still a puzzle in his mind, but each story, each recounting, however small, had fostered an awakening.

"Your grandfather was an outcast," his mother laughed, "as smooth-talking as your dad. He swept my mom off her feet and off the reserve to a little place in Saskatchewan."

"Where?" he had asked.

Not sure," she replied. "A farm of sorts, small, maybe a rental, I don't know, on the outskirts of a town I've never gone back to. My dad had chickens, did road work, odd jobs for the town a few months of the year. My mom grew vegetables in a small garden, and stayed close with me. It was tough, and there was never much, but I remember we got by."

"What about the reserve?" he had asked. "Why didn't they stay?"

She had looked at him hard then. "I don't really know. I guess they felt there was nothing there for them. He and my mom needed to be somewhere, anywhere, but there. Being Metis meant for my parents that 'home' might not really be anywhere. I was never there, she said, born somewhere else, maybe on the road to where we ended up. It was all a mystery that I didn't have the words or thoughts or time to untangle."

"What do you mean?" he asked. And it was here that another truth had emerged, an extension to a story that he had never heard before, the elaboration of a tale that his mother had kept closed off for years.

"Because I was taken. Sent off to school to get Christianized." She spat out this last word as if she was trying to dislodge some parasite from her body.

"Taken?" Dash was confused. He had heard her use this word before, but it was an odd word to use. People don't just take each other. He remembered school history classes about slavery. Those people had been kidnapped, pure and simple, taken from their homelands and spirited away. It couldn't have been like that. He knew enough about the law given his past infractions to understand that this should be wrong. Of course, maybe it was like marriage when you go through the rituals as man and wife, he thought, the "Do you take this woman to be your lawfully married wife?" kind of taking. Maybe the group home and the school had a right to do that. After all, he had to go to school by law, at least until he was sixteen. Still.

She looked at him. "If I'd had a choice then, if my parents had had a choice, I wouldn't have gone."

"I thought you said it wasn't that bad, at least not for you." He was digging, but not sure what for. Her response was short, like the crack of a pistol. "I lied."

"Lied. Why?"

At this, she looked away, brushed some imaginary crumbs from the table they were sitting at, her hand finally coming to rest on his. "I didn't want you to know, didn't think you needed to know." He started to interject, but she stopped him. "I was angry, ashamed, humiliated, afraid, lost. I still am sometimes when I think of what went on there, and what it cost me."

"What it cost you?"

She pulled her hand gently away from his and sat back in the chair. "It cost me my parents, first off. Things turned for them in a bad way after I was gone. A tidal wave of pain just up and carried them off. Their memory of me became more and more clouded with drink. They slowly faded from me over the years." Dash's mom paused, then tried to clarify her words for him. "You have to know that these were the stories I was told when I was away, that were filtered through to me from the lips of nuns puckered tight by their own beliefs and prejudices. Best if I forgot about them, they said. Can you believe that?" She rubbed at her eyes, pushing away at the salt that had suddenly risen. "By the time I was old enough to get away, any traces of them had disappeared."

Dash shifted in his seat. He wanted to reach out and touch her, but instead pulled each of his wayward hands through his hair, then clamped them to his legs. "What else, mom?"

"What else?" She clenched her fists on the table and stood up. "It cost me my self-respect and my dignity too. I was abused, Dash. I was. Priest and nun both. Physically and mentally. This wasn't a normal school, it was a school for the Indians where all of the Indian could be washed away, where our sins would become white as snow," she said mockingly. "Those ten years cost me and everybody else in there a chance to be and to know who we were." She stood, kicked her chair back, and moved to the cupboard for a glass and some water. She laughed bitterly, "I guess they did a pretty damn good job because I never got who I was back again."

Dash was still groping in the dark, "But…"

"No more, Dash," she said. "Not right now. Maybe some other time." But then she brightened, reiterated another truth that he never tired of hearing, "You make everything all right, though.

Always remember that." And she turned and kissed the top of his head as she brushed past him. "By the way, when Eric gets back, he and I are going out for the night. Some dinner party at friends of his outside the city. That OK? We won't be that late."

"Sure. Whatever you want. I can look after myself. I'm not a kid."

"I know. You're a young man with a job and a future. Remember that too."

* * *

Eric had come home in a good mood. *Not unusual for him,* Dash reminded himself. He was good for his mom. They got along, laughed loud together, argued loud too, but always made up, always recognized the importance of their relationship, the need for compromise, the need to let petty things go. Dash had watched his mother exit for the evening. She was not a young woman anymore, not old by any means, but her youth had been gobbled up one crow's foot at a time, maybe even snatched away at infancy as he thought of her earlier revelations. But she was still beautiful, could still turn eyes with the right clothing and a hint of makeup adorning her face. Tonight, she was simply attired. Nothing formal about dinner with a friend who wore jeans all the time and whose wife moused around in greys and browns, trying to avoid the trap of ostentation. "Nothing wrong with a little colour," his mother had said. Flo, the woman in question, just needs to open up, she had told Eric. He suggested she might try to be less opinionated, but his mom had waved her hand and continued. "She's pretty enough, but why amble like a cow when she can prance like a thoroughbred?" Eric had rolled his eyes, his mother had laughed, pecked his cheek, and twirled to show off her own look. A light cotton summer dress, sunny yellow with bursting floral reds hugged her figure, a designer jean jacket accompanied it to ward off late August's current evening cooling trend, long feathered gold earrings and a necklace complimented her olive coloured skin, and sandals and red painted toenails completed her look. A vision of comfortable elegance. Dash was impressed at how little it took to return the lustre to his mother's eyes.

"Have fun," he called out to them as the door swung open. His mother had run back to him at this, given him a hug, an "I love you" and returned to Eric with a "we will" from her and a "see you, kid" from Eric. Then the door had closed. It was barely 6:00 p.m. Dash noticed as he looked at the stove clock. "What to eat?" he muttered out loud. He opened the fridge. Some leftover pizza caught his eye, and he grabbed it. That and some chips in the cupboard would do the trick. He noticed a lone beer at the back of the fridge and decided that too would be good. Eric was not a teetotaler. In particular, summer brought out a desire for a cold one or two from time to time, but he was not a lush. A couple of beers, a glass of wine on special occasions, and he was good. His mother had followed suit and, aside from a few slips, had maintained her sobriety under pressure. Much of that recent pressure, Dash acknowledged, had been of his own making. Tonight, he had noticed a bottle of red wine leaving with Eric. The mantra of drink responsibly had echoed in his head. He knew they would be fine. Note to self as well as he cracked the bottle and took a swig.

He had been drunk several times in his young life. Many he couldn't quite remember, and this had troubled him. Each time had been with Manny, and mainly at parties. Some dope and beers, and he had been off and away from the reality of his day to day existence. Most of the time, he would crash where he was or at Manny's, but his mom always knew what he had been up to when he returned. She had a sixth sense that amazed him; her ability to pick up on his physical cues was uncanny. In hindsight, he had to admit that coming home in the early morning with a stumble, red-eyed and reeking of his night's activities did not require great sleuthing on his mother's part. He smiled. It was the knowledge of her own frailty, her own susceptibility to the demons enveloping him from time to time that splashed him with enough cold water to bring him back. "Don't make this a habit," she had said. "Don't let it control you." Her light from a rocky shoreline had helped so far.

When he had eaten and satisfied his thirst, he wandered into his bedroom. He opened the bottom shelf of his nightstand and lifted the case out. Maybe it was the fact that he had a job as a painter, going flat to flat, house to house, mixing, cutting, brushing, rolling, the colours bleeding out onto walls and alcoves and closets of different shapes and sizes, that had returned him periodically to the smaller, more intimate confines of his art kit. Maybe it was the fact that he was working with different tools and textures, pencils and charcoals, and erasers and paper hunkered privately over a table with no daily quotas of completion staring him in the face, without the public scrutiny of performance, lurking over his shoulder like a vulture waiting to pick his mistakes to death. his mistakes to death. Maybe he just enjoyed the quiet opportunity of personal indulgence afforded him in moments when he was alone. The feel of the objects he freed from their confinement and laid out slowly around him, waiting for the ceremony of creation to begin; the sound of the various leads as they embraced the page and swept and arced or fidgeted with precision; the fingertip smudging and blurring that accented changes or fiddled with errors before erasure. Whatever his reasoning, he bundled the kit from the bedroom to the kitchen and placed it on the table. It had travelled with him faithfully for years, had suffered at his hands the adversities of neglect, frustration, and anger, but also the joys of enlightenment, accomplishment, and satisfaction. It had been a friend and an enemy, a chronicler of life and death, a vault of images imprisoned, yet free.

Dash lifted out a piece of paper, his current effort, and placed it aside. As part of his infrequent ritual, he would first skim through his body of historical works, a pile of remnants, like corpses on a battlefield, all needing some form of attendant care. Most were animals and birds, singly rendered or within a hastily scrawled landscape, sometimes a simple flower or two, a river curling along an embankment. There was an incomplete picture of a crow frozen in death settled on top of the drawn and quartered head of a horse, both attempts recorded and archived as part of the actions of past nemesis, Billy the Tormentor. He had never thrown them out. He also reflected on his mother, captured years ago in a state of sleep—an earthy Cleopatra still needing the touch of a more skilled artisan to do her justice. Finally, and always last, he would reach for something not his own, the circle ever-tightening and darkening to its inevitable point of puncture, drawn in a moment of anger by his mother, her story told in thirty seconds, dark matter spinning into a background of white. He would let his hand glide over the lines and feel the furrowed ruts of the wheel ever-deepening on the page until his finger found the hole at the centre, the minute pinhead bursting through the papered façade, a ragged perforation of her past. Only at this point would he return to the present.

The picture he was drawing lay in front of him. He had marked up the paper with a ruler in a grid pattern, large enough on the page to work from a photo or picture, an early lesson he had noted in the kit's small instruction booklet. A good idea to do, it said, when trying to learn perspective. Get it framed. Start with the head if doing an animal. Draw the basic shapes to help define the image. Work from left to right to avoid smudging. He was right-handed, so this had worked. Start filling in details when you have completed your outline. He reached for the small photo he was using, which had been stored in the kit. It was a small 3 x 5 picture taken years ago by his mother with a disposable camera. A close-up of Digger sitting on the front step, his face transfixed, Dash guessed, by the camera positioned in front of him. Dash must have been nearby, but couldn't remember. It was a grainy representation even at close range, but a record nonetheless, the only one he had. His mother had given it to him when the roll was developed, and he had kept it amazingly intact and secure in the box ever since. Only recently had he decided to try to capture the photo again, but in a different medium. Another rule came to mind before he began. Reaching for the small sharpener, he ground his pencil to a point. It was time to bring more of his dog back to life.

* * *

They had feasted on barbecued chicken and ribs, roast potatoes, corn on the cob, salad, and generous portions of Flo's apple pie and ice cream. Conversation throughout the evening among the eight had been light-hearted, never straying too close to politics for long. There had been some gentle ribbing of Eric and Miriam about their desire to remain in Edmonton which the other guests felt had gotten too large and unsafe. "Leduc here is close enough for us," Mike had said. "We have a nice little house, some acreage, and it's only about a forty-five-minute drive to the heart of Edmonton when I need to go there." He had left the trades for the quieter life of early retirement and part-time work at a building supplies company in town. His wife kept books for a few local businesses, and between the two, they both had time to relax, make the odd trip here and there. The two other couples had always been from the area, unknown quantities to Eric and Miriam, nice, friendly, but totally invested in the comforts of a smaller community.

Eric had just laughed at the banter and reminded Mike and the others that he and Miriam, of course, were much younger and more free-spirited than they and, therefore, more able to enjoy the pace of the larger centre. "There may come a time," he said, "when Miriam and me will want to join you and poke around here in the outback." Miriam had been quiet for most of the evening, polite, talkative on occasion when speaking to one person at a time, but deferring to Eric in the larger setting. She had been good with the drinking, she and Eric consuming only two glasses of wine at dinner and a cold beer each when they had first arrived. By the time they had left close to midnight, declining an offer to stay over, they were happy and clearheaded.

Alberta's Highway 2, the main artery connecting Calgary to Edmonton and beyond, pumps traffic back and forth between these largest of the province's cities at a fast pace daily, pouring into and out of smaller locales like Red Deer, Lacombe, and Leduc along the way. The roadway is open and flat, with farmland stretching out on both sides for most of the trek. At night, darkness envelopes the driver in stretches between communities, lights from vehicles sweeping off into the median between lanes, the asphalt ahead and the ditches and fields beyond. A quiet, except for the occasional car coming in the opposite direction, envelopes the rider and can lull travellers into a sleepy complacency, tires purring on the roadway beneath like a cat snuggled on a lap.

"Would you ever consider moving out to a place like Leduc?" Miriam asked, her head leaning back against the truck seat.

"I don't know, maybe. Not now, for sure," Eric said. "Don't have enough saved for a house yet, even out there." He glanced over at Miriam and grazed over her sleekness. She was fetching. Fetching. What a word. Something his dad would have said, something attached to a dog command. Fetch. Get that stick, boy. God. Beautiful. That was better. She was that. "Why?" he asked. "You interested?"

"Not really. Least I don't think so. Who knows, right? Where we are is good enough for now." She put her hand out to brush his arm. "Besides, what would I do there? I like my job at the clothing store, and I'm getting used to the city. It's home." She sighed. "And there is Dash."

"Dash is what, almost nineteen?" Eric replied."He's doing good at the moment. Might even decide to move out sometime, find his own place, his own life."

Miriam straightened and turned her body more toward him, "Your point being?"

Eric gave her a look. "Nothing. Just saying that you can't base your decisions on Dash and what he might or mightn't do. He's a young man now with his own road to follow. Christ, Miriam, I was up and gone from home at eighteen, and never went back."

"Well, good for you. Doesn't fuckin' matter what you did, though, does it? He's been through a lot in his life, a lot of it based on my decisions. He can leave when he wants and not before." She slammed her legs up against the dashboard, folded her arms, and turned her gaze out the window.

"You're right, you're right. Sorry, honey. Came out the wrong way, that's all." He put his hand out to touch her shoulder. His eyes focused on her for just a second, and when they returned to the road, there it was, in front of him. A large coyote, red-eyed and unmoving, had shot up out of the ditch. In the tiny window of decision-making allotted to him in this game of chicken and chance, he made the wrong one and veered.

"Jesus Christ!" He pulled left, the tires complaining, and hit the soft shoulder of the median. Miriam's "Eric!" pierced through the cab and beyond. At thirty or forty kilometres an hour, he might have been able to pull back onto the road, maybe even stop. They were doing one hundred, and the trajectory of the vehicle took them into the median and down, the truck beginning its roll almost instinctively as it plowed forward. Three times it circled in its dance before coming to a rooftop finale, wheels pointing skyward into the night, lights flickering into the grasses. There was silence both inside and out as the carcass lay crumpled between roadways waiting for discovery. With its nose raised into the air, the coyote briefly took note, then loped off across the fields in the opposite direction.

* * *

Picture #10: *Refrigerator*

Observer's description: A couple stand in front of an open white refrigerator. Both are nude. It is late evening, possibly early morning. The woman holds the door, her back, buttocks, and legs defined as she peers inside. Three cats congregate at her feet on black and white floor tiles, hoping for food. The man faces frontward, his body fully visible to the viewer. His right arm is stretched across the top of the fridge. His other arm holds a glass of milk, which is raised to his lips. Their poses are relaxed; their bodies sculpted, naturally rendered in golden tones that warm the white and dark around them. They share an intimacy and sexuality, a comfort that exudes outward from them. Perhaps it is a hot evening, and they want the cold contrast of fridge air and fresh milk to refresh them. Perhaps they are breaking from sex, moving easily together from one need to another.

Chapter Ten

DAY FIVE

THE PRESENT

Coyote had felt a tug, a pull just then that had roused him from his sleep in the park. Its origin had come to him through a dream that spanned great distance and floated out of the past. He recognized the terrain; he might have travelled it once. It differed from the small isolated cloister of trees, benches, and walkways that he found himself sheltering in, surrounded by the shrieking horns, harsh brakes and abrasive smells of metal objects belching at him from all sides in the growing morning light. These were tied to the remnants of his thoughts, a twisted wreck upended in the quiet darkness of a summer night, pushed to the fore but drifting from him now as he stirred into the present coldness of this fall city air. He needed to disappear back into obscurity, let Crow circle and spy and make sense of the day. The evening had been uneventful, but his stomach was full. Late-night dining on a raccoon too intent on opening a garbage container to sense his presence had satisfied his need. One hunger eradicated by another. They have lost their edge, *Coyote thought,* these creatures foraging in this human environment. *Instincts. Most haven't got them anymore.*

*   *   *

I am dishevelled and out of breath when I arrive. Securing my bike, I whip off my backpack and helmet and blow inside, a fall leaf red-faced and tumbling toward my desk. I pull out my water bottle, take a quick drink, and begin to settle, my dewy complexion starting to evaporate. Only fifteen minutes late, not the end of the world. But I hate being late, anywhere. Part of a control mechanism, I suppose, an only child complex passed down to me from parents who were nothing if not punctual. Never late for work, an appointment, an invitation, a planned night out.

"So, Henry, we have tickets for the show at eight and dinner reservations for six just around the corner from the theatre," my mom as the organizer would say. "That will give us lots of time to eat and get there without rushing." My dad would simply nod. I look at the pile of paper I need to shuffle through. "So, June, is this our night for sex? We won't be home until well after eleven. Hope I'm up for it," and my dad might chuckle. I laughed out loud, drawing the attention of one of my colleagues close by.

This last thought I had invented, but I wouldn't put it past my parents to plan their sex. Some initial groping, tentative hands in the dark, seeking flesh, a few words of encouragement or maybe an "Oh, Henry, just get on with it." Dad obliging with a teeter and totter, a bump and a grind, a wham and a bam, a shudder and a roll, the circus theatrics ended, packed up and put away until the next planned engagement, the next ticketed show. I shook my head at this. Perhaps it was not this way. It's hard for children to imagine their ageing parents having sex at all, but they had a youth once and with it, passions. And who was I to say that they managed sex the way they managed their bank accounts, with periodic checks to make sure everything was in order, automatic deposits and withdrawals performed without thought? Maybe they still exuded desire when the mood struck them, spontaneously and without reservation. Why not? I took another drink from my thermos, allowing the cold water to release me from these images. I needed to get down to work.

But I couldn't. I was Scrooge on a Christmas morning. One of my favourite seasonal movie images had popped into my head like a vision of sugarplums, Alistair Sims dancing in his bedroom with an epiphany and a desire to stand on his head. What the fuck? But fuck it was, and I had been stood on my head.

Dash and I had made love and took the plunge into uncharted territory, two boats unmoored and drifting together, both part of the same tidal flow. It had been tense and awkward at first, a slow unravelling on the couch from a kiss to a touch to mutual disrobing to a trail of discarded clothing leading to the bed. His fingers found me, opened me, entered, retreated. I stroked his cock and guided it into me. "Jesse, oh, Jesse." Had he called to me?

"Jesse?" I shuddered. Jesus, it was Cindy at my desk with a request. I snapped out of my reverie.

"Sorry Cindy, I was somewhere else, not quite awake yet, I guess. What can I do for you?

* * *

Dash was pissed. Anger had swept over him when he stepped out on the porch, threatening to send everything up in smoke. He was already going to be late. *Fuck.* The last thing he needed was to have his bike staring up at him useless and deflated like some poor animal waiting to be put down. And idiot that he was, he had not gotten around to getting a pump for his bike yet. Luckily, Jesse had calmed him, reminded him that she had one, and after several minutes, he had mounted his steed and ridden off. He still simmered as he rode. Some tool had intentionally messed with him, but he was lucky. His bike could have been stolen, or his tires slashed. Could have just been a bunch of kids out on a lark or a dare. He'd had experiences of his own growing up that would make this a likely possibility. Suspicion in him put it down to something else, a coincidence running too close to home for comfort. But he shrugged off his intuition and focused on a more important reality, Derrick's reaction to the fact that on the first day of his solo flight, he was sputtering to even get off the ground. He roared up to the front door of the office, a Y.E.S. man he still hoped.

Surprisingly, Derrick was chipper and cheery when Dash busted in.

"Well, at least you made it," he said, giving Dash a brief nod. "I wasn't sure if you would."

Dash looked at him. "What do you mean?"

"For the last two days, you were attached to Blake's hip. Today, the umbilical cord is broken. You're on your own. Some guys decide to pack it in once they realize this. They just don't show up for work."

"That's not me. If you want to know, I'm late because somebody let the air out of my tires last night. Nothing serious, it just took me time to find a pump."

"No excuses needed. You're here. That's the main thing. Besides, things are slow at the moment. Only Blake and Rod have headed out so far." He turned to shuffle some papers. "But don't get too relaxed. Once the Financial District starts to wake up, you'll be out chewin' and bein' chewed."

"Chewin' and bein' chewed. Have to remember that," Dash joked, "the next time I feel hungry."

"A little history lesson for you, Dash. The Financial District in downtown Toronto was originally called New Town around 1796 or so, an extension of the Town of York at the time. Now, it's bounded roughly by Queen Street West on the north, Yonge Street on the east, Front Street on the south and University Avenue on the west." Dash nodded along. "Everything out there clustered together pulsates like a galaxy filled with stars. Bank towers, corporate headquarters, large legal and accounting firms, insurance companies, stockbrokers, advertising and marketing agencies, the whole economic heartland of the city, hell the country for that matter, circling each other daily through the gravitational pull of money. Add to that the underground network of pedestrian walkways, PATH for short, arteries of retail outlets for shoppers and commuters, and you've got a hell of a lot of people and power coursing through the core of this city, sellers and buyers, winners and losers, the wealthy and the wannabes." Dash had covered pieces of this ground with Blake over the last two days but hadn't had Derrick's picture painted for him in this way yet. "And you're one of the tiny wheels, literally, I guess that helps keep this monster turning." He laughed. "And by the end of the day, when you feel like the bug that's been stepped on or the morsel that's been chewed up, remember that you are not alone. Most poor shits out there are on the same bike, churning their asses off."

Before Dash could respond, a phone went off, and Derrick answered. In seconds, he had finished.

"OK, Flash, time to earn your pay. Pickup and delivery. A short run between 350 Bay and 1200, but you have to get there first."

"Right." Dash made sure he had his phone. If his training was any indication, he would be fielding calls from the road and not be back here again until day's end, if at all. His backpack was already clamped on. He headed for the door.

"Remember, Dash," Derrick reminded. "Take it easy out there. Don't take risks. If you're late, you're late. It's not worth blowing up over a deadline. We're around if you need to check in for anything, OK?"

"Got it, boss," and Dash gave him a grin. It was soon wiped off his face as he grabbed his bike and turned into the world around him. He was on his own, anonymous, a small bit of detritus spewing out onto the roadway, pulled along by the collective mass. No matter. Pushing his way along with the glacial tide, he eventually found Bay Street and headed up it, a drop of mercury heated. This rush of adrenaline brought him back to last night: the bed, white sheets, the warmth of her body and embrace. Unplanned, unforced, it had both been what they wanted. A release. He hoped it would lead to more, to something real, something other than just a need to satisfy an urge, to scratch an itch they both had.

Tania had been an itch and others before her. A mutual clawing at the skin; an attempt to forget. But not Jesse. He peddled on. One step at a time. A delivery truck pulled in front of him, jerked to a stop, and put on its four ways. Jesse dissolved in an instant, Dash forced into a split-second decision to whip out into traffic and around the intruder. "You stupid fuck," he screamed as he shot passed, the driver offering him a shrug and a finger. "Let it go," he muttered. His first stop loomed up ahead. Jumping the curb, he rode up to the entrance and dismounted. He took a gulp of water from his bottle before going in, wishing it was stronger.

* * *

Greg stood in the bathroom at the company office and stared into the mirror. He had been pulled from the road. "Just for the day," his manager said. "We're doing inventory and need an extra body to help with the task." Bullshit. It was something else, had to be. He was a driver, a delivery guy. That was his job, not some clerk tallying up sheets and counting beans with the rest of the parts department losers. Sighing, he pulled the bottle of Tylenol out of his pocket and knocked back two more. It was true he looked like shit, an observation not lost on his boss, although he didn't say as much. But that was none of his business. He put his head back. *Fuck.* He thought of Jesse, and her pal, Hiawatha, wondered how his day had started with two flats to deal with. Whenever he felt sorry for himself, he would look to others and make them responsible. It wasn't him, God no. His mind pulled him back to his family. Images of gatherings at Christmas, Easter, a summer trip, or stay at a cottage. He was always the one left out. His parents never asked how he was doing, never included him in conversations, never encouraged him in ways that his brother and sister had been, everybody always too busy with their own lives to pay him any real attention. His was the world of instruction and command, a "shape up or ship out" military approach to development and staying in line. Well, fuck it, he'd had enough, gone AWOL and here he was, his own man. It hadn't stopped him leaning on his parents for money every so often. He hadn't been back for Christmas since he'd left, a couple of years for sure, and had missed his birthdays at home. On these occasions, he had asked for money and got it, as well as substantial amounts at other times, his father stipulating that these were loans, interest-free, of course, which needed to be paid back. Sure, Pop, whatever you say. What do you need money for? You've got lots. You fix up your apartments and houses, and for what? To give to deadbeats, immigrants, and Indians rather than your own flesh and blood?

"Well, fuck that," he said out loud and slapped the wall. Just then, the door opened, and Graham, the manager, walked in.

"You're needed out there, Greg." He moved toward a urinal and unzipped. Greg stood there for a moment and then turned toward the door.

"You all right?"

"I'm fine. Why?"

"Nothing big. Just that you peeled out of here yesterday like some maniac, and a couple of people have noticed you look a little off at times." He zipped up and turned toward him. "You're sure everything's all right?"

"Yeah, I'm sure. I just like being on the road and not stuck in here, that's all."

"It's just for the day, right?" and he moved to the sink.

"Right." Greg started through the door.

"Hey." Greg stopped and looked back over his shoulder. "Performance reviews are coming up soon, remember? That's when we'll talk some more, OK?" Graham ripped some paper towels out of the dispensary, wiped his hands, then headed out. Greg looked at his retreating back, moving off in another direction, an image of his father walking away. Another person out to get him. "Review this," he whispered out loud and threw up his middle finger. One consolation about today, he thought as he made his way to parts, was that he would be finishing up early. He would scrape the shit off this day, hop in his car, and motor down to see Jesse at her workplace. He would be reasonable, make his case calmly, keep it under control. If he had time, maybe a drink beforehand just to steady him. Three o'clock couldn't come soon enough.

* * *

My morning had been uneventful—a couple of scheduled clients, who had magically remembered their appointments, and a few dishevelled walk-ins. The regulars gave me some hope and made me think I was making a difference, heading them in the right direction with either good advice or a reputable contact. These were people with strikes against them, sure, but who were coming up for air. They wanted help, wanted back inside, had shaken off enough of their current world to make an effort. But they were few and far between. Most were pinballs, the walking dead. They tilted in and out, bouncing off one agency to the next until they exited onto the street, reloaded, and shot themselves up and in again, repeating and repeating, following the same worn path. They collected no points, saw only momentary lights and sounds as they travelled with their afflictions and addictions into and around the rabbit holes we provided in the city.

For a time when I was growing up, there lived a man in our neighbourhood. Not indoors, but deep in the ravine of parkland that ringed homes in the area. I would see him on his bike, a box tied to his rear pannier, scavenging the streets for bottles or cans to turn in for money. Once, looking out our living room window, I had seen my dad on the sidewalk holding up his hand to stop him. He had pressed money into his palm before returning to the house. I learned that others did the same, passing him money, sometimes food. Everyone considered him a harmless soul, down on his luck. My father said he was someone who chose to be alone. He preferred the outdoors, the security of the trees to the walled enclosures we resided in. If he passed me on his bike—his clothes always a little worse for wear, his face sporting the scruffiness of beard—he always smiled, his eyes twinkling with some unacknowledged insight. Eventually, I never saw him again. Perhaps he had moved on. I never really thought to ask.

My thoughts turned to Dash and our night together. My colleagues would be shocked if they knew of our budding relationship. Risky, unprofessional, ill-advised would all be words circling my desk. But no one needed to know. It was my decision. I only hoped that he was on his way out of his last burrow.

I looked at the clock. It was almost lunchtime, a break I planned to take outside the office today. I would eat at my desk when I returned. I had a purpose in mind, and I was excited. Dash had wanted a sketchbook, and I was going to get it for him. A surprise, a gift, no payback required. We were to go looking together after work, but there may not be time, and I didn't want to put it off. Strike while the iron is hot, something my father would say. Besides, we were out of food, and I needed to get some groceries as well. There was an art supply shop not too far away that I could get to quickly enough by bike.

I jumped ahead to Saturday when I was scheduled to begin my own return to the world of art. Maybe I will have time to look around a bit for myself, get into the mindset. I see myself in my apartment, working on a canvass, with my brushes, paints, and palette at my side. Dash sits on the couch, sketching. "Jesus. Get a grip for Christ's sake," I mutter to myself. "You're not Snow White, and he's not some prince come to charm you." I glance around, pretend to straighten my desk, and then beeline it for the door, my fairy tale still just an apple with a bite out of it.

* * *

What a racket. Only three hours in and Dash was already fuming. Why did he let these situations get to him? If he was a tennis ball, he would have been into the net twice already, if a baseball blasting foul into the stands, if a football missing the goalposts wide, if a hockey puck ringing off the iron. He had made three deliveries so far, but each with their own moments of turmoil. His Bay Street drop-off had been easy to find, straightforward like Derrick had said, but once inside, he had been forced to wait. It was like he was invisible, the person at the desk failing to notice him, intent more on conversing banally with a colleague. His eventual slamming of the package on the counter jerked both heads into his line of fire, his report of "delivery" going off like a gunshot and ricocheting around the lobby. He pulled himself together with a smile and goodbye before quickly looking for cover, eyes following him until he once again merged with the street.

His phone had crackled to life just as he reached his bike and he was off in another direction, a three to four block ride to an ad agency office on Wellesley Street and then over to an office somewhere on Gerrard Street. He had struck out with good intentions but became wedged in traffic behind a lethargic truck and an uncooperative stoplight. He opted for some sidewalk shortcuts. Pedestrians were not amused. One jerk grabbed aggressively for his handlebars. Dash shoved at him as he passed and kept going, a barrage of profanity nipping at his heels like a pack of wild dogs until he made a corner. He was out of control and realized it. He found the street again and humped his way to the destination. Before entering, he stopped, had water, and checked his watch. His time was good. "Get a grip, get a grip. Relax. Fuck." He picked up and delivered this second package with relative serenity, and he breathed again. "Just let the day happen," Blake and Derrick both had said. Both guys were cool, Dash had to admit. Blake and his reggae; Derrick and his 60s and 70s stuff. As he churned through the morning, he tried to think of an old song Derrick had mentioned, some obscure group that had only this one big hit at the time. Thunderclap Newman, that was the band's name. Derrick would hum this tune and sing the refrain often enough that some of it stuck to Dash. Now, he mimicked what he recalled. He continued his revolutions, pounding out strokes to this and other tunes.

As noon approached, there was definitely something in the air. Dash needed to do something else—something personal. On his last run along Dundas Street, he realized that he was just a few minutes from Mutual Street. It had only been three days since walking out on Tania. The memory was bittersweet, the right call, but still unsavoury. His abrupt departure was not well thought out, and in his hurry, he realized later that a few important possessions were left behind. Clothes were one thing, mementos another. Stupidly, he had forgotten the envelope lying on the top shelf of the bedroom closet and the dream catcher hanging from the bedroom window. Personal stuff from his past. Such an idiot. He meant to go back, and this seemed like the best time to do it. There was a good possibility Tania would not even be there. If the door was unlocked, which it usually was, he would go in quickly and quietly, get what he wanted, and leave. No harm in trying. He hoped she had not tossed them both in a moment of anger.

Dash lashed his bike up to the tired, weathered porch rungs before climbing the three steps to Tania's front door. Everything here could use a facelift, a coat of paint to add some colour. Taking a deep breath, he knocked and waited. Nothing. He heard the crow before he saw it. It settled on the railing of the porch next door. Dash was transfixed. They searched one another's eyes. The crow tilted his head toward the door as if to encourage the action. Dash turned and knocked again, then tried the knob. It opened. The crow flew up and away. Pushing into the front room, he surveyed an all too familiar sight. It reminded him of a poorly tended squatter's camp, the refuse of belongings tented around him in makeshift piles. There was a body strewn on the couch, another curled uncomfortably on a chair. Either could have been him just a few days ago. Neither was Tania. He moved around the evidence of another party, maybe the same one, bypassing bottles, cans, and discarded clothes, snaking for the bedroom. The door was closed but slightly ajar. He nudged it open enough to take in the bed. He recognized the contours of his former girlfriend, nakedly exposed, her body still appealing. Someone else was with her, the tuft of a head peeking out from under the blankets heaped up on top. Male or female. Not sure. His dream catcher was still hanging from the window partially obscured by a hastily pulled curtain. He smiled. An image of his mother popped into his head. It lingered for a moment until he blinked to clear it.

He made for the closet first and silently opened it. It looked untouched. Some of Tania's clothes hung from hangers; assorted shoes cluttered the floor. A box that he remembered still perched on the shelf, a repository for winter hats and scarves. He felt to the left, and there it was. He pulled down a manila envelope and looked inside. All there. Expelling a breath, he moved toward the window. His dream catcher hung on a thin bent wire, easy to lift off and place in the envelope. He pulled back the curtain and brushed the dangling feathers. Sliding it up and off, he inserted it into the envelope and turned to go. It was here that his stealth deserted him. An inadvertent kick to the bedpost roused the prostrate nude just enough to waken her from fog to a clearer reality. Like a poorly conceived play, the scene began to unfold around him.

"What the fuck?" *Pause to elevate outrage.* "Dash, you prick. What the fuck are you doing here?"

A clambering for position on the bed ensues as head beside stirs and reveals itself. A guy, Dash notes, vaguely familiar, but the name on the list of dramatis personae escapes him.

"Just came by for a couple of things I forgot," Dash spits. "I know the way out."

Guy raises himself to a sitting position and stares blankly. Tania pole dances her way onto the floor and follows Dash into the front room. Guy on bed collapses again and pulls covers over his head, tuft of hair reappearing.

"Jesus Christ," the horseless Godiva blusters. "You can't just walk in here and take what you want."

Bodies on furniture begin to stir and follow the pair as they dance around them toward the door. Quickly, the audience loses interest and drifts back into the arms of their respective stupors.

"My stuff, Tania," Dash retorts. "Don't worry, I won't be back again." *He reaches for and opens the front door, thinking the scene is over, but she follows him onto the porch for an unexpected encore. He can't help himself when he sees this.* "You're not on the clock now, Tania. You can put some clothes on."

She screams her first of several obscenities at him. A couple on the street stop and stare, their detailed reviews soon to be released in the gossip columns to neighbours and friends. Dash inserts the envelope calmly into his backpack, grapples with his bike, and begins to ride off. Tania's immodest rant continues to trail him until the city's curtain of noise falls, and her cries evaporate. The scene ends.

Chatter from his phone pulled him back into what remained of his working day.

* * *

Crow made one final circle, his sides still aching with laughter. He had watched the spectacle unfold from his premium seat, a balcony position at rooftop level. He was not sure what he had seen—tragedy, comedy, satire—but he knew that he had to laugh. Humour was the only thing that kept him going when darkness threatened to envelop too much of the world. You laughed, played jokes, tried to look at the brighter side of situations. The man and woman had enacted a drama below him, their words and gestures flying up to him and then disappearing. They left him coated with an all too familiar feeling of frustration, the oily residue he often wore when thinking of people and their personalities. Everything was on display, in this case, paired down to public vulgarity and nudity, usually considered violations of human decorum. Maybe he should consider it art. In all its absurdity, he might have missed something. Maybe it was art. After all, most bystanders at this scene, the few caught as passing observers to the moment had just watched, or jeered, or clapped, then walked away. A stage act, amateur theatre rather than the trappings of life. As if in agreement, he tilted and turned to follow the rider. Whatever had just happened, he had been entertained. Perhaps that was all that the fickle and flowing mob below him wanted: entertainment. Whether conscious or not, they all played a part in the travelling show. As did he.

* * *

I had returned from my excursion elated, success within my grasp. A small black sketchbook for Dash—not too large, good paper, elastic band to keep it tightly closed, and a flexible spine that allowed it to open and remain flat. Thirty dollars. What the hell? I hoped he would like it and not be upset that he hadn't picked it out. Or worse, get all guilty on me because I had paid for something yet again. Too late now, he would just have to suck it up and live with my decision. It made me smile until I settled into work. My afternoon had been rough but was drawing to a close. There had been an unexpected insurgence, a migratory influx of the needy that had left me buffeted. From my desk, which seemed to pitch and toss like a raft on a rough sea with each new arrival, I reached out and attempted to pull them on board. Some flailed at me, threw back my offerings, and floated away in anger; others pleaded, grappled, shouted, and held on until our process finished. I was growing tired of the verbal soaking we all endured, this mutual humiliation via process and policy. It was as if we had all been hung out to dry, but in a perpetual downpour of rain. The waters pummelled us until we shrivelled up like prunes. Sometimes everybody drowns.

It was then that things got even worse. As I emerged from the office, an iceberg loomed up in front of me. I felt the waters turn cold. It was the titanic moment of my day. I couldn't move. I couldn't avoid the collision. My body started to shut down, but I managed to look around. No lifeboats.

"Hey, Jesse. We need to talk." Hard aport! Hard aport! My brain tried to guide me around the object and to my bike, but no luck. There was no room to move. I stood there, momentarily stunned. He got up close. "D'you hear me?"

Finally, I spoke. "What are you doing here, Greg? You stalking me?"

He sneered at this. "Whatever it takes to get you to listen to reason."

"Reason." I laughed. "I can't reason with someone who won't listen. I've told you. Leave me alone. I don't want to see you anymore." I started to step away from him.

Then he grabbed my arm. "C'mon, Jesse. I've stopped drinking, that should be a sign of my good intentions, right?"

"Stopped drinking. Funny. Seems to me I can smell booze on your breath." I wrenched myself away from his grip and made for my bike. My heart was pounding.

"I just had a quick one after work to calm my nerves. It's not easy to have someone walk away from you for someone else, especially that guy."

I'd had enough. "I didn't walk away from you for anybody, Greg. I walked away because of you, only you. I made a mistake hooking up with you. That's it. Find someone else who will put up with your shit, but leave me alone."

He stopped for a second, long enough to let me start moving. I bent to untie my lock, but as I did, he recovered. He lunged, and I thought he might hit me, but instead, he grabbed my handlebars. "You think you can just ride away? You think you can treat me like some loser, like that red you're shacking up with?"

I couldn't believe it. At first, I just stared, my jaw hanging open, I imagined, like some poor climber dangling for life from a precipice. I managed to regain my mental balance, push my fingers into bedrock. "Get out of my way," I said as calmly as I could.

"Or what?" He didn't move.

"Do you want me to scream, here in public? Call the cops on my cell? Happy to do it." I was shaking, but more with blind rage than fear. He seemed to get the message and stepped away just enough. I walked my bike a few steps before stepping over the frame.

"Don't come near me again, do you understand?" He simply stared at me as I peddled away. I didn't turn, merged onto the street, and rode toward home, but I felt his eyes burrowing into my back, an unwanted passenger on a bicycle built for one. "Goddamn it." This had to be the end of my nightmare. It had to be.

* * *

The final notes of Dash's workday sounded in a crescendo. An intersection punch up between a car and a van turning into one another. No injuries that he could tell, and he left the growing jam up to sort itself out over the coming hour. *Great to be on a bike*, he thought as he roared up Queen Street intent on getting home. Home. The word had just come out, materialized into a form he hadn't recognized for a long time. There were only two places he had belonged before. Both had contained his mother; both had contained love. He was making a big assumption in thinking it now, believing that it was a solid, tangible concept, a possible reality. But he couldn't help it. The end of his first day in charge, no Blake to rely on, had been good—great, actually. Granted, some hectic riding had been needed at times to get to his locations, but it had worked out. Above all, after his brief altercation with Tania, everything had seemed like chocolate drizzling onto a dish of ice cream. He had his most prized possessions intact and back in his hands, and he was heading home. Derrick had crackled out an invitation to join him and a few riders at the Duke of Richmond for a drink and some chat, but he said he'd take a rain check. He had things to do. His boss had been fine with that. No pressure, maybe tomorrow, and Dash had left that possibility to percolate as he rode. Another sign of acceptance, he hoped. His refusal today, though, had been more about Jesse than anything. She was the one he had wanted to celebrate his success with. She was the gauge he wanted to measure his inflating sense of self-worth against, and so home he went. Maybe it was love that he felt for her. Why couldn't it be?

He found the door locked when he arrived, unusual in that Jesse had said she would be home well before him today. Her bike was there on the porch. Maybe she had gone out again on foot to run an errand she had forgotten about or to pick something up. They were supposed to go shopping together, though. No matter. His own key was zipped into a pocket in his jacket, so nothing to worry about—another sign of the growing trust that was generating between them. He locked up his bike and opened the door. But Jesse was home. She was sitting on the couch, leaning forward, arms resting on her knees. She stared at the coffee table in front of her, hands locked together in a ball. A glass of wine waited to be picked up. Finally, she looked up at him, attempted a smile and gave him a feeble, "Hi." It was clear something was off.

* * *

"I didn't think you were home with the door locked. You OK?"

"Not really," I said.

"What happened?" Dash dropped his backpack by the door and moved toward me. It was hard to pull myself out of the funk I was in. My slow response to his question had him interjecting and posing more.

"Bad day at work? Some bad news?"

He was trying, but I didn't know how to tell him what had happened. I didn't know how he would respond. Finally, I decided to just let it out like the sudden release of air from a punctured tire.

"Greg confronted me outside after work. He was waiting for me, not sure how long. We had words." As I said this, I watched him grow tighter and tighter, a snake coiling, his hands clenching, and his jaw turning to concrete.

"That miserable fuck!" He paced around the room, indignant, outraged. I appreciated his outburst, his concern; it made me feel whole and warm.

"It's all right, Dash. I'm good. A little shaken at first, but I can handle it." However, he didn't buy it.

"What if this jerk decides to keep at you? I told you he's not going to go away."

"I appreciate your concern. I told him to leave me alone, to never come near me again." I sounded confident when I said this.

"Not gonna happen," he replied. "I know his type. He won't stop until somebody stops him."

I got a little alarmed at this. "Dash, I don't want you to do anything, OK? Leave it alone. Worse comes to worst, I'll call the cops on him." I hoped this would set his mind at ease. Again, he didn't accept my logic.

"Can't trust cops." His words shot out like bullets. He continued. "They aren't going to do anything until it's already happened. You'd have to have bruises all over your body before they'd take you seriously." I took this in without comment. It was a barrage of words I recognized and had heard in different forms before. My workplace was filled with faces uttering the same sentiments.

I stood up and put my arms around him. We held each other until we both started to calm down. "Forget about him," I said. "I'm starving. Let's go out and grab some groceries. We'll cook, have some wine together and you can tell me about your day. Sound like a plan?"

He kissed me on the forehead before releasing me, then gave me that gorgeous smile. "Good idea. Let's do it." I put my wine in the fridge, and we moved out into the early evening, hoping to put the day behind us.

* * *

Picture #11: *French Cross*

Observer's description: A large metal French cross rises up and fills the painting on the right side. It is embedded in a three-tiered slab of concrete. It sits in a relegated corner of a field. Four metal posts at each corner enclose it with ropes, but anyone could duck under and move closer to stand by or touch the structure. A fence line separates the cross from another field along which rides a young girl on a horse. The girl is looking back over her shoulder as she passes at the cross and the plaque attached to it, perhaps gleaning what it says. The grass is green below the cross and its pedestal. The adjoining field is green as well except for a brown trail that has been made by passing horses or farm vehicles. A tranquil, isolated feeling is evoked through the depiction of this dark cross looming upwards, the lone rider moving slowly by, canopied under an overcast sky.

Chapter Eleven

THE PAST

Dash had painted himself into a corner in more ways than one. Paul had finally had to let him go. He had given him two weeks, paid no less, to deal with the trauma of his mother's death, told him to come back when he was ready. Paul had even said part-time would be fine until he found his feet again. That had been six months ago. He had returned, but only pieces of him. His work had been shoddy as if he had forgotten all the lessons he had been taught. Drink, drugs, and depression had a way of commanding his actions now. In the beginning, he had tried to stay clean at work, setting aside the weekends to sink into oblivion and forgetfulness. But like a river dammed upstream by a falling tree, his practices began to swell the banks of Monday, then Tuesday, and on. Although clarity trickled through sporadically on some days, his increased tardiness, carelessness, and general malaise became increasingly evident. Paul had had enough when he stumbled in one day last week, leaking booze and proceeded to knock over a paint can and ladder in quick succession. His erosion had become complete.

"That's it, son," Paul had simply said. "I can't use you like this anymore. Go home." At this point, Paul shoved an envelope into his hand as though he knew this moment had to come. Paul had looked at him, kindly but hard. "This is a bit of severance for you, holiday pay if you want to put it another way. But it comes with a suggestion. Get some help, lad."

Dash had looked at him, swaying, a sapling bent and about to break. "Sorry I fucked up on you. Thanks for this." And he turned away.

"Just get better," Paul had hurled at his back. Dash knew the gesture had been meant in support but wondered how he would do that. He had become known to the police again, his notoriety taking the form of a nuisance only, which had been a relief to date. Disturbances they responded to, a banging on his door on a Friday or Saturday night as he lay passed out on the couch, often found him in a holding cell well into the next day. He had been released from these perditions with warnings, some officers even laughing at his plight or spicing up their interjections with stereotypical racist language. These revelries were intermittent; they woke him up and brought him to attention for a moment. His job loss was now one such interval, and he had paused since then, a miraculous span of two days, to take stock of his current situation.

On the table in front of him were three items. Dash had kept them safe and together in the corner of his closet. Twice in the months that had passed, they called to him, and he had pulled them out, sat on his bedroom floor, and touched them. He had cried then, deeply and movingly, curled into himself and wailed staining the rug beneath with his salt, letting the rivulets dry on his cheeks. This was the first time he had taken them from their sepulchre, thought of opening them in the light of day. He knew their contents but had refused to exhume them until now. It was time.

Central to this triumvirate was a small wooden box, the urn that contained his mother's ashes. Its polished golden brown finish reminded him of wheat nodding in distant fields, honey extracted from a buzzing hive. When held, it hummed with warmth and life, her essence still radiating within. There had been a service at a Protestant church, Eric's familial choice and Miriam had gone along for the ride. But while she had been remembered in prayer, spoken of with practiced deference and charity by the minister, she was not to be laid to rest in a plot. Beechwood Cemetery, a long rectangular swath of land encased north-south by the Yellowhead Trail and 124th Avenue and west and east by 107th and 97th streets, was to harbour Eric's body and stone; Miriam was to have a simple marker. Afterwards, her ashes would travel to different locations for proper dispersal. This was made clear in the second item, which Dash had lifted from the table.

The living will that his mother had constructed lay unfolded in front of him. Dash had to hand it to his mother. She had prepared herself for this eventuality. Although simple in scope, it laid out her wishes succinctly. He, Dash, was the sole beneficiary of everything that she had. If Eric as executor did not survive her, then Dash would fulfill that role as well. The name of a lawyer had been attached, someone his mother had obviously contacted before. He stared blankly at the paper in front of him. He couldn't believe that she had been so organized, so aware of life, death, and the passing of time to have created this moment when she had acted on her feelings for him. He had always viewed her as somewhat of a free, troubled spirit not often tied to the real world. Both could be true, he supposed. Now, he would have to act, hold himself responsible and accountable, move forward with her wishes, visit this lawyer and determine his fate. Laying the page down, he turned to the final offering and removed it from its paper sheath.

He had only recalled his mother's handwriting a few times before, scratched out like hieroglyphs. Grocery lists, notes to teachers, reminders on fridge doors, a paltry collection of her penmanship abilities. In front of him was a letter, written with care in a scrolling eloquence that reminded him of gently flowing river water, white clouds billowing overhead. It was composed in pencil. He wondered if she had used one of his, a borrowed remnant from his own box once held dear. Even her choice of utensil, something that could smudge, that could be more easily erased, that could be etched more naturally across white than pen, seemed appropriate to his mother, Dash thought. His hand shook slightly as he held it. Just the DTs, he wanted to think, a brief tug that implored him to have a drink before he proceeded. But it was more than that, he knew. It was the unravelling of something his mother had left him from beyond the grave, an inventory of personal insights that she had wanted him to have. It was like uncovering something from an ancient dig that he knew was important, revealing, precious. He was nervous and excited. Putting the mental tug of beer and pot behind him, he moved into the moment.

My son,

You have always been my light, and I have always tried to be yours. If you are reading this, you will know that most of my light has gone away, but I want you to know that I am still here, burning. As long as you walk this earth, I will be with you. Think of me, and I will be tussling your hair in the wind, caressing you with the sun's rays, and speaking to you from the darkness when it tries to seek you out. Dash, do not sink into despair. I wish you had known your grandparents. I wish you had known your father better. I wish I had taken the time to teach you more about me, but I did not. The glimpses I had of myself came to me like pieces from a broken mirror, fragmented reflections of who I was. But it was me who chose to not put those pieces back together. I was a puzzle that I didn't want to complete, and I am sorry for that.

There is much about you that is so good. You are bright, creative, compassionate. You must build on those components to make yourself strong. Despite everything you've been through, search for your true self along the road that you now must travel. Do not desert your heritage like I did. Although some of this loss was taken from me unwillingly as I have tried to tell you, I did not pursue renewal on my own when I had the chance. I wish I had, both for my sake and yours.

Make a life for yourself, Dash. One that is not filled with hate or regret. One that is not beholden to the addictions that took me for a time. You must rise above these obstacles, put a mark on yourself that makes you and me proud. If there is a spirit world, as I believe there is, then I will be watching you. Don't get creeped out. It is only my love that will be following you. Look to nature, the animals, and those you hold dear as you move forward, and I will be there.

Always and forever with love.

His mother's words bled together suddenly. Tears welled up in his eyelids, threatening to overflow their banks and topple to the page. He pushed the letter away. Dash stood up and walked a circle around the table, looking from one item to another. He touched the box, brushed the will, and picked up the letter again. But now, his anger surfaced, pushing his mother's thoughts upward and away from him. For an instant, his fingers closed on the paper intent on crumpling and tearing. Finally, he allowed it to float to the table before taking four steps and heaving his fist into the living room wall instead. Each blow echoed with a series of cries, simple "whys" that lacerated the air along with his hand. She was gone and he didn't know what to do. His only constant, the only star that had guided him had flickered and gone out. He walked to the kitchen sink, allowed cool water to wash over his broken flesh. He moved his fingers, clenched and unclenched his fist. Nothing broken. He needed to forget again. His mother's words would have to wait. Grabbing his coat and checking for his wallet, he headed to the front door.

* * *

Dash felt the poking and prodding before he heard the words "hey, buddy" finally creep into his consciousness. He flailed at it. "You OK? You need some help?" He rolled toward the arms that were placed on his shoulders and cracked his eyes open, two oysters shucked. He felt cold concrete running along his back and groped to make sense of his surroundings. When he tried to speak, only mumblings escaped from lips and a tongue that felt embedded in sand. He choked and coughed and looked around. Propping himself up, he found his back resting against a wall. He made out the outline of what looked like a door across from him, a bin and some garbage cans beside it. *Jesus.* He was in an alley.

"Here." The voice interrupted his thoughts again. "Have a coffee and a sandwich." The hands placed two items on the ground beside him and pulled away. His reaction time was slow, but he brought the figure into focus—a middle-aged guy, and behind him and off to the left, a female and somewhat younger figure. Shifting his gaze down the alley to the street, he noticed a van.

"Who are you guys?" The words came out in a rough chunk that he expelled at his feet.

"Volunteers," the man said.

"With St. John's Ambulance," the woman added.

Dash just nodded and reached for the paper coffee cup. It was hot in his hand, and he cupped it in both for a few seconds before taking a sip. The heat trickled down his throat and began to bring him out and into the world again. Funny how something as simple as a shot of coffee can bring you back to yourself. He took another sip and laid his head back against the wall.

"What time is it?" he asked.

"Just after three in the morning," the woman answered.

Three in the morning? How long had he been passed out here? He tried to remember. There was the apartment. He had left, angry and determined, with money in his pocket, to get to Jasper Avenue and must have hit a bar or two for a few drinks. He pulled at the coffee again. His right hand was a bit sore, and when he looked at it, he saw it was skinned and scraped. He then patted his coat pocket and felt the outline of his wallet. *Thank fuck.* Still there. He set the coffee down. Extracting the thin, frayed cache, he opened it. Nothing there. "Empty," he muttered. "All gone." Whatever he had started with had been spent. He patted his pant pockets, felt the outline of a key, maybe some coins. "Well, that's somethin' at least."

"Sir?" He slid his head up and toward the female voice. "Can we take you somewhere?"

"Yeah," said the man. "We could drop you at the Mission just a few blocks away. You could get inside for a few hours."

Dash secured his wallet again and picked up the coffee. He shook his head. "Not interested in any Mission. When I finish this and get my legs again, I'll head home."

"So, you have somewhere to go?" asked the woman.

He nodded. "I do."

"You sure there's nothing else we can do for you?" chirped the man.

"No. I'm good. Thanks for stopping by." They nodded and turned back toward their van. He chuckled at that point. Thanks for stopping by. Like they were friends who had dropped in for a visit. Come again anytime. Don't be strangers. *Jesus, what a tool.* He watched the van pull away, and then he sunk back into reflection. The last few hours were still a blur. He couldn't remember how many drinks he'd had or how many holes he'd visited. Must have been a few. Sighing, he slung himself into a stand and inched his way down the alley toward the street. He reminded himself of the sandwich he had left behind, turned, and promptly threw up, spraying his shoes with a generous bile, an indistinct reminder of his past activities. The sandwich could lie there for another to find. Dash lurched onto Jasper Street from the alley in a diagonal pattern that increased with momentum until the bumper of a parked car halted his trajectory. He laughed, spun off the impediment like a pinball, and braced himself for the street crossing to come. Luckily, the roadways were deserted, 3:30 a.m. being a relatively dead hour for everyone but those like himself. Spirits, halfway between life and death, in a limbo land between guilt and redemption. He paused momentarily by a light pole to map out his direction.

He couldn't remember how many times he had been like this. A lot with Manny, but that was just because of the partying.

They had passed out in apartments, in cars, in parks, but never in alleyways. Never alone either. But Manny was gone and so were his friends. He was a solitary drinker now and just wanted to get home. He patted the pole and started to move.

His mother came to him then, speaking from the light winds that blew into the treetops he was passing underneath. On his way through a small park, he found a bench and deposited himself there. Puke was rising in him again, but he pushed it down. "Mom? Look at me, eh? Not what you wanted." Shaking his head, he rose and pushed on, mushing along, head down, his imaginary dog team yelping into the morning air. "Look at me," he mumbled again to no one. Suddenly, he thought he saw a dog appear in front of him. He couldn't be sure. It loped along, occasionally turning to make sure he was following. It was larger than Digger, naturally wild-looking, but not intimidating. Dash smiled and took it as a sign. "That you again, mom? Well, I'm game. Lead on. I'll follow."

* * *

Coyote had been wrapped for hours in the darkness that surrounded him. He had remained quiet and still, following the short but erratic pathway taken by this human from one watering hole to another. It had not been difficult. The young man's pain was chained to him so tightly that two city blocks were all he needed to dull his feelings. Then the open maw of a laneway had engulfed him, and he had entered and collapsed. A few others had passed by, drunks and loners as well, but they had not joined him, preferring to stumble on to howl at the sky or mark their territory with a piss somewhere else. Coyote was prepared to wait until dawn, but two others had arrived to help. They brought the man sustenance and raised him into consciousness. Coyote's stomach growled. When they left, he watched red-eyed as the man emerged and ricocheted across the street toward him. He was slow enough, his direction tentative. Good, *Coyote thought.* Enough time to double back for that sandwich. *Human food. Better than nothing.*

He snapped away his hunger in two bites, then appeared part dog, part shadow to participate in the man's remaining journey.

* * *

Two days had passed since Dash's night of humiliation. His salvation was that he did not remember much. It was as if the entire event had been a miserable dream, an action performed in a trance. He had been under a spell brought on by the absence of thought and the presence of drink. He had bathed himself in alcohol, shrivelled his brain to the size of a raisin and plunged into the void. This had been his initial response to his mother's letter, an angry retort and complete denial of her words. Once back at the apartment, an epic undertaking that took two hours of plodding up and down streets looking for familiar terrain, he had immediately dropped like a stone onto the couch and remained there inert until a pounding in his head pried him awake at seven that evening. "Christ," he muttered into the sleeve of his jacket not yet removed. Rolling to the floor, he had grabbed his head and pressed, hoping the pain would subside. He had needed water and had crawled the expanse of his desert floor to reach the kitchen sink. The refreshing cold of the tap spewed over his head and into his mouth, pushing him into the present with each raising of his bevelled hands. He had spent the rest of the night regaining his equilibrium. A warm shower, more water, some Tylenol found in the bathroom, more water, an attempt at food, Cheerios and milk, and he had started to recover. At 10 p.m., he had made tea, a drink he rarely had, and afterwards, fell asleep in bed. Twelve hours later, his head cleared, he sat at the table reviewing his options. It was time to act. Swallowing his fear and uncertainty, he found the number and placed the call.

* * *

Owen and Dodds. His mother had contacted this firm north of Jasper and south of 104th Street. It was easy enough to find. The appointment was at 2:00p.m. Dash had been smart enough to set up a time later in the day. It provided him with the opportunity not only to get there on time but also to back out if he felt so inclined. He was not sure if he was ready for this. He didn't know what to expect, what he would find out; most of all, he felt nervous around lawyers. To him, they were smart, powerful, driven, virtually his opposite. But his mother had had the courage, intelligence and determination to set these wheels in motion, so he needed to suck it up and ride toward whatever lay ahead.

The office was a converted two-storey house. Owen and Dodds maintained the ground floor consisting of a large outer waiting room surrounding a central secretarial space, which two women occupied. Upstairs were two bachelor apartments accessed by a side stairway. Dash had flung himself into one of six available chairs after announcing his arrival and waited, bouncing his knees in time with his nervousness. Within minutes, he was ushered efficiently through a door and directed down a short hallway to a room where he was greeted. Standing and reaching across his heavy-looking wooden and paper-laden desk, the man extended his hand and announced himself as William Dodds, the latter half of the lawyering duo. Dash accepted the handshake, then was gestured to sit down in one of the two chairs provided. Formalities quickly dispensed with, Dodds moved on to specifics.

"Your mother's estate is quite straightforward, actually. She had two accounts at the bank, one in her name and one in yours." He paused here to look briefly at Dash over his glasses, a look that felt scrutinizing. Dash simply nodded, and Dodds took this as a sign to continue.

"Your mother's personal account is simply savings, and at this time, it has two thousand eight hundred seventeen dollars and thirty-two cents in it." Dash swallowed. This seemed like a lot of money. He was surprised she had managed to scrimp this much together. But she had been working steadily since their arrival here, and Eric had certainly been big in the way of support. His train of thought was interrupted as Dodds moved on.

"The other account in your name is a little different. Your mother had been putting money into this one for you, one hundred dollars a month since you arrived in Edmonton. With interest such as it is, and the fact that you are closing in on twenty years of age, that leaves you with a sum of sixty-eight hundred and forty-two dollars." Dash sat back in his chair, his mouth open but not ready to articulate anything. *Jesus,* he thought. *How had she done this? What had she had to sacrifice to drop a hundred dollars a month into an account for him?* He tried to think. Food, rent, clothes. Where had she found the means, the will power to do this? True, Eric came to mind again, and Dash had contributed some for rent and food when he had been working, but still. And the biggest mind blow of all, he hadn't known a thing about it. When was she going to tell him? How long would she have continued doing this for him? Until he was twenty-one? Longer? He felt his cheeks begin to flush, and his eyes begin to water. Shame and love mingled together. He needed to get out of here. Dodds was astute enough to notice his discomfort and brought him back to the table.

"Since your mother's will is very explicit, there is no reason that these funds cannot be in your possession within a week or so. There will, of course, be my bill for services to cover, but I am not aware of any other debts in her name. I will be in touch with the bank, and I will get you to sign these documents saying that you understand and agree to what we have discussed, but I think that's it." Dash nodded and pulled himself together enough to sign where he was told to.

"Any final questions, Dash?" Dodds had said this with a level of compassion in his voice.

"No…thank you." And they had both risen and exchanged handshakes.

"Well, you know where I am, and you have my number. Make sure my secretary has your current address and phone number just in case, and I will be in touch with how and when you can get your money. Good luck."

Outside in the fresh air of the afternoon, Dash breathed in deeply and exhaled. He took in the sights and sounds, the bustle and activity as if everything was new to him. His mother was gone, but she had done so much to try to keep him safe and whole, and he hadn't had the inclination or the time to recognize and appreciate this. He would go home with a new determination, he told himself, and wait. Wait for the money. Wait for a plan to materialize. And while waiting, he was going to draw and give his heart some time to heal.

* * *

Chapter Twelve

DAY SIX

THE PRESENT

We had had a good evening. Cooking together had brought us closer. He cut up the vegetables and chicken; I sautéed and did the rice. Afterwards, with a glass of wine and a plate of macaroons, we kicked back our feet and talked. Wading through the ups and downs of his day, painted a clearer picture of how he was dealing with the job. It also gave me an insight or two into his life with Tania. Nothing in what he recounted really surprised me on that front. Many Tanias had come through my door, so I knew the type. I also knew what he had been through over the last year or so himself, struggling as he was with his darker influences. Here we were, three days into a new job, almost a week into change. I didn't know if the temptation of alcohol was wise on my part, but he seemed to be coping. Since arriving, he had certainly not been up in the nights secretly scarfing down my bottles of Pinot Grigio or cans of beer. As long as he was with me, I could credit myself with his slow transition, a weaning off certain habits that were not so good for him and onto one that was—me. What I felt was a coup, an acceptance from him that I was becoming a more intimate and integral part of his life, particularly when he opened up about his earlier days and memories of his mom. It had started with the package he had gone back to Tania's to retrieve and pulled out of his backpack.

"That's beautiful," I had said. "When did you get it?" He had been holding a dream catcher. He offered it up to me, and I turned it in my hands, brushing the feathers, admiring the colours and weaving, outlining the circle with a finger that brought everything together.

"At the local stampede we had in town one summer. Before we moved. It was a gift for my mom."

"How old were you"?

"Around fourteen, I think." He paused to take it back from me at that point. Put his hand on it, covering it gently. "Seems like a long time ago."

"Nice gift. What did she think of it?"

He looked at me and smiled. "She must have liked it. Had it hanging in the window of her bedroom until we moved and then again in Edmonton."

Dash put it aside then and reached into the package for what remained. A series of sketches had popped out. Animals primarily. Dogs, horses, birds, rough landscapes here and there, and a woman—his mother, it turned out—in repose on a couch. Some were in worse shape than others, pieces missing, edges discoloured or curled like they had been torn from a larger book. Maybe the sketchbook that he had once told me was part of an art kit he had. "These are pretty good," I had commented. It reminded me of my own desire to get back into sketching and painting myself.

"If you say so," was all he had said.

"I do say so. You've got some talent. You should keep at it." His animals were particularly life-like, the woman on the couch just needing something more to finish it. They had all been folded repeatedly and smudged with time but obviously carried from place to place without thoughts of letting them go, like old photographs telling stories of a past.

He had nodded, turned to me and said, "Well, I'll see what I can do."

I wasn't sure at that point if I should ask, but I did. "These pages sure have gone through a war. You must have had them in a book at some point."

He sat stonily silent for several seconds, then acknowledged that they were.

"What happened?"

"I was in a town, think it might have been White River, trying to get further south. I'd had enough of the North by that time. Couldn't decide whether to jump on a train at that point or continue to hitch." Dash had stopped to let the clouds circle his thoughts. He needed to get back into the darkness to carry on with the rest. "Not much of a place, White River. A few hundred people maybe, a motel, diner-type places, and a couple of shops. Least, that's all I really remember. But it's on the Trans-Canada Highway, and it's a railway stopping point."

"I've never been there myself," I said, "but then I haven't been too far north in Ontario, believe it or not. Tobermory, across on the Chi Cheemaun ferry and then on to Manitoulin Island and Sudbury and back. That was when I was younger, and I was with my mom and dad travelling by car to see some relatives. I loved some of the scenery and the boat ride, but that's about it. My parents weren't big outdoor types then. They still aren't."

"Like I said, you aren't missing much. Unless you like a lot of bush and rivers. Fishing and hunting would be good around there, I suppose."

He seemed in no hurry to return to his story, so I nudged him back in that direction. "You were telling me about your layover."

"Not much to tell. I had walked along the main street, I guess it was, and across some tracks to a small train platform where I could sit. I was thinking of checking out train times and tickets." He stopped again to look down at his hands. "Three guys showed up in a truck nearby, parked, and got out. At first, I didn't think anything of it, but they must have been following me 'cause they came over and started givin' me a hard time."

"What kind of a hard time?"

He looked over at me. "C'mon Jesse. The usual stuff I get from certain whites. Insults mainly, but at that time, I had a fuse, and it didn't matter if I was outnumbered. Anyways, they decided they wanted to check out my bag, the big backpack I was toting around on my travels. It had my clothes, personal shit, and my art kit. I landed a few good punches before one of them cold-cocked me with a lucky blow, and I went down. They dropped a few kicks on me, tore everything apart, stomped on my kit, ripped up my book, left stuff all over the platform, and took off. Broad daylight, but of course, nobody was around. Who knows if anybody saw anything."

"Jesus, Dash. Did they take any valuables, any money?"

"They weren't out to rob me, Jesse. Just to teach me a lesson, tell me to keep movin' on, I guess. There are lots of Native reserves in the North, and one was near White River. I guess it's all about steppin' up the hate for some. And those boys felt they had a code to maintain, maybe a score to settle. Lowlifes with too much time on their hands. Anyway, when I recovered enough to put stuff back in my bag, these were all that I came away with. I've carried them around ever since, so they've gotten a little more beat up. Never thought of sketching again until I met you." He smiled. "You, Colville, and the AGO. Who'd of thought?"

It was then that I remembered my purchase for him. "Speaking of Colville and art in general," I had said as I got up and walked over to my bag, "I got you this today. Almost forgot in all the excitement of running into Greg. Here you go."

He reached out and took it. Turned it over, examined it, ran his hands over the front and back, opened it, laid it out flat. "You shouldn't have done this, Jesse. I told you I was going to get one and pay for it." I had detected a note of irritation rising in his voice.

"I know, I know, and you can pay me back if you really want. Consider this a new beginning, a start to your new drawing endeavours. You can redo some of the pieces that you already have if you want."

"Thanks. I am going to pay you back." And as if taking my suggestion, he tucked his pages carefully inside the sketchbook and gently closed it.

Making love afterwards was its own reward for my good deed. He could thank me as often as he liked this way. I thought of how quickly our relationship had developed. It had only been a few days since he had knocked on my door. My wasted time with Greg had barely cooled, and here I was hot with Dash. It had all been so quick and still so uncertain. Yet, it felt right. I was smitten, a word my mother might say. I smiled. It had probably happened the first day I laid eyes on him. Time was a funny thing.

But I was into Thursday now, and my daydreaming had to quit. Pushing last night's activities aside, I made for the coffee pot in the work area, poured myself a mug full, and headed back to my desk to start the day. Thursday. The weekend was just appearing over hump day and onto the horizon. *Let's get to it*, I told myself as I dove into the paperwork in front of me.

* * *

Greg had had another rough night. It was not so much the drink this time. Granted, he'd had a few in his apartment throughout the evening, but not enough to tank him. He'd spent a few hours cranking out his favourite bands, The Who, Lynyrd Skynrd, Slayer, until he got people hammering on his wall to tone it down. None of these modern bands for him. He wanted edgier stuff, anthem songs that would mix and match with his current state of mind, slice out the mellow, and interject the mad. He ended with "Won't Get Fooled Again" for a second time and the final swig of a fourth beer before allowing a neighbourly truce to settle in. He had crashed just before midnight, but the beer had not subdued him. He tossed and turned restlessly, reviewing his encounter with Jesse in a semi-state of sleep until the alarm clock read six. Cursing into the blue of early morning, he pulled himself out of bed, pissed, showered, dressed, drank some orange juice, had some cereal, brushed the remnants of the last hours out of his mouth, and headed for his car.

He sat in it now, an hour later, on Beverley, nursing a coffee he had picked up, waiting for signs of movement. Had he always been this way? Possessive? Never wanting to let go of what he thought was rightly his? He flashed back to high school and his first girlfriend. It was Grade 11. Paula. He thought she was hot. Unfortunately, so did a few other guys. She went out with him for a few weeks before things soured. He hated Shakespeare, but they were studying *Othello* at the time. Jealousy started getting the better of him. He started following her when they weren't together, seeing who she spent her free time with. He got angry when she talked to other guys, laughed at their jokes, did assignments together with them in the library. Anything could set him off. Why couldn't she be exclusive? Just want to spend time with him? He was not like that black bastard in the play, but eventually, his controlling nature and occasional outbursts broke her down. She had told him to get lost. It seemed that every woman had been the same since then. He took a sip from his coffee. Jesse had to be added to the pile. What was it with these women? What did they see in their choices of men? Losers like this Indian she enjoyed being with so much. Well, he was going to track this guy, but good. Even if he was late for work, he would find out where he went in the morning.

Ten minutes later, he lucked out. Jesse appeared on her porch with her new shadow. Greg scowled. She locked the door, and they each unlocked a bike and came down the steps, ready to leave. Then she gave him a kiss, not a peck but a lingering search with her hand tucked behind his head. "You bitch," he breathed into his cup. He finished his coffee and turned on his car. They left together, but Tonto, Greg noted, needed to set a quicker pace and so waved to Jesse and had taken off. Greg let Jesse disappear and stayed on his rival's tail. He kept him in sight until he saw him cut off, mount a sidewalk, and dismount outside a building. Two other guys on bikes greeted him with a fist bump, and then all went in. He found a spot to pull over, locked up, and quickly froggered across a busy Bathurst Street to inch up close enough to see the sign on the door. Your Express Service. Was this guy a bike courier? Not wanting to draw too much attention, he sauntered back to his car. Fuck work, he wanted to know. In a few minutes, Dash emerged, a package in hand that he quickly transferred to a backpack. He adjusted a phone on his chest and took off. *I'll be damned*, Greg thought, *a bike courier*. And he laughed out loud. What am I worried about? This guy can't stack up for long. With a sigh of relief, he got ready to turn his engine over but then had a second thought. Loping back across the street, he entered the building and casually approached the woman at the desk.

"This a courier place?" he asked gruffly.

"That's right. What can I do for you?" Greg noticed her tattoos and was immediately turned off. Not his type. Why did women have to mark up their bodies like that?

"Nothin' really. I just had a few questions about workin' here."

"You mean as a courier? There are only a couple of in-house jobs here, dispatcher and service rep, and they're filled."

"Yeah, sure, as a biker."

"You'd have to come back and talk to Derrick at the end of the day."

"What's the end of the day here?'

"Guys usually finish up around five. He should be in by then." A phone call drew her attention, and she brushed him off with a "got to pick up." Greg grunted and just walked away. Back in his car, he prepared to head north and to his job. If things worked out, he planned to come back, have a few choice words with Jesse's mistake, and set him straight on a few things. Looks like he had a plan. Reaching for a CD, he wound himself up with Rush and

"The Spirit of Radio." He'd offer up some excuse to his boss about construction and lane reductions for his lateness. Not like it hadn't happened before. Smirking, he found a hole and shot out into traffic. Driving was such a release.

* * *

Dash began his day with an uneasy feeling. It first came when he was leaving Jesse's apartment. It had resurfaced on and off until he was well into his first run through Little Italy. He finally felt he had shaken it by mid-morning as he moved out of an Ossington stop and was zigzagging over to a James Town pickup. He had felt he was being watched. A crow had startled him then, swooping down between parked cars and rising quickly to a place in a tree above him. It had unnerved him enough to give Jesse a quick text on his phone, simply asking how her day was going so far.

An eventual response some fifteen minutes later indicated she was good but busy and asked him the same. He had dropped his worry just then and responded, saying his day was great and that he'd see her later. By the time another pickup and drop had been made, it was noon, and he was going to take a break for a bite of lunch. Jesse had made sandwiches for them both, popped in a hard-boiled egg and an apple, and they were good to go. He thought of his recent good luck as he sunk his teeth into the ham and cheese. She had been a lifesaver, and he was determined to stay on track for her. For himself too. The urge to drink, to get hammered, to hoover up some pot or hash for good measure, crawled into his headspace, but never escaped to run amuck. He had felt his mind clear a little more each day since Jesse had allowed him in. He thought of his mother for a moment. She was always there, as she said she would be, watching over him. He hoped she was proud of him at this turning point in his life. Only a week, he knew, but a good start. The weekend was a stone's throw away.

Just then, a foodie on a bike passed by, gave him a wave, bounced up onto the sidewalk, scurried down a few storefronts, and pulled to a stop. Some lunchtime delivery, it looked like, with his square backed bag full of pizza or Thai or a bunch of subs. Who knew? Dash had heard some of the disgruntled chatter emerge at the office over the last few days. The fact food couriers were springing up all over, taking away the purity of the bike courier mantra. Blake had had run-ins with a few, entitled wannabes that lacked a definable code to the road, as he put it. A couple of the other guys, like Tod and Blair, agreed with Blake, but Derrick and a much older part-time rider that Dash had just met and couldn't remember his name, were a little more understanding.

"Live and let live," Derrick had said at one point when the debate had come up at end of day. "They're new to the game, and they aren't in our wheelhouse as far as competition right now. Plenty of room out there for all of us." That had settled the discussion for the moment, but all it took was a day on the road where a foodie had pulled a bonehead stunt and the debate was back on the table. Dash had no opinion one way or another. He was so green himself that he was sure bonehead stunts were around any corner at any given time, and he could be the culprit. He would save his ire for heavy metal objects and two-footed wayfarers who, stuck in mindsets and actions of anger or stupidity, got thrust in his way.

Suddenly, a woman screaming for help cut through the air. Dash had just finished lunch and started looking around for the source. He heard the scream again and pinpointed it. Across the street was a woman moving back and forth along a row of parked cars. A man had come out of one of the buildings nearby and was approaching her. She continued to scream, inching further away from the man. Passersby were few at this point and were simply onlookers like him. The woman finally turned and made as if to run, but the man sped up and grabbed her from behind. Dash decided that he should act and bolted across the street. Grabbing the man who had wrestled the woman to the ground by then, Dash pulled him off her. The woman, dishevelled and flailing, got to her feet, looked momentarily at her saviour, and then ran between two parked cars and disappeared into a side street.

"Get your hands off me," the man cried as he tried to manoeuvre away from the arms grabbing at him.

Dash pushed him back. As the man turned toward him, the word "Security" looming above the pocket on his shirt front caught Dash's eye. "What's going on?" he growled, still crouched, ready for an assault.

The man glared at Dash sizing him up, then brushed at his pants and put his hands on his hips. "Great job, moron. Someone inside saw that woman trying to break into these cars. I came out to confront her and you gave her a chance to get away. Thanks for that."

"Why was she calling for help then?" A logical question, Dash thought.

"Why does any nut bar on the street do anything? Fucked if I know." The guy continued to groom himself, tucking at his shirt and adjusting his collar.

"I thought somethin' else was going on. Sorry, man."

The security guard just waved it off. "Forget it. She didn't get anything. Happens all the time." He turned to go back inside. The smattering of gawkers that had stopped to witness the sideshow had moved on.

Dash just shook his head and returned to his bike. The first time he tried to get involved in helping somebody out, and it back fired. Typical. From now on, he would just stick to riding and doing his job. He glanced down the alley as he made off for his next run, hoping to catch a glimpse of the woman. But the cupboard was bare. It could just as easily have been him a couple of weeks ago peering through car windows, checking doors casually for one left unlocked. With the spin of a wheel, how things can turn. Jesse loomed up in front of him, a green light ushering him through the intersection. He breathed this reality in and out as he churned off south and east toward Regent Park and into the rest of the afternoon.

* * *

Graham just happened to be entering the building when Greg screamed in off the street and headed for the back to park. "Jesus Christ," he muttered. "Has he heard of the word subtle?" He would have a chat with him again; this attitude of his was starting to piss Graham off. When he arrived at his office, removed his coat and checked his phone for messages, he decided to go for a walk and speak to Greg before he left on his route. Grabbing a coffee from the urn outside his door, he headed for shipping. He noticed Greg leaning on a counter, arms draped over a box he had yet to pick up. Judging from the time, he was already thirty minutes behind on his schedule.

"Hey, Greg, a word before you get going." He approached with the intention of a courteous interaction, but when Greg simply maintained his posture and acknowledged Graham with only a sideways glance, everything changed.

"I noticed you came in late this morning."

Greg slowly stood up, tucked the box under his arm and began his rehearsed excuse, "Yeah, the traffic…"

"How many times is that this month?" Graham interjected. "Three? Four?"

Greg frowned and shifted his feet. "There was construction and…"

"And what about roaring in here like a wailing banshee in that car of yours?"

Greg's car and his driving were off-limits if criticism was involved, even if it was from his pasty-faced boss. He drove a Mazda for God's sake. "She's a beauty, right? Too much power for her own good," and he smiled. "Built for speed."

"Not the point, Greg. The parking lot's not a speedway, OK?" Greg said nothing.

"Look, I just wanted to tell you to knock off the showmanship when you come to work, and no more lates." Before Greg could reply, Graham added, "Oh, and one more thing. Your performance review is tomorrow. We'll do it first thing, so be here on time." And with that, he finished his coffee, chucked the cup in the receptacle nearby, and walked off. Greg stood there for a moment watching him retreat, flipped him his middle finger for good measure, and headed off to his van. Everybody was out to get him. The rest of the day rose up in front of him like a tidal wave that he had to fight to crest.

"You prick. You bastard." The words that Graham had spoken were totally forgotten as he tore out of the parking lot, squealing his tires across oncoming traffic and into his lane. "Eat that, you snivelling douche bag." It took him eight city blocks, a series of horn blasts, two near misses first with a slow turning female driver and then with a cyclist who, in his mind, was too far out in the lane to warrant protection, before he brought his blood pressure down to a simmer. Five o'clock couldn't come soon enough. As he pulled into his first drop off, he remembered his promise to hook up with Jesse's courier buddy. A little revenge could be sweet at this point, he reasoned.

* * *

Forlorn? Perhaps too severe a feeling to use as my day had progressed, but it had not been a good one. I had felt isolated, an island under siege, the waters around me shark-infested. My regulars had come in numbers unusually high with their seas of concern, uncertainty, and paranoia. There was no escaping the desperation that rushed toward me wave after wave, breaking across my desk and threatening to pull me out into the undertow of their lives. And above me on the wall opposite, the clock had continued to remind me through its two-armed assault that time was moving imperceptibly. When I finally witnessed a lull, brought on by the generosity of a passerby who had carried in two boxes of doughnuts for the courtesy table and which had momentarily gained the full attention of the troubled around me, I seized the opportunity and made for the bathroom. Heading for the sink, I splashed cold water on my face and gazed into the mirror.

Again, I was not sure of the words. Dowdy? Frumpish? These were old-school terms, something my mother might use to describe clothes certain people wore, both men and women, to functions she was forced to attend. Uninspiring? Unimaginative? Plain? Could these be more relevant to how I perceived myself in this moment? I tucked a strand of hair behind my ear. Maybe I could stand to use a little more make-up even though I loathed wearing it. Maybe accessorize my attire with some brighter features: a colourful scarf, some earrings, a nice jacket. Instead, I wore the garb of my surroundings, of my job, unfurled around me like a flag in defeat, fluttering at half-mast. *Well, I was trying to fit in*, I told myself. I should not be a walking advertisement for a fashion magazine when my clients often came in wearing ensembles resurrected from Salvation Army bins, patches and fragments cobbled together to keep out the cold and provide a modest sense of dignity.

Suddenly, another image from *A Christmas Carol* entered my mind, the ghost of Christmas Yet to Come, revealing to Scrooge a scene from a destitute quarter of London on presumably Christmas morning. The undertaker, the charwoman, and the house servant all in attendance at "the shop", a sketchy rusted, metal enclosure the size of a large garage filled with piles of clothing and various objects. Dirty street urchins sitting in filth sorted through the remnants, coughing in the soot-coated environment while the owner/father/manager of the "shop" sat scratching his flea-infested legs and waited to have Scrooge's stolen cache of goods presented to him for suitable appraisal. The image passed quickly, but it was an accurate enough reminder of my reality here.

Struggle was not a word that came to mind when I thought of my upbringing. Instead, comfort, security, privilege had surrounded me like fluffy pillows on a queen-size bed. I had not wanted for anything. My parents, though busy and often aloof, had always been there for me in their ways. Love, though not often tangible, was in the air, as the song went.

I ran the list of clients through my head that I had seen that day as I reached for paper towels to dry my hands. There was Ethel, the resident bag lady, timing her arrival at her usual hour of nine, grimed from a night of wandering the streets but charming in her own way. Not a problem but someone who needed more than we could offer. Hers was a habitual need for companionship at a place she regarded as safe. I was often her target, someone she could approach for a bit of conversation. Granted, we had had to stop her attempts at panhandling within the building, her roaming from desk to desk to solicit change. Once boundaries had been established, she was willing to come in for visits and the chance of a coffee. There was Paul, a young schizophrenic bouncing in and out of rehab and in and out of our office looking for work, trying to stabilize a portion of his life that was still often out of control. And Amie, I couldn't forget her. Tentative, quiet, head down Amie entering the building with a shuffle, the marks of self-inflicted knife wounds often evident on her arms. My heart went out to them all, these apparitions of need traversing the sidewalks. But then there had been an influx of first-timers, adults and their children, new arrivals trying to gain a foothold in the city, many with limited skills and education. In their eyes, I also saw a look that evoked histories of hardship. All I could do was try to help and point out some possible solutions. But on this day, I felt like a wayward compass having lost the ability to find true north. Forlorn. Perhaps the right time for that word now.

Both my parents at different times in our conversations, either in person or on the phone, had asked me why I continued to do the work when its toll on me could be so high. Was the job safe, and if not, why would I place myself in jeopardy? There must be another career path I could find that would be equally satisfying. In their worlds, they had been economically successful by remaining relatively unattached to anyone but themselves. While not selfish, given that they supported various charities that they believed in, they were not active, never personally engaged or involved. They had a handful of good friends, but social circles, in general, they orbited out of necessity, a gravitational pull they used to keep their positions of respect intact. Despite my love for my parents and their well-intentioned nurturing, I was trying hard not to be them. I left the washroom and wandered back to my desk. There would be no prisons and no workhouses on my watch. I would finish up with a flourish and then look forward to seeing Dash. Let's hope his day had been better than mine.

* * *

Dash had been told by either Derrick or Blake that the Regent Park area used to be located on parts of the old Cabbagetown neighbourhood. Technically surrounded by Gerrard, River, Shuter and Parliament streets, it was begun as a community housing experiment but became so much more. Businesses, shops, restaurants and cafes peppered the area, adding vibrancy to a diverse downtown component. After completing a run on Sumach Street, he had ventured into the park nearby, slowing his pace and enjoying a moment of green space. There were so many spots he saw as if for the first time; his awareness stimulated by his changing circumstances, Jesse, and this job. However, he was still not out of the woods. The urge to have a drink other than the water he carried had risen up daily. Whenever he passed a bar or noticed an advertisement looming up at him from a sign, a craving surfaced in him. He had shared wine and beer with Jesse, but sparingly, and in her presence it had been all right. Alone for too long and left to his own devices, he wasn't so sure. He had heard people say that the best thing to do to stop a habit or addiction was to hit it head-on, cold turkey. He didn't think so, at least not for him. He had tried that before; it lasted a couple of days. No, for him, it was another thing: the support he had from Jesse. He thought about it, she had been there from the day he walked into her office. He just hadn't seen it, a spark that was turning into a flame. Because of this, he was giving himself time to heal. He now found himself pausing to reflect before acting, to deliberately think through past experiences, to remember what excessive drinking and drugs had cost him over the years as he had tried to pull himself together. And right now, as he looked around, it seemed to be working.

His mother came to him then. She floated in from across the floor in their old bungalow. Jeans, red top, bare feet, her smile blooming for him as she hummed a tune that engaged them both. Only good memories of her had surfaced lately, no darkness. The words of her letter still echoed deep within him, pounding across his chest like wild horses. He missed her. He wished he could talk to her, let her know how he was doing, have her meet Jesse. But these thoughts soon dissipated in the cool breeze that blew across his face. He took a sip of water from his bottle and readied himself. The next stop was a "long bomb", as Derrick called it, a pickup beyond the six-kilometre radius of their usual rides, this one out beyond the Don Valley. He should be back by five if everything went well. Day four would be history.

* * *

Coincidence. This was a word that Crow had long been familiar with. He was aware of patterns shaping themselves in such a way as to seem remarkable. That these two bodies in space should coincide in time could appear to be almost otherworldly, a spiritual intervention.

But there it was unfolding below, these rivals within blocks of each other. Fate. Maybe. Just another flip of the coin. He had been kept so busy throughout the day moving from one to the other, leaving the third attached to her desk that he had been unaware or had perhaps forgotten of this possible occurrence. It was still unlikely that their paths would cross. Each had their own destinations, and there were many streets, buildings, and lights intervening in the flow necessary to gather them to a specific point. But a passing could happen, like ships in the night, one not seeing the other. Crow was excited, but his sphere of influence was limited. He would simply watch and see what unfolded. There were still cards to be dealt. He thought of Coyote out there somewhere, waiting for him to finish and pass on the vigil. Not yet. There was still light left in the day. Crow circled in the wind, his black eyes searching.

* * *

It was unusual for Greg to find himself down this far. His routes tended to crisscross more northerly trajectories. But a delivery was a delivery, and here he was, travelling down streets looking for a dealership. Not that far from where he hung out when he was downtown, but the thought of being in an area overrun with Blacks, Hispanics, East Indians, people sponging off Canada's good nature, coming here with their crazy cultures and traditions was too much. Of course, it was this way almost everywhere you went. Toronto had too many of these areas popping up. And our own Indigenous. The worst. Indigenous. A stupid politically correct word, overused and overrated.

Calgary. Now, there was a city making its own mistakes. Granted, a lot of the immigrants had been making their homes out in the growing suburbs, but there was still a blight in the downtown area, and his good old dad wasn't helping. What the hell was he thinking? Greg always shook his head at every one of his dad's new renovations, which were all about making living spaces more accessible for everyone. Fine, all well and good, but did it have to be for everyone? Couldn't his cracker of a dad get Whites, true Canadians, in there as a priority? And he wasn't alone in this thinking. He had been online to a few sites, people like him, hard-working and nationalistic, patriots who just wanted what was best for the city and their country. People voicing their opinions, some even willing to take action. Good old dad, with his vision of fairness, was part of the problem and not the solution. C'mon, what was fair about what he was doing?

The bleak cloud permeating Greg's mind suddenly lifted. He was on River Street, and an LCBO came into view. He would make a quick pit stop and pick up a six-pack for after work. Then he would find this dealership, drop off his last package, and head back. He slowed, signalled to turn right, and a bike courier blew by. "Fuck. You stupid prick. I had my signal light on. Christ." He banged the steering wheel, turned into the small parking lot, giving the receding rider a long look. There was something familiar about that guy, he thought. Whatever. He glanced at the dashboard clock. It was almost 4:30p.m. If he wanted to have a chat with Jesse's two-wheeled warrior, he would have to do his last drop off and then head directly back across Dundas Street with the company truck and find a spot close by to watch for the guy. Could forget the beer. Nope, not an option. He'd just be late coming back with the truck. No worries. Dipshit Graham would be long gone by then. He'd make up some excuse for his late sign out in the morning. *Fuck 'em.*

* * *

I was just dotting the "I" on my last form of the day when the text from Dash arrived. He was going to be late. Sometime between seven and eight, he figured. Did this put the meal of my design out the window, something I had been thinking about all day to keep me from spiralling into the doldrums? It involved a stop on the way home to get fresh fish and then some recipe checking, but would also fulfill my current desires of awakening the man with food. Dash loved fish, or so he told me. I was going to get pickerel, a white fish he said he used to catch while growing up. I planned to prepare it simply, the way his mother had when he had come home on his bike all smiles, hoisting the two or three lovelies that he had taken stealthily from the lake. He had told me this story quietly, a memory pulled from the water with some struggle, but then arching into the light and spraying me with insight. I held onto it.

He said he was going on an outing for no more than an hour or two to The Duke of Richmond for an after-work drink with his colleagues. I had suggested, in a not too dictatorial manner, I hoped, that he have, perhaps, only one beer before donning the wheels of his trade and returning. I reminded him that his means of transportation involved lung and leg power plus hand and eye coordination. While this was all tongue in cheek and meant to arouse nothing but smiles when he read it, I was crawling with anxiety as I cycled toward home myself. He assured me that he had everything under control. Deep inside, I trusted him, but that didn't help my worry. So many variables could change things, beginning with the simple camaraderie of acceptance. Laughter, jokes, and storytelling, relaxing the guard with new colleagues, could easily lead to a few more rounds. *Shake it off,* I told myself as I stopped at the market. Get the fish and let him take care of the rest.

* * *

Dash had been past Old City Hall countless times, had been into the Eaton Centre and wandered around, but he had never been inside The Duke of Richmond. He had seen people congregate outside, either standing for a smoke or sitting on the few patio chairs available along James Street. But it was late September now, and a cool wind swept along Queen Street, ushering everyone who wanted a drink or some food at The Duke through its doors down a few steps and into its spacious surroundings. It reminded him a little of The Rex, the pub he had been to with Jesse almost a week ago. This one was a little less tired looking, the clientele more the lunch and after-work crowd from the businesses around, filtering in for their daily reprieves from the grind. This one was more likely to have tourists drop by or shoppers pop in as well, its proximity to Toronto landmarks within stumbling distance.

A large bar straight ahead was what he first saw upon entering. In typical British tradition, extensive dark wood carved itself into various shapes along walls, tabletops, and the backs and bases of chairs and booths. Gold and red coloured seats, their cushiony softness ensuring a comfortable sit, invited butts of various proportions to place themselves into service. People could spread out in collections of twos, fours and more, depending on group size, either to the left or to the right and then down toward the back. If here on one's own, a generous row of stools lined themselves up at attention along the bar like the Queen's Guard waiting for patrons to throw up a leg, lean over the gleaming counter and place an order.

The place was busy, but Dash had been told when he arrived to wander around the corner and down toward the back where Derrick would have a table set aside. He knew some of the guys were here as he had seen their mounts chained up outside, waiting patiently for their return. And so, after taking in his surrounding for a moment, he walked on. At the bend, he looked down and over the heads of the already huddled until an arm went up and directed him toward a familiar voice.

"Good. You made it," Derrick called out. "Grab a seat." Dash gathered himself, pulled back a chair, and plunked down beside Blake, who was taking a pull at his London Pride.

"Nice to see you still on your feet, rookie," he joked as he put his glass down.

Dash smiled. "Week's not over yet."

"That's true. You could be on your face this time tomorrow."

"Don't mind him, kid," a voice Dash didn't know piped in. "I've been bucked more times than I can count over the years." This guy was much older, lean and weathered, someone, it looked like, who had spent years getting to know the streets from the outside.

Derrick chimed in then. "Time for introductions. You know Blake and me, of course. I think you met these two guys," pointing to Tod and Blair. Both were young, but still several years older than him, Dash guessed as he nodded. "But the two relics at the end, I don't think you've come across yet." Derrick said this with affection. "Kenny and Phil are old horses," he joked, "but I can't seem to put them out to pasture. Phil is sixty-three, but Kenny, a part-timer now, is an ancient. Still pumping around this town on the job at seventy-four."

Kenny laughed at this, a grin that showed the lack of a tooth or two. "Derrick's right, kid, I've been at this a long time, but it comes and goes with the seasons now. I've done other things in life, but I always come back to the riding." He took a swig from his beer and added. "No more winters for me."

"Yep, Kenny's a fair-weather man," chirped Phil. "Leaving the hard sloggin' to youngsters like me."

"Ah, go fuck yourself," Kenny replied. "You're a part-timer too, you old goat."

"Yeah, but I'm not givin' up on the winter like some delicate flowers I know."

Dash ordered a beer for himself and settled into the banter that began circling the table. He soon felt part of the group, adding to the conversation when asked about his week, taking good-natured ribbings but heeding the advice that occasionally came his way. The first forty minutes passed quickly. Dash was mindful of Jesse's words. He would compromise and would not have three beers. He would just have this second one in his hand

and then call it a day. Getting home when suggested was not going to be a problem.

* * *

Greg had been forced to find a parking lot a block and a half from the pub. Tailing the guy there through traffic during rush hour from the courier shop had been a nightmare, but he had managed, thanks to his aggressive approach. The gauntlet of fists, fingers, and horns he had ridden through only heightened his senses and his persistence. He had pulled over briefly across from the pub, put his flashers on, and watched to make sure his target was going inside. Having a company truck was a bonus in situations like this where passersby thought he was making a delivery, something tolerated a little more than some guy in a car who had just double-parked to run into a store. It still cost him money to park, and the walk back was a few minutes, but he told himself it would be worth it. He could use a drink anyway, the one he had while waiting for this guy to show up back at his base was getting a little warm, and he didn't like warm beer.

Inside the pub, a part of him was immediately cautious. The place was familiar enough; he had been in a couple of times with a friend or two when at the Eaton Centre, but he didn't want to be seen by this guy just yet. Where was he? Not in the front section which was easily surveyed from the steps coming in. Greg headed to the bar and sat on a stool at the end. This way, he could see down both sides of the pub. He ordered, and after casually taking a sip when it arrived, focused on one table in the far corner. A group of seven guys yukking it up in cyclist attire. And there he was, the cocky Comanche, smiling away, taking it all in as if he had done nothing. He took another long drink, his thirst unsatiated. He wanted him alone, in the bathroom, or outside when he was leaving—just a few choice words, a warning to stay away from Jesse and to get lost, head back to the reserve.

"You must be thirsty. You want another?" The bartender brought him back. She was good-looking, someone he might be able to score with under different circumstances.

"Sure, babe. Another would be great." He polished off the remainder of his first and settled in.

* * *

"So, where you livin', kid?" Kenny asked. Their discussion had covered everything from sports, particularly the Leafs' chances this year, to politics briefly, and with enthusiastic malice. "Politicians are all bums" was the consensus. Then it was on to music and Blake's assertion that the 60s and 70s were not dead, which produced much head-nodding, although he couldn't get everyone to agree with him on reggae's place in the orbit of those decades, and finally to travel, which generally meant local because money was everyone's enemy for the most part. Life was simple and good if you could accept that only the lottery and a lucky ticket was going to change anybody's fortune.

"With a friend right now," Dash replied and took a drink.

"Male or female?" Kenny quipped.

Phil butted in. "Does it matter, Kenny?"

Kenny smiled and looked back at Dash. "Maybe."

"It's OK," Dash said in reply. "Female, Kenny, and really nice too."

"There you go, that's all I needed to know." He paused, "Well, maybe not everything."

Dash laughed out loud this time, a genuine burst that echoed around the table. "That's all you're gettin', Kenny."

The chatter continued for another twenty minutes or so, some work stories of the day casually inserting themselves into the mix until Dash had finished his drink. It was time for him to go. He let Derrick and the others know.

"I'm going to hit the head and then ride out, guys. I'll straighten up before I leave."

"No need to do that," Derrick said. "These are on me. You made it through the week. You earned it."

The other guys piped up in agreement. "Good to have you on board, kid," Kenny added. "Course next week, the tab is on you." He raised his glass.

He nodded at Kenny. "Thanks for the invite and beers, Derrick. I still have one day to go before I can call it a week, though."

Derrick looked at him. "Remember what I said about guys who can't cut it quitting after the first day or two. You're still here. Tomorrow? Piece of cake."

"Right. See you tomorrow, then, guys." He rose from the table and headed to the john.

* * *

Greg took another gulp and slid off the stool. Now or never. He ran a hand through his hair as he made for the washroom. All he wanted was to get in his face for a minute. He pushed open the door and saw him at a urinal. He hadn't looked up. *That's it,* he thought. *Shake it off. Good boy. Turn around. Here we go.*

Dash was zipping up as he turned, then heard Greg say, "'Member me?"

"No," and he moved to walk by. Then a hand came up and into his chest, halting his progress. He took a harder look.

"Sure you do, pal. I'm Jesse's boyfriend, in case you forgot." And he gave him another tap.

Dash simply looked at him. "Not anymore," and stood his ground.

"Listen, red. Time to move on, say your goodbyes." At this, he gave Dash a shove, hard enough to send him back a step. He'd had enough of this jerk.

"You don't get it," and Dash moved toward Greg, unintimidated. "Jesse doesn't want you in her life…ever again. She doesn't want to see you or hear from you. It's over. Leave her and me alone."

He moved to pass, and then it happened. Greg grabbed him and rammed him up against the bathroom wall. "It's over when I say it's over, you prick."

Dash latched onto his arms and tried to swing him off, but Greg's anger gave him extra strength. They scuffled for a few seconds before Dash freed his right hand and landed a punch to the side of Greg's head. Momentarily stunned, he let go, and Dash lashed out again, hitting Greg square in the face. He doubled over, grabbing his nose.

"You fuck." His hand came away with blood on it, and he moved to the sink, all thoughts of continuing the skirmish gone. No one else had entered yet, and Dash wasn't waiting around for another round. He exited the washroom, a range of mumbled epithets following him out. Head down, he breezed by his table without stopping. Pushing through the door, he released his bike outside and rode off. Disbelief, frustration, even a little worry mixed in with the traffic as he moved along. This was getting serious and out of control. There was a lunatic on his tail. He needed to get back to Jesse, make sure she was all right. Maybe bringing in the cops wasn't such a bad idea.

* * *

The bleeding had stopped, but a few drops now darkened Greg's shirt. No matter. He looked at his face. His nose was sore, but didn't seem broken. He noticed a small scrape under his eye where the bastard had landed his first lucky punch. Not sure if his eye would go a little yellow or black. He rested his hands on the sink but quickly turned away when somebody entered. He left the washroom, slapped some money down on the bar for his drinks, grabbed his jacket and left. The eyes following him soon returned to their own lives. He was incensed, beyond rage, but there was something else, another feeling perhaps even more pronounced. Shame. This was not the shame he felt when singled out by his teachers for stupidity at school, when belittled by teammates for a costly mistake, when reprimanded by his boss at work. This was a different kind of shame. This was the shame of being bested by an inferior. As he walked, it was all he could see. It had happened to him another time in the Sault. Well, never again. He clamoured into his truck and started it up. For a second, he thought of tearing over to Jesse's apartment, showing her what her new man had done to him, but that would be pathetic and just show weakness. No, he needed to be smarter than that, think a little more on what his next step should be. It was after seven. First thing's first. This truck needed to be returned, or he'd be in deep shit. He grabbed a beer, opened it and took a long swig. Warm, but what the hell? He needed to calm himself down for the drive back. There was always tomorrow.

* * *

There were so many fresh fish to choose from when I entered the market on my way home. I wanted pickerel, though, and settled on three generous sized fillets. I wasn't sure how hungry Dash would be, so two for him, one for me. Add to this the rice and vegetable stir-fry I was planning, and we were good. My decadent side didn't stop there. Before getting home, I had slipped into a bakery and snagged two cinnamon buns for dessert. While I waited for Dash to return, I had ripped off a small piece of one bun just to satiate my sugar needs. Scrumptious. I forced myself to stop at one extraction. If I didn't, I would pick away at it, a crow hunkered down on road kill, until only a pile of desiccated crumbs remained.

My thoughts strayed to this evening. I hoped I could encourage Dash to open up more about his past. This could be good therapy for both of us. I would do this after dinner and clean up by introducing art into the equation. I wanted to take out some of my supplies in preparation for the art class on Saturday. In doing so, I hoped to engage Dash in the same, get him to open the new sketchbook I had gotten him, maybe the Colville book he had stashed away. I decided to start cutting up the vegetables and throwing the rice into a pot to get a jump on prep. I poured myself a glass of wine first and then began to rummage.

Twenty minutes later, I heard him on the porch securing his bike. I looked at the stove clock: 7:26 p.m. He had done it. His first salvo with colleagues into the public domain of drink and he had surfaced intact, or so I hoped. I would wait for his entrance to determine that for sure. In the brief interim I had, I would quickly bread the fish.

When the door opened, it was not the face I expected. There was no smile, not even a greeting. He removed his jacket, kicked off his shoes, gave me a quick look laced with concern and made for the couch where he sat down, leaned forward, hung his arms over his knees and stared at the coffee table. It was almost like his posture the first time he had walked into my office and sat across from me, only this time I was standing. I left the kitchen area tentatively and sat down beside him. We said nothing until he finally looked over at me and broke the silence.

"I had a run-in with your ex today," he said matter-of-factly.

It took me a few seconds to register before I responded, "Greg? Where?"

"At the pub. The Duke of Richmond, where the guys went after work."

I was flabbergasted. "Like, he was there, and you just bumped into him?"

He spread his fingers out in front of him. His right hand seemed a little red, even slightly swollen. Things started moving in slow motion from then on.

"No. It was weirder than that. He came into the washroom behind me when I was having a piss and getting ready to leave. It was like he followed me to the pub."

"Followed you to the pub?" My brain was flying off in different directions. "But how? Unless he just happened to be there, and you didn't see him when you walked in."

"I don't know, but I don't think so. I think he somehow figured out where I work." Dash stood up at this point and started walking around. I could see that he was still agitated.

"What happened?"

He hesitated again, taking a few steps toward the window in the living room and looking out before turning toward me. "He grabbed me, and I ended up throwing a couple of punches, bloodied his nose."

"Jesus Christ, Dash. What happened after?"

"Nothing. I just left and came straight home. I don't know what he did after that."

I got up and came over to him. I put my arms around him, and he quickly reciprocated. We held each other for a minute or so, not speaking. He caressed my hair and kissed me on the head before letting go. Then he asked the question I knew I needed to answer.

"Jesse, how the hell could you hook up with a guy like that?"

"That's the million-dollar question, isn't it?" I stepped away from him and sank down onto the couch. "I'd need to see a shrink to figure that one out."

Dash sat down beside me and simply waited. I had to try to explain.

"He wasn't like this in the beginning. We were attracted physically. He was funny, charming even. It wasn't until we became intimate that I started to see the cracks appear. His drinking became more apparent, his attitudes clearer."

"Why didn't you give him the boot then?"

"I should have. But a part of me, this is going to sound crazy, thought I could change him, reform him, turn him around. Maybe

I was testing my own moral ground, seeing how strong my own convictions were."

Dash grabbed onto my hands at that point. "Two things, Jesse. One, you're nothing like him; two, you'll never change a guy like that."

"I know. It was a mistake that never should have happened. My bad."

For a moment, I erased Greg from my mind and substituted Dash. The same scenario could be playing itself out with us. My initial attraction toward Dash had kept me interested in him more than most of my other clients; my hope to change his trajectory and his outlook on life more of a personal mission. This could just be another need I couldn't readily explain, a shortcoming in myself I needed to exorcise. No. Not true. Dash was changing…working hard at becoming whole. I knew and could feel this. I broke off these thoughts and misgivings abruptly and stood up.

"What is wrong with him?" I started pacing. "I never thought it would turn out this way. We've got to talk to the police. Fill them in. Register a complaint or something." I sounded desperate.

Dash stood up and stepped into my path. "I was thinking of that too, but I want to wait."

"Dash, why? This could get ugly. Christ, it already has."

"I know, but I was the guy who threw the punches, and nobody saw us. We were in the john by ourselves. I want to wait a day, see what happens. Maybe he's calling the cops about me. Turning his stalking of us on its head."

"But I can stick up for you. Tell the cops about my own history with Greg. He's been in my face twice in the last few days, too, remember?" I didn't want to let this go.

Dash put his arms out and held my shoulders gently. "Look, Jesse, let's have dinner, chat some more, give it some time, then we'll see. You got any ice?"

"Ice? Sure, in the freezer. For what?"

He held up his right hand. "I just want to wrap some cubes in a cloth and cool it down."

"God, Dash." I was still reeling from the conversation but pulled out a tea towel for him. The mood of the evening had come to a crashing halt, but it was Dash who was determined to bring it back.

"I notice you've got fish there. Looks great. I am starving." And he gave me his signature smile.

I focused on the food in front of me. "Absolutely." And I took a gulp of my wine. "You want a glass?"

He shook his head. "Not now. Maybe with supper. I'll see how I feel."

And with that, we began the process of satiating our appetites. We would see where the evening took us. Was retreating into art still a possibility, something to take the edge off? Dash came up beside me, his hand secured with the towel and ice.

"Anything I can do?"

"Yeah, give me another hug. Then set the table."

* * *

Coyote was hugging the fence line between houses and the park. He surveyed the sky. Darkness was settling in, and he was starting to breathe easier. He would let Crow drift northwards to shadow the other. His obligation remained with the two, and he preferred this. Both had arrived home at an interval of an hour or so apart. There was a tension obvious in the latter that had Coyote remain vigilant. Would they leave or stay in for the night? He hoped they would stay, his creaking bones only wanting to find a space to rest quietly and observe without the need to wander. His hunger was evident, and he might have to scavenge at some point. He would not attempt this until later when the city had slipped into sleep, and only nightcrawlers like him were abroad. A walker led by his pet, a surly looking mastiff, passed on the street not more than one hundred feet away. It sniffed the air as if aware of his presence, then lifted its leg against a tree and moved on. Something smaller, much smaller, was all he wanted. At that moment, he thought of wide-open spaces where he could run more freely. That dream would have to linger on the horizon. Patience was what was needed now and an eye to tomorrow.

* * *

Picture #12: *West Brooklyn Road*

Observer's description: In the foreground of the picture is an overpass, the name West Brooklyn Bridge clearly visible as signage on its railing. To the right of the sign, the outline of a figure in grey is waving down at the traffic below. The road comes curving up slightly on an angle, the landscape of trees, water and then the purple hue of hills in the distance a part of the ribbon it creates as it flows off into a cloudy sky. A tractor-trailer is cresting the incline and moving toward the viewer, who is almost under the overpass, taking in the scene as a passenger through a vehicle window. The large company name KING is emblazoned on the trailer. Does the man know who he is waving to? Or has he simply stopped to take in the view and gesture anonymously to those on their own journeys? How long has the truck been on the road? What is it carrying, and where is it heading? Is the driver alone in the cab, or is someone there for company or relief?

Chapter Thirteen

THE PAST

There had been nothing left for him there. Whatever bridges he had hoped to build over the years had burned and turned to ash like his mother. The money had come. Doing a smart thing, he had followed his lawyer's instructions and placed it in a bank account. It was safe and accessible from any branch or ATM he might run across. He had thrown his belongings into an oversized backpack—art kit, mother's urn, dreamcatcher, and a bit of clothing—and closed the door and walked away. Dash had no specific plans, only that he would head east and see what happened.

He had done one more thing before departing—the first gesture in a series he wanted to fulfill to ease his mind. The day of his leaving had been bright and clear, wisps of cloud dusting the sky to break up an otherwise blue canopy. *Fitting*, he thought, *perhaps even a good omen.* But his visage darkened, and his footsteps became heavy when he reached the marker. Likely the last time he would come to this cemetery. He had stood for an eternity, staring at the small stone before opening his backpack and taking out the urn. *Not all*, he had told himself. Enough to lay down a sprinkling, a powdery rain that would remain until the elements determined otherwise. She was a part of that realm now. As if to acknowledge this new reality, he noticed a crow that had settled on a gravestone two rows away. He fingered the lone feather that hung from his pack as he held the bird's gaze. Eventually, it lifted off with a cry to perch on the branch of a large oak shading a corner section of the cemetery. Returning the urn to his pack, Dash had stood a moment longer, then turned, meandering past other stones before exiting the grounds.

He had never learned to drive. His mother had encouraged it. Eric had supported her, even offered to teach him, but he had refused. Walking, biking, hitchhiking, and public transit were the four domains of movement that he accepted as all he needed. He had never flown like a bird either, travelling by plane being too costly. But one day, it was something he would like to do. He remembered in his younger days, the many trees he had climbed. The perspective of being twenty or thirty feet higher had impressed him at that age. He had gone one better and managed to get out on the rooftop of Manny's apartment complex with him several times, beers and joints in hand, to stare out over the city. Back then, his feeling had been one of freedom, the exhilaration that he was above the world and could do anything. He was free again now, but in a way, that was more paralyzing. He was on a crumbling ledge rather than a strong branch or solid rooftop. Fear of falling rather than soaring filled his being. He was a fledgling, leaving the nest on wings that could barely hold him up.

Dash left the city by bus on the Yellowhead Trail, which ultimately turned into Highway 16. He rode it in silence, rubbing elbows with an old man who smelled the part and whose hands were gnarled like the roots of an ancient tree. The old man sat ramrod straight, gazing ahead or occasionally out the window, his hands all the while secured like talons to his knees. Dash wondered what he was thinking and what history resided under the drying bark of his rigid trunk. As they passed through Elk Island National Park, Dash had stood up, made his way to the front of the bus, and asked the driver to let him off. This was not a regular stop, he had been told, but it didn't matter. He wanted off. He watched the bus disappear on the horizon until it was a speck.

He had stopped here because his mother's voice had told him to. They had come as family years earlier on their trek to

Edmonton, enjoyed a moment of respite where they had taken in the surroundings, the animals, whatever they could see in the short time they allowed themselves before moving on. His decision to disembark had been spontaneous, and now that he was here, he didn't know what to do. He decided to walk along the roadway at the park entrance until he reached the visitor's centre. The park was huge, with various lakes and trails tucked into its expanse. This was where driving could have had its advantages. He was like a returning ghost, a final punctuation mark on that experience. In a secluded spot, he had removed his mother's urn, sprinkled more of her by a trail at a forest's edge, taken a piss at the visitor's washroom, and walked back along the road to the highway. His entire layover had been about three hours, and he was now without transportation. Sticking out his thumb, he decided to give hitching a try, and after twenty minutes, a young couple picked him up. They had been talkative, and he had tried to be engaging, but his responses soon became monosyllabic and window gazing his past time. They took him as far as Lloydminster, where he decided to stay for the night. It turned into six months.

Like the town, which maintained a dual identity by straddling both Alberta and Saskatchewan, Dash invoked two personalities while in residence. He had worked a coin laundry at the motel where he stayed. His mundane job of mopping floors, cleaning the toilets, bagging garbage, and keeping an eye out for vandals was also split in two like the town, four hours between ten and two during the day, and four hours between ten and two at night. His job was to clean everything up twice a day. It was a good enough job because he was left alone, and the manager, noting his quiet, withdrawn personality, had offered it to him soon after his arrival on a week to week basis. His earnings covered the weekly rent and left him with a few dollars extra for food. Dipping into his bank account only occurred when he drank. This happened several times a week and was tied to his shifts. Self-control on his working days was key. He kept two offerings on hand in the small bar fridge in his room: beer and rye. If he decided to stay in his room for the afternoon and evening, he might have a couple of beers. If he decided to go for a walk through the streets, head to a small park in town, he would mix up a "traveller" of rye and Coke in the Coke bottle before beginning his wanderings. At night as he mopped and cleaned, he might also bring along a liquid sidekick. Only on his day off might he forget himself and drink more than he should. A happy enough drunk at these times, he might find himself waking up under a tree, on a park bench or, even once, face down in a ditch. He had always managed to get up, get his bearings, bumble back to his room, grab a shower, and draw minimal attention to himself. Dash would maintain his commitment to the job and the lifestyle for almost two months until a new friend arrived.

Willy was a couple of years his senior and a "Lloydminster lifer" he had joked. He had driven up in an old two-door army surplus jeep and hauled two bags of laundry out. Dash had eyed him closely as he mopped an area at the back in front of the washroom. Whistling as he dropped his bags, he looked around and waved Dash over almost immediately.

"First time in here. Usually go to the one further down on the other side of town. You got a coin machine somewhere?"

Dash had nodded and pointed to the wall behind the door.

"Thanks, pardner," and he had sauntered over. There was nothing hurried about his actions. Everything happened in slow motion. It was as if time didn't exist for him, or he had so much of it in reserve that he could dole it out slowly like a dealer at a poker table. Dash had been back at work for a while before he felt a presence behind him. Turning, he found the patron leaning up against an empty machine, his own loaded further down, plugging into conversation.

"What the hell have you gotten yourself into that life has come to this?" he quipped.

Dash was unsure how to take this until he noticed the smile and then knew he was kidding. He relaxed a little but was only able to shake his head and say, "Never planned to get a job. It just came up."

Willy had stood for a moment sizing him up and then asked, "You never planned to get a job, you not from around here?"

Dash stopped and leaned on the mop. "Nope. Was just passing through. One day turned into another. I got this, and here I am." He put the mop into a bucket and wheeled it to the side.

"Where'd you breeze in from?"

"West of here. Edmonton."

"You left Edmonton for this?" And at this point, he had reached into his pocket and pulled out a joint. Dash had looked around as if eyes had suddenly appeared from everywhere, but Willy had just sparked it up as if he were at home.

"You can't smoke in here," Dash had reminded him, pointing at the sign clearly visible on the wall at the entrance.

"Relax. Nobody in here but you and me. Have some." He held it out, an offering of friendship. Dash shrugged, and their relationship had begun.

Willy's life as he liked to refer to it, which had encompassed Lloydminster for the better part of seven years, involved little to no work and little to no ambition as far as Dash could make out. According to him, he had left a dysfunctional home and useless school to wander south and ended up here. There was a pause at this point as he took a long toke on the joint before passing it over to Dash. He had fallen in quickly with a posse of ne'er-do-wells as he called them, locals and drifters who had melded into a loosely constructed but amiable group, purveyors of drugs in a variety of forms to those with ready cash and the wisdom of discretion. They kept their operation small, dealt mainly in the safer elements of marijuana and hash, and relied on the local RCMP's spotty abilities to keep them in business. It was this establishment that Willy had coaxed Dash into within the week, severing his ties once and for all with the motel and his present life of soap suds and toilet bowls.

The few months spent tailing Willy in his world were funnelled through a haze of haphazardness. He lived in a roomy but dilapidated frame house with occupants who turnstiled in and out, casual acquaintances for the most part, who seemed to exist for the sole purpose of a party. They would show up with or without Willy, crank music, siphon dope and booze into their bodies, and pass out or move on. Dash came to realize that he was no more special as a friend to Willy than any of the others who had turned to him for release, escape, connection or meaning. He folded more and more into himself, heading out to parks or water in and around the border town. When lucidity and creativity had emerged, he had even taken out paper and pencil to sketch. Then he had drawn various loose landscapes, tried to capture the odd bird, crows mainly as they seemed to come to him, even wait as if posing, allowing him to capture as much of them as he could. Twice, across an open field, he had seen a coyote, perhaps the same one each time, he wasn't sure. Unhurried, it had stopped each time and looked in his direction before moving on. It was in one of these moments that his mother came to him again, pure and clean and true as he nodded under a tree in the emerging springtime of the community. Her words were simple, straightforward, and swirled up around him like the wind in the grasses.

"Go home, Dash. It's time to go home."

He cried then, deep sobs racking his chest, the recognition of his lonely, empty existence haunting his every breath. In time, he put his papers away, stood and walked back to the house. With a resolution he had not felt since his arrival, he grabbed the remainder of his things and left. He had gone only half a block when the familiar roar of Willy's jeep sounded in his ear and pulled up beside him.

"Hey, my man, where you headin'?"

Dash looked over at him. "Time to go. Had enough of this place." And he continued to walk.

Willy inched forward in his vehicle, keeping pace. "Hold on, hold on. Where are you goin' exactly…or do you even know?" He said this in a friendly enough tone. Dash had never felt threatened by Willy; he had never put pressure on him to do anything. Dash had helped with the distribution of dope here and there, but he had done so willingly and only when he wanted. He almost felt guilty now telling Willy he was leaving.

"I'm going back home."

"What, to Edmonton?"

"No, my first home. Where I grew up." He continued to walk.

"Here. Look. Stop for a minute, will you?" Dash complied, and Willy snailed over to the curb and parked.

"Where exactly is home?" he asked in earnest. When Dash mentioned the name, he was surprised at Willy's response.

"Throw your stuff in the back and get in." Dash had hesitated for a minute until Willy had followed up with, "It's only a couple of hours from here. I'll take you." And they had driven off midday to a place in time almost six years in the past.

* * *

The first indication that they were getting close to town was the two-grain elevators rising up to greet them. To Dash, it felt like he was looking at an old photograph or a watercolour painting on a wall. Everything was the same, familiar but faded. They drove down Main Street past storefronts and offices bearing the same names, past people looking and walking the same way. There was a slowness to each passing, to each movement, time itself harnessed to a wagon rutted in the mud. The eyes that followed them, flitting from vehicle to faces, pegged them as outsiders. It was a feeling Dash had felt through most of his life here, and it rose in his chest, bubbling there like hot water in a kettle.

"Anywhere you want to go?" Willy finally had broken the seal in their silence. Dash had pointed him along a couple of side streets on a loop that would take them back out to the edge of town. Some of the dirt side streets he noted had been paved, a small parkette at the town centre had been installed as a new aesthetic endeavour, and around nine or ten new houses had popped up along the road to their old home. This all came as a surprise. Dash recounted the population as they had entered the town. The census that was taken some time after their departure had seen fit to add another two hundred and eighty-three to the total. Growth was occurring. He certainly couldn't understand why.

A pickup suddenly appeared ahead of them. It had exited the reserve they had begun to approach, squealed tires onto the main road, and shot on toward the town centre.

Dash made a quick call and barked, "Turn in to the reserve!" Willy obliged by laying on the brakes, chirping to a crawl, and easing onto the dirt track that passed for the road in.

"You believe in givin' a guy a warning," he chuckled as they bounced along over a rise and onwards. The reserve, a small collection of fifty to sixty homes, stretched out in a large square of four streets about half a kilometre ahead. Kids could be seen on one or two of them, playing in the dirt and gravel. Laundry bucked and lurched in the stiff breeze that blew them dry. As they drew closer, a few dogs came loping along toward them, yapping at their arrival.

"You wantin' to stop somewhere in here," Willy asked. "Have a word with somebody you know?"

"No. Don't stop." Dash began to feel self-conscious. "Just drive down to the end of this street, turn up the next one, and we'll get out of here." He didn't know what he expected when he had Willy turn in. They passed a large field at the end of the street that housed a ball diamond. Beyond this and ringing the reserve was a grove of trees. He had been out this way with Digger a few times when he and his dog had been wandering. It looked different from this angle somehow.

As they headed back up the adjoining street, adults began to appear, coming outside or from behind a shed or garage. One held a wrench he had been working with, the hood of a pickup raised to invite his tinkering; another held fishing line that he was curling onto a spool. Two women simply brushed back their hair from front doors where they stood with their arms crossed. The houses were predominantly small wood-frame bungalows, much like what he and his mother had lived in closer to town. Some were in better shape than others. They all looked tired, though, Dash noted, in need of some paint and general reparation.

"You come in much when you lived here?" Willy was moving his jeep along at a slow pace but sensed that his friend wanted to speed up a little.

"My mom had a couple of friends she used to visit occasionally," Dash responded. "They would meet at their homes or over there at the community hall." A two-storey building appeared on their right as Willy drove by. It had a couple of gas pumps out front and a general store on the ground floor. The community hall was upstairs, a large space where people gathered for whatever events happened to take place in the small community.

"It's not much of a place, is it?" Willy commented as he drove back out and over the rise.

Dash felt himself flush, his face becoming heated. He never said anything but thought he should have. His guilt at this failure was broken when they turned out and back onto the main road.

"So, where's this house of yours?" Willy blurted as he geared down at the bend.

"Around this corner and on the right."

A couple of hundred metres on, the laneway appeared, leading up and toward the bungalow. At a quick glance, it looked the same. Willy slowed and made to turn up the lane.

"Maybe we shouldn't go in," Dash said.

"Why not? You'd like a closer look, right?" He moved up the lane as he spoke.

"Yeah, but we're trespassing."

Willy scoured ahead of him. "Don't see a car or truck around. Could be nobody's home. Besides, if anybody comes out, we'll just say we're lost and head out."

By the time he had finished talking, they were in front of the house. Not much had changed. A new coat of paint had been slapped on, he noticed, and the old shed out back had been torn down. A large swing set and slide stood in its place. A sandbox littered with a plastic shovel, a pail, and some cheap toys awaited occupants. The one disappointment he observed was that the doghouse was also gone. No Digger flying off into the fields that still surrounded the place. No Digger barking up a storm at someone's arrival. No Digger to piss off or please his mom.

"Let's go," Dash announced.

No one had come out to confront them in their short time there, but there was nothing else he wanted to see. Willy wheeled the jeep around, and they headed off, the bungalow disappearing in the rearview mirror. For an instant, Dash imagined he saw his mother waving to him from the front door. It was then that he asked Willy to stop. Reaching for his bag, he pulled out the urn. Taking a small amount of ash, he walked a few steps back up the lane and sowed it into the mixture of dirt and protruding grasses at the edge.

It was now mid-afternoon. He did not want to stay in town and so asked Willy to take him to the highway, where he planned to hitch again.

"Are you sure about this?" Willy had asked as he dropped him off.

Dash nodded. "Yeah, I'll be fine." Willy was the closest person to a friend that he had had since Manny, but he needed to move on. He still wanted to leave, to get farther away from the old and into something new.

"All right, pardner, you know best," and they left it at that. Dash watched him drive away, knowing he would never see him again. He turned and waited for luck to arrive. So far, he figured he had spent over two thousand dollars of his savings and inheritance over the months since he had left with nothing to show for it but countless parties, some random sexual encounters, and occasional nervous brushes with the law. He always vowed, when he rose out of the murky depths, that he would do better. His mother would not be proud of him so far. The electrical van that stopped, picked him up, and drove him until dusk into Regina might lead to his next chance at redemption.

* * *

Training, that's what he needed. This was the advice given to him by middle-aged Hank, who had picked him up. Hank had been away on a job for two weeks, wiring rooms in a new motel just being finished in a town west of here. When Dash had told him that he had done some painting in Edmonton where he was from, Hank had launched into the advantages of having a trade. "There's plenty of work out there," and he had gestured expansively with his left arm as if it was growing on trees, waiting to be plucked like a piece of fruit, "if you get the training." Dash had nodded dutifully and let the topic run its course and drift off toward sunset.

"Tell you what," Hank had said as he pulled into a service station on the outskirts of the city for gas, "take this card of mine. There are a couple of jobs painting that I can probably set you up with if you want. What are your plans?"

Dash just shrugged at this and said, "Nothing particular."

"Where you staying?"

"Nowhere at the moment."

"You got money?"

Dash nodded, "Enough."

With that, Hank drove on until he came to a city bus stop. "You know the city at all?"

"Never been here before," Dash admitted.

He saw Hank hesitate, give a big sigh, and look at his hands. Dash spoke first.

"Look, man, I'll be fine. Thanks for the lift." And he opened the door before Hank could respond.

"Give me a shout if you want some work," he managed to call out as the door closed. Dash waved, walked over to the bus stop, and watched Hank disappear. The drive had taken just over three hours. He was hungry. He would grab a bite to eat, find a place for the night somewhere, and decide on his future here after that.

* * *

Dash had stayed just one night, but not where he planned. In those few hours, he realized he did not like where he was and he would not call Hank. That evening, the city bus had taken him along Albert Street, a major thoroughfare into the heart of Regina. He had opted to disembark around Dewdney and grab a bite to eat in a small diner where the food was cheap and filled his stomach. It was getting dark and cooling down, and he had wanted to get inside for the night. And so, he had walked, not sure what he was even looking for, hotel, rooming house, until a cop car had torn up beside him and stopped.

"Where you going?" an older white cop barked from the window of the passenger seat.

Dash had looked around momentarily, then bent down to remark, "Just walking around." He realized later that he should have been more specific.

The older cop had looked at his younger partner in the driver's seat and chuckled, "Just walkin' around. You been drinking?"

"No."

"You live around here?"

"No." Another mistake.

"No," the cop had mimicked. "Well, where are you from?"

Dash had shuffled his feet a little. "Came in from Edmonton earlier."

"Came in from Edmonton. How?"

"Started out by bus and then hitchhiked. I'm just lookin' for a place to stay."

The cop acted like he hadn't heard what had been said. Instead, he opened the car door, eased himself out and said, "What you got in the bag?"

"Just personal stuff, clothes and stuff." Dash guessed he had looked nervous or something at that point because the cop had motioned for him to open it.

"What's this, then?" the cop had asked, opening and poring over his art kit. He turned and smiled at his partner, who was now also out of the car and standing close by. "You an artist?"

"Not really. I just like to..."

"That really yours," the young cop interjected, "or you lift it from somebody?"

"No, it's mine." The young cop had just smirked.

"And this?" The older cop had pulled out his mother's urn.

In a moment of growing frustration, Dash had blurted, "Gimme that," and reached out to grab it. Immediately, the young cop had put his hand on his hip and unclipped his gun.

"Settle down, chief," the old cop blurted and held out his hand. "What...is...this?"

"My mother's ashes."

He opened the container and looked inside. "Yep, they're ashes, all right. Can't rightly say whose, though, can we?" and he laughed. "And you've been carting these around with you, have you?" He put the stuff back in the bag, opened the back door of the cruiser, and threw it inside.

"Get in."

"Get in?" Dash was dumbfounded. "But I haven't done anything."

"That's for us to figure out, isn't it? Lot of crime around this part of town, and guys like you seem to always fit the bill."

"What do you mean, guys like me?"

"Why, Indians, son. Seem to crop up a lot of the time when there's a problem. Drinking, fighting, crime. Now, get in."

"Where are we going? I want to know."

"You wanted a place to stay? Well, we're givin' you one. Now, get the fuck in."

When the door closed on Dash, he felt a feeling of suffocation course through him. There was nothing rational about any of this. He had been randomly picked up because of who he was. He reached out for his bag and drew it closer. He tried to block out the dread, the uncertainty inside him. Hooves pounded across his head and down along the ridges of his shoulders. He looked out the window at the unfamiliar buildings and streets pass and waited for the ride to end.

After another hour of vague questioning at the precinct, he had been thrown into a small cell. He had been asked if he had anyone he could contact. Hank came to mind, but he decided no. Around ten, a burger, fries, and a drink had been delivered, and he had attacked the food ravenously. When a cop came in to remove the tray, Dash had asked how long he was going to have to stay.

"Don't know for sure. Overnight, I expect, so you may as well get comfortable."

"Overnight? Man, I haven't done anything."

"Your ID says you're not from around here. Checking up on you could take a while."

Throughout the night, Dash slept fitfully, walled in like an animal. The noises around him of doors slamming and voices yelling woke him periodically and served to remind him of where he was. His past had been expunged. There was nothing he was running away from except himself.

In the morning, he was released. No apology. No explanation. Just a warning to stay clean. Even in a city this size, he felt he was now marked and known, that no good could come of him staying. He found out where the bus terminal was, dropped a chunk of money on a ticket, and sunk into a seat for the seven-hour trip to Winnipeg. His bank account was dwindling. He wanted out of Saskatchewan, past Manitoba, and into Ontario. Then maybe he would be far enough away to start over, to find a place where he felt he fit in.

Two hours into the trip, Dash noticed a coyote loping across a stubbled field. What was he tracking in the openness? Gophers, mice, a carcass pushing its remnants up out of the earthen fridge that had kept it frozen through winter? He craned his neck backwards to follow it until it was gone from sight. He thought of his dog for a moment, and in doing so, instinctively pulled his backpack off the seat beside him. He had been lucky that not every seat was filled. Not everybody was leaving like him, and he had luxuriated in the space. Placing a sheet of paper on his kit for stability, he had doodled in a corner, unsure of what to draw. When he finally began in earnest, he pulled from memory the wildness he had passed—a field; an animal, panting and padding across it, alone and living in the moment; a crow or two etched in the sky as observers. Afterwards, he had dozed, head resting against the warmth of the window, and dreamed of running and flying, his body furry and feathered and floating away.

* * *

Dash reflected on the city as he disembarked. Motoring along Portage La Prairie, he had been given an indication of Winnipeg's size. It was big enough, but he had been warned by Willy who knew people from there that the train tracks that coursed through its heart, opening and closing in places like the zipper on a jacket, had two sides. "And you," he had said, "will end up on the wrong side." With that life lesson echoing in his head, Dash had gone in search of a ticket seller and a question about the route to Kenora, Ontario. After a scrutinizing look, the teller had sold him a ticket for a journey that wouldn't depart for another six hours, a 10:35p.m. exodus that would get him there around 2:00 a.m. He scanned a large map erected on the station wall that he assumed was for travellers like himself who needed direction. Still, when he left for a walk, he had no destination in mind. Two hours later, after meandering north where the Red River and Coronation Park could be sighted, he found himself on Marion Street. He didn't want to go too far anymore before returning. His feet were getting tired. Just then, a Liquor Mart appeared, and he quickly made a decision. Entering, he bought a mickey of rye, shoved it in his backpack, and left. At a convenience store he had passed, he purchased two large bottles of Coke, some chips, and a suspect meat sub. Returning to the depot, he headed for the washroom, emptied out half the Cokes and filled them with his new elixir, discarded the empty mickey, and went out to sit. He had about an hour and a half left to kill. Dash passed the time eating, drinking, and skimming magazines and brochures he found lying around. He knew how to be stoic, to relax into time, to wait, observe, blend into his surroundings. He hit the can again before his scheduled bus departure, saving the second bottle for the journey. His time in Winnipeg had been scant and disappeared uneventfully within minutes out his side window.

Dash crossed into Ontario in the early morning dark, an immigrant bent on a new life. He entered as a shadow needing definition, a feather plucked. Consuming the last few drops of his drink, he would bookend another few hours inside the small terminal waiting for sunrise. Then, he would determine his next course of action. He slept fitfully on a chair, drifting in and out of murky images that he couldn't hold onto, wispy clouds that dissolved quickly. When the light began to appear through the windows, he roused himself and made off in search of food. A diner offering the staples of breakfast and coffee popped into view, and he entered. Bacon, eggs, home fries, toast, and coffee helped settle him, put him into the right frame of mind to explore. Dash still had no purpose, no idea what his next steps would be or where they would take him. As if to prove this, his feet carried him out the door, along Park Street and into a green space wielding the same name. He noted either lack of imagination or laziness on the town's part in their naming protocol and hoped he hadn't made a mistake in leaving Winnipeg behind. *Too late now,* he thought as he entered Kenora's Park with a shake of his head. Here, he hoped to get his bearings and focus on a strategy. As he stood to survey the scenery around him, a figure approached, casual, nonchalant, unhurried.

"Hey, man, you got a smoke?" Dash took in the figure in front of him. He was about his height, a little scrawnier, dark, unkempt shoulder-length hair, and a three-day growth, which he scratched briefly after his greeting. Jeans, running shoes, and a brown bomber jacket completed his ensemble. Likely his age too, but he couldn't be sure.

"Don't smoke," was all Dash offered.

"Shit. Been dying for a smoke all morning, but that's OK, man."

Dash thought the guy would move on after this exchange, look for another figure that might have what he wanted, but he didn't budge.

"You from around here, man?" He stuffed his hands in his pockets at this point and swayed back and forth on his feet, a metronome guiding an invisible pianist.

"No, just got here a few hours ago."

"Yeah? Where from, man?"

Dash wasn't sure he wanted to divulge too much, but couldn't see the harm in generalizing, so he settled on "the West."

"Oh, yeah, that's good. I've been out West myself a few times. Nice part of the country."

Dash knew that he shouldn't ask because he wanted to get free of this guy, but he did anyway. "How far did you go?"

"Kenora." Dash looked at him like he was from Mars. Then the guy burst out laughing.

"Kidding, man. Just kidding," and he stuck out his hand. "Name's Dunstan."

Dunstan. What kind of a name was that? Dash thought, but he reciprocated.

"Dash."

"Cool name, man. You a runner?" And then he laughed again. Dash felt his defences drop a little as he smiled.

"What are you doin' here? Visitin' someone?"

"Don't know anyone here. Thought I might stay for a bit, look for some work."

"Work!" The word shot out at Dash like a bullet so fast that he almost ducked to avoid being hit by it. "Really."

"Yeah. Anything wrong with that?"

"Not at all, man." And then Dunstan's speech pattern began to miraculously evolve. "I too, have found an occasion to work now and then. Never liked it much, I must say." And he laughed in such a way at this honest assessment of his own character that Dash couldn't help but smile again. He went on. "You see, Dash, I consider myself a dabbler, a man of many talents. I have not, historically, been able to settle upon merely one form of work and so, over the last two years, since a brief and unsuccessful tenure at Confederation College, I have been a man of leisure, odd jobbing it here and there until I could pad my resume into one that allows me to pocket pogey in the winter months in this fair town."

"What?" Dash had never heard any friend or acquaintance that he could remember, not Manny, Willy, Eric, his mother, who talked like this guy. He was quickly being forced to reassess Dunstan in terms of his recent oratorical outburst as not just some street person who had stumbled toward him for a smoke some ten minutes ago.

"Let me rephrase, my perplexed and confused looking friend." Here, he stopped for a few seconds while he fished a cigarette pack out of his pocket and lit one up.

Dash gave him a hard look. "Thought you didn't have any smokes?"

"Just an icebreaker. Wanted to see what you were like, you know, gauge your reaction to me."

"You always walk up to strangers like that?"

"Not always, only those I judge to be of sound character," and he smiled. Dash said nothing to this, and so Dunstan continued.

"And so, back to my original point. I am currently unemployed, but," and here he looked at his wrist where he pretended to scrutinize a non-existent watch, "I will soon have employment once more should I choose to pursue it."

"What do you mean by should you choose to pursue it?"

"Well, therein lies my tale," and he took a long draw on his cigarette before expelling the smoke skyward, "for this was not supposed to be my final destination. Like you, I am a traveller, a transient bent on going elsewhere should the shoe fit or the mood strike."

Dash was about to ask his new and strange acquaintance to get to the point, one he felt had somehow been lost or misdirected a few sentences ago when, after a final drag, Dunstan flicked his cigarette away and began a short history of his last few years. It seems his parents were both university educated and had instilled in him an expectation to continue in that vein. Halifax was his home, a beautiful enough city that offered water and scenery in abundance and so, not having any particular post-secondary plans, he had followed his parents' advice and entered Dalhousie University for a three-year general arts program, something so vague and uninspiring that he had left after the first semester. Frittering away the next few months, working for the city in the Parks and Recreation Department, he had managed to save up enough money by summer's end to bid goodbye to mom and dad. They reluctantly gave their blessing on what was to be a short excursion westward to Vancouver to find himself before deciding on his future—a future his parents insisted should still be a degree of some kind. Like a voyageur intent on searching out new territory, he had ventured westward, stopping for short bursts in Montreal, Ottawa, and Toronto, enjoying the various experiences these different cities had to offer before wending northward until he had hit Kenora.

"That was two years ago now." He stopped his reminiscing long enough to spark another smoke.

"Two years," Dash interjected. He looked around at what he had seen of the town so far. "Why are you still here? I thought Vancouver was where you were headed?"

"Four words, my friend," and he flicked ash into the air, "Lake of the Woods."

"Lake of the Woods?" Dash was once more baffled and bemused. Listening to Dunstan was like grappling with a large walleye reluctant to be landed. You thrashed around with him hoping to understand where he was going.

"Turns out," Dunstan elaborated, "that Kenora is surrounded by a beautiful network of rivers, forests, and lakes. Once I investigated a little, it started to feel more like home. If you love the outdoors, you can get out of the town, which is not that spectacular for sure, and relish in the openness and freedom of nature, something I didn't realize I truly missed."

"So, what about Vancouver?"

"Oh, I'll get there. Don't you worry. I'm just not sure when." Dunstan paused to enjoy his cigarette.

"And this job that you say you can get if you decide you want it?" Dash remembered what initially had gotten them on this turning wheel, and he wanted an answer to that particular spoke in the conversation before Dunstan rode off on some other tangent.

"I have continued in my seasonal endeavours working for Parks and Recreation," Dunstan confided.

Dash encouraged him to continue. "And what does that mean…exactly?"

"The job involves springtime cleanup of the brush in and around camping areas, clearing of roadways, then the maintenance of campsites and grounds through the season when the hordes arrive—all in all, not a bad job except for some of the yahoos who pass through thinking that the park is party central and, therefore, their own personal dump.

"Well, good luck. Sounds like you've got a plan for the next while, at least," and Dash made to walk off.

"Hang on. Don't dash off," and he laughed. "Where are you going?"

Dash shrugged. "Not sure. Unlike you, I don't have a plan."

Dunstan crushed his recent smoke into the ground. "Then come with me."

"What do you mean?"

"Just what I said, man. I can get you a job if you want. At least for the spring and summer. Doing what I do, you know? Working campsites, doing housekeeping if we end up at a camp with cabins and such; any number of things that would get you some cash."

"I don't know. Where do we stay?"

"We stay where we work, which could be in any part of the large expanse of woodland and lake areas around. But I also rent a house in town a few blocks north of here over the tracks. It's my place in the off-season when I want to come back for a bit of unwinding in a different way.

"Over the tracks." Dash was reminded of Willy's Winnipeg comment, but this was Kenora. How bad could it be? "OK. I'll check it out with you and give it a shot."

Dash followed his new friend up 7th Avenue until they reached Railway Street, practically named again, he thought, as it paralleled a band of several tracks going east/west. Here, 7th Avenue narrowed and burrowed under Railway Street and the tracks, emerging on the other side. The landscape of the streets had changed during their short subterranean journey and took on a more worn and working-class feel.

As if to interpret Dash's thoughts, Dunstan initiated him into his community. "Lots of Ukrainians in this area, my friend. Good people, hard-working. There's a Ukrainian church, of course, a school, even a literary society. But there are lots of other cultures as well. I kind of like the vibe the area gives off." With that, they had turned onto 4th Street and a few houses down came to Dunstan's home.

"Welcome to my humble abode," he said. Dash was pleasantly surprised. It was a two-storey frame house. A few steps up, and you were onto an expansive front porch with four chairs positioned randomly on it. Prying open a screen door, Dunstan had pushed open the front door, which was ajar, and walked in.

"Not too worried about security?" Dash queried.

"Not at all. What's yours is mine." And then he had laughed. "I mean, look around. What's to steal? A few sticks of furniture, maybe my CDs, player, and small speakers over there," and he had pointed to a corner of the room occupying those assets. "Of course, nobody wants my books." Dash was amazed at a bookshelf lining another wall that must have held several hundred paperbacks. "What can I say? I like to read, but not too many of my acquaintances do."

Dunstan had then given him a quick tour of the kitchen and another smaller adjoining room, which had a table and chairs and served as the dining area. Down a short hallway was a door to a small downstairs bathroom. A door at the back opened onto a small backyard. Dash noticed a fire pit in the ground, some lawn chairs balanced precariously around it, and a small aluminum shed. "Don't use this much unless there is a party in the offing." He led Dash upstairs, where there were two bedrooms and another small bathroom, but this one with a shower.

"Thus endeth the tour. Home sweet home," Dunstan joked. "Like I said, I'm mainly here during the off-months, the months when winter keeps me hunkered down here more. It can get a bit crazy at times when people know I'm around, though. Always dropping in to share some weed or to drink." Dash had been offered a bedroom, a space of his own. He threw his backpack onto the bed, and life there had fallen in behind.

* * *

It had been some of the best of times and some of the worst of times. Dash paraphrased in his mind this line from a book that Dunstan had quoted once. He had to admit his new friend was well-read. He had thumbed several of Dunstan's collection, even managed to complete a couple that Dunstan thought he might like because they were shorter yet descriptive and captivating, *Treasure Island* was one, *For Those Who Hunt the Wounded Down*, the other. Both novels had embodied struggle, colourful characters, and a healthy mixture of hope and despair. Most of all, though, Dash preferred to absorb quick overviews of books with Dunstan as the storyteller when they were deep into the effects of a couple of joints.

Work had begun about a week later. His friend had been right. The job had been tolerable, the scenery incredible, and, even more so, his education expanding. The Lake of the Woods area, as Dunstan pointed out, had several Indigenous reserves dotting it. Some of their workmates had been Indigenous, and he had been introduced briefly into a world he had never really known. Dunstan knew several of them as friends, and in the off-hours, whether at camp or back in town, they would interact together. Dash found he was opening up in ways he had never done before, questioning, trying to retrieve something of his own past through the stories he heard that could connect him to the emptiness he had always felt about who he was.

Dunstan, this white male who had singled him out as a possible friend, had never broached his identity with him. It didn't seem to matter. But others had. Some understood, when they talked, what it was like to not know much about heritage. In particular, Kenny, an older Cree in his late twenties who worked in a small lumber mill outside of town and who had met Dunstan much like Dash had on the streets of Kenora, was sympathetic. He and two of his siblings had been taken at different times and adopted into different families, their connections to each other erased and with it, any form of cultural identity. Kenny had sought answers over the years and pulled up a handful of seeds that he hoped would grow into something more substantive. As yet, he told Dash, he was still a nomad of sorts, wondering and wandering. Others Dash had met from reserves when their paths had crossed insisted he continue to search. These had been women like Sharon and Eileen, with stories much more tied to the earth, their pasts something they insisted needed to be woven into tapestries that they could wear with pride. They were strong, fun-loving individuals who instructed Dash in ways that reminded him of his mother. If only she had been able to have these kinds of conversations with him. What a difference that could have made for them both.

These moments, a nurturing of the soul that made Dash think he might never leave, were always tempered by other forms of interaction. The white-hot heat of insults flung from cars as occupants drove past, the disparaging jokes of campers after too many beers, the random trajectory of an empty can or stick or stone barely missing its mark, all reminded Dash of the other side of reality, of what it was like to be seen as nothing more than a face that needed a foot on it. This image he had remembered from another of Dunstan's books, one he had skimmed with interest. He had been caught leafing through it, and his friend had said, "Good book. Pretty dark that Orwell guy, but insightful. Imagine a boot stomping on your face, forever; one of the great lines in there. Enjoy." But Dash never had. It was not an easy book to get into, he had found, so he had put it down. It was enough for him to know that he would always have the image of life that the author described, boots hovering above him from hateful pockets of society bent on crushing his spirit. This, in turn, made him angry. At August's end, despite the friendships he had attained, he decided he should move on and race the coming colder weather toward Toronto.

"I want you to have this," he said to Dunstan. They were sitting out on the front step on a Sunday evening recovering from the effects of a weekend party. Dash had not announced any official goodbyes but was not returning to work. He had been squared for his efforts to date, the last cheque in his wallet ready to be cashed. He had broken even over the last months here, another good sign, he felt. Dash held out his offering to his friend.

"I can't take that," and instead pulled out a smoke as a diversion. Dunstan knew what it was. "I appreciate it, but I can't."

The urn was placed at his feet nonetheless. "I've decided to move on, Dunce." He had coined this nickname after their meeting, the implication humorously evident, but the opposite of what Dash truly believed. "Not going back to work with you tomorrow."

There was no attempt at dissuasion, no evident surprise. Dunstan took a long drag, blew the smoke upwards and simply asked, "Where to?"

"I've always wanted to see Toronto. Check out a big city."

"The Big Smoke, eh?" And another cloud wafted into the atmosphere.

"Yeah, I guess."

"Here's a tidbit for you." Dash readied himself. When Dunce started off with this phrase, it meant you were in for a lecture. It might be thirty seconds or thirty minutes. You had no way of knowing. In the end, though, it was generally educational. "Toronto has had many monikers: Hogtown, Muddy York, Toronto the Good, and, of course, The Big Smoke." Here, he paused to take another haul on his cigarette. "But Sudbury and Hamilton have also been called The Big Smoke because of INCO and Stelco and the great chimneys that fill their skies and spew their toxins. Vancouver has also been given that title because of the persistent fog that marks their terrain. It was a writer for *MacLean's* magazine, I believe, who coined the Big Smoke allusion for Toronto. He wanted to use it as a reference for a city that was large and full of potential, but which couldn't live up to the hype."

Dash didn't know how to respond, so he simply acknowledged that, once again, Dunstan had outdone himself with his trivia-based insights. "I still want, no, need to get there," he confided.

"Not what it's cracked up to be, you know, Dash. But then, maybe Vancouver isn't either." He left his convincing at that.

"Yeah, I hear you; still for me, it's time to go."

Dunstan looked over at his friend, then flicked his butt onto the street. "Understood." He got up to stretch. Afterwards, he bent and picked up the small box. "Like I said, though, I can't take this. You should have it." He pushed the urn gently into Dash's stomach. Dash lifted his hands but thrust them firmly into his pockets.

"My turn for a story, so hear me out." He stepped down onto the street and looked back up at his friend. He smiled. "I've been leaving pieces of my mother at different places since I left Edmonton. There's some of her in the cemetery there, some in a park we visited years ago, some at our old home, and now the last evidence of her scattered throughout Lake of the Woods." He paused and looked down at his feet to let the reality of this sink in. "That box was just a container. She is where she would want to be, out there, sprinkled into the earth and in here," and he pointed to his head and heart. "Put that on your shelf with your books, fill it with something else. I've got everything I need from her rattling around inside me."

Dunstan turned the urn over in his hand, weighing its importance. "Well, since you put it that way, I accept." He came down and embraced his friend. "Best gift I ever got. Now, come inside. We need to have a joint and decide where this can best be displayed."

* * *

Dash hopscotched from Kenora to Thunder Bay by bus in a series of stopovers and moves that took him almost twelve hours. He took in the sights of forest and road along the way and transferred impressions from time to time onto his notepad, pencilled incisions of greys and greens cutting into the pages. On one, Dunstan appeared perched on a rock beneath a tree, cone on his head marked with symbols, a wand in one hand and a cigarette in the other. They had promised to stay in touch even as the distance between them widened with each turn of the wheel. Maybe he would take a picture of it on his cell phone and send it to him. Maybe.

Thunder Bay appeared in the distance at night, a spewing of lights held in check by the landscape around it. Lake Superior was here but remained hidden, its waters churning in the depths and lapping eagerly at its lengthy shoreline. Dash would see it at daylight as he moved on. With Toronto in mind as a goal, he had opted to save money and stick out his thumb again. After a long wait on Highway 17, an 18-wheeler shuddered to a stop and offered him a ride. When he opened the cab door and climbed aboard, he was greeted by a woman.

Darlene was not who he had expected. Her dirty, long brown hair was pulled back from a weathered face into a ponytail. Long and lithe, she worked the controls around her cockpit in a comfortable, confident way that suggested years in the seat. She shifted them slowly and effortlessly back onto the road before she turned to him and offered her first words.

"You can throw that pack of yours in the back if you like." Dash glanced behind and quickly gathered in a small bar fridge, neatly organized bunk, a small TV, and a few magazines and books on a shelf." He dropped his contents onto the cab's floor behind them. The seats were leathery and plush, a necessity he eventually understood as they were propelled along. He looked out and down from a height that he imagined birds might enjoy.

"Where you headed, young man?" Her words were lilting and kind. He looked over at a pair of twinkling eyes, their gaze only on him for an instant before turning back to the road. He quickly felt his tension release, and he leaned back into the embrace of the seat.

"Hoping to get to Toronto."

"Still a long trek. I can get you to White River before I stop for a bit. Been driving for too many hours to push much longer. Need a break." She reached for a pack of cigarettes and offered Dash one. He declined. She threw the pack down on the console between them and cracked the window before lighting up.

"Smart not to smoke," she said. "Tried to give them up two or three times, but they're a part of me now, just like this rig." She began to talk then, recounting her life to Dash as if he were an old friend or an intimate relation. He did not need to interject or to query, only listen. Maybe, it was what she needed, the ears of another simply within range of her voice acknowledging and storing the information she was passing on. He wondered how many others on her journeys had been picked up and regaled with her stories, her short wave going out on the air to anonymous travellers. Darlene was a mother of two, a boy and a girl, grown up and away, one in Montreal, the other in Kamloops. She would see them a couple of times a year, if lucky, at Christmas or a road stop drop-in. Otherwise, it was a phone call or a text exchange. They each had different fathers. Neither one was in the picture. She regretted this. One trucked like she did, the other was dead for all she knew or cared, a good-for-nothing who drank too much and talked with the back of his hand once too often for her, so she left with her son in tow. But they were good kids, pulling their own in life, working, both happy and in relationships, thirty-somethings with dogs for children.

When Dash finally had a chance to talk, he asked how long she had been driving. She laughed and said, "Longer than I care to remember, but if you want a number, fifteen years." She said she got the "bug" when she went on a couple of road trips with her second partner. She took her own training when her kids were teenagers and could fend for themselves and stay on their own more. She loved being out and driving, but it cost her a second relationship and the intimacy of a home life.

The miles clicked by for them both. Sometimes there was silence. Only the crackle of her CB or the hum of the engine would interfere with the scenery around them. Two hours in, Darlene elevated the tension for Dash, an electrical shock that caught him momentarily off guard.

"You Indian by any chance?" She had pushed the word out of her with ease like the way she blew smoke from her lungs. It drifted up into the cab and around Dash, who momentarily turned away to avoid the sting. His silence initiated a response that brought him back to her. "Stupid. I didn't mean any disrespect. It's just that I hear the word so often on my runs that I forget. I meant Native, or I guess even Indigenous would be better."

"Good guess." He smiled weakly. "I'm Metis, but I can't give you much history. My mom didn't know too much herself."

"So, where is she now, your mom?"

"She died a little while back. Car accident."

"Sorry to hear that," and she reached for another cigarette.

"That's OK."

"What was she like, if you don't mind me asking?"

"Beautiful. She had her moments when she could be like a storm raging around you, but more often, she would open up into bright sunlight. You'd bathe in a warm glow that made you feel safe and whole."

"Sounds like quite the lady."

"She was. I wish we'd had more time together."

"Time is a thing you can't hold onto. It disappears before you know it."

"Sometimes, I wish I knew more about myself." Dash looked over at Darlene. "It might help me understand where I fit in."

Another cigarette sparked to life. Dash could tell that Darlene was going to make another pronouncement, a philosophical insight of some kind. Surprising for a truck driver, but again, maybe that was his prejudice surfacing. But first, she asked his name. When told and she had laughed at the uniqueness of it, she carried on.

"I'm not saying we share a similar background, Dash, and I don't presume to know anything about your pain. I know it's real. I'm sure it is because I've seen it on so many faces like yours over the years." She took in a long pull of smoke, the ember of her cigarette retracting quickly like a fire scorching earth. The release enveloped her face for an instant before the ghostly wraith was sucked into the unseen air beyond the cracked window. "I have an Irish background, so I've been told. My parents led me to believe this, but I never checked any of their stories or history out."

"Why not?"

"Didn't seem important, too much bother, I didn't have the time. Excuses, that's all it was. I sometimes wish I had. The thing is the closest I've gotten to my heritage over the years are the fries I eat when I stop for lunch or dinner." She laughed and then launched into a brief coughing fit. "Really got to quit talking and smoking at the same time. Can't do it." Frustrated, she lowered the window and pitched her unfinished cigarette. "Here's what I do know about the Irish, so take it for what it's worth. They had their troubles. They were displaced, driven off their land, forced to migrate, were stereotyped as drunks, useless, no good, untrustworthy, lazy." She looked over at Dash. "Ring any bells? It can be hate that drives people to do what they do to your people, to anyone they think is different, inferior, impure, but it's also ignorance and fear." Here, she stopped as she reached for another cigarette. "And, of course, above all, people like that are assholes, pure and simple."

Dash turned Darlene's words over and over in his mind. He thought of Billy, his childhood tormentor, and wondered what he would do or say if he met him again. Could time have changed his outlook? Not likely, he reasoned. There was too much asshole in his bones.

He put his head back and slipped into sleep and dream. His mother resurrected. She was sitting in the front passenger seat of a car, Dash in the back. The open window was blowing her hair back, and she was laughing, talking a blue streak and pointing out the sights and sounds around her. Finally, she turned her head to him and whispered, "We're here," and he rose upright to take a closer look.

"We're here." It was Darlene who spoke these words now. "Didn't want to interrupt your nap."

"What?" Dash straightened and looked around.

"You've been under for the last thirty minutes or so. Thought you could use a break from my chattering. This is White River."

"Not much of a place," he noted.

"Only to those who live here, I guess. Originally, it was set up as a rail town in the 1880s. Mainly logging took place here. There wasn't even car access connecting up the Trans-Canada Highway until the 1960s. Pretty isolated like a lot of the small northern towns. But if you like wild, natural beauty all around you, rivers and lakes and forest, then you've come to the right place."

"Yeah, I came from a small town myself. Larger than this. It had its good points, like when I could ride off on my own to the bush or the lake. But you have to fit in, and we never really did. So, we left," and here, he glanced over at Darlene, "for bigger and better things."

"Bigger and better can be good," Darlene agreed as she signalled into an area large enough to house her rig, "unless you end up getting lost."

Dash inhaled and let out a sigh. "Yeah."

"So, listen. This is it for me for a few hours. I'm going to grab a bite and then some rest in the back before hitting the road again. My destination is the Sault, another three or four hours away. I'll take you on if you want to wait."

"Thanks, Darlene, but I'm going to look around, walk over to the train station." He reached back for his pack and opened the door, "but if I'm still at the side of the road somewhere along the way feel free to stop and pick me up." He smiled as he stepped down.

"Well, everything is within walking distance, including my truck. If I see you hanging around when I wake up, I'll assume you want a ride. Take care, Dash."

* * *

Darlene had been right. Dash could cover Main Street and take in all the sights, motel, gas station, restaurant, homes, and small businesses in under twenty minutes. The town wore age on its sleeve, the buildings sagging with wear. When he crossed the series of tracks and noticed rail cars lined up and waiting in lines for an engine to arrive and couple them into motion, he could see Darlene's brief history lesson come to life. He wandered over to the station to check out VIA Rail passage, a travel option he had yet to experience. The place was deserted except for a lone employee, who told him that, yes, there was a train going through to Sudbury but not until the next morning. His follow-up question informed him that it would take about ten hours to get there with all the stops along the way. He had gone out to find a place to sit in privacy and ponder his next move when a pickup truck bounced across the tracks and stopped nearby.

Dash paid little attention to the arrival until he heard the doors open and slam shut. When he looked up, three men approached him, casually looking around as they did so.

"Hey, man, what you doin'?" This came from the driver, the smaller of the three.

"Just sittin' here, gettin' my bearings." He had shifted his feet at the time, moving one closer to his bag.

"You ain't from around here as far as me and the boys can tell." He said this as if he were a border guard or cop bent on checking ID.

"No, I'm just passing through. Thought I might take the train out."

"No train 'til tomorrow, chief," barked the largest of the three from behind his friend. "Looks like you're goin' to have to stay awhile."

"Or hitchhike. We saw you get out of the rig that pulled up," said the third.

Dash perked up then. He began to feel buzzards circling around him. He wanted no trouble. "Yeah, you're right. I'd best be movin' on. Thanks for the advice." He stood and reached for his bag.

"We saw you walkin' down the street too," barked the driver, "lookin' into a couple of places. What you got in the bag? Anything you shouldn't have?" He sneered when he said this.

"Just personal stuff." Dash continued his movement to pick it up.

"Well, let's have a look to be sure." When he reached to grab the bag, Dash put his hand up.

"Don't."

"Don't. What do you mean, don't, chief? I want to see what's in the bag." This time when his hand went up, Dash pushed him away.

"Leave it alone." He tried to move past the three at that point, but his moment had passed. When he was spun around, he lashed out with his fist and connected. The driver stumbled backwards and into his friends. Dash dropped his bag and tore into them as best he could. A few punches were all he could deliver before one of them suckered him. Once they put their boots to him, he was stilled. He lay on the ground, stunned from the blows. It took two minutes for everything to end. The tearing and smashing around him sounded like the frenzy of feeding animals. He tried to get up but was hammered down each time. The last sounds he recalled before drifting into numbness was the spraying of gravel around him, a final coating of dust.

* * *

Crow sat perched atop a boxcar intent on the spectacle. Coyote lay underneath in the shade of its rusting bed. This was the closest they had come to a meeting, a crossroads in their journey together. They waited until the truck sped away, searching for a reaction to the episode that had just unfolded before them. But none came. No one peered out of a window at the man on the ground, no one passed by or came running. They had wanted to intervene, to rush out at the three with beak and teeth bared, but this was not their world. And so, they ventured out in the aftermath carefully into the upturned and defiled landscape. Crow flew downward and landed, pecked at the remnants of paper and pencil and the wooden fragments of the container. Coyote padded close to the man, sniffed hair, face, clothing, and nuzzled into back and leg. When breathing was detected and stirrings began—jerks of the body, the clenching of hands in the dirt, the slow movement of the head—they pulled back to their vantage points. They waited for the woman to come striding, then running across the tracks, a spirit they knew could help before each arced off in their own direction.

* * *

Dash had felt himself drifting; an out of body experience. He was floating, looking down from above, winged, a bird surveying. He noted the trio, the triangle he was in, his body stretched between three points waiting. Then he had descended, changed into fur, and breathed more closely his inert body, taking in the smell of his defeat, the unforgiving pebbled mattress that bore his weight. As he stirred, wing and fur melded into one, and he became lost in the swirling. Finally, a voice not his own pulled him slowly back into the world of wakefulness.

"Dash. Jesus Christ. What happened?"

The voice was familiar. He rose to greet it as best he could, but his head protested. He coughed, spewed words that made no sense to him and attempted to rise.

"Just hang on. Take it slow. Can you sit?"

They were not stated as commands, but he found himself following instructions, testing each part of him to ascertain compliance. As sore as he was, nothing seemed to impede him, no mental cue from his brain, still foggy, seemed to evade him. His body obeyed, and he grappled with balance. He rose like a newborn colt to feet that barely supported him. He shuddered and stood blurrily, scanning his surroundings, shaking off the placenta of a violent birth. The refuse around, scattered in all directions, reminded him of a tornado. He tried to recall what had just touched down. The arms supporting him broached one of the questions again, this time with more resolve.

"Dash! What the fuck happened to you?"

He looked in the direction of the voice and recognized it. "Darlene. Where did you come from?"

"I was coming back from lunch, saw this pickup truck screaming out of the station parking lot, and sauntered over to look. It wasn't until I got close that I realized there was a body on the ground, and not 'til a few steps later that I recognized the clothing."

"Well, thanks for stoppin' by. Wish I could offer you something, but I'm fresh out of everything." Dash tried to smile, but the effort caused pain to shoot up through his ribs.

"C'mon. Tell me. Did that truck that tore out of here have something to do with it?" She had let go of him and was glancing around at the debris left in the wake of whatever had happened.

Dash nodded. "Three locals, I'm thinking, with lots of time on their hands and a particular dislike for Indians."

"Maybe we should check to see if they took any of your stuff," Darlene suggested.

"This wasn't about a robbery, Darlene." Dash felt the kindling inside him begin to catch, and he started to burn. This gave him more energy. He stretched and twisted, gauging how far his pain would let him go. "This was about me being who I am."

He bent to retrieve what remained of his kit. The truck had made good work of the box, turning it into firewood mostly. A few pencils were strewn unbroken, and he reached for these. Darlene picked up several sheets of paper and pictures that were not ripped to shreds.

"Didn't know you were an artist," she said as she handed them over to him.

"I'm not. I play around when I get the chance, is all."

"Yeah, well, some of your playing is pretty good." She noticed him stagger a little as he went for his bag.

"Let's get you to my truck. You can sit a spell in the cab 'til you feel better. Sure you're OK?" They started to walk.

"I think I will be."

She offered him bottled water from her small fridge when they were settled. He rolled its coldness over his face, forehead, and neck before cracking it open and guzzling most of it down.

"I'll take you on to the Sault if you like," she said matter-of-factly. "You shouldn't be out on the road. You never know where those shits still are."

"I wouldn't worry about them. They've had their fun." He said this more with resignation than rage. "But you haven't had any rest yet, I don't think. Unless I was out cold for longer than I thought."

"I don't need to rest now. I'm wide awake. Besides, the Sault is only another four hours. I'll rest when we get there."

Dash did not argue. A renewed tiredness had sunk into his body. He listened to Darlene's movements as she started the truck, flipped switches, and pushed her rig into gear. By the time she had lit a cigarette, he had slipped into a wilderness of sleep.

* * *

The pecking had started as soon as they arrived at Sault St. Marie. Darlene was having no arguments, and like a mother hen, ushered Dash into the emergency at the hospital. He was going to be checked over whether he liked it or not. She was not letting him go anywhere until he got the OK from a doctor, and, yes, she was going to wait for as long as it took. Her trip over the bridge to the States was not a priority anymore.

By the time the poking and prodding had been completed, it was after 10:00 p.m. Dash had been stuck here for six hours and was starving. The prognosis had been good, though. Nothing was broken, but a couple of ribs were cracked, and he was bruised and banged up. The doctor had prescribed some painkillers and sent him on his way. Darlene was in the waiting room when he came out, a couple of subs and bags of chips in hand.

"Not sure what you liked. Figured I couldn't go wrong with meat and cheese." They walked out the doors and down the street to where she had found a better spot for her truck. They sat in the cab and ate. "What's the verdict on your check up?" she asked between mouthfuls.

"Good. Got a couple of cracked ribs, which will take a bit of time to heal. No fighting for awhile." He looked over at her and smiled.

"What are you going to do now?" Darlene reached for some chips as she spoke.

"I'm still heading to Toronto. Just not sure how yet." The food had given him strength. He didn't feel as worn out.

"You got money?" Her question was tinged with concern.

"Yeah, like I said, Darlene, those pricks weren't after my money. I got a bit of cash," and pulling out his wallet, "a card. All of my millions are still on it."

Darlene laughed. "Good, well, here's what you're going to do. A bus leaves from here tomorrow morning, close to the hospital. It'll take you to Toronto with some stops in twelve hours or so. Get on it. I don't want you hitchhiking."

"Yes, ma'am," and Dash gave her a mock salute.

"I'm not kidding," and she lit another smoke. "Just to make sure, you're going to catch some sleep in that seat overnight as best you can while I stretch out in the back and do the same. My truck, I get the bunk. No arguments." Dash nodded, and they finished off the subs, chips, and some water in silence. By midnight, they were both enveloped in darkness.

Dash watched Darlene pull away in the morning. He had offered her some money for all she had done, but she refused, and he knew better than to argue. He smiled when he thought of her, cigarette in hand, shifting stick and bearing down on the highway. Her temperament reminded Dash of his mother, and he stood and watched her retreating trailer until it disappeared completely from view over the winding bridge. He had had to wait for a couple of hours at the stop, but when the bus arrived, he had boarded with his bag, insisting on keeping it with him, and settled in. He felt for the prescription he had filled, a small bottle of relief, and took two. There was nothing to do now but finish his journey. Toronto was down below, the largest city he had ever been in. He didn't know what to expect. Try to get a job, find a place to live, but most of all, just blend in. This could be where things would get better. Dash listened to the hum around him and hoped. That's all he really had left.

* * *

Picture #13: *Seven Crows*

Observer's description: Seven crows are circling above the yellow, brown, and green markings of field grasses below. Some of the crows are larger and appear in the foreground distinctly rendered; others circle lower and are in the perceived distance, more like black slashes cutting into the canvas. Pushing back behind them is a loose configuration of the fence line. Behind that, further into the observers' sightline, are marshier areas flanking a meandering river that winds itself off into the final image of tree-lined hills. The sky is overcast grey. The crows glide effortlessly on the wind, their wings fully extended. They share a collective search of the world around them and the ground below. Their camera eyes capture everything and record it for future interpretation. There is something in the freedom of their flight that pushes beyond the boundaries contained by the painting. The viewer can only surmise what it is they truly see.

Chapter Fourteen

DAY SEVEN

THE PRESENT

The evening had turned out better than I had initially thought. After dinner and clean up, we had drifted to the couch. Dash had opened up more about his past, the ups and downs of his existence and being who he was. The minor difficulties I had incurred growing up, a shunning or two from entitled teenagers like myself whose actions lasted a month or two at most before nails were retracted and words patched us back together, were nothing compared to what Dash endured. But he had spoken of darker episodes as if they were in the past, and was determined not to let them back into his world. Even the recent chapter on Greg had been closed like a book and shelved. Instead, we had taken out others and spent an hour or two skimming through *Colville* and a book of mine on anatomy and drawing. Then we practiced for a time, our pencils dancing across paper at the coffee table or on our laps until we had strewn the area with creations either destined directly for the garbage bin or the possibility of reworking. When bed had beckoned, we left our efforts unattended and in the dark to whisper to each other, while we did the same until sex and sleep claimed us. Now, in the emerging light of day and with Dash's arm across me, I did not want to get up. I nestled into him for another minute before urging myself fully into wakefulness.

"Seven o'clock, Dash," and I rolled over the top of him to the floor, "time to get up."

"You makin' pancakes?" he muttered, "just felt like I was being flattened."

I laughed. "Good one. Hadn't thought about it much. Not a bad idea." I made for the bathroom. "Make yourself useful. Look for the ingredients."

He groaned. "But, I need to get to the can too."

"Won't be long," I called from behind the door. "Just get up and get moving."

Breakfast was a triumph—fluffy pancakes with bananas, raspberries, and real maple syrup to top them off. Yummy. We headed into the day knowing it was Friday, a weekend beckoning just hours away. I had told Dash we were going out tonight, maybe to the gallery if he wanted, and then to dinner. My treat, I said, something for us to look forward to, a one-week anniversary of his job and our few meaningful days together. "No argument from me," he had said, then offered up a kiss before cycling away. I put my apprehensions behind me and pushed out onto the street.

* * *

Greg hated Toronto's traffic. It didn't matter what time of day it was, he could always count on getting jammed up behind assholes who didn't know how to drive. He was already pissed, a feeling he knew all too well. It usually sprang from a night of too much drink and the resultant foggy embrace of a morning that had him starting out angry and complaining. Last night had been even worse, though, because he wore the results of a confrontation he had lost; a sore face and slightly puffed-up eye. The world was against him, and Friday made it feel no different. Topping it off was the realization that even with his driving expertise he would be punching in late. Worst of all, he'd forgotten about his review this morning. He was determined to pull in and park quietly and hope that Graham had his head up his ass somewhere out of range and had forgotten it himself.

Arriving and parking seemed to go well. No one took notice as he signed in and headed out again to get his truck. It was then he noticed that it wasn't there. *What the fuck?* He strode back inside and approached Nigel, one of the mechanics who did maintenance on their fleet of vehicles.

"Hey, man, where's my truck? It's not where I left it last night."

Nigel gave him an uncomfortable look. "You're to go and see Graham about that. He told us to send you in once you got here."

"Graham. What the hell does he want?"

Nigel just shrugged and went back to work.

Greg tried to calm himself as he headed down the hallway; there was no point in getting riled up until he knew what was going on. He could smooth talk Graham concerning his review, but his truck being elsewhere was something else. The door to Graham's office was open, so he turned in off the corridor and entered. Graham was scribbling something on a pad of paper at his desk and didn't look up.

"Nigel said you wanted to see me."

Graham finally stopped writing, looked up, tossed his pen onto the desk, and sat back. "Yeah, I did. Sit down."

"What's up? I noticed my truck wasn't out back when I came in."

"You were late again this morning." Graham began tapping his fingertips together in front of his face, elbows resting on his chair arms. "Forgot my reminder yesterday to be on time."

"Traffic was a bitch this morning."

"Right." Graham went on. "And last night, it seems you didn't check out until, let's see," and he glanced down at a note on his desk, "after seven."

"Yeah, I had to do some errands on the way back. Figured I'd just use the truck." Greg started bouncing his left knee.

"Your eye looks a little swollen, by the way, kind of yellowy too."

"Woke up with it. Probably just an allergy to something, I guess." Greg wanted to get off this merry-go-round, so he got to the point. "So, what happened to my truck? Time's money, right? I should be getting out on my deliveries."

"About that, Greg. I sent Paul out early this morning to check out your truck since it came back in late. I just wanted to make sure everything was all right. No problems with performance, unreported scrapes and dents, stuff like that." Here, he gave a long pause before continuing. "Anything you want to say before I continue?"

"What have I got to say? The truck was fine when I brought it back. I added a bit of mileage doing those errands I told you about. That's it."

"That's not quite it." He sighed, reached down below his desk, and hoisted up the remainders of a six-pack. "Any ideas about this? Looks like three are missing."

Greg shuffled around in his seat, hoping to gain some time and an excuse. "No idea, Graham. Not mine. Somebody must have broken in. Had a little party overnight." He tried to smile but found the gesture unnatural.

"Nope. Doors were locked. No attempt to get inside."

A couple of plausible alternatives percolated in Greg's mind, and he poured them out. He might have left the doors unlocked when he was in on a delivery, and somebody got in or on one of his after-work errands. Whatever. He insisted on punctuating his case with another denial. Those beers were not his. Graham had simply let him finish before reaching for his pad of paper.

"You've been with us for a while now. Always had a chip on your shoulder, but I let that pass. You did your job well enough in the beginning. Over the last few weeks, though, your attitude has deteriorated even more. People around here see it. Employees have made comments to me, Greg. You come in late, peel in and out of here like you're at Daytona, and now this, something by the way, that I think has been going on for a while."

There was more writing now. Greg's mind watched the scribbles and loops as they moved off Graham's pad and seemed to start filling the walls. He tried to get out in front of it, erase it as it gained momentum, but all he could see was a hand moving inexorably toward an exclamation point, which Graham vocalized.

"There's no room for this behaviour here, Greg. I can't keep you on. You're a driver for God's sake, and it seems you drink on the job. Not a great combination. You'll get holiday pay for the time you've worked with us for this year. And I'd suggest you get some help, maybe some counselling. You've got problems."

A ragged edge crept into Greg's voice. "I haven't got problems. At least nothin' I can't handle."

Graham looked at him for a second. "But you're not handling them, are you?"

"Yeah, but…you don't…"

"Listen to me, Greg. I can't take a chance on you anymore. It wouldn't be responsible of me. Not at this point. You do whatever it takes to get your head straight, but it can't be here. That's it. Take care of yourself."

Greg sat there, stunned for what seemed like an eternity. He clenched at the arms of his chair then rubbed his hands along his pants. He did not say anything as the heat of the room engulfed him, and his face flushed red. He wished he had a gun, just for a second. The disgruntled employee whose actions periodically make the six o'clock news came racing into his mind. He pushed into a stand and exited Graham's office, the sound of a rushing waterfall filling his senses. Nothing was said to the employees he passed. *Fuck them.* Placing the keys in the ignition of his car, he sat there, composing his thoughts as best he could. It was a hell of a week. He'd lost his job, lost his girlfriend, and lost a scuffle with an Indian. He had no doubt that the pittance he was still owed would be directly deposited in his bank account, but he would need another job somewhere soon. He gripped the steering wheel and wrung it like the neck of a bug-eyed turkey. But today, he now had time on his hands. It was a little after ten. Turning on the engine, he sat revving his car. Then he shoved it into gear and screamed out of the parking lot. Home first, change, settle into a plan. A drink or two would help him focus. Then it would be on to step two, revenge in some form or another. The opportunity just had to present itself.

* * *

Crow was high in the air, working a large circle that would grow ever smaller as the day progressed. His flight was not an easy one. The wind had picked up, gusting around him, forcing him to work harder to stay in control. They would converge at the woman's apartment where Coyote already lay nestled and hidden, then flair out again for a few hours like a sunburst before settling into darkness. This was what they knew. There was to be a general pattern of movement between the humans that would eventually bring all three to a gathering, a point where everything would become crystal clear. What came after would vanish into a story, a recounting of sorts by unreliable narrators.

* * *

The day was going well. I took my lunch with colleagues, an unusual opportunity to catch up without the distraction of crises that so often interrupted these moments. There was an apparent calm as we joked and gossiped, running the gauntlet between personal life and general client information. I was forced to divulge tidbits about my new love interest; an insight Julie, a colleague I was close to, had gleaned from two sources: a particular glow I seemed to be wearing as the week had progressed, and the periodic smiley daydreaming she had found me immersed in when quietly at my desk. I couldn't deny that I was happy, but it was early stages. Luckily a distraction came through the door and sought us out at that point, and our afternoon began in earnest.

My evening plans with Dash were front and centre as the hours ticked by but would be a little disappointing in one instance. The AGO, I had remembered, would not be open this evening. We would go out for dinner, though, to a place just north of Bloor Street that boasted an array of East Indian dishes. Something a little different. I would suggest we cycle there, which would give us more time to enjoy the evening out together. I tried to keep Greg's recurring image at bay as a wispy cirrus cloud high in the sky that would pose no threat, a mare's tale it was sometimes called, that would simply gallop off into the sunset and disappear.

* * *

Dash found himself racing through the day, wanting to get to the end. It had been quiet, his runs straightforward. Perhaps Fridays were less crazy than other days. People were leaving early or taking the day off or generally in better frames of mind because the weekend was approaching. Amazingly, he had only yelled at three drivers and only gotten the finger or the horn twice. It was hard to believe he had ridden through the week without wanting to quit or wanting to sink into drink. That would have been his typical road to follow if not for Jesse, who had put up highly visible stop signs for him along the way. The thought of her made his pedals light, his heart skip, and the smile come to his face much more frequently. Such a good person had entered his life. He was turning over a new leaf; he could feel it. There was much more hope now rather than self-loathing and despondency. Derrick had told him this morning that he was doing well, and this had also helped, but Jesse was the key, and he couldn't wait to get home. Jesse, dinner, and the gallery sounded like an unbeatable combination right now, a trifecta that he had bet on and won. He settled into the remainder of his workday. Only the nagging presence of Greg from behind, a coarse bridle that kept biting into his mouth and pulling as he bent into his ride, prevented him from revelling completely in his new fortune. Most of his day had been spent looking over his shoulder, trying to dislodge the unwanted passenger.

* * *

Coyote was still nestled in the back corner of the park, a daytime position in this locale that allowed him a full view in front but provided the security of shadow. People might walk within several feet of him but never notice his blended obscurity. With his head and ears down and his body hugging the ground, he could pass for the earthy decay of autumn foliage. He saw the first of the three arrive, black car gliding along the street until it stopped and inched backwards into an available parking spot. Coyote knew it by its predatory shape, but more so by the white strafing across the roof, telltale signs that Crow had visited earlier in the day. Suppressing the desire to laugh, Coyote remained vigilant. The car's occupant remained inert and inside, expecting the arrival of the two. Higher up in the sky, Coyote noticed a black form taking shape. Crow was descending, making for one of the trees that lined the street. That meant the others could not be far behind. Coyote thought of their roles as watchers. Shapeshifters striding two worlds. Ethereal feathers and fur.

* * *

He had managed to maintain his truculent attitude throughout the day. This had primarily been because at home, Greg had consumed a couple of beers and a shot or two to keep him edgy. When it was time to leave, he had prepared further concoctions, mixing rye with two bottles of Coke he had left over in his fridge. These would come with him. Travellers. An old trick while driving. A simple sleight of hand, allowing him more public access to booze. As he waited in his car, sipping at his beverage, he realized that he really didn't have a plan. His actions would have to be decisive, but what would that be? He could take the tire iron out of his trunk, charge into Jesse's apartment when they arrived and lay a beating on her new man. Neither would expect that. He could kick open the door now, simply lay waste to the apartment, and take off, let them stew over what had happened. The more he sat and drank and waited, the more he realized that his ideas were stupid. He would have to find an opportunity that made sense and would leave him in the clear if possible. So, he sat tapping the steering wheel with his right index finger, mimicking the noise in his head.

* * *

I arrived moments before Dash, barely having time to position my bike on the porch and unlock the apartment door. It was just pushing 5:30 p.m. Lots of time to freshen up, relax for a bit, then head off. I had made a reservation, just in case, for 6:30 p.m. Our ride over would only take fifteen to twenty minutes.

"Nice timing," I called from the open door as he rode up. He smiled and nodded and bounced up the stairs with his bike.

Once inside, I outlined my plan. His disappointment at the AGO's closure was evident, but I reminded him of tomorrow.

"Remember I told you a couple of days ago that I was going to take an art class? Well, that starts at the gallery tomorrow. It's a morning session for several weeks that will hopefully get me back into painting." I headed for the washroom as I spoke. "You could join me if you want." I didn't wait for his reply, knowing what it likely would be, but the idea was out there dangling if he chose to grab for it.

He was sitting on the couch when I returned, fiddling around with the pages on the coffee table that we had left strewn about. "I don't think I'd be interested in the classes," he had said. "I'm more of a loner when it comes to drawing. Besides, it's too late now, and I don't have the money anyway."

"Excuses, excuses," I joked. I reached out, grabbed his chin, and gave him a kiss. "But I understand. Maybe another time. You can still come to the gallery with me when I go and do your own thing there if you want."

"That I could do." He smiled at me, got up and headed for the bedroom. "I'm gonna grab a quick shower and change if we have time."

"Sure. We don't have to go for about half an hour." I started skimming through an art book as I waited for his return, thoughts of this evening and tomorrow merging into an aromatic bouquet.

* * *

Greg had exited his car and wandered across the street. He settled himself onto a bench far enough into the small park to see everything and not be seen easily. Hunched over with his arms on his knees, he swirled the bottle around before straightening and taking another swig. Almost gone, but there was still another under the seat in his car. What to do? He was getting tired of waiting. Maybe they weren't coming out, weren't going anywhere else tonight. Then he would have to make a move at the apartment. Could get the tire iron out of his trunk, go up, knock on the door or better yet, just burst in, scare the shit out of them, or catch them in the act, his dick in her hand. "Fuck!" He yelled this into the growing night air. He was losing it, going around in circles. He had just had this conversation with himself a short while ago—the tire iron; the apartment mayhem. He had to get a grip. He stood up, stretched, and threw the empty bottle out into the street. Pacing back and forth behind the bench, he watched the door for a sign.

* * *

Coyote watched the animal in the man grow. It was fueled by a rage he could not control and the liquor he continued to pour into himself. When he began to pace, it reminded Coyote of a caged beast. He had felt this way himself at times but had never lost control. Control is what kept him focused; it was what kept him from lashing out without thought. Emotions needed to be managed, or they would run away with you, like a herd of buffalo stampeded into flight by fear, the need to escape, the need to do anything but stay calm and think, and always, always the funnel narrowing and narrowing until a cliff's edge greets you and you can't turn back. Crow was up above making the same assumptions, drawing conclusions about the man below and where his emotions and this night could go. This man infused with so much anger that it burned inside, waiting for release. More fuel was only going to increase the flame, giving it the ability to fan out unpredictably, a brush fire unrestricted, bent on scorching out its own path.

* * *

They left the apartment at 6:10p.m., and all six eyes followed them. Reactions to their departure differed in speed and intensity. They were heading up Beverley Street, Jesse leading the way. Then they would cross Dundas Street, meander along St. George Street through a section of the University of Toronto before ultimately reaching Bloor Street and turning right for a couple of blocks. The trip was not long or arduous but would sharpen the edge of their increasing hunger. As they began their cycle north, Greg's movements were immediate. An erratic run to his car, a fumble with the keys in the ignition, and an illegal U-turn with a bit of rubber left behind found him stopped at the lights but still in plain sight of his adversaries moving on.

* * *

Crow lifted off into the up draught of gentle winds that floated him along without effort, his tracking a simple aerial ballet of twists and turns performed at his own leisure. Coyote gauged his terrain more painstakingly, with daylight still a worry. He would follow, not as Crow flew, but as he hunted, using scent and sight, cunning and quiet, to ultimately find his way.

* * *

We kept it simple at the restaurant. I didn't know where Dash would draw the line on food I wasn't sure he'd like. We started out with some pakora and samosa appetizers and moved on to a tasty butter chicken entrée with rice and naan. Simple enough fare, but he enjoyed it. He reminded me that, while his palette may not be as refined as mine, he had sampled more than burgers and fries in his life.

"My mom used to make some great fish dishes. Mainly trout, bass or pickerel, and we'd have it with this," he said as he scooped another forkful of rice.

I knew this from earlier conversations. "What else?"

"Sometimes, one of her boyfriends would drop off some caribou or deer, and she'd cook that up. I never liked it as much as fish, though." He became a little quieter then and turned to the chicken.

I laughed. "Neither of my parents cooked much, and when they did, it was pretty bland. My dad would barbecue a bit in the summer, but most of the food I recall was easy to prepare, frozen or pre-packaged. We ate on the fly, or we ate out. The benefits of having busy parents, I guess."

Dash nodded. "We never had the money to do much of that." He smiled. "But even if we did, there wasn't anywhere much to go—the local greasy spoon. Take out. I preferred cereal, Kraft dinner, and Pizza Pops." He took another bite of buttered chicken and then held up his fork. "But this is pretty good too. Good call."

"Glad you like it." I thought I would remind him of something now. A date. Something specific that only I remembered it. A Monday. Maybe that's why it had a feel. "Guess what?"

"What?" He dipped a piece of naan in chicken sauce and popped it in his mouth.

"This is an anniversary of sorts for us. A year since we first met."

He chewed slowly to take this in. Finally, he said, "You're kidding. Wow."

"Yeah, I think that's incredible too."

He reached out and covered my hand at that point. "Thanks for sticking with me. I never could have gotten here without you. It was a Monday, right?" He pulled his hand away.

"You remember?" I must have looked shocked because he broke into a huge smile.

"Of course. I locked onto you when I walked in right away. I said, 'That beauty's for me. Got to go over and introduce myself'."

"Get out." I could feel myself blushing.

"It's true. And look at us now."

"Yeah. Look at us now."

Our dinner continued casually and covered the better part of two hours. We kept the conversation light. I didn't want to pressure Dash into talking about his mother and his growing up unless he wanted to interject with something. We were getting there, a little more each day. Our personal histories could be fleshed out later. There was plenty of time as we got to know each other better. We had passed on beer or wine, opting to wait until we got home, but finished off with a sweet plate of spongy cake balls dipped in syrup, three each. Enough to leave a sugary taste in our mouths and not regret the extra poundage for the ride back. It was dark and sliding past 9p.m. when we left.

* * *

Once he knew where they were headed, he had circled and circled until a spot appeared on the street about a block away. Greg could see the entrance if he sat in the passenger seat. He put his head back, cranked up some Nirvana, and sipped on his drink. Nursing it would be difficult. When two hours had passed, he started getting frustrated. He had gone for a few short walks to pass some of the time up the other side of the street and back, checking out shops and peering over into the restaurant when he passed. Their bikes were out front. How long did it take to eat? With his drink gone, he now needed a piss. Luckily, he had the empty bottle, and with a few deft moves back in his seat, he had his dick out and was relieving himself. Once finished, he could open his door and drop the bottle, piss and all, against the curb. He frowned then at a memory. He'd been at a party back in Calgary, and two friends had offered him a beer. He should have been smarter. They'd gone into the kitchen for it while he waited, came back quite a bit longer than he expected with smiles on their stupid faces, and gave the opened bottle to him. It was a little warm when he took a drink and a bit salty, but what the hell? Then they'd broken up laughing like idiots. He finally figured it out. What a tool he was. It took him weeks to live the humiliation down. He was angry again, just thinking about it. It seemed he was always being played. He was about to get out of the car for the third time when he noticed them coming out. After unlocking their bikes, lover boy had reached over and planted a kiss on Jesse's lips before mounting his bike. "We'll see who gets the last laugh this time," Greg muttered as he turned on his car and inched out into the street.

The traffic was thinning out even on Bloor Street, and once they turned back onto St. George Street, it became even quieter. Dash knew the return route and had gotten out ahead of Jesse by half a block. She sensed the car behind her and wondered why it hadn't passed. Maybe it was searching for a parking spot. It didn't concern her until it revved its motor a couple of times. She looked over her shoulder and into its lights, and then it took off toward her. She cried out and aimed for a space between two cars. She managed to nose through and bump the curb, but the car caught the rear of her bike, spinning it into the bumper of a parked car and flipping Jesse onto the sidewalk. She lay there, stunned, not sure what had just happened. However, the sound of metal crumbling further down and tires squealing away forced her to ease into a stand. She looked herself over, began to walk around tentatively, sensing for pain in her arms and legs. Nothing much. But a sickness began to grow in her stomach, wretched bile forcing itself up into her head and flooding her senses. Dash. She traced the outline of parked cars lined up and down the street until her gaze centred on an object positioned like a piece of sculpture in bent and contorted repose by a fire hydrant. She stumbled forward in a half-run. As she got closer in her ambling trajectory, she recognized the bike and nearby, a body slumped into the street. This time, her cry sliced the air in a howl. "Dash!" He gurgled a response as she cried out his name and fell to hold him. Others began to appear in ones and twos, and an ambulance was called. The scene slipped into chaos.

* * *

Coyote had been behind and to the left of the vehicle when it took off. Loping in and out of the shadows, he had been mimicking the moves of an animal intent on its prey. He anticipated the acceleration, the moment of impact when evasion was impossible, the sinking of claws and teeth into flesh. Crow could see another angle from above, one of explosion when a large object pushes another outward, in this case, in two directions. The aerial shot looked like a fork to Crow with the body flying out right and slamming into the rear of a parked pickup, the bike careening left and embracing a fire hydrant before bouncing back, its front wheel twisted skyward and spinning uncontrollably.

Both saw the aggressor fishtail off, its red eyes flashing twice before turning and disappearing into the night. Both noted the heaped and crumpled masses several feet apart. Coyote sniffed both the man and the bike before turning toward the approaching woman and then slipping away.

Turning and turning in a widening spiral, Crow elevated himself to a higher plane. Winds buffeted him. Trees and buildings obscured a clear view. Things fall apart, he knew this, but he continued his cries. Below him, Coyote, eyes turned upward at Crow's sounds, howled his own refrain. He pursued a similar path, enlarging his retreat from the scene, street by street, putting the gathering people and sirens behind him. The circle had not closed completely yet. There was still hope, still a chance for renewal. The rough beast, its red taillights out there somewhere, could still be brought down—just not yet. Coyote and Crow would move out of this frame for now and back into their own landscapes and world. A second coming would be announced. They would return when the painting was finished.

* * *

Picture #14: *Church and Horse*

Observer's description: At the centre of the painting stands a one-storey, white frame church. Three dark, stone steps lead up to the white front door. A worn black plaque above the door frame indicates the church denomination and dates. There are no windows visible. The church is surrounded by a field of yellow grass. There is no pathway leading to the steps. To the side, almost at the very edge of the painting, is one lone cemetery stone, standing, grey, thin and on a slight angle. The image of the church suggests one of abandonment. In the immediate foreground and flanking each side of the picture is a wooden fence, its painted posts worn, cracked, and flaked. A metal gate is seen open, hanging, bent. Approaching the gate from the right in the foreground is a beautiful black horse, galloping toward the open gate, its mane flowing and eyes flashing deep and dark. The image is one of freedom and grace as the horse moves toward what is assumed are more wide-open spaces. The contrast between white and black is powerful and holds the viewer's gaze between two distinctly different worlds.

* * *

He could smell dog, then a cold nose touching his cheek. Was it Digger? He tried to open his eyes to look, but a sticky substance held them closed and so he imagined the animal standing in front of him, watching as he bent to gather in another stone before launching it into the field. Digger was full of energy today, racing this way and that, nose to the ground. Later, he promised he would take him out across the fields, and they would roam together. It was a sunny summer day. He looked over his shoulder and noticed his mother watching him from the screen door. She had her hands on her hips, and she was laughing at them. She was so beautiful. He turned back toward the field and saw someone coming toward him, but couldn't make out who.

Above him, wheeling in the sky, he noted several birds black against the sun. Crows. A murder of crows. Funny, that word, murder. *Where did that association with crows come from?* he wondered. *Why not a silly word like gaggle for geese? Or serious like parliament for owls?* Oh, well, what did he know about history or words or where things came from? He heard his name called, echoing down a long dark corridor. Then it was close, really close, muffled whispers, a cat's purr. He tried to speak but found that nothing would come out of his mouth. Arms were securing him now. They felt warm and inviting. He decided he would rest for awhile here and continue his dream.

* * *

DAY TWENTY-ONE

AN ENDING

The days of Colville are coming to an end. His exhibit is scheduled to close in less than a week. I had returned to the gallery several times since that night trying to make sense of the event, my life, and where I was heading. I had dropped out of the art course I had planned to take to focus on Dash, on his immediate needs and mine. There would always be other opportunities. But I had not put down my sketch pad. I carried it with me each time I returned to the gallery now. I would find an alcove, a quiet corner, and draw, usually trying to capture something that the art on the walls or the building itself provided for me.

Today, I am focused on a particular painting in front of me.

* * *

Picture #15: *Dog, Boy, and St. John River*

Observer's description: In the foreground, a young boy stands with his back to the viewer facing the river. Behind him a dog, perhaps a yellow lab, tail raised in excitement and anticipation, stands among the grasses, wildflowers, and scrub brush that lines the shore. It is late fall as indicated by the lack of foliage, the dried decaying wildflowers, and the boy's heavier hooded coat. The outline of a shotgun, barely visible, lies cradled and broken in the boy's arm, a suggestion that violence has been abandoned in favour of reflection. Together in the early evening, the boy and his dog look out at the river's rippling deep blue as it moves off toward the distant hills of the far shore. In contrast, the sky is a beautiful robin's egg blue with wisps of darkening clouds overhead absorbing the golden light of the setting sun. There is an air of peace and calm that has settled around the landscape, a moment framed, yet timeless.

* * *

From the picture, I create a memory in my mind, my formulation, my truth, of Dash as a boy. A moment of innocence and oneness, a moment tied to nature in all its forms. I will bring this to life, into the light using Colville as my inspiration.

Dash is wandering the gallery somewhere, watching and smiling, breathing in his surroundings. I can feel him, and I long for his return. I hope he loves what I am about to create.

I pick up my pencil, gather myself and begin.

Acknowledgments

I would like to thank the many friends who read parts or all of my manuscript and offered their advice and encouragement; the Guelph Public Library and the Art Gallery of Ontario for use of their archival materials; the Toronto bike couriers whose interviews gave me insights into their day-to-day working lives; the members of my writing group who kept me plugging along; and finally, the Tellwell staff who helped mold my vision into a palpable form.

CPSIA information can be obtained
at www.ICGtesting.com
Printed in the USA
BVHW032058280421
605984BV00001B/1

FRAMEWORKS

David McConnell

Frameworks
Copyright © 2020 by David McConnell

Tellwell Talent
www.tellwell.ca

ISBN
978-0-2288-3309-3 (Paperback)
978-0-2288-3310-9 (eBook)